PORTAL
OF A
THOUSAND
WORLDS

PORTAL
OF A
THOUSAND
WORLDS

DAVE DUNCAN

OPEN ROAD
INTEGRATED MEDIA
NEW YORK

Copyright © 2017 by Dave Duncan

Cover design by Mauricio Díaz

978-1-5040-3875-1

Published in 2017 by Open Road Integrated Media, Inc.
180 Maiden Lane
New York, NY 10038
www.openroadmedia.com

Dedicated to my wife, Janet, who, as always, was my first reader and in-house editor, to the many friends over the years who have acted as second readers for so many books, to the copyeditors I have driven crazy, and (especially!) to the fans who have bought my works, enjoyed them, and recommended them to other people.

CONTENTS

THE CALENDAR

Years	Moons
Vulture	Wolf
Nightingale	Ice/Budding
Raven	Hare
Firebird	Fish
Sparrow	Nightingale
Phoenix	Lotus
Peacock	Thunder
Finch	Harvest
Swan	Chysanthemum
Quail	Falling Leaf
Jackdaw	Fog
Bird of Paradise	Cold
Heron	
Albatross	
Pheasant	
Osprey	
Eagle	
Cormorant	
Crow	

Note: An extra "Cuckoo" moon is inserted periodically to keep the lunar calendar in step with the solar year.

PORTAL
OF A
THOUSAND
WORLDS

— 1 —
THE YEAR OF
THE JACKDAW

At the side of a busy street, a small boy had taken shelter from the drizzle under a barrow whose owners were selling cuts of meat. The boy was almost naked, vermin-infested, and seriously undernourished, but he had tasted meat so rarely in his life that he found the stench more nauseous than tantalizing. Flies liked it and it kept them away from him. Carts, horses, people, and barrows jostling by in a clamor of wheels, hooves, and curses. Rich and important people were borne in rickshaws or palanquins, frequently escorted by armed guards.

Peering through all this bustle of legs and spokes, the boy was studying the great gateway at the other side of the road. The archway was a very imposing entrance to find in a district of vice, dirt, and slums. The courtyard beyond it was grand, spacious, and well tended. It was gloomy, though, being enclosed by large buildings and roofed by sepulchral evergreens.

The courtyard also bustled in a hushed, well-orchestrated way. A funeral procession was being organized by a group of monks and nuns in gray robes. The rest of the cortege wore white—white horses to pull the hearse, white rickshaws and palanquins to carry the family mourners, white-clad musicians and professional keeners. Dusk was falling, and soon it would be time to start.

When all was ready, the drums began to beat and the shengs to wail. The horses leaned into their collars and the whole procession unwound like a giant snail emerging from its shell, oozing out through the gateway. The crowds in the street fled from it, taking refuge in doorways or passages, hiding from ill-omen. Carts, rickshaws, and litters halted on one side and sped up on the other, clearing the street until the cortege had wailed and thumped and rattled out of sight and earshot. Then the crowd healed up behind it as if it had never been.

When the courtyard was empty and the crowd returned, the boy squirmed out from under the barrow, dodged across the muddy street, and walked boldly into the yard. The buildings' grandiose bronze doors were closed, the paved driveway that looped around the big clump of trees in the center was deserted. Two boys with shovels and a barrow were cleaning up after the horses, but he ignored them. The only other person in sight was a monk, sitting cross-legged on the steps outside the left-hand door. He wore a gray robe that covered one shoulder and left both arms bare. His feet were also bare, his eyes shut, his head shaved. He was too far from the great trees to be sheltered, but he seemed oblivious of the rain.

The boy said, "I'm hungry."

The monk opened his eyes and smiled. "Many people are hungry, little brother." He pointed to the gate. "Go back out and turn this way. Ask at the kitchen door around the corner."

"I'm not a beggar! Gray Helpers kill people, don't you? I'll kill someone for you if you promise to feed me. I can sneak up on anyone! No one will suspect me."

The monk did not scoff or rage, but gave the proposition solemn consideration. "An interesting offer. Good killers are always in demand. I need to be sure you're nimble enough, though. You go and catch a pigeon in the square and bring it back here—alive—and I promise you the biggest meal you ever ate in your life. Off you go."

The boy returned in a very brief time, with a pigeon clasped in the straw-thin fingers of both hands.

The monk said, "Now kill it."

The boy had obviously watched chickens' necks being rung. With one fast yank, he produced one dead pigeon.

The monk floated to his feet. "Nicely done. I am Brother Moon. From now on, your name is Tug. Come in."

He delivered Tug to two boys not much older, who deloused him by shaving his head, scrubbed him until he glowed, salved his scabs, wrapped him in the largest garment he had ever worn, a cloth that reached from his waist to his ankles, and delivered him to a very long hall, which they told him was called the refectory. Brother Moon was waiting there, all alone, sitting cross-legged in the center of the tiled floor. He greeted the boy with a smile and pointed at the floor in front of him to show where the boy should sit.

Another monk hurried in with a steaming bowl of rice and a beaker of water, which he laid in front of the boy. He smiled, also. The boy distrusted smiles because he had seen so few of them.

"Eat," Moon said.

The boy needed no second command. Ignoring the chopsticks provided, he used both hands to make the rice disappear. The monk watched in amused silence, asking no questions.

The bowl empty, the boy drank the water. "Wasn't the biggest meal I ever ate," he grumbled hopefully, but perhaps truthfully.

"There's lots more to come," Moon said. "If you are a good worker, you may stay here and never be hungry again, but if I let you stuff yourself too quickly, you will become very sick. I'll give you a job to do, and when you have finished that, you can have more food, lots of it."

He rose and led the boy to a place that smelled very bad, like a seriously neglected cesspit. It was long and narrow, with a row of stone tables along the middle between two gutters; naked bodies lay on about half the tables. The same two boys who had cleaned the newcomer were waiting for him, grinning, and as naked as the bodies.

"You must remove your wrap and hang it on the pegs over here," the monk said. "We do not allow our clothes to be defiled by touching the discards. And you will always bathe when you leave this place."

"What do I have to do?" the boy asked warily, wrinkling his nose against the stench.

"You have to wash a corpse," Moon said. "Happy and Tooth will show you how to do it."

Instructed by Happy and Tooth, Tug washed the corpse without losing his meal. He was bathed again, fed again, and then told to wash another discard, still without ill results. He was fed a third time and admitted to the order as a postulant.

Months later, when he confessed that he had stolen the pigeon from a dovecot in the next street, Brother Moon said, "Of course you did. That's why we keep the dovecot there."

This insignificant event occurred in the Year of the Jackdaw of the two hundred forty-seventh cycle, being the seventh year of the reign of Emperor Absolute Purity of the Eleventh Dynasty, in a city whose name was written as Felicitous Wedlock of Waters, but spoken as just Wedlock. The Gray Helpers maintained Houses of Joyful Departure in every town and city of the Good Land, earning their name by helping the immortal sparks of the recently dead to escape from the now-useless husks that bound them and thus to head onward to the blessed Fifth World. The house to which the boy had been admitted was a very large one, befitting a city of great wealth, for Wedlock stood at the junction of the Jade and Golden Rivers, in the province of Shashi, near the felicitous center of the Good Land. The training received by Postulant Tug—later Novice Tug—was, therefore, as fine as any that the order could offer.

Tug learned the rituals of the dead, from collecting the body and purifying the family home to preparing the corpse and taking it in procession to the burning ground. He learned how to build a proper balefire, whether a communal heap of green timber and trash for the poor or a magnificent geometric pyre of fragrant sandalwood for the rich. He learned the appropriate music and chanting of sorrow and later of jubilation as the sparks flew up to accompany the deceased's ascent to the Fifth World awaiting amid the stars. He learned how to oversee the triumphant return home and the banquet to celebrate the deceased's ascendancy. He participated in thousands of funerals, sang at them as treble and later baritone, wept at many more as a keener. He learned to wash cadavers, sew their mouths shut, plug their orifices. He helped make coffins, cook for banquets, care for horses. He chopped enough wood to build a village. He gathered bones and dug pits for them, the discarded reminders of the deceased's brief sojourn in this, the Fourth World.

He also received clandestine anatomy lessons, dissecting corpses unbeknownst to their former owners' sorrowing families, until he knew the location of every organ in the human body and the effects of all major diseases. He learned how the farewell gifts should be packed into the pyres so that a decent proportion of them remained with the living, meaning the Gray Helpers, and how to palm the jewels that were placed in the corpses' mouths for their use in the Fifth World. He was given a firm grounding in the pharmacology of potions and acquired many other curious skills, including playing the sheng, fighting with blade or firearm, and understanding numbers as well as any scribe. In the final year of his novitiate, he was taught two hundred fourteen different ways to kill people, thirty-seven of which would leave no trace.

— 11 —
THE YEAR OF
THE VULTURE

CHAPTER 1

Sunlight walked out on the rampart and looked down at the town and the crowd waiting there. Four Mountains was an ancient fortress, reputed to be the most impregnable stronghold in the Good Land, a bastion of granite blocks on a mountain spur, flanked on three sides by a raging mountain river. The crowd that gathered there every day was too far off for him to recognize faces, but it was certainly larger than it had been six moons ago, and probably larger than the entire population of the town, so people must be making pilgrimages in from half of Qiancheng, perhaps from farther away than that. Small wonder that the mandarins were worried.

He shivered, for the wind was cold and sharp as a knife.

The watchers had seen him. They were cheering, waving their arms from side to side in a motion that soon spread through the whole throng, as if they were grass. The wind prevented any sound reaching him, but he raised his hand to bless them. Now they were starting to kneel. Every day at noon, they came, in baking heat or pounding rain. They would probably still come when the winter blizzards blew, to kneel in the snow. He would still be here, unless the government changed its mind.

What had they come to see? An Emperor robed in glory? A mighty warrior? No, just a boy of fourteen, with only his head and bare shoulders visible over the wall, and too far off to distinguish his features. But they had been told who he was, and they wanted to believe, so they came in their thousands, assembling every morning to wait for his appearance at noon. Every day, he came out and raised his hand to give them his blessing, an empty gesture, which he knew to be worthless, but they treasured so that they could tell their grandchildren.

The town itself stood farther away, because, for centuries, the keepers of the fortress had kept that clifftop meadow clear of trees or buildings to give the castle's archers a clear view of any approaching hostiles. The first fort at Four Mountains had been begun by Half-Dead Tiger, back in the interregnum after the Fifth Dynasty, when the landscape was untamed forest. It had been completed by the second Emperor of the Sixth, a hundred years after Half-Dead Tiger's name had fallen short of reality. It had grown considerably since then and the town had grown up to supply it and purloin its name. The hills were treeless now and terraced to grow rice.

Most days, he came out to the little courtyard behind him and ran around it for an hour or so to work up a sweat. Two laps clockwise, then two counterclockwise so as not to get giddy. Repeat and repeat and repeat. He would do gymnastics, turn cartwheels, walk on his hands—anything rather than just sit in his cell all day. Other boys of his age were working in the paddy fields or poling boats or chopping wood, already being useful in the life of the Gentle People. Starting to drop hints to their parents about girls who would make suitable wives for them. Sunlight was in jail.

But two nights ago, he had seen Chrysanthemum Moon in the sunset, and the weather had taken notice already. Today was too chilly for exercise for a boy wearing only a loincloth. He was shivering like a bird with a broken wing. Besides, it looked as if the crowd had begun to sing a hymn to him, and he could not have that. He waved good-bye and went back inside, closing the door.

Come back tomorrow, friends! The nights were growing too long to sleep through and he was so terribly bored. The warden disapproved of his prisoner's daily audience. He had tried to put a stop to it once, back in Lotus Moon. There had been a riot in the town—boys throwing filth at the castle gates, shots fired. Fortunately, the imperial government in Sublime Mountain had either not heard of this disturbance, or was not sufficiently bothered by a few dead rioters to order reprisals.

Sunlight's room was shabby but generously large, with a rack of books, comfortable furniture, and windows looking out toward the town. All in all, it was as good a jail as he had ever known. The guards were forbidden to speak to him and the lack of company was irksome, but he had endured as much before. He had known prisons much, much worse. Only the boredom truly bothered him. He had read all the books downward, upward, and sideways.

Every tenth day, his mother was allowed to visit and she was already overdue. She was a simple soul and believed every word he told her—not that he ever lied to anyone, but he tried not to worry her. The husband she believed to be held somewhere else in the castle was almost certainly dead.

The locks on the outer door began to clatter. Sunlight paused to inspect his hair in the mirror. It dangled to his shoulders now, uncut for three years, but it was changing as the straight black hairs of his childhood fell out and were replaced by the wavy brown locks he would have as an adult. The result was a mess, and would be for the next year or two. Quail fussed often that her son did not look tidy. His face was becoming bonier, less rounded, more familiar. He noticed—amused at his stereotype adolescent interest—the first hints of lip fuzz.

The door creaked open; he spun around to smile and hold out his arms to his mother. Quail had been name enough for a peasant, but the authorities decided that it lacked dignity for this prisoner's mother and some unknown official had added the name of their village, making her Quail Long River. The larger name had not made her any bigger—not enough of her to feed a half-grown tiger, her husband had joked. He had been a big man, a good man, not one who had deserved the bitter jest that Heaven had played on him.

"Mother?" The boy frowned at her red-rimmed eyes as she ran to him. Her cheeks were still shiny and she had not brought him anything. Usually, she came laden with books and flowers from well-wishers. He wrapped her in his ropy arms. "What's wrong, Mother?"

She gulped, sniffed. "They are telling lies about you! They say you are disobeying the Emperor, that the Emperor is angry at you."

That was true, but she would never believe that the Son of the Sun could be in the wrong. Disobedience was unthinkable for any of the Emperor's children.

"Are they threatening you?" Sunlight asked, evading the point.

He was taller than she was now. She sobbed against his bony chest.

"They are going to send me away if you do not do what the Emperor says!"

"Come and sit." He led her to the bench and sat her nearer the door, so she had her back to it and he could watch it. It had not been closed behind her, so there was more bad news to come.

She was still mumbling about the Emperor.

"Mother, do you know how old the Emperor is?"

She looked at him in bewilderment. She probably could not think of the Emperor as anything less than a godlike, all-wise grandfather.

"He's only eighteen, Mother! I very much doubt," Sunlight said, a little louder than necessary, "that His Imperial Majesty Absolute Purity knows anything at all about my being here. I doubt even more that he has managed to impose his will on the mandarinate yet. Or the eunuchs." There would be guards outside in the corridor, and it wouldn't hurt to sow a few doubts there, even if it wouldn't do any good, either. The last time Sunlight had visited Sublime Mountain, even Zealous Righteousness, probably the strongest Emperor in two centuries, had been as much in the power of the palace eunuchs as most of his predecessors.

"Eunuchs?" she repeated.

"Geldings, Mother. The palace is always riddled with eunuchs and they get into everything, like roaches." The problem wasn't that eunuchs were stupid or incompetent; it was that they were too smart, too competent, and too efficient at blocking anyone else from interfering with their private empire-within-an-empire.

She was looking at him blankly, and probably the eavesdroppers outside the door understood no better. Oh, poor Quail! She could not be much more than thirty, but wrinkled and bent by work and weather. Sunlight had not been her first child, and two after him had died in infancy. With her eroded skin, her hair already graying and crudely cut, her threadbare cotton dress, she was absolutely typical of the great underworld of the Good Land, the lowly peasant mass that supported all the glory in the palaces.

A drum marked a slow beat out in the corridor. That was ominous.

Now boots thumped and guards marched in, followed by two men in elaborate silken robes and scarlet slippers, and finally an even greater glory, a mandarin of the third rank. That was a worrisome sign, for his predecessor had been a lowly mandarin of the first rank. Thirds were often governors of entire provinces, not insignificant forts like Four Mountains. Fat cushions were arranged appropriately on the floor, like chessmen, so the great one settled at the front, flanked by his aides, and the pawns stood at the back with their muskets. One of the lesser clerks consulted a scroll.

"Sunlight Long River!"

The prisoner gave his mother a squeeze and stood up to face the officials. He folded his arms. "I am the one you call by that name."

The flunky read his warrant, inevitably beginning with the Emperor's seventeen major names and titles, ending with a terse statement that wardenship of Four Mountains Fortress was now entrusted to the blessed, honored, et cetera, Sedge Shallows, wise and trusted mandarin of the third rank.

Sunlight was still only a boy, so he knelt and tapped his forehead three times on the floor, then sat back on his heels to await the great man's pleasure. When adult, he sometimes chose to respect authority and other times chose not to.

The new warden was a man of around fifty with silver in his dangling mustache. He was a monument of multicolored embroidery, of perfectly arranged folds, cords, and pleats, but he had not been chosen for his affability. He must resent being posted to these barren hills, far from the intrigue and the opportunities for graft and promotion in Heart of the World. He must also resent having to come to the prisoner, instead of having the prisoner dragged before him in chains, but the imperial authorities were being very careful with this captive and must have given very specific orders on how he was to be treated. Now the old warden had been withdrawn or demoted and this new one sent to apply more pressure. How much more? In many small bites or one great gulp? Sunlight had met his type oftentimes before, and memories brought dread.

He wondered if Emperor Absolute Purity himself might be behind this new appointment. Had he actually started to assert himself and break free of the regency? A few others had managed it at about his age. Most Emperors who succeeded as minors never succeeded in being more than puppets. Dynasties often died when the heir was a minor.

The floor was cold and hard under Sunlight's knees, but he had met harder and colder.

The warden spoke, using Palace Voice, which would not be understood by the guards or peasants like Quail. "Sunlight Long River, you have been commanded in the name of the blessed Son of the Sun to answer certain questions concerning the so-called Portal of Worlds."

Sunlight replied in the same dialect. "I have explained many times, Noble Scholar, that I will speak of such matters only to the Son of the Sun in person."

"You expect me to summon the Emperor for you?"

"Take me before the Golden Throne, where I have stood many times, Eminence. I will not try to escape on the way, I promise."

Quite likely Sedge Shallows had never set eyes on the Golden Throne, despite his exalted rank. Possibly he never would. He scowled. "You will force me to apply sterner measures."

The boy shrugged. "I force nothing."

"Have you forgotten that the Courtly Teacher said, *Refusal to act is to act*?"

"He also said, *Every man desires rank and wealth, but if they can be retained only by evil means, then they must be abandoned*."

Parroting old texts was the mandarins' own game and the warden sneered. "He also said, *Ministers in serving their ruler must serve his cause above all*."

"But the Humble Teacher said, *When the ruler does not direct his ministers according to laws of goodness, he must answer for their sins*."

The warden hesitated. "You dare call the Son of the Sun a sinner?"

"Not I, Eminence, but the Courtly Teacher also said, *The gentleman who ever parts company with good conduct is not worthy of the name*."

"Enough!" The mandarin nodded to his flunkies. "Proceed."

One had produced a brush and ink block to write.

The other unrolled another scroll and read out, also in Palace Voice, "First question: Who made the Portal of a Thousand Worlds?"

Sunlight sighed. "I will tell the Emperor, not you."

The warden said, "Bid farewell to your mother, boy."

Sunlight stood up and reverted to the common tongue. "Am I to fall on my face and beg for mercy? For me or for her? Where is she going?"

"She is not your concern."

Another guard entered, ushering a workman with a bag of tools. The room was becoming crowded.

"Good-bye, Mother." The boy she had named Sunlight went to her. He bent and kissed her. "Go with my blessing always."

"No, no!" She clung to him fiercely. "You must answer their questions! They will let you go free if you will answer the Emperor's questions."

No they wouldn't. He wondered what they had in store for her. She was of no importance, but all the fires of history illuminated no limit to human cruelty.

"Go, Mother, please. You have been a good mother to me, one of the best I have ever had. But you have done your duty and must go. I release you. No doubt you will be blessed for your service. Go."

She crept away, so bowed by sorrow that she hardly seemed taller standing than sitting, a tiny monument to human suffering.

The workman had pulled back the rug in the center of the room to uncover a metal ring set in the stonework. He began hammering, closing the first link of a chain around it. The chain was rusty but looked strong enough to hang a horse. It was barely as long as Sunlight's forearm.

He looked around in dismay and caught the warden gloating. This was becoming serious. An adolescent body was much more vulnerable to maltreatment than an adult's.

"I am fourteen years old, Scholar. I need exercise to grow properly."

"Let us move to the second question, then. Secretary?"

The flunky read out, "When will the Portal next open?"

"The people look for me at noon every day," Sunlight said.

But of course the new warden had foreseen that difficulty. "And they will see you at noon every day, except it will not be you. The eagles in Heaven may notice the difference, but the rabble won't be able to tell. Will you submit or be forced?"

The workman had stopped banging. Now he knelt beside his chain, staring up at the prisoner with an expression of horror, or terror, or both. He was young and repellently thin. He was of an age to have many tiny mouths to feed. Sunlight walked over to him and offered an ankle for the manacle.

The warden said, "Your wrist."

Sunlight would not be able to stand upright, perhaps not even kneel properly. Remembering the last time this had been done to him, he sat down, crossed his skinny legs, and held out his left hand.

"The other one."

For a moment, the boy considered refusing. No, it was too soon, his time was not yet. He must be patient. He smiled and used his right hand to give the workman his blessing. "You are not to blame."

The man gasped in relief, blinking away tears. "Oh, thank you, First—"

"No!" Sunlight laid fingers across his mouth. "Do not call me that! They will punish you. Now do what they want." He offered his right wrist.

The warden rose from his cushion and moved closer to watch the hammering. When he was satisfied that both ends of the chain were secure, he sneered. "Third question: Who will pass through the Portal when it opens?"

Sunlight was neither doctor nor magician, but his experience was beyond comprehension. At close range, he could recognize the shadow of death on the new warden.

"Either hand works," he said, and used his left to bless the man.

"If you ever do that again, I will have your wrists clamped behind your back and you will have to eat like a dog. *Who made the Portal?*"

Sadly, the prisoner said, "You will not know in this life, Honorable Scholar. You have very little time left."

The warden pointed at the rug. "Remove that," he told a guard. "Move that forward, and that. The prisoner will be fed every two days. Every ten days, you will put the Emperor's questions to him again."

"Take me to the Emperor and I will answer them."

At the door, the mandarin fired a parting shot. "Meditate on the wisdom of the Humble Teacher, who said, *The Good Land is a dragon and the Emperor is its head; he will lead, but we are the limbs that must obey and support him.*"

"No, he didn't! That nonsense was inserted into his teachings about a hundred years after he ascended. He would never have said that."

The warden left; guards followed; door slammed. Locks and chains and bolts clattered. The Firstborn was left sitting on bare flagstones. He still had the books, the comfortable bed, the view, and all the rest of his comforts, only he could reach none of them. He had a water jug and a bucket. He had a loincloth but no blanket. And winter was coming.

CHAPTER 2

"Have you ever killed a man, Tug?" inquired Rice Straw.

The question was not entirely irrelevant, as Tug had him firmly gripped in an armlock and was holding a knife at his throat. Just because they were in a training session in the seniors' gym did not mean that the blade was not razor sharp.

Tug said, "Yes. Do you want to be the next?"

"No. Please."

Tug released him and returned the knife. "Then tell me what you did wrong this time."

Two days earlier, Rice Straw had been promoted from postulant to novice. Having been taught everything he could ever need to know about the Gray Helpers' official business of cleaning up and cremating corpses, he had now embarked on learning about their private sideline, part of which was creating them. So far, his efforts to make a mock victim out of Tug had all ended in mock disasters.

Tug himself was still only a novice, although overdue for initiation to full helper status. His training had indeed required him to advance a man, but it had been on Brother Providence's contract; Tug had inserted the knife as directed, but the outing had counted on Providence's score. Tug's still officially stood at zero.

The sun was setting, and even at noon, the seniors' gym was never bright, for the exercises performed there belonged to darkness and shadow. Tug was aware that a third person had entered, but Rice Straw was not, and he jumped like a flea when a raspy voice spoke his name.

"Rice Straw!"

The boy shot across the room and flopped down on his knees before the newcomer. Master of Archives was a plump, soft man with badly rotted teeth and a face scarred by smallpox. He sprayed when he spoke, and his breath was recognizable at five paces.

"We have a logjam of discards developing in the washing room. Go and help clean it up."

Rice Straw snatched his robe off its peg by the door and vanished without even bothering to put it on. Tug had by then arrived in front of Archives. He offered a three-quarter bow.

"Master?"

"Good news. As the venerable Abbot has told you several times, we have been delaying your initiation until a worthy client appears, and it seems very likely that one will come calling on us this evening. If not tonight, then tomorrow. If he waits longer than that, it will be too late, and he will not be worth saving."

Excellent news! Tug managed to hold his heartbeat at its normal level, although that required as much effort as it had when he performed that outing for Brother Providence. He tried not to lean backward as Archives continued his fetid narration.

"You will recall that you conducted funeral rites for a merchant, Jade Harmony 6, last year."

"Certainly, Master." It had involved the Ritual of Supreme Desolation—not one of the very highest, but lavish enough, and for a mere postulant to be put in charge had been a great compliment. That scale of funeral implied considerable wealth, if not quite first rank in a city as rich as Wedlock. The Emperor's death tax would have pushed the deceased's son even lower in the standings.

"Then go and watch at the door this evening. You will recognize Jade Harmony 7 if he comes?"

"Certainly, Master," Tug said again.

"And you are confident that he will not recognize you?"

Tug let a thin sliver of indignation show in his voice. "Of course!" The director of lamentation at a Ritual of Supreme Desolation must be a very senior Helper, which is how the mourners would have seen Tug.

"Then go and prepare."

Tug strode back to his cell and attended to his toilet. He wrapped himself in a fresh gray robe of flimsy summer cotton, leaving his arms and left shoulder bare. He sat cross-legged before the mirror and contemplated his appearance until he was satisfied that he seemed appropriately juvenile and innocent; he must not appear to his prospective employer as in any way threatening, despite the Gray Helpers' sinister reputation. He then padded to the great door, where old Brother Moon had the watch that evening. He glanced in surprise at Tug and then smiled and nodded, guessing why he had been sent.

It had been Moon who had admitted Tug nine years ago, so his presence tonight felt as if it should be a favorable sign. Truly, this might be his naming day at last!

By its very existence, the House of Joyful Departure condemned its environs to becoming an area of penury and ill omen. No wealthy merchant would be seen dead there unless some very close relative was, in fact, dead there. Jade Harmony 7 would certainly not come in daylight, for that would add the danger of finding his way blocked by a funeral procession, a most dire augury.

Night had fallen, but the air felt like hot blankets, and was equally hard to breathe. What excuse, Tug wondered, could a man such as Jade Harmony invent for venturing into these insalubrious surroundings at all? To order a one-year memorial service for his father? He could arrange that by sending a runner from his home, although to attend to the matter in person might be seen as a meritorious display of respect for ancestors.

Aha! Tug heard a distant clang of a gong signaling to the unwashed and unworthy herd to clear the way. It grew rapidly louder, until its source ran into the tree-shrouded courtyard in the shape of a lithe and very sweaty youth. He was followed by a grandiose palanquin borne on the muscled shoulders of four well-matched hulking young barbarians from the Outlands, no doubt prisoners taken in some borderland disciplinary action. Behind them came no less than eight guards in bright plumes and lacquered armor, equipped with muskets, pistols, and swords. They ought to deter any evil-intentioned rabble away from serious violence, but might well invite well-aimed airborne handfuls of dung.

Brother Archives had prophesied that Jade Harmony 7 would come calling this evening, so the occupant of that palanquin was undoubtedly Jade Harmony 7.

The doorway to the Gray Sisters' quarters being closed, the gong beater knew to trot around the courtyard and halt before the steps where Brother Moon kept watch, and where two postulants were already unrolling a red carpet. The Gray Helpers' efficiency and propriety were legendary. The bearers set down their burden with obvious relief. By then, Tug had already gone, for he knew exactly what was about to happen.

Jade Harmony would be conducted by two novices bearing lanterns along passages of stark and somber stone—a curiously long way, much longer than the path that Tug used to reach the same destination. By the time the merchant arrived at a secluded cloister, smelling of blossoms and incense, and made private by the tinkling of some nearby stream and a choir rehearsing nearby, the angular figure of Gray Abbot himself would be there to welcome him. Gray Abbot was very old, his face long gone past wrinkles to the leathery texture of the truly ancient, lacking even eyelashes or eyebrows, although he did seem to have retained most of his teeth and his gaze was shrewd. Tall, thin, leaning on a staff, he stood like some ancestral apparition in the weak gleam of a pink and green lantern. At his feet, two cushions and a tray of refreshments were already set out for a conference, another display of the legendary efficiency. Tug stood unseen in the shadows, waiting for his cue.

Jade Harmony had changed since his father's advancement to the Fifth World—he had gone from prosperously plump to overtly obese. Perhaps he was getting more to eat with one less mouth to feed? His embroidered silks must cost as much as his train of eight guards and four bearers. Just from memories of that funeral he had arranged, Tug doubted very much that the man could afford such display.

After a brief argument over precedence, the two men settled on their cushions. As decorum required, they began by exchanging pleasantries while sipping warm wine, but suddenly the Abbot said, "If Your Eminence has come upon some private matter, then our conference at this time should be brief."

Such directness verged upon the indecent, but the merchant clearly saw the wisdom of it in this case. He drew a deep breath. "I do have certain troubles, Reverend One. Your counsel would be of inestimable value to me."

Birdlike, the ancient head nodded. "I can offer experience and wisdom, yes, but for action we must rely on the young."

Without turning his head, he beckoned to Tug, waiting behind him. Tug padded into the light, silent on bare feet. He sank to his knees and touched his shaven head to the paving, directing his reverence midway between his superior and the visitor.

"With respect, Reverend One," Jade Harmony protested, "discretion—"

The ancient raised a skeletal hand. "I assure you that, despite his admitted youth, I have enormous confidence in this man, one of our finest initiates in several years. If you need the sort of assistance I think you need, Eminence, you will find no better aide than he. Regard our guest, Brother."

Tug sat back on his heels and fixed dark eyes on the merchant, still portraying a childlike innocence belying the gruesome tales whispered about the Brothers' shadier activities. Surely no one could suspect him of anything!

"I trust your judgment implicitly, Holy One," Jade Harmony muttered.

"Then," said the Abbot, "let us quickly summarize your problems for the boy's information. Your daughter's marriage brought her husband a dowry that was the wonder of the bazaars, but tragically, soon after that happy day, your honored father unexpectedly released his spark to ascend to the Fifth World, glorious be his memory among us. By now, the governor's clerks will have collected the Emperor's death tax and some generous share for themselves. Doubtless many of your father's contracts included penalty clauses exercisable upon his demise; those may have proved expensive for you. In short, and I trust Your Eminence will understand that only the need for a speedy resolution compels my lapse into crudity, you probably find yourself, through no fault of your own, in a financially vulnerable state. And we all know that every harbor swarms with rats."

Appalled, Jade Harmony let out a long breath and then shrugged dismissively.

"Who in particular threatens?" asked the Abbot softly.

"Lemon Grass 3," Jade Harmony muttered. Now there was no doubt where the discussion was leading.

The old man smiled. "I expect there are others, but he is your most immediate oppressor?"

Jade Harmony nodded, now looking so miserable that Tug had trouble withholding a smile.

The Abbot looked to him. "If so directed, you could assist the noble merchant in this matter, Brother?"

"Yes, Father." Tug kept his voice low but confident.

"Then, Eminence, I think you may put your mind at ease. We will appoint this fine young monk to assist you. First you must name him."

"*Name* him?" Jade Harmony repeated, bewildered at the way the discussion had taken off like a spooked horse.

"Certainly. Give him a name that you will remember, one that will not clash with any names in your household or business dealings to create misunderstandings. A name that resonates with good fortune for you alone and will not draw others' attention! Think back to some of your travels or triumphs, perhaps?"

Jade Harmony held Tug's steady gaze for a moment. Contemptuously, he said, "Silky."

Tug-who-was-now-Silky genuflected to him. "My ears are honored to hear this name you grant me, Eminence. I will serve your needs in all things and ahead of all other loyalties."

The old man clicked teeth in satisfaction. "An excellent name! Congratulations, Brother Silky."

"He reminds me of my first concubine," Jade Harmony said. "The one my parents gave me on my fifteenth birthday. He has the same cow eyes."

"Quite," said the Abbot. "Serious matters are best dealt with expeditiously. I will have a contract drawn up, Eminence, and Brother Silky will bring it to you tomorrow if that will suit. Our terms are standard, but there are always details to discuss."

"And things are always clearer in daylight. However, Your Reverence . . ."

Tug-Silky had a strong suspicion that Jade Harmony 7's conscience was now demanding to know what fit of insanity had brought him to such an abomination as murder for hire. Whatever he had been about to say, the Abbot forestalled him.

"He will not be wearing his present habit. What guise will you sport, Brother Silky?"

Silky flashed a boyish, extremely juvenile smile. "Do you ever sponsor sand warriors, Eminence?"

Jade Harmony shuddered. "Of course not." Barbaric!

"Sponsoring sand warriors can be an extremely profitable public service. I will bring you a business proposal on the subject tomorrow."

"I look forward to it," Jade Harmony croaked. "One hour past noon."

His house would be quiet then. Even if the crazy impulse that had brought him here was already fading, he could go home and sleep on it and decide tomorrow. He moved to rise. Instantly, Silky was on his feet, offering assistance. He placed his hands under his prospective employer's elbows and raised him. He caught a twinkle of amusement from the Abbot. Jade Harmony 7's impressive girth advertised his prosperity for all the world to see, but he had failed to notice how little effort the newly named Silky seemed to need to lift him with those reed-thin arms.

He who had been Tug and was now Silky ushered the fat man out to the courtyard where his guards and palanquin waited. Kneeling with head bowed, he watched unobtrusively as the wretched Outlanders hoisted their load of lard shoulder-high for another journey. He touched his forehead to the ground in obeisance as the parade moved away. Then he went back inside, heading into the true monastery, not the part that visitors saw.

He walked slowly, practicing calm. He had been named at last, so he was now a full brother in the order. Very soon, he would make his first credited score, and he was annoyed that the prospect had raised his pulse above its normal rate, although that was only half of a layman's. This time, he might still have to tolerate a supervisor, but the score would go on his tally, and it would be a very easy one if—as seemed most likely—the fat man himself was to be the subject.

Silky! A wonderful name from a lackluster client. The fat man was probably already regretting his impulsive leap out of mediocrity, but Silky's first contract would be very short-lived. Pity! It would have been interesting to teach the fat man the advantages of the Helpers' unorthodox business methods.

The abbey premises were much larger than realized by any outsider, even the governor's tax assessors; they housed one of the largest chapters in all the Good Land, ranking as a house of 400-ply. Large was not endless, though, and he came to the door of the Abbot's reception room at last. It stood open, so he slipped through the bead curtain beyond and sank down in obeisance. By day, this was a magnificent chamber, furnished in silks and precious woods, decorated with jade, fine porcelain, tiles, and stone. It was a safe guess that the mandarin governor himself had nothing to match it, nor would that blubbery client of Silky's, for all his vaunted wealth.

By night, it was a mysterious universe of its own, lit by a single colored lantern hanging at head height near the far side. The Abbot and Brother Archives sat on cushions below it. They were visible, as was the low table on which their tea set stood, but all the rest of the great room was a darkness twinkling with points of reflection from gems or porcelain or mother-of-pearl.

"Enter, Brother Silky," the Abbot called. "Close the door and come join us."

Silky obeyed, dropping to his knees on the tiles near the table, although farther from it than the elders sat.

The old man—who did not look as old as he had earlier, but was still old—poured a bowl of tea for him. "Congratulations on your contract, Brother. I see it being enormously profitable, both for our House and for yourself. Officially, if the question is ever asked, your client came to negotiate a one-year memorial for his father, but Brother Archives has been expecting for some time that he would soon come calling on more serious business."

Silky said nothing.

"He is a fool," Archives said. "The moment he got his hands on the family seal, he started making very rash ventures. He should have spun out his daughter's dowry payments for years. Lemon Grass and Distant Cloud are planning to split him between them."

Silky waited, confident that the Abbot would know what bothered him.

The old man did, of course. "You have questions, Brother?"

"Father, is not the merchant Lemon Grass a client of our house?" The brotherhood never tolerated conflicts of interest, and Lemon Grass was one of the richest men in Wedlock and, thus, in all Shashi Province. By asking for his death, Jade Harmony should have condemned himself to becoming a routine score on Lemon Grass 3's contract.

"Indeed, yes." The old man turned the leathery mask of his face to Archives. "How many years have we been assisting him, Brother?"

"Six, Father. His count now is seven routine and only three requests. He is a shy man." The archivist's laugh was foul but his memory was legendary.

"So he is ripe, you see?" the Abbot said. "We should gain little more by waiting until the end of his contract, whereas I foresee great things from Jade Harmony 7. You have heard of the Portal of Worlds?" For a man of such antiquity, his eyes were amazingly bright.

Silky knew very well of the Abbot's obsessive interest in the Portal, but not why he thought it important. He had not expected to be discussing stupid legends on this, the night of his naming.

"Only stories, Holy One. Some say that it is due to open again soon."

"Not in my lifetime here, I am afraid, but certainly in yours. There are signs! Celestial Rose breathed fire last year, during Thunder Moon. It is recorded that before every opening of the Portal, either Black Dragon Mountain or Celestial Rose will breathe fire in the Year of the Crow and the Emperor will send propitiatory offerings."

So far as Silky knew, either Celestial Rose or Black Dragon Mountain erupted every two or three years and the Emperor always sent propitiatory offerings. He bowed his head in homage.

"I am elevated by this gift of lore, Holy Father."

"Yes. Jade Harmony may be able to assist us in our preparations for that epochal event. Now, about tonight . . ."

"Tonight, Father?" Silky asked very calmly. He was fairly sure that he had not twitched as much as an eyelash.

"It must be done before you call on our client tomorrow. Natural causes, please. Any questions?" the Abbot demonstrated a saintly smile.

Very many questions! Lemon Grass 3's aide was Sister Freshet, and Silky had no wish to find himself on the wrong end of her knife.

"I have great respect for Sister Freshet's skills, Father." The standard contract set no obligation on the Order to defend the client from third parties, but it was understood that it would normally do so to safeguard its own interests.

The old man chuckled. "So you should. She is a very dangerous woman, as she has demonstrated many times. But you are a very dangerous young man now. And you are named, Brother Silky, so it is permitted to reveal the last great secret to you. Recite to me some Outlandish poetry."

Silky sensed that the old men were laughing at him, but he had been taught long ago not just how to suppress anger, but how to dismiss it altogether. The thought of a last great secret was intriguing, although there would undoubtedly be other, greater secrets behind that one.

"I confess that I cannot, Holy One, not a line." Yet, ever since he had been admitted to the Order, he had attended the Abbot in his chamber once a month for the purpose of being instructed in Outlanders' poetry. He ignored the Abbot's gentle smile and Archives's rotten-tooth leer. Of course it was understood that those one-on-one sessions were also a chance to complain about any brother or sister who had behaved badly, although Silky had never been rash enough to do so. Outlandish poetry? Not a line. "I must assume that the purpose of those sessions was otherwise than I was led to expect—and allowed to remember," he added uneasily.

"Well done. You have taken that revelation much better than most do. Have you ever heard of a leash?"

"Only as a restraint for an animal, Father."

"It is also a restraint for Gray Helpers. The poem the Order uses is very long and exceedingly bad, as you would expect. It is never likely to be quoted for its own merit. Sister Freshet's leash is, I believe, lines twelve, thirty-nine, and seventy-four?" the Abbot looked inquiringly to Archives, who nodded. "Very well. When you meet her, you repeat these two lines:

"The heron and the swan against rain-dimpled water . . . Up golden ladders to the moon. Dreadful doggerel, but she will at once go into submission, and you may then give her your orders. Be quick, for you will have only a few moments before she lapses into coma. You bring her back with the release: *Morning star that dies when its task is done.* She will remember the incident with resentment unless you have instructed her not to, but either way she will obey your instructions with zeal." He did not insult his new monk by asking him to repeat the words. "And tomorrow, I will call her in to change her leash and remove any residual compulsions you have implanted. I can't imagine Freshet refusing a wholesome young man such as yourself if you asked her nicely, but if you plan to abuse your transient power over her, you had better do so tonight."

"I would not do that, Father," Silky said. "It would betray your teaching and my loyalty to the Order." He had attended Sister Freshet on her sleeping mat twice, but both times at her command, never by his request. Besides, he could guess that the Abbot had ways of finding out when the leash was used; that ability to control must itself be controlled.

The old man nodded approvingly, but then his face had probably not betrayed his feelings once in the last fifty years. "Freshet can advise you on time and place and method and you should listen carefully, but you make the decision. This one is yours. You may dismiss her beforehand and do it alone if you wish. Archives?"

"It shouldn't be too hard. Lemon Grass is a man of predictable routines. Don't leave before I have shown you plans of his grounds and defenses."

As if Silky would be so stupid! "Thank you, Brother."

"Go, then." The Abbot gestured their joint dismissal. "I envy you this night, Brother Silky. One's first score is a great milestone in one's life, a memory to be savored and enjoyed. May your ancestors guide your hand and bless your venture."

Silky had no ancestors that he knew of. He must just hope that they knew him and had heard the Abbot's prayer.

A thick mist had rolled in from the river, which was a good omen for a young assassin on his first outing. No one could have told Silky from an artisan's apprentice going home after a long day; his hands were dirty and callused, his walk depicted physical exhaustion. All the equipment he would need was in a satchel on his shoulder. He carried no visible weapon, but anyone who tried to rob him would not survive long enough to look surprised.

If this first contract turned out as profitable, as the Abbot had hinted, then Silky's share would be substantial. Brother Bursar would invest it for him, and the Gray Helpers' investments paid much better than most, because they could apply all the inside knowledge they gathered from their clients. Two or three good contracts and Silky would be rich enough to buy a priory some-where—not a 400-ply abbey like Wedlock's, of course, but even a 20-ply would eventually make him rich if it were well managed.

He thought back with amusement to that impudent, starving waif who had offered to kill somebody for Brother Moon. The Tug who had been born that day had died this evening. *Silky!* What a glorious, wonderful name for an assassin! He could not remember any of the names he had used before he became Tug. And what would he be tomorrow? An anonymous flunky in the Harmony mansion? Cook? Maintenance man? Guard? His tal-ent was weaponry. He hoped his client could be persuaded to take him on as a sand warrior, fighting in the arena. That would be both an exciting life and a very convenient cover for his real work.

He had never visited the Lemon Grass mansion before, but Brother Archives had shown him the layout down to the last tree and closet. Although it stood in spacious grounds surrounded by spiked walls and well patrolled by dogs and armed guards, any Gray Helper knew how to deal with those.

Nobody registered the killer's arrival at the wall. He found a place well shielded from view by a bush, then blew on the whistle to summon the dogs. He could just barely hear the tone himself, but no one much older than he would hear a thing. The dogs came to investigate, growling and snuffling; he tossed the bait over to them. While he waited for the drug to take effect, he changed into all-enveloping nightwork clothes that left only his eyes visible.

The spiked wall was a joke. The dogs were snoring.

Rummaging through his memory of the house plans, he located Sister Freshet's window. Having poked a twig through the shutter lattice as a signal, he climbed into a nearby tree, and settled in for a long wait. In fact, it was little more than an hour before chinks of light appeared around the shutters.

According to Archives, Sister Freshet had been assigned as aide to Lemon Grass at the start of his contract six years ago. She had rapidly promoted herself from servant to concubine, a post she still held without complaint—Archives suspected that she was genuinely in love with the man, a complication discouraged but not unexpected. She found Silky's signal and, in a few minutes, came strolling around the corner of the building, silent but not furtive.

He removed his hood and dropped gently to the ground behind her. Had she been his subject, she would have died instantly. Knowing what to expect, she was unsurprised and turned calmly.

"Tug? Nicely done. Is this for real?"

"Absolutely!" he said indignantly.

"Who's your subject?" she demanded, her voice in the night suddenly crackling with suspicion.

He said, "*The heron and the swan against rain-dimpled water. Up golden ladders to the moon.*"

She winced and doubled over as if struck by sudden belly pains. "Oh! Rot me! You turd!" She sobbed a few times. "Stop it, stop it!"

"I have instructions for you."

"Tell me! I'll obey. You needn't do this to me."

"Yes, I do, because my subject is Lemon Grass 3."

She groaned. "Please, please! It's getting worse."

He plunged ahead. "You will obey all my instructions, answer my questions truthfully, and you will not betray me or hinder my escape."

"Yes, yes! Just make it stop."

"Do you understand?"

"Yes."

"And you will obey?"

"Of course I will obey, anus worm! Didn't he tell you? I'll eat shit if you tell me to."

"Not necessary. *Morning star that dies when its task is done.*"

She uttered a faint breathy sound, a whisper of relief, and then straightened up. She bared her teeth, but she did not try to knife him.

"Lemon Grass is a client!"

"There's a conflict and he lost."

She sighed. "I see. Then it's over. . . . They gave you a big one to start with, Brother! The town will buzz tomorrow. What's your name now?"

"Silky."

"Good one! What do you need, Silky?"

"Advise me. Natural causes."

She snorted. "He's taking his usual exercise and Starry Pink gets the honor tonight. When he's done with her, he'll go to his own bed. Never varies."

The novices' toast: *May all your subjects be predictable.*

"What does he wear in bed?"

"Nothing. A sheet on top. He keeps a quilt handy in case he feels cold."

"Show me where," Silky said.

It was going to be drastically easy. Knowing the geography of the Cloud mansion, he could have done it alone, scrambling up the stonework to a window and lying in wait to break the subject's neck when he returned, but he had been told repeatedly that safest and simplest were always best. His orders were that it had to be natural causes.

He followed Freshet indoors and up the stair to the master's bedchamber. Then he sent her away, because he wanted to enjoy every moment of this, his first real score. He had worked hard and long to get to it.

A rich man like Lemon Grass slept on a raised bed of bricks, into which braziers could be placed during cold weather. Wearing hood and gloves, Silky drew back the quilt and sprinkled powdered wolfsbane on the pillows and the topmost rug. The subject would ingest a fatal dose through his breath and his skin. He would be found there dead in the morning unless he awoke with hallucinations of flying and hurled himself out the window.

Silky had already warned Overt Operations. The Gray Helpers would be summoned to prepare the body, and they must make sure the deadly bedclothes claimed no more victims. He went back downstairs and let himself out. The dogs showed no signs of waking. No one saw him go over the wall.

His first outing was done. Not quite boring, but close.

He was home at Joyful Departure within the hour, finding a party to celebrate his naming already in progress. He was quite touched by all the cheers and little speeches, but he had displayed his own talent for hypocrisy at such events often enough to distrust most of them. Of course, he was having a double celebration—name and first score on the same day was unusual—so he got to kiss all the girls twice.

Sex was just another business technique to the Order, a craft that needed practice like any other. The wall dividing the nunnery from the monastery was of polished glass, topped with razor-edged spikes and regarded by novices on both sides as a skill-testing question. Any adolescent boy or girl who did not regularly break the rules against promiscuity would be recognized as unsuitable material and duly expelled, dead or alive. The only true prohibition was a visible pregnancy, for which all three parties involved would be put to death. Thanks to good pharmaceutical instruction and a shoddy lock on the pharmacy door, matters never went that far.

❋　❋　❋

Following tradition, Silky announced that he must rest up for a busy day ahead and left early. The female novices then drew straws to see who would help the newly blooded brother celebrate. It was dark in his cell, and the girl who joined him there wouldn't tell him her name. That didn't matter, because he knew her scent and texture. After it was over, he slept very well.

Jade Harmony slept very badly. He thrashed and repeatedly wakened himself by crying out in nightmares for reasons he could not remember. His concubine was too pregnant to be of any help—he had limited himself to one as an economic measure—and he never lay with his wife now, not wanting more legal children to support.

He eventually gave up and went up to the rooftop shrine to pray for help from his ancestors. The sky was clear, and the uncountable worlds looked down on him coldly. How many of them had his ancestors reached? How many of those ancestors were advanced enough now to help their troubled descendant still trapped down here in the Fourth? He prayed for wisdom, but nothing changed.

He left early for the harbor, after issuing strict orders to set the dogs on any caller touting business ventures.

Rumors about Lemon Grass began to circulate by midmorning. Before noon, the criers had the news, and the governor ordered the trading floors closed. Nauseated and feverish, appalled at how easily he had been hoodwinked, Jade Harmony summoned his palanquin and guards and went home.

In Wedlock, the slums of the masses huddled near the water; the palaces of the rich stood on the uplands, enjoying vistas, cool winds, and springs of sweet water. Most of the palaces had been built by princes and were now owned by merchants or retired mandarins. Jade Harmony 7's residence was not one of the best, but it was still a palace. From it, he had a good, if distant, view of the river traffic, a few modern paddleboats and stern wheelers spewing plumes of black smoke in among the swarm of traditional junks.

The thought that he might have lost all this but instead had saved it by complicity in a murder tore him to pieces. Poverty was unthinkable, but the death of a thousand cuts was even worse. Suddenly, he felt an unbearable urgency, and signaled with his drum for maximum speed. Unsatisfied, he signaled for even more, until he heard the crack of the guards' whips on his bearer's backs.

Arriving home, he gave instructions that a man named Silky should be admitted, blessing his foresight that he had not mentioned that name earlier and hence could not be seen to be countermanding his own orders. He declined food and again sought reassurance in the shrine of his ancestors. A right-thinking man should never order a murder, and yet the sense of relief that Lemon Grass was no longer holding a knife at his financial throat was undeniable. The very sunlight seemed to sparkle brighter.

Eventually, Jade Harmony crept out to sit in his water garden and wait for his visitor. Bamboo swayed gently in the breeze, caged birds sang, waterfalls purled their silver songs, and all he could think of was the execution ground before the governor's mansion. That was where evildoers were sliced to death, immobilized in wooden cangues, screaming their lives away amid the mockery of the crowds. The spectators would lay bets on how long he would take to die, and bribe the tormentors to make the show last for days.

Surprisingly, First Musket himself came to announce the visitor. "A sand warrior, Eminent One, calling himself Silky! He refuses to surrender his weapons."

Sand warriors paraded around festooned with fearsome shiny blades of all shapes and sizes, like walking bower birds' nests. Jade Harmony could not imagine the doe-eyed boy he had met at the monastery adorned like that. "I hope you didn't laugh too hard?"

First Musket blinked in bewilderment. "No, Eminent One." He glanced around at the shrubbery. "You wish us to admit him? And stay close?"

"*No!*" More calmly the merchant added, "I will receive him in private. He is known to me."

The old musketeer's mustache bristled in outrage, but he rose from his knees and withdrew, backing and bowing. It was unheard of for any man of status to receive a male visitor alone, armed or not. Jade Harmony wondered uneasily if loyalty might override obedience in this case, resulting in forbidden eavesdropping, but then the sight of his visitor drove all other thoughts from his mind.

No ash-gray robe now. No boy, even. He wore the scarlet knee breeches and leather boots of his pretended profession, and the traditional collection of weapons—at least a score visible, probably more hidden. A long sword hung on his back and two shorter ones at his waist. Baldrics forming an *X* across his chest were loaded with throwing knives while more were strapped to his forearms. Several paces away he drew his longest blade to salute, then went through the correct ritual of bowing and scraping until he was kneeling in the sand before Jade Harmony 7's cushion. It was undoubtedly the same youth, the one he had named Silky, but he seemed to have aged several years. Arms and chest . . . even his neck looked thicker and more mature. His raven-black queue was gathered in the traditional topknot of a sand warrior, tied with purple and white ribbons.

Jade Harmony stared at that more than anything. "Last night, your head was completely shaven!"

Silky smiled disarmingly. "Last night, the light was not of the best, Eminence."

There was nothing wrong with the sunshine now. "This is what you really look like?"

Again the boy showed a perfect set of teeth, a rarity in Shashi. "This is what I look like when I am dressed as a sand warrior. Last night, you saw me in a monk's habit. People are happiest when they see what they expect to see."

"Sorcery?" Jade Harmony whispered. His scalp prickled. It was unmistakably the same youngster—face, voice, eyes, oversize hands. He recalled now how easily those hands had lifted him.

The warrior shrugged today's broad shoulders. "A minor occult skill."

"Purple and white? Whose colors are those?"

Silky smiled, as if amused by his ignorance. "The House of Humble Followers of Martial Ancestors. There are six warrior lodges in Wedlock, but they are legal fictions. In fact, each sand warrior is sponsored by a gentleman of quality, one already licensed to maintain armed retainers. I will never sully your own noble colors by wearing them in the arena."

No, he wouldn't. The ritualized swordplay of the sand warriors was an entertainment for the masses, never gentlemen. "But everyone here would know what you are!"

"Officially, I would be, say, a clerk of accounts. I can look like that, too, but your household may be allowed to know that I am a sand warrior. Only you will know that I am a Gray Helper. May we proceed to the contract, Eminent One?" He stretched forward to offer a scroll.

Jade Harmony began to unroll it; exquisite brushwork swam before his eyes. He closed it. "Lemon Grass had a major seizure in the night. There is word that he may not live."

The boy sighed. "He *does* not—the Helpers were summoned at the third hour. A funeral of the Most Exalted Grade is being prepared. May he prosper as well in the Fifth World as he did in the Fourth."

"You killed him!"

Last night, the boy's smiles had looked innocent.

"I helped him advance on the staircase of worlds. Does this not relieve the worst of your troubles, Eminent One—as we agreed?"

Yes! Yes, it did, and the thought was sickening. "I did not agree! I agreed to nothing. Now you expect me to pay you for committing this murder?"

"Not now, Eminence." The killer looked quite shocked. "Our terms are explained in that scroll."

Jade Harmony 7's stomach churned like the river behind a sternwheeler. Again, he unrolled the contract and tried to read it.

"There are no names written here!"

White teeth flashed again. "Of course. No names given and no signatures required. That is purely a statement of terms already agreed between a gentleman and his servants."

Jade Harmony could not read through his tears. He could not think. "Tell me briefly what it says."

"All our contracts are for seven years or seven requested outings, whichever comes first. We may provide other incidents, at our discretion. We call those 'routine' and do not count them. An aide, meaning me, is assigned exclusively to your attendance during that time. I work to promote your interests and no others.'"

"'Outing' means 'murder'?"

"We prefer to call them outings, or 'incidents.'" The assassin smiled again. "We offer many more services than just murder, Eminence. Our information is unmatched in Wedlock and throughout the Good Land. For example, we know that the governor assessed your deeply lamented father's worth at 473,000 taels and levied a death tax of 95,000 on it. Fortunately, his assessors overlooked your rice lands at Great Salt River and the silk partnership in the Mulberry Islands, not to mention the emerald collection your father had been amassing in his last years. The sudden, tragic advance of Lemon Grass offers several opportunities for those who can act quickly, of which the most promising will be a drastic drop in the price of salt, because he and some partners were holding it back from the market and the others don't know how much he had in stock. I do." And so on.

Jade Harmony listened in amazement to a display of financial virtuosity such as he had not heard since his father died. The monk child never hesitated or stumbled as he rattled off prices, amounts, locations, dealers, profits, or prospective partners, nor was he merely parroting a lesson, because whenever Jade Harmony asked a question, he answered promptly and lucidly. At the end, he raised an insolent and amused eyebrow to invite comment.

"When do I pay you and how much?" Jade Harmony asked hoarsely.

"You pay the House of Joyful Departure, Master. It allots me a share."

"How. Much. Do. I. Pay?"

"There will be a settlement at the end of the contract."

"*How much?*"

"One quarter of your worth."

"My . . . *Quarter*? Of my *entire worth*?"

The boy spread his hands as if to show that he was hiding nothing. They were the thick, callused hands of a warrior, not the small, soft hands of a monk. Or so they seemed at that moment. "We estimate your true present value at a conservative 500,000 taels, Eminence. We guarantee that it will increase manyfold during the life of the contract."

"And if, in the meantime, the governor has cut us to shreds in the Place of Execution?"

Silky laughed. "The Emperor, bless his name, does not appoint fools to be governors! The last attempt to put a Gray Helper on trial was a hundred years ago in the city of High Vistas. The governor's replacement's replacement's first act was to burn the indictment."

"The Son of the Sun—"

"The Emperor knows that he is mortal also," Silky said impatiently. "Do not worry about the Emperor or his minions. They will not trouble us. Now, you will see that it is to our mutual advantage for me to have some independent position in your household, so that I can come and go without having to ask leave of some servant or endure this absurd rigmarole over weapons every time I must speak with you. Sand warriors are very profitable for their sponsors. For example, last month's bout between Carmine Fangs and Implacable Dragon . . . Mayhap you have heard of it?"

"No." The mere thought of watching armed men fight made Jade Harmony 7's skin crawl.

"Admittedly, it was a match to disablement, which is rare and more profitable than most. The two sponsors—including their shares of the gate and the book, but before paying the purse to the winner and a settlement for the loser's widow—regrettably, he bled to death, which was quite unplanned—anyway, between them, the sponsors shared more than 7,000 taels. The winner's sponsor netted 4,000 clear." The monk smirked at Jade Harmony 7's expression. "I do not lie to you now, Master, and I never will. Not a bad return on room and board, you must agree."

"That is all? A room and your keep?"

"That will do to start with. As soon as you see the profits rolling in, you will be ordering me to expand your stable, hire trainers and so on. Most sponsors rapidly become enamored of the sport."

How had Jade Harmony ever thought this young killer looked innocent? Trapped, trapped! This must be how it felt to blunder into quicksand. Public bloodshed and private murder! What would Jade Harmony 6 have said? What must he think if he was watching now? Better to think upon Jade Harmony 1, who had been the next worst thing to a pirate and who would approve. He had died on an impalement stake. "What choice do I have?"

"None, really," Silky said sadly. "Last night, you asked me to kill Lemon Grass and I did. He did not suffer and the Good Land is better for his ascent. The contract is in force. Believe me, you will not regret it, Master, once you have adjusted to the idea."

This was absurd! An illegal conspiracy in an unsigned document? Such a contract could never be enforced. But the gleam in the young killer's eager eyes warned Jade Harmony that it was extremely enforceable.

"And who is next?"

"Master, that really is not a wise—"

"You said you would never lie to me!"

Silky looked sulky. "I did not say I would tell you everything."

"But you will tell me this!" Jade Harmony shouted.

The sand warrior pouted for another moment and then shrugged. "Very well. The eminent merchant, Distant Cloud."

The merchant wailed. "My son-in-law? My daughter's husband?"

"Who is merely five years younger than your honored self," Silky said snidely. "What did your fifteen-year-old daughter think of her gouty, baggy-faced, thrice-married bridegroom? In a year, he has not gotten her with child, which tells us much. Like you, he is a client of ours. A good financial match, you thought, but right after the wedding, Distant Cloud asked us to advance your father, his wife's grandfather, which we did. Today, I requested—and received—permission to return the compliment, since your contracts are now likely to come into conflict. I think I will advance his sons first, and then him, because it will be tidier if your daughter returns to you bringing his entire estate intact, except for taxes and his bequest to the Gray Helpers. I will use some means that will not make three deaths close together seem suspicious. This program will triple your assets within the month and bring your daughter back to her mother's loving arms. That should stop some of her moping. Do you see any flaw in this proposal, Master?"

Silence. Jade Harmony stared into the abyss. Triple?

Triple his assets?

Within the month?

Shut up Morning Jewel and stop her never-ending griping?

"Master?" Brother Silky muttered.

"You murdered my father?"

"Oh, not I, Eminence! You are my first client."

"But Distant Cloud paid your House to have my father murdered?"

"He ordered your esteemed ancestor's death and will pay for it in the manner I just explained."

After another long pause, Jade Harmony whispered, "I approve your proposal, Brother Silky. Does that make the proposed incidents requested or routine?"

Suddenly, the boy was back with his eager childish grin. "Since I already proposed them and received the Abbot's approval, they won't be charged to your account, Master. You still have six outings in hand."

CHAPTER 3

Siping, northernmost province of the Good Land, was the site of its capital, Heart of the World. The city itself was an ugly sprawl of shanties and slums whose sole reason for existence was to provide services and goods to the imperial palace, Sublime Mountain. Sublime Mountain justified its name by occupying the entire surface of a large mesa, a yolk around which the city lay like the white of an egg. But even Sublime Mountain was not the true center of government, for the palace was divided into the Great Without and the Great Within. The Great Without was the abode of the mandarins who ran the courts, enforced the laws, and gathered taxes. The imperial stud, armory, printing office, library, archives, and army headquarters were there. The Great Without was about work.

The Great Within was concerned with pleasure. It covered a much larger area, and comprised many parks and palaces, where the hundreds—or in some reigns thousands—of imperial concubines, Empresses, their female children and juvenile male children, plus thousands of female servants and eunuchs to guard and tend them, dwelled. Only one unaltered male lived there: the Emperor himself, currently Absolute Purity, Son of the Sun, Denizen of the Golden Throne, Lord of the High and the Low, et cetera.

The Empress Mother looked out with deep disapproval at the snow swirling past her window. A blizzard in Falling Leaf Moon!

Winter had come too early, and storms as violent as this one normally raged across most of the northern provinces. There would be dead livestock, flooding, and probably famine before summer. She could do nothing about the weather. She could handle almost anything else, though, and today she was to set in motion events necessary for the survival of the Eleventh Dynasty.

A score of women and some eunuchs had labored for hours over her toilet, from bathing in rose water to the final delicate touch of paint on her faded eyelashes. They dressed her in enough embroidered silk to carpet a palace and jewels that could have graveled a courtyard. A hundred artisans had worked for a year to create her costume. Now, with perfect timing, her carrying chair arrived. She rose from her bench and minced two steps in her platform shoes—a striking, even terrifying, figure in her imperial-yellow finery, with her tall hat, elaborately bedecked hair, and starkly painted face. Two women adjusted her folds and covered her in a thick fur rug, four eunuchs lifted the poles, eight eunuch guards took up position, and the Empress Mother of the Good Land was borne swiftly from her quarters, having spoken barely a word so far that morning.

No one saw her as her bearers trotted through the Great Within complex, up and down stairs, from building to building. To avoid the snow, they skirted the open courtyards, going by way of covered cloisters and secret tunnels. It was possible, even likely, that these courts and halls were, at most times, thronged with scores or hundreds of people, all of whom had been hastily cleared out to allow the Empress Mother unseen and untroubled passage. The Empress Mother neither knew nor cared.

Her destination was the room called the Emperor's Eye. It was tiny and very private, its only function being to provide a view through an ivory screen into the Abode of Wisdom, the meeting hall of the Great Council. This was, in effect, a window from the Great Within into the working palace, the Great Without. If the Emperor did not wish to preside in person, he could watch from the Eye while remaining unseen, or he could choose to stay away altogether and no one would know the difference. In fact, the present Emperor had never been even to the Emperor's Eye, let alone the Abode of Wisdom; his mother always came in his stead. His father, Zealous Righteousness, had watched proceedings from that room a very few times, but had never presided over the council. Unlike ordinary mortals, the all-powerful need not endure boredom.

As her attendants withdrew, leaving her alone in the little room, the princes were entering the hall, joining the mandarins already assembled—the timing was always perfect, but whether the meeting was adjusted to her toilet or her toilet to the meeting, the Empress Mother neither knew nor cared. Anyone approaching the throne was required to do so barefoot and in an undignified scamper. On reaching his place, he must kowtow, which involved kneeling and knocking his forehead on the ground three times, repeating the procedure twice, for a total of nine knocks.

The councillors' rugs were arranged in arcs facing the throne on its stage, to the watching Empress Mother's right. The throne—a minor throne, not the Golden Throne itself, which stood in the Hall of Celestial Peace—was concealed behind an even larger and more intricate screen because an Emperor would lose face if he ever entered before his courtiers did, and even more face if he fussed with the hang of his elaborate costume. Any Emperor who ever did attend would be revealed only when everything was ready to proceed.

The most ornate of the rugs lay close to a corner of the dais, reserved for Venerable First Mandarin. The company bowed in reverence as the old fox entered. Despite his trailing white beard, First Mandarin was spry enough when he wanted to be, but as a tribute to his high office, he was allowed to approach the throne slowly, with ancestral dignity.

Of the twenty-four men present, only four really counted—First Mandarin, who ran the government; Chief Eunuch, who ran the palace; Supreme Guardian, who ran the army; and Court Astrologer, who could advance, retard, or totally prohibit just about anything. These four formed the Small Council, which ruled the Good Land in the name of the Emperor.

The Empress Mother ruled the Small Council.

Following centuries-old ritual, First Mandarin ran the meeting without a wasted word. Each official, in turn, was recognized and produced the reports he had brought, one by one. Only the titles were spoken: "A demon wind has made great havoc in the Mulberry Islands." "A catalog of tributes sent to the Son of the Sun by certain Outlanders of the west." And so on. A deaf-mute page would gather the file and lay it before the throne with much ceremony. Rarely, First Mandarin would issue orders or call for comment, but those were kept equally terse. He ordered money sent to rebuild the imperial docks destroyed by the typhoon, for example. And so on.

The Empress Mother listened and watched. Any report that mattered had already been read to her in private and now she was mainly assessing people. Despite all their practiced inscrutability, she had a very good idea of what every man in the room thought of every other one—envy, distrust, loyalty, or admiration. Incompetence, excessive ambition, and especially alliances must be detected and dealt with before they became dangerous. She especially watched the four princes in attendance. None of them was closely related to her son, because over the years she had methodically pruned the sprawling imperial family down to a manageable size. Nonetheless, if her son were to die or be deposed, then one of those four would succeed to the throne. They all seemed loyal enough, but she kept them under close watch and never trusted any of them.

What did not happen in the Great Council mattered more than what did. Unrest attributed to the Bamboo Banner insurrection had now spread to two provinces, but both governors' month-end reports were logged in as routine. The new warden of Four Mountains Fortress had recently confessed to a complete lack of success in coercing his prisoner into cooperation and requested permission to proceed to sterner measures, but that affair had never been mentioned, even in the Small Council. The Empress Mother handled it personally, through First Mandarin.

At the end, First Mandarin made a ritual call for new business. In a shocking breach of tradition, Supreme Guardian raised his hand. The current blizzard was making roads impassable, he said. The ways up to Sublime Mountain itself were very steep and he was concerned that the palace would experience food shortages unless the storm ended soon. This announcement produced no panic in the chamber, because none of the grandees present would ever go to bed hungry even if the lesser staff were starving. First Mandarin just told him gently to remind the army of its duty to the Son of the Sun. In a world of hyperbolized civility and circuitous euphemisms, that was a brutal public rebuke.

The Empress Mother felt a tremor in the webs. Supreme Guardian might have been aiming his barb at Chief Eunuch for not making sure that the imperial larder was adequately stocked, which would be a normal enough political catfight. On the other hand, the general and First Mandarin had kept daggers drawn for years, and might have staged this public spat to conceal a secret rapprochement. She made a mental note to keep that possibility in mind.

As the meeting adjourned, she went out to where her bearers waited to convey her to her next appointment.

By the time Chief Eunuch was ushered in, the Empress Mother was sipping tea, comfortably seated on the modest throne in her audience chamber. The old man was obscenely obese, as round and soft as a ball of fresh dough; he waddled when he walked.

Palace flunkies were not normally required to kowtow, but he must when he was formally summoned like this, unless she bid him come forward. Today, feeling spiteful, she left him to it, not letting him off a single twitch. By the time he was kneeling on a rug at her feet, he was streaming sweat and puffing like a steamboat.

For months, even years, she had been procrastinating over the problem of her son. Procrastination was second nature to her except when she was faced with imminent danger, but time was running out. If Sublime Mountain did not shortly declare that the Son of the Sun had fathered an heir—or even a daughter, which would be a great relief to the Empress Mother and a huge disappointment to everyone else—then people were going to start believing the rumors of impotence or idiocy or insanity. Thousands of men labored in Sublime Mountain, thousands of women, girls, and eunuchs worked in the Great Within, and yet no more than four dozen people had ever set eyes on His Imperial Majesty Absolute Purity since his accession as a child. The enormous deception was becoming too obvious. There was speculation over who was next in line to the throne. The rabble dissidents in the south calling themselves the Bamboo Banner were claiming that the Emperor was dead. There were demands that he appear in public.

In fact, Emperors almost never did appear in public, and no one dared look at them when they did. The Emperor was the Son of the Sun, above all other men. He must not be seen to spit or cough or display any form of weakness. Inside the Great Within, he was seen by no one except women and eunuchs. Eunuchs were universally despised, half-men, little more than spayed animals, and it did not matter if they saw the Lord of the High and the Low with a head cold or a hangover. They were everywhere in the Great Within, and yet very few eunuchs, even, had ever set eyes on Emperor Absolute Purity. When an Emperor proceeded outside the Great Within, he traveled in a covered palanquin, carried by sixteen bearers and surrounded by a troop of guards, all of whom would be eunuchs. Crowds groveled in the dirt as he passed, and any head that was raised would be chopped off.

Finding her back to the wall, the Empress Mother had made a decision. In fact, she had made two decisions. Two plans were always better than one. Typically, of course, she would reveal only one of them to Chief Eunuch, at least at present.

The moment the servants withdrew and the two of them were alone, she went straight to the point, giving him no time to catch his breath. Only she could cut through ceremony like this, and it pleased her to demonstrate her power.

"Which girl do you recommend, Chief Eunuch?"

But even that could not catch him off his guard. "If it please Your Majesty, Snow Lily."

"Why?"

He adjusted his facial blubber into a mawkish smile, which did not reach the little pig eyes; none ever did. "She is so sweet, so dainty! So *delectable.*"

"My son is not expected to eat her, Chief Eunuch."

He wobbled his jowls politely at her joke. "To have served His Majesty and his greatly honored father all my life has been a peerless honor. My only regret, you know, is that I cannot have sons to continue my service after I advance." Lying was food and drink to him. "And to have had a daughter like Snow Lily!"

He would have sold her at twelve or younger, the Empress Mother decided. No one in Sublime Mountain had fewer scruples or more crimes on his soul than the fat man. Zealous Righteousness had called him a leather bag of night soil, but he had not hesitated to employ the eunuch's many talents.

"They are all highly qualified. Why should Snow Lily be first?"

He simpered. "She is lyrical and agile, well cultivated in art and classical poetry, a credit to the finest courtesan school in the Good Land." He clasped his hands, fingers like great white slugs, and paused as if wondering whether to point out that the Empress Mother herself had graduated from that same establishment. Apparently, he decided that discretion was safer and didn't. "During the demonstrations, she was the first to start touching herself. That is always the sign of a lustful nature. Their clothing is examined afterward, of course, and her shift was the dampest."

The Empress Mother had noticed that fondling also. She could remember her own training, and how shocked she had been when she had first been required to witness the mechanics of human copulation. She had never been warned that men did to women what ganders did to geese and dogs to bitches, if in different positions. Her body had known, though, and had soon reacted to the demonstration. In her innocence then, she had not realized that there were other candidates watching the same performance from other spy holes and that the watchers were themselves being watched. The training required had been simpler in her day, too, for Emperor Zealous Righteousness had been a mature man and still virile, with wide experience of women. The current class was being instructed in rousing the reluctant and elevating the limp.

It was past time to introduce Emperor Absolute Purity to the joys of concubinage. Hundreds of girls had been considered over the years, delivered to the gates by proud, rejoicing families and later returned privately, rejected and in tears. Nobody outside the Great Within could keep tally, so nobody outside realized that not a single girl had been accepted. But the hoax could not go on forever. A final six had been examined in the greatest detail. They were all mature—meaning fifteen or even sixteen in that context—all physically perfect virgins. They were also petite, for His Majesty tended to be alarmed by large people. Five would be rejected; one must go to his bed.

"I agree with your choice, Chief Eunuch," she said. "I will receive her."

"Now?" Was he bluffing, or had he prepared for even that surprise?

"At noon. If she pleases me, I will present her to His Majesty directly."

When important matters were in play, the Empress Mother liked to allow time between appointments so that her confidants would not run into one another in the antechambers. She therefore sent for a secretary and had some reports read to her before calling for her next visitor, Lady Twilight.

Twilight was close to forty, spare of build, with a face like a cleaver and an overall look of hard wear about her. Officially, she was His Imperial Majesty's chief food taster, which was fitting, because she probably knew more about poisons than anyone else in the Good Land. She had entered Sublime Mountain at eighteen as food taster to the Pearl Concubine, this being a standard palace precaution for any of the Emperor's women who conceived. They had been together ever since. The Pearl Concubine had been promoted to Junior Empress and now Empress Mother, but it had been thanks to Twilight that she had survived the so-called Scorpion Summer that followed Zealous Righteousness's death. Poisons had swirled around Sublime Mountain like plague, wiping out nine-tenths of the imperial family. No one had doubted that Twilight was behind many of the deaths or that she was a Gray Sister. It had been the Empress Mother who so aptly named her, of course. Now, after many years, the Empress Mother needed the Gray Helpers again, and Lady Twilight was still her liaison.

No kowtowing and kneeling for her—she was much too dangerous to provoke, even if her own daughter was now the Empress Mother's taster. She must always be treated with wary courtesy, allowed to sit on a cushion before the throne, the highest honor granted a commoner. Tea was brought, the flunkies dismissed, the weather deplored, but then the Empress Mother cut straight to the point.

"I have decided to risk your proposal." The second plan.

Lady Twilight bowed her head. "Your Majesty does me great honor."

"I am still doubtful that it is possible, though. The hazard is mortal for all of us."

"I am confident that it can be done."

"How much?" Brutal, but the lethal topic would make delicacy even more hypocritical than usual.

Twilight laid down her tea bowl and tucked her hands in her sleeves. "Too much to pay in money."

The Empress Mother nodded. She had expected this. "The city of White Rapids in Jingyan. Population: about eight thousand. Official tax revenue: forty-four thousand taels per year. You pocket that plus whatever else you can squeeze. And the rents."

Twilight displayed her Gray Sister training by showing no reaction whatsoever. "I believe it could be managed for that."

It certainly should be. The offer was staggeringly lavish. There was the minor problem that the Bamboo Banner might sack the town in the very near future, but news moved slowly along the length of the Good Land and here in Heart of the World only the government knew the extent of the Bamboo problem. The government was the Empress Mother.

"However . . ." Twilight murmured.

A ghostly warning bell tinkled ever so faintly, like a wind chime among the stars. "However?"

"So generous an assignment may be difficult to conceal? Perhaps rather two smaller donations than one so large?"

Ah! This promised to be interesting. The Empress Mother had often wondered about the division of income within the

Gray Order. That its overall wealth must rival that of the throne itself there could be no doubt, and its expenses likewise, for it must have half the mandarinate on its payroll. She held out her bowl for more tea.

"What ratio would you prefer between the two parts? Your own share, now . . . would be how much?"

Twilight refilled the tea bowls in silence and then ventured to glance up and meet the Empress Mother's eye. That was a breach of protocol, of course, but they were old . . . well, not friends. Never friends. Fellow conspirators, more like. Twilight dropped her gaze and pursed her lips, apparently recognizing that she had set her foot in a trap that would not open until the Empress Mother wished it to.

"The normal division," she conceded reluctantly, "would be two-thirds for the contributing abbey, with the remainder divided between the originating officer and the assigned aide."

"You being the originating officer and the youth you are to find for me being the aide?"

"That is correct, Your Majesty."

"Divided equally?"

"More or less equally. . . . It varies."

The Empress Mother would bet the Empire that it varied. "But in this case . . . ?"

Twilight sighed. "In this case, to assign any share to the aide would seem to be superfluous, would it not?"

True. He would own the Empire. He could pay himself whatever he wanted, for as long as he continued to breathe. Suddenly, the sheer immensity of the hoax they were planning snatched the Empress Mother's breath away. She had considered the dangers and the odds of success very carefully, without giving much thought to how far it would go or what would happen afterward. Then she caught Twilight's eye and saw that her personal assassin had already foreseen where the plot must eventually lead. Several people were going to die. How many and which ones would be established by events.

"I see your point. I will locate two properties of approximately the same total value as White Rapids and you will decide which is to be yours. How will you proceed?"

"I will go to Chixi," Twilight said. "You need Outlander stock, and there is plenty of that in the hill country. Stalwart men." Meaning big brutes.

The Empress Mother nodded again. She had worked that out for herself very easily. The Eleventh Dynasty had been of Outlandish origin and Zealous had been very big, although rarely a brute to his concubines. The first time he had dropped his full weight on her and begun thrusting, she had thought that she would be crushed and her bones shattered. She had learned otherwise and could now look back on the terrifying experience with amused nostalgia.

That Twilight hailed from Meritorious Aspect in Chixi was good fortune.

"And it is remote," Twilight said. "Poor communications, less gossip. No one travels at this season without urgent cause. My sister in Meritorious Aspect is failing, and Your Majesty has graciously granted me leave to go and visit her."

"The abbot of Meritorious Aspect is . . . ?"

"*Abbess.* She is my sister."

"Ah, good!" Truly, Twilight was a treasure. Of course, she had always denied having family, but truth was a seasonal fruit. "And when you are there?"

"I will personally send out appeals for candidates to all the minor chapters in Chixi. Some of them must have novices of the right size and age. I will choose the best fit, of course."

"How soon can it be managed?"

Twilight turned to scowl out at the blizzard. "In this weather?"

"The hill will soon become impassable. You must leave at once. The Grand Canal and the river should still be navigable, and by the time you reach Chixi, the snow will have melted."

Twilight nodded. She would not dare argue very hard, but her ready acceptance suggested that the Empress Mother had offered too high a price. No matter, the future of the dynasty was at stake. Twilight took her hands out of her sleeves but did not rise.

"Anything else?" the Empress Mother demanded.

"If I need to send word to Your Majesty, what name should I use?"

"Use your own name. The sick sister is a perfect excuse, if anyone dares wonder." She chuckled softly.

"But a code word for your new aide, Majesty. How about *Butterfly Sword*?"

"So obvious an oxymoron would be too memorable."

"You have not heard the expression? A butterfly sword is a large dagger, intended to be hidden in a sleeve."

The Empress Mother did not encourage humor. "As you please. You have our leave to withdraw."

Both plans were now under way.

The idea of being nice to someone was very alien to the Empress Mother. She had employed every trick in the book and most of the crimes in the legal code during her rise to power, both before the Zealous Righteousness's death and after it, so the hand of friendship hiding the poisoned dagger was part of her stock in trade. She was well aware that she might be creating a future rival in Snow Lily, but the risk was low and must be taken. The child had to be befriended, at least for now.

The Empress Mother summoned her army of body servants and had them remove two-thirds of her decoration. When the noon gong sounded, she was no more bedecked, bejeweled, bedizened, and bespangled than the wife of any senior moderately corrupt mandarin. She felt naked.

For this interview, she had chosen a modest meeting room looking out on an ornamental lake. The blizzard still raged, so the water was stark black and everything else white, with snow piled up in head-high drifts on roads and roofs and bridges; reminiscent of a painting by the minimalist Cherry-Tree Master. A dozen large braziers made the chamber toasty. Inviting. Homely, even.

As the trembling child was led in and shuffled forward to the place where she would begin her kowtow, the Empress Mother actually smiled in welcome. A venerable servant, catching an edge of that smile, almost dropped a priceless porcelain tea service.

Snow Lily was everything Chief Eunuch had called her, a small dream of young womanhood, understandably nervous but not gibbering in terror. Her face paint could not mask a perfect complexion and features of classical delicacy. As soon as the servants had withdrawn, she was given leave to sit on a rug, a great honor for a candidate concubine.

"I won't eat you, you know," the Empress Mother reassured her, thinking of Chief Eunuch's gastronomic vocabulary. "In my youth, I went through very much what you are having to go through."

Not quite. There had certainly been no tea party, for the Empress Mother of her day had taken no interest in her son's numerous bed toys. One night, when the omens were auspicious, the latest approved candidate had been stripped naked to ensure she bore no weapons, wrapped in a sheet, and carried into the imperial bedchamber. Her first night had gone quite well. Zealous Righteousness—never shy about his duty to breed heirs, although rarely successful at it—had taken to his new girl with unusual enthusiasm. He had called for her the following night and she had done even better. She had won promotion to a higher rating. Nine months later, she had given him a son and the world had opened for her like a blossom.

Snow Lily sipped tea with peerless lips and nibbled cake with flawless teeth. She had been taught to make conversation. She was talented. She might grow to be a rival if she managed the highly unlikely feat of producing a Grandson of the Sun, but the Empress Mother was confident that she could deal with that threat if and when it arrived. As Empress Grandmother for an orphan Emperor, she would have another twenty years of autocracy ahead of her.

Yes, the girl would do if any girl could do. The older woman bent the conversation away from the palace art collection to matters more pertinent.

"You have seen my son in processions, I expect."

"I have had that honor only once, Your Majesty. At the Acclaim of Imperial Ancestors."

And at a distance. There were some ceremonies that even the most reclusive Emperor could not evade without provoking speculation that he had died, but there were ways of keeping secrets even then.

"You will meet him soon."

The child took it well and spoke of unimaginable honor.

"Before you do, I must tell you something, my dear. You will be surprised. This is a state secret—that you have not only been chosen to be one His Majesty's concubines, but you will be the very first."

Snow Lily's eyes widened as if she had been jabbed with a bamboo eel spear. It was well known that the Son of the Sun had been born in the Year of the Nightingale and the birthday he had recently celebrated had been his eighteenth. Most noblemen became fathers at sixteen.

"Very soon after his dear father ascended to the Fifth World," the Empress Mother explained, "he was stricken by a serious disease." The nature of the disease had never been established but had probably included snake venom and quicksilver. "The astrologers almost despaired of his life. It slowed his development, but he has caught up now." Meaning that his voice had broken and he had produced a few pubic hairs. The eunuchs insisted that he did sometimes have erections. In theory, it was possible.

"I have frightened you, child. Come, let us go and call on him right away."

The Empress Mother actually took Snow Lily's hand for the short walk this visit entailed, which was another singular honor as well as a precaution against either of them falling over in their absurd court shoes. Absolute Purity had been moved to a room nearby for this occasion. As they crossed the hall to it, the Empress Mother heard baritone screaming and guessed that the Son of the Sun did not approve of the break in routine. The moment the guards opened the door, china shattered and it was clear that the Lord of the High and the Low was throwing things again.

She had promised Snow Lily a surprise. She had not said it would be a pleasant one.

CHAPTER 4

Face to the Sun was the most southerly city in the Good Land, the largest in Dongguan Province, and the greatest port in the world. From dawn to curfew, its streets were rivers of people: rapids of darting pickpockets, pools of plodding porters, whirlpools of babbling beggars, peddlers offering trinkets and snacks, stinking night-soil collectors, itinerant barbers, fortune-tellers, astrologers, cobblers, rag merchants, harlots, and thousands more. Wagons, rickshaws, mule trains, palanquins, and overburdened camels came swirling along like logs in the torrent; barrows and stalls constricted the flow like rocks. Shouts and curses mingled with the sound of pipes, gongs, and bells in a deafening clamor.

Through all this reeking confusion, the esteemed and learned Mountain Water, mandarin of the second rank, was being transported in his painted cart. He had two carriers in tandem to pull it, a gong beater and two guards out in front to clear the way, two secretaries trotting behind. Mountain Water was an extremely important man, senior deputy to the city governor. Being late for his luncheon of rice and fish sauce, he had ordered maximum speed, but that was barely faster than a walk in the noontime turmoil, no matter how eagerly his gong beater gonged or his guards wielded their bamboo rods.

As his guards were bracing themselves to fight their way through the absurdly narrow Gate of Prosperity that led into

Celestial Vista Square, a gunshot rang out ahead of them. Then another. Then three in quick succession.

Firearms were tightly controlled in the Good Land, but apparently people knew them from fireworks. The crowd in front surged back like a tidal wave. A great mob rushed away from the gate, trampling all before it. Screams of terror drowned out all the other mingled dins. Children seemed to fly through the air. Mountain Water's entourage was forced to a halt, and his guards found themselves in a real battle. Switching from flicks of their rods to vicious head strokes, they fought to protect their master from being overrun by the human avalanche.

"Floor them!" the senior guard barked and his helper obeyed, taking a two-handed grip on his bamboo and striking to hurt. In a few moments, they had felled a dozen or so semiconscious men and women to provide a barricade. Latecomers tripped over them and were struck down to add to the heap. Mountain Water was a very important personage and must be protected.

The flow faltered and the noise level dropped.

"Senior guard!" Mountain Water shouted.

Man Valor turned and squeezed his way back along the shafts, past the terrified gong beater and the panting bearers.

"Most Honored Master, we should be on our way again in just a—"

"No, no! I want to know what is going on and who is firing guns. You go and investigate and hurry right back here." Truth be told, Mandarin of the Second Rank Mountain Water looked almost as frightened as his gong beater. More, even.

Man Valor saluted and retraced his steps to the front. The crowd had gone and most members of the human barricade were already back on their feet. Some had limped away, some were still lying injured, but he pushed his way through and trotted along to the Gate of Prosperity. The immediate area of Celestial Vista Square was deserted, as he had never seen it, but an immense crowd had gathered in the center. Drums were beating. A gang of young men there had erected a human pyramid, as if they were celebrating a festival day, and even as he watched, another acrobat shot up from the midst of the crowd and added himself to the top. The onlookers roared approval.

Then there was another shot. And another roar of approval.

Man Valor had no idea what to make of this.

He started to run. His master would want a complete report.

Man Valor's father had been a soldier, leader of a hundred. He had named his firstborn Man Valor because, as he had explained to the boy when he was old enough to understand, valor defines a man. A man without valor is useless. A man may be strong or clever, but if he is not valorous, he is dirt. Man Valor could barely remember his father, but he remembered that.

When he was ten, the honored governor had sent ships to destroy a nest of wicked pirates and Man Valor's father had died bravely. Man Valor, escorted by his mother, had gone to the governor's palace to receive a small bag, which he had been told contained his father's ashes. He had thus become head of the family, responsible for his mother and sisters.

He had been working like a man ever since. He had done many things, some not very honorable but necessary. He had been a runner and grown nimble. Working in the docks had made him strong. Eventually, some approving ancestor had sent him a job as one of the honorable Mountain Water's personal guards. Now he was chief guard and twenty-four years old. His sisters were married off at last, his mother did not have to work quite as hard as she used to, and he was thinking of taking a wife.

He arrived at the back of the big crowd. He could hear drums and shengs and men singing. The pyramid had added more men—lithe young men, bare-chested, wearing only cotton trousers and green headbands. The crowd was chanting a name: *Bamboo! Bamboo! Bamboo!*

Man Valor pushed into the crowd. He was not tall, but he was strong and his tunic would not close around a tea bale. He went through the people like a boat through reeds and no one tried to stop him. He reached the front just in time to watch the human pyramid dismantle, its parts dropping nimbly to the ground, landing on bare feet in perfect formation. The drums thundered and he joined in the crowd's wild cheers. He had always adored watching acrobats; as a child, his fondest dream had been of being one.

There was much more going on—acrobats running, leaping, vaulting over one another, or turning somersaults in mid-air; singers and musicians; and dozens more men in the same unbleached cotton trousers and green headbands, holding back the crowd with bamboo staves heavier than the one he carried. There must be more than a hundred of them, possibly two hundred. Who were these people and where had they come from?

Remembering that he had come to find out who was using firearms, Man Valor grabbed a spectator beside him, obviously a porter, for he had a pack by his feet. "Who are these men?"

The porter glanced angrily around, recognized Man Valor's tunic as the governor's livery, and flinched. "I do not know, Guardsman."

"They are the Bamboo Banner!" said a woman with a child on her hip. "From up-country."

"Who are the Bamboo Banner? Who leads them? What—"

The porter snapped, "Watch!" He pointed to where a band of drummers was beating a wild tattoo, rising to a climax, turning all heads. One of the Bamboo Banner men was prancing around in the open space, arms wide, drawing attention to himself. Another watching him held a gun at his side, butt on the ground.

Satisfied that he had the crowd's attention, the first man stopped prancing, turned to face the gunman at a range of four or five paces, and spread out his arms. The other went down on one knee and raised the gun to his shoulder. It looked like a modern rifle. Man Valor shouted, "No!" and a few other spectators also cried out. But most did not. They had seen this done already.

The gunman fired. *Crack!* His victim staggered as if he had been punched, but he did not fall. He laughed and spun around, showing that he was unhurt. The crowd roared.

"How do they do that?" Man Valor yelled. He meant to ask the porter, but one of the Bamboo Banner crowd controllers had noticed his livery and was suddenly there.

He was young, tall, and bony, with close-cropped hair and very bright eyes under his green headband. He held his staff horizontally with both hands, as if about to push Man Valor backward. But he was grinning, showing a broken tooth.

"Heaven preserves us, Guardsman! You want to see? Hit me!"

Suspecting a trap, Man Valor leaned on his own staff and said, "Why should I hit you?"

"Because you cannot hurt me. Go ahead. Hit me with your stick, anywhere you want." His grin grew even wider. "Except between the legs. I am not senior enough to take that one yet."

This was a trap. The kid had some pink welts across his chest, but he would not be so amused if Man Valor broke a few ribs for him and he had a lot of friends handy.

"No."

"A coward!" the boy said with disgust. "Here!" He held out his bamboo rod to the porter. "You hit me. Hit me hard."

The porter shook his head, snatched up his pack, and backed away into the crowd.

"Are there no real men in this city?" the boy wailed.

"There are now!" said one of his comrades, arriving at the scene. He was older and heavier; he was also the one who had just been shot and ought to be dead. "Front or back, Leaping Serpent?"

"Both!" Leaping Serpent said. He turned sideways and

hunched his shoulders, bending slightly. The other man raised his stick overhead and brought it down two-handed across his victim's shoulders with a crack that made Man Valor wince and several of the spectators cry out, as if they had felt the blow themselves. It certainly looked genuine, but the youth hardly reacted at all.

He straightened and put his staff behind him. "Again!"

The strike came sideways this time, whistling like a sword cut, and took him full across the chest. He staggered backward a step and Man Valor thought he saw a wince, but it was gone in an instant. The blow should have laid him flat on his back.

"Now will you hit me?" Leaping Serpent asked him mockingly.

The acrobats were building their pyramid again, but Man Valor had to deal first with this inexplicably indestructible youngster. "With my own stick?"

"Certainly." No hesitation.

"Then hold out your arm and I'll break it for you."

At once, Leaping Serpent extended his right arm to the side. "Hard as you can."

Man Valor looked warily at the other man.

He nodded. "Go ahead. Heaven preserves us because we serve the Good Land. Serpent is far along in his studies. You cannot hurt him."

Man Valor raised his staff two-handed and brought it down on the boy's forearm as hard as he could. The arm moved, of course, but there was no trickery. He both felt and heard the impact.

Leaping Serpent said, "Thank you! Not a bad smack." He wiggled his fingers to show that he had taken no hurt. "Will you let me do the same for you?"

Man Valor's tunic was thickly padded to protect his arm, but he shook his head. He could not work if his arm was broken; he needed wages to eat.

The crowd was applauding the acrobats. He looked to see how the pyramid was coming along.

"Why not?" asked the older man, stepping close. His eyes were as bright as the boy's under thick dark brows. "Are you afraid of being hurt?"

"Yes." And if he did not get back to report to his master very soon, he was going to be hurt with a whip.

"We are not afraid of anything. We follow the Bamboo Banner and no man can hurt us."

"I don't believe you."

"You don't trust your own eyes? You saw me shot? A big strong man like you cannot break a boy's arm?" He lowered his voice and moved his face very close to Man Valor's. "I am Chestnut River, patriot of the third proving, of the Pearl Army."

"I am Chief Guardsman Man Valor."

Chestnut River raised bushy eyebrows at the inappropriateness of that name. "The Emperor is dead." His breath bore a sweet smell of spices and his teeth had a green stain on them.

Sweat! Here was treason! "No! Not true! Long live the Emperor!"

Chestnut River nodded solemnly. "The palace lies to us. The Good Land is being ruled by a *woman*! Do you wonder that Heaven is enraged? That we have storms and floods and terrible omens? We must restore the Golden Throne. Bamboo himself leads us."

Man Valor just gaped at him. Men who could not be hurt? The urgency of the drums seemed to have merged with his heartbeat, filling him with a strange, confusing insistency. He was shaking. The pyramid was four men high now and obviously heading higher still.

Chestnut River took his arm in a grip whose power was appreciable even through the armor padding. "Come with us, Man Valor. Follow Bamboo; follow the Bamboo Banner. We will have you as top man of a pile like that one inside two weeks. In three months, you will laugh at blows and bullets and sword cuts. Join us!"

"My master . . . I must go and explain first and then—"

"No, you must come now." Already Chestnut River was leading him across the square and he was putting up no resistance. Leaping Serpent strode along on his other side, grinning joyfully.

"But my mother . . ."

"No one may turn back when he has taken the first step. Do you need to prove it with a gun? I will gladly let you try to shoot me, but it will do no good, as you saw. Bamboo had made us invincible. Will you be one of us, Man Valor? Are you worthy of that name you bear?"

Man Valor kept on walking.

CHAPTER 5

Day in, day out, Prior Fraise of Sheep Rocks was not a happy man. He ministered to the mortuary needs of the largest parish in Chixi Province, but his flock was spread over endless hills, inhabited more by sheep and goats than people. At least half of those people were semibarbaric nomads who dug pits in the ground and buried their dead whole, without caring in the least that their sparks might not yet have fully escaped and would need ritual help to ascend to the Fifth World. The few permanent settlements were mostly isolated ranches and mining camps. They did not bring their dead to Sheep Rocks; they expected the Order to go to them.

That morning, Fraise was in a particularly sour mood. Two nights ago, he had conducted a farewell for a wealthy rancher, but nothing had gone right. The cost of importing firewood into that blighted, eroded, deforested land had all but wiped out the Order's profit. Fog Moon had lived up to its name, making the timber wet and obscuring the stars that should preside; without wind to help, few sparks had risen, making the mourners tearful and angry.

Worst of all, the discard had borne an unmistakable gunshot wound in the back of his head, and so had obviously been a casualty in one of the hill country's age-old blood feuds. Yet his heir had ignored all hints that the Gray Brothers could help him obtain his revenge in return for a trifling fee. The stupid amateur would probably get himself killed instead. Admittedly, that would mean another ritual for the Order to organize, but an outing as well would have been much more profitable.

After a whole day on horseback in wind and rain, Fraise had returned to the monastery exhausted and frozen to find a letter awaiting him from the Chixi mother house in Meritorious Aspect. Almost certainly it was another warning that he was behind in his remittance. The financial Helpers there never seemed to understand that a large parish did not necessarily mean a large income; the abbess of a 300-ply house evidently had no idea of the problems of a 10-ply priory like Sheep Rocks. Some months, Fraise could barely feed his tiny community, as well as remit his dues to Chixi, let alone put anything aside to further his own career. He had inherited the priorship two years ago simply because nobody else wanted it. It had brought him no happiness or respect. The older initiates still kept forgetting and addressing him as "Brother Fraise" and the novice sisters were no more cooperative than before.

He had finished his morning tea and rice. The tray had been removed by the half-witted postulant, so he had no further excuse not to open the scroll. Yet still he dawdled. He was tempted to burn it unread.

The northeast corner of the roof was leaking again.

His room was probably the finest in all of Sheep Rocks, because the priory was the only stone building in the village, all others being crumbling wooden shacks. In summer, he had a pleasing little garden, tended by the two postulants and he owned a silk rug not too obviously faded. When the weather permitted, which it currently did not, he had a fine view of snowy mountains. Yet, by the standards of abbots or abbesses, these quarters ranked as a dog kennel. His shelves held a few small carvings of nephrite, which had belonged to his predecessor and which the ignorant might mistake for true jade, but no real *collection*. A man of worth always collected something: antique scrolls or porcelain or ivory, usually of some particular time or provenance. These he would display for visitors to praise while he expounded on their specific qualities. That was what gentlemen *did*.

The prospect that Fraise could ever amass enough wealth to buy himself a modest abbacy seemed as remote as the stars. He was doomed to remain rooted forever in these ghastly hills, and even that might be better than whatever the abbess of Meritorious Aspect was about to threaten him with.

Sad and apprehensive, he broke the seal and unrolled the scroll.

Dearest Brother, guard our words within your heart alone. We yearn urgently for a brother or male novice counted on these fingers: thumb, that he stand more than eight spans, less than nine . . .

Prior Fraise stopped, blinked, and went back up to the beginning again.

The characters still read the same and the calligraphy was very fine, very precise, not ambiguous at all. Eight spans? Very few men of the Gentle People were as tall as that. Fraise himself was not and he had never considered himself short. Nine-span giants were rare, even in Chixi.

Index, that he be of Outlandish stock and appearance.

That went without saying if he was more than eight spans tall.

Middle, that he was born in the Year of the Nightingale, or very near.

She was describing Novice Horse! No! Never! Fraise could not visualize himself trying to run Sheep Rocks without Horse. Horse was wonderful with the livestock. He could dig a bone pit in a third of the time anyone else took and he chopped more firewood than all three other novices together.

He ate more, too.

Fraise read on.

Ring, that he have a leaping heart. Pinky, that he be a skilled seemer.

Hmm. Horse was very good at seeming magic within the limits imposed by his size. But a leaping heart? If she meant ambition, well anyone with a leaping heart would not voluntarily hang around here in Sheep Rocks to rot, which was a cruel appraisal of Fraise himself. It was true that he was holding back on initiating Horse, although he hated to admit it even to himself, but that was not because he feared that the kid would gallop away over the hills to greener pastures. Horse was too amiable and easygoing to do anything so drastic. Fraise was delaying because Horse was far too valuable as a novice. An initiate brother was excused from the more menial tasks in the priory, and Horse did most of those all by himself. It would take three youths to replace him.

But if leaping heart meant dutiful, painstaking, and eager to please, then Horse qualified again.

If you cannot satisfy our need, Brother, let fire eat this paper and rain wash your memory.

This was a very good day for rain and a cozy, but expensive, fire.

If you have, in your care, the youth we seek, speak to none of this but bring him in haste, covertly, to the priory

*at Huarache, two days west of our house, and believe
that our gratitude toward you will be without bounds.
May your spark shine ever brighter in this and all higher
worlds.*

The characters swam on the page. She was telling him to
name his own price! A conch of taels? A 50-ply abbacy? Let some
other fool try to run this priory without Horse?

The prior rang his bell and when the buck-toothed postulant
answered, Fraise told him to send in Novice Horse immediately.

He was tempted to leap up and pace the room as his excitement mounted, but that would imply a lack of tranquillity and
dignity. Why had the request come to him, in this flyspeck ham-
let? Just for secrecy? But there were many obscure houses closer
to Meritorious Aspect, so he must assume that many identical
letters had been dispatched. It could even be that the hunt had
so far failed to find a youth fitting all those very specific requirements, so now they were beating the hinterlands.

It was going to be an imposture, obviously, possibly even an
impersonation. Outlanders with enough money to hire an aide
from the Order could only be nobility. Half the lowly cattlemen
and horsemen of Chixi were of Outlandish stock and despised
because of it, but ever since Falling Mountain had led his horde
in from the Outlands three hundred years ago to overthrow the
Tenth Dynasty, most of the aristocracy had been of Outlandish
stock. Anyone sneering at them did so a long way behind their
backs. Most noble families were well diluted by Gentle blood by
now, but some retained their size and rocky features. Even the
imperial . . . Fraise shied away from that treasonous idea. The
Order would never risk *that*! But some young noble not too far
from the throne was a possibility. The risk must be appalling, but
just thinking about the potential rewards made his head spin.
His share would certainly make him rich.

And Horse himself? Well, he might get discovered and suffer the death of a thousand cuts, but success would surely bring wealth beyond dreams.

Fraise sighed. He tried to be a meritorious person as the teachers defined that slippery term. He was aware that men had more faults than fleas, as the Humble Teacher wrote, and he tried to rise above his own. But the truth was that he was jealous of Novice Horse, of his never-failing cheerfulness, the way the novice sisters looked at him . . . Horse should have been initiated at least half a year ago, but who could possibly replace him?

The bead curtain jingled. Novice Horse put his head through at about knee height, touched it to the floor, and stopped. His close-cropped hair dripped rainwater on the floor.

"What are you doing, fool?" the abbot shouted.

"Honored Father . . . You said to come at once, but my feet are muddy."

Fraise laughed in silence. Let Deputy Prior Evening Fade worry about the mud!

"Never mind that. Enter properly."

Horse's head withdrew, then he parted the beads and strode in. He must have been tending the horses, because he was soaking wet and coated to the knees in more than just mud. He wore only a breechclout, also muddy. He dropped to the floor and kowtowed. Suddenly, the room reeked of stable.

Moved by a sudden whim, Fraise strode over to the wardrobe chest and dug out a monk's robe. "Stand up."

Horse stood up, and up. He frowned uneasily, suspecting something wrong.

"How tall are you?"

"Eight spans and a hand, Father . . . perhaps a little more." He sounded apologetic about it.

"When were you born?"

"In Lotus Moon in the Year of the Nightingale."

They couldn't ask any better fit than that.

The prior handed him the robe. "Put that on and make your-self seem respectable."

Horse clearly guessed that something unusual was afoot, for his face was completely expressionless. He took the robe and walked over to the mirror in the corner. In about two minutes, he returned for his superior's inspection, properly garbed—one shoulder covered, the other and both arms bare. His face had lost some of its heavy boniness and melted into the softer, reas-suring features of the Gentle People that layfolk expected and would find more reassuring in times of bereavement. His head was now clean shaven, his arms no longer bulged so conspicu-ously with woodsman muscle, and although his feet were still grubby if Fraise deliberately stared at them, he would not have noticed them otherwise. In fact, he would not even have noticed that this humbly smiling young monk was damp.

Who could not be jealous of such perfection?

"Excellent!"

Horse bowed. "Your Reverence is gracious."

"Merely truthful. I am"—Fraise omitted the *probably* he had been about to insert—"about to grant you your initiation. Let me try one more test. How are you at impersonation?"

The novice gave him a steady look. "I have had no training in that skill, Father."

Clever answer. Seeming was the art of assuming a general type—putting on a monk's robe and seeming to be a monk. Duplicating a particular individual was so impossibly difficult that novices were strictly forbidden to try it lest they become dis-couraged and lose confidence in their seeming. But there were tales of initiates who had been able to do it.

"But you have tried, in private." Everyone did. No novice in the history of the Order had been able to resist trying.

"A little, Father."

Fraise removed his prior's headdress and held it out. "Be me."

Still expressionless, the youth walked back to the mirror. This time, he needed longer and eventually Fraise went to stand beside him and provide his image as a model. Horse's reflection stopped wavering, and then there were twins. Yes, he had very nearly achieved the impossible. No longer Outlandish, he was now one of the Gentle People; his face was the prior's and their eyes were level; the great height and breadth had somehow disappeared, sedentary flab had replaced the remarkable musculature. The strain was obvious, though. Now sweat more than rain beaded his forehead, sinews corded his neck. The illusion was not perfect and not quite steady, but Fraise would never have believed that even this much was possible. It might well deceive anyone who did not know him—and it have been achieved with no preparatory study!

If the abbess of Meritorious Aspect did have an imposture in mind, she could ask for no better seemer than Horse.

"How long could you hold this?"

"Not long, Reverend Father." He spoke through clenched teeth, as if in pain.

"Must I find out?"

"Forgive your errant servant, Father. One hour, maybe, but not two."

"It is very well done."

Fraise's nearly double-bowed his head. "Your words fill me with joy and the hope that I may someday be worthy of your teaching." Even the voice matched!

"You may return."

With a *whoof* of relief, Horse inflated to his former size and shape. His hands were shaking as he returned the prior's headdress.

"Very well done. There may—and I stress *may*—be a profitable first contract available for your naming. You and I are going on a journey. Change into traveling clothes, then saddle the two best horses. Tell no one. But first send Deputy Prior Evening Fade to me."

The arrow flies!

The appalling realization that the mysterious summons might be a vicious practical joke did not occur to Fraise until he and Horse arrived at Huarache. That they arrived at all was no less than a miracle, and entirely due to Horse. Fraise would never have made it by himself or with a less resourceful companion. As the never-ending rain turned trails to swamps and brooks to torrents, Horse coaxed superhuman efforts out of the weary mounts. He took infinite pains to keep them healthy and more than once seemed to drag them across fords by his own brute strength.

Initiates who traveled were sure of hospitality at any House of Joyful Departure along their road, but there were few of those in northern Chixi. Inns were nonexistent. The only recourse was to beg for shelter, and for that they must seem to be other than what they were, for no man, neither prince nor peasant, would knowingly invite ill-omened Gray Helpers under his roof. In those cases, it was always Horse who charmed their way in, often volunteering to cut firewood to earn their board, even after a grueling day that had left Fraise half-dead with exhaustion. When anything special was available in the way of hospitality, it would be offered to Horse. If the luxury was only a spare bed mat, he of course yielded it to his superior. If more intimate pleasures were offered, then they were invariably offered to Horse, and those he did not refuse. Fraise was left to sleep alone and curse himself for his wicked jealousy.

The Humble Teacher said, *To those who want least is the most given.*

In the final week of their journey, Fog Moon gave way to Cold Moon. Rain stopped, skies cleared, and the world seemed to freeze solid instantly. They had to endure days of bone-cracking cold before they rode into Huarache.

Or rather into what had once been Huarache, for three quarters of the little town had vanished in a fire two years ago, according to a passing mule driver they asked for directions. The abbey had closed down; the Gray Helpers had gone, he said.

Despair froze Fraise's bones even colder than the wind did. Who could have played such a trick upon him? Was he so despicable as to provoke such spite? And who in the world disliked Horse enough to hurt him also? The prior slumped in misery on his horse and wanted to howl.

Meanwhile, Horse had kept his horse walking and the other had followed.

"There it is, Father!" he said cheerfully.

"What?"

"The monastery! Smoking chimneys, see?"

True enough, the skinner had been wrong. The Order was still ministering to the few remaining inhabitants of charred Huarache. Sprawling and stone-built, the Huarache House of Joyful Departure stood up bold and strong amid the ruins to welcome its visitors with a delicious aroma of cooking. The community must be much reduced, for the frozen mud in the big courtyard indicated that traffic had been light before the frost came, but two brothers came running to answer the bell.

Fraise noticed them notice Horse and then exchange glances. He wondered what they were thinking: *Here comes another one*? Or perhaps it was, *This looks like the right stuff at last*? He was so travel-weary that he did not care much anymore.

The monastery was obviously designed for at least a 40-ply community, but the two brothers, Hawthorn and Western Mountain, seemed to be the only people around. One took the horses, and the other led the visitors to impressive guest quarters. There they could indulge in hot water, dry clothes, and thick fish soup. Life suddenly became worth living again. By then it was close to winter sunset, but the abbess sent word that she would receive Prior Fraise and Novice Horse whenever they were ready.

Knowing that they had arrived at their destination, Horse must surely be excited, but he was concealing his emotions admirably. He limited his display of emotion to a slight frown as he asked, "Where is everybody, Father? I thought 10-ply was the smallest house allowed?"

"I expect we will find out in good time," Fraise said contentedly. The security was admirable. He was certain now that this house had been abandoned after the fire and had been opened up exclusively to interview and inspect the candidates called down from the hills by many copies of that cryptic summons. Whatever conspiracy was afoot was calling on remarkable resources, and that meant that it was aimed at a considerable pay-off.

Brother Hawthorn came to report that the abbess would now receive the reverend prior and his novice. Her name was not mentioned, but that was not unusual.

She wore the headdress of a high abbess, but she was not the abbess of Meritorious Aspect, whom Fraise had met a few times. Her room was spacious and completely barren of furniture except for one silk cushion and two rugs, equally spaced around a glowing charcoal brazier. She knelt on the cushion and gestured the visitors to take the rugs, so that the heat was divided evenly among the three of them. She was about forty, with sharp, hard features and an abrupt, uncouth manner. She wasted less than a dozen words on greetings and inquiries about their journey.

Fraise kept his replies equally laconic. He hoped he was managing to seem as inscrutable as Horse, but he had trouble keeping his heart rate down.

"So"—now she took notice of Horse, who kept his face

lowered respectfully. Compared to her he seemed to fill half the room—"what did you bring me, Father?"

"What you asked for, Mother. Exactly in all respects." Fraise returned the scroll before she could ask for it.

She unwound it enough to confirm that it was the genuine article, then laid it on the brazier to burn. "Stand up, Novice." She had not been informed of Horse's name, but that must be about to change anyway. "Turn around. Good. Down again, please. It hurts my neck to look at you when you are standing."

Horse knelt again, smiling respectfully at the jest.

"What do you enjoy most in your duties for the Order?"

Fraise wished she had not asked that, because he knew what the answer was going to be and she would not like it if she had an outing in mind for him. It was very hard to imagine Horse ever hurting anybody.

His face lit up with enthusiasm. "Comforting people, Mother. I mean when the bereaved are weeping and full of sorrow and we can explain again about the spark rising up and they see the stars waiting for their loved ones and know that she or he will be reborn in a better world. They dry their tears, and I love that."

The abbess did not comment. "Can you speak Palace Voice?"

"I have had almost no experience of it, Reverend Mother. Just the imperial tax gatherers, when they come around."

"Try that one for me."

"Peonies bleed against the green
A kite circles.
I open the gate. Children come running."

The abbess winced. "That is terrible. You sound like the hill country bumpkin you are. What other voices can you do?"

Horse quoted a few more lines of poetry in Qiancheng

dialect, which he had picked up from passing traders overnight-ing at the priory, and then in a southern jabber he had learned from Brother Wavelet.

"Better," the abbess conceded. "Quite good, even. Have you advanced anyone yet?"

"No, Mother."

"Would you, if your client requested it?"

Horse did not hesitate. "If my client's interests required it, yes. Not if the request was motivated by spite or trivial dislike."

"Why not?"

"Because it would bring an unnecessary risk of disclosure."

That was the book answer. She nodded, and appeared to be thinking.

"The novice is a very good seemer," Fraise volunteered. "He does remarkable impersonations." He shrank back from her burning glare.

She said, "Neither will be necessary. As you said, you have delivered exactly what I requested. I did not stipulate an accent, because that can be taught and he seems to have a good ear." She turned to Horse again. "If you can learn that, you will do very well for the contract I have in mind. It is not for me, though. I am not your client, who does not wish to reveal her name at the moment. I am authorized to speak for her. Release him to her, Prior."

Fraise hesitated. "We have not discussed terms yet, Mother." One could not extort fees from a high abbess as one could a client of the laity. Again, she scorched him with her dragon-fire look.

"They will be more than generous. Do you doubt me?"

He wilted. "Of course not. I appoint this monk to assist the client you presently represent, Mother. Name him."

For the first time, she actually smiled. "My client directed that his name be Butterfly Sword."

The new Butterfly Sword kowtowed, narrowly missing the

brazier with his forehead. "My ears are honored to hear this name she grants me. I will serve her needs in all things and ahead of all other loyalties."

"And you will be very greatly rewarded, Brother Butterfly Sword." The abbess rang a silver bell. "We have a novice in this house who speaks excellent Palace Voice." That could hardly be a coincidence. "You will make that your primary study, as a matter of extreme urgency."

"I will work at it day and night, if that be permitted, Mother."

"It may be," the lady said with a smile that began by seeming cryptic but was understandable when the novice entered. She was petite and lovely. She carried a tea set, which she set down gracefully between Fraise and the abbess. She glanced at Horse— and then took a second look, the way all girls looked at Horse.

"Moth," the lady said. "This is Brother Butterfly Sword. You are to teach him Palace Voice and palace ways. He says he is willing to study by day and by night."

Quite unabashed, Horse was grinning, a shocking breach of decorum in a solemn naming ceremony.

Novice Moth grinned back, so they looked like a pair of naughty children.

Fraise felt the bite of jealousy again. He could guess what they would be studying tonight, and it would not be child's play. They left together and his star pupil never looked back to say good-bye or thank you.

"A fine day's work," the abbess remarked, pouring tea. "I agree that you met my requirements exactly." She passed him his bowl. "You should see some of the dwarfs and geriatrics who have been paraded through here. I was starting to get quite worried! What is his leash?"

"We have not yet settled on terms for this contract," Fraise muttered desperately. Horse's leash was the only hold he had left.

The abbess shrugged. "What do you want?"

He drew a deep breath.

If Horse was exactly what she had been looking for, he had lots of bargaining room. "A 100-ply abbacy."

"Sorry. I don't have one to offer." She smiled at his anger. "I want you far away from here. You must have some idea by now of what is in the wind, Father, so you can guess why. I counteroffer with a 220-ply abbacy in Shiman. The climate down in Shiman is much more clement than Chixi's, almost tropical. Interested?"

Fraise thought of all the novice sisters there would be in a 220-ply, all eager to please the abbot. He felt almost faint. And beaches, perhaps. "Then we have an agreement!"

"The boy's leash?"

"Lines seventeen, seventy-one, and one twenty-four."

The lady raised her cup in salute. "To your swift promotion, Father Abbot!"

"To your future prosperity, Mother Abbess!"

The tea was very bitter, but he was much too excited to—

Oh!

Oh, what a fool he had been. . . .

—III—
THE YEAR
OF THE
NIGHTINGALE

CHAPTER 1

Lady Twilight returned to Sublime Mountain on the last night of the year, which marked the Death of the Vulture, and she thought it might mark hers also. She burned with fever, her chest gurgled with every breath, and she ached as if she had been beaten with hammers all over. Blizzard after blizzard had assailed her ever since she left Meritorious Aspect.

Had she been on any normal mission, she would never have started out. She would have stayed on in Huarache until blossom time, but the Butterfly Sword contract was both too vital and too dangerous. Any delay or departure from the plan might bring disaster. While she had lingered at Huarache, waiting for the perfect candidate to appear, runoff from the exceptional rains had raised North Water to a full spring flood, never expected in winter. The boatmen had demanded extortionate danger money to venture out on it, and the normally leisurely trip downstream to Meritorious Aspect had been completed in two nightmare hours.

From there, a boat on the Grand Canal would take her back to Heart of the World, but the canal was already starting to freeze over, something that normally happened only in Ice Moon, if at all, and the abbess told her she was crazy to continue. The only person in the Good Land who would not accept that the weather had closed down travel was Lady Twilight's lifelong client, the Empress Mother. Death was the only excuse for failure, and also the reward she assigned for it. So Twilight carried on with her journey as if her life depended on it, which it very well might. By then she had begun to cough. At the last sunset of the year, she reached the palace gate more dead than alive, in a palanquin that her bearers had dropped repeatedly as they struggled up the icy hill from Heart of the World. The guards were reluctant to admit an obvious invalid, even when she showed her imperial warrant, because sickness was never allowed near the Emperor. Entry to the Great Within was even more difficult. Senior eunuchs were summoned and at first failed to recognize her. Twilight screamed and wept and coughed her heart out, and finally won her way to her quarters. There she collapsed into bed under the frowns of two physicians.

She did not truly expect to sleep on that night of all nights. No one did. The death of one year and the birth of the next were marked by the Festival of Snowy Owls, the white bird that flies in the time of darkness. It was celebrated with kites and the finest of all firework displays, needed to scare away demons. The Emperor provided the greatest barrage in the Good Land. People banged pots and danced in the streets until dawn and the sky was filled with the sparks and smoke of the fireworks. If the real stars came to join in, that was an especially auspicious start to the year.

Fed and drugged and warm at last, Twilight did sleep, for a space that somehow seemed to be half a year and yet no more than a few minutes. She was awakened by a shrill scream.

"*Why did you not tell me you were back?*"

What? Where? Who? Oh, horrors, a demon with a hideous painted face lit by subterranean fire . . . the Empress Mother in her festival finery, holding a lantern.

"I asked you a question! How dare you return and throw yourself into bed before you have reported to me?"

Twilight's answer was a paroxysm of coughing that went on and on until she collapsed back on her pillow, gasping for breath. She had not known the Empress Mother to come calling on her since the murderous days of the Scorpion Summer. What could have gone wrong?

"Now answer!" said her tormentor. "Quickly! It is very dangerous for me to stay here. I might catch your disease. *Did you find him?*"

Twilight nodded and stretched vainly for the beaker of water. Reluctantly, the Empress Mother edged just close enough to pass it to her at arm's length before quickly retreating.

The background racket sounded like guns firing. Much pot beating and drumming. Just fireworks? No, those were gunshots. . . .

"Well? Describe him!"

"Perfect. Right age, size . . ." Moreover the boy bore so marked a resemblance to Zealous Righteousness that Twilight had even wondered if the late Emperor might have gone dragon hunting in the Chixi hills at about the right time. It would be very dangerous to ask, though. The Empress Mother would take umbrage at the implications. "More like his . . . father than . . . Just perfect." Twilight went back to wheezing and gurgling.

"Is he *fertile*?"

"Didn't wait to . . . find out. If he . . . isn't, won't be for . . . lack of trying."

"Didn't you *ask*?" the Empress Mother snapped.

Twilight just shook her head. In a house as small as the priory of Sheep Rocks, paternity would always be debatable.

"Well, after tonight's disaster, we can't wait," the Empress Mother announced ominously as she reached for the door handle. "As soon as you feel better, you will go back and fetch him. It's very urgent." Darkness fell; the door closed.

Twilight went back to sleep.

Snowy Owls was one of the Empress Mother's favorite festivals, one of the great social events of the calendar, both in the palace and throughout the Good Land. There were receptions outdoors, if the weather was cooperative, and many more of them indoors, where one could eat and drink to one's heart's delight and still watch the fireworks.

This year's was an epochal catastrophe. After weeks of cloud and snow, the sky cleared at sunset just in time for everyone to see the thin crescent of Wolf Moon, the sign that the Year of the Nightingale had begun. That was hailed by Court Astrologer as a very good omen. Old fool! But no sooner had the sky darkened than the demons came, even before the Emperor had lit the first firework to start the festival.

Of course it was not the Emperor who rode in the curtained palanquin to the Tower of the Four Quarters to light the first fuse. Any loud noise threw Absolute Purity into fits of screaming terror, so that every year he had to be drugged senseless before the fireworks started. His stand-in for the lighting ceremony was Court Astrologer. After so many years of that substitution, very few people were aware that it was a substitution and the others assumed that there was some continuing ritual reason for it—the lack of any official explanation merely showed that they ought to know what it was.

The Empress Mother presided in the Hall of Tiles, greeting the guests after they kowtowed to her. The turnout was thinner than she had expected because many invited guests had been unable to manage the roads. And the hall was so cold that everyone had to stay muffled up, hiding their spectacular robes under cloaks of sable, ermine, and sea otter. The formal procession was just lining up to emerge onto the Heavenly Terrace and see the start of the fireworks when some woman glanced out a north-facing window and started screaming.

Demons! Demons dancing in the northern sky—green demons mostly, with flashes of red. Lines of them swirling, marching, suddenly vanishing and just as suddenly returning.

Another eruption in the south . . . Soon they covered the dome of Heaven from skyline to skyline. Howls of terror and despair.

"Start! Start!" the Empress Mother yelled. Men and eunuchs ran to light fuses. The carefully planned choreography of the display was forgotten in the desperate need to frighten away the demons before they could work their evil. Sky spirits were baleful at any time, but never more so than at Snowy Owls, when they could blight a whole year. With booms and starbursts, the palace fought back against the diabolic invaders. Every flunky in Sublime Mountain, every thief and beggar in Heart of the World, had found a pot to bang or a bell to ring. Every lung screamed defiance and spells of exorcism.

The demons ignored it all. They danced in draperies, in plumes, fires, fountains. They wore green or red or violet—blue or white, demons of all colors and aspects joined in the frenzy of evil. Even the blessed stars could barely shine through their brilliance.

Eventually, the supply of fireworks ran out, long before the normal climactic firestorm. The Empress Mother sent word for the guards to fire their muskets, the army to fire their cannons! Fire bombards! Fire anything! Still the demons swirled and marched and danced.

It was hopeless. Half frozen in her chair under a mountain of ermine fur, the Empress Mother quit the field. She ordered her bearers to take her back to her quarters immediately, as fast as they could run. In a melee of guards and bearers and miscellaneous flunkies, her train rushed through courtyards and halls. Never could she recall an omen so obvious and so terrifying. The whole nation would panic, even if the demons had been seen only in Heart of the World. This was where the Emperor was, and the message was intended for him.

The dynasty must be trembling on its foundations, and the fault was her son's, for being a mental cripple, a useless idiot. The

Empire needed an Emperor. Heaven and ancestors could not be deceived by an endless series of substitutions; they were not being honored properly, and now they were showing their displeasure and threatening to withdraw their mandate, if that had not already been done.

She sent word to the Small Council to assemble immediately in the Abode of Wisdom. She had her servants strip her of much of her state-occasion finery, especially the absurd shoes that made walking near impossible. When she was capable of moving more or less normally, she settled in her chair and called for the bearers. Chief Eunuch came waddling in ahead of them. He minced odiously close to whisper in her ear that Lady Twilight had returned.

Indeed?!

The Empress Mother gave orders that she was to be taken first to Twilight's quarters. *Then* to the Abode of Wisdom.

By the time she reached the Abode of Wisdom, she had recovered from her first shock. The Empire might tremble, but it need not fall. Thanks to Twilight's good fortune, they could yet have an Emperor. It might take a month or longer to fetch the boy and smuggle him into the palace, but his presence would immediately bring everyone else into line. He could reign and she would continue to rule.

The Small Council had assembled, all kneeling and facing the throne—First Mandarin, Chief Eunuch, Supreme Guardian, Court Astrologer. A few young eunuchs were running around lighting lamps, and others were bringing in braziers to warm the hall, but it was still very dark and icy. Not tonight would the Empress Mother hide in anonymity behind the Emperor's Eye. Nor would she presume to take the throne, although that was her privilege as sole surviving member of the regency committee. No, she had her chair carried right in among the assembled councillors and set down there. Never mind cold and dark! She was warm enough under her fur robes. She barked at the bearers and they fled, while the startled ministers rearranged themselves to face her unexpected location. The last door closed.

"Court Astrologer! What is the meaning of this obscene demonic exhibition?" The gunfire had almost stopped. Even the pan bangers seemed to have given up in exhaustion.

The old man wailed and wrung his spidery hands. "It means trouble ahead, Your Majesty. Disease, famine, unrest."

"I do not need *you* or all the demons of the *nine hells* to warn me of that! For the last four months, the weather everywhere has been disastrous! Flood here and drought there, storms everywhere . . . Of course, we must expect famine and plague and unrest!"

"But the harvest was good," Chief Eunuch wailed. "Many governors reported it bountiful. The unusual rain did not begin until after the harvest was gathered. Next year's crop should find ample moisture, surely?"

Even if he was just terrified by the demons, that quivering bag of fat had no right to interfere in a subject that was not his responsibility. Supreme Guardian and First Mandarin exchanged glances to see who would get the pleasure of puncturing the wind bladder this time.

"The harvest was indeed bountiful in many provinces," First Mandarin explained patiently, "but then unseasonable rains turned the roads to mud and the rivers to torrents. In many places, there was no way to move the crops to market. Heaps of grain rot in the fields while cities starve."

"The demons!" the Empress Mother shouted, whipping them back on topic. "Why so many demons on the portentous Night of Snowy Owls? What does it *mean*? Tonight you proclaimed the sighting of Wolf Moon a good omen, and then with the words barely out of your mouth, this happens! Why did you not warn us, Court Astrologer?"

His watery eyes bulged like a dragon's and he pawed at his snowy beard. "The demons themselves are a warning, Majesty, of course. I cannot warn you of warnings, or the second warning would be superfluous, indeed redundant, and therefore not necessary. And if there were to be no second heavenly warning, how can I be expected to foresee the need beforehand . . ." Evidently, there was enough light in the hall for him to understand the terrestrial warning in her expression. Brought to bay, he tucked his hands in his sleeves and sat back on his heels with a bland smugness. "It means that the Portal of Worlds will soon open."

In all the years she had known the old moth, the Empress Mother could not recall him ever making a solid, unequivocal prediction like that. The other councillors were staring at him with unmasked terror.

"You are certain of that?" she demanded.

Court Astrologer smiled modestly. "As certain as I can be at this stage. I first began to suspect that an opening might be coming when a guest star was seen in the Constellation of the Wagon, back in the year of the Osprey. It seemed too early to alarm Your Majesty, so I did not speak up at that time. However, Your Majesty will recall that I did mention the possibility when Celestial Rose breathed fire in the Year of the Crow. That is not necessarily a portent that the Portal of Worlds will open, but it is guidance to us, a warning to be vigilant. All this unreasonable weather is another. Plus, of course, earthquakes and civil unrest. There was that earthquake in Jingyan last Thunder Moon, with substantial loss of life. And the Bamboo Banner rabble has not been returned to obedience." He blinked moistly over his glasses at Supreme Guardian to indicate whose fault that was.

"Demons at the Snowy Owls Festival foretell an opening?" the Empress Mother demanded.

"One of the most reliable portents, Majesty. There are many listed in the archives, not all of which are restricted to warning of the

Portal of Worlds opening, and not all of which, it appears, are necessary. But the weight of evidence has now become quite convincing."

The Portal opened only in Firebird Years, so the old scoundrel had three clear years before he could be proved wrong. At
his age, that must seem like a lifetime. If he were wrong, it *would*
be his lifetime.

"And what does the opening itself portend?" Dynasties fell
when the Portal of Worlds opened. The Third had, she knew, and
the Seventh, and a couple of the minor ones. Barbarian hordes
emerged from the Portal. One Emperor had vanished inside it,
taking his army with him.

"Ah, Your Majesty, I am interpreter of the future; I defer to
the historians who are custodians of the past." Court Astrologer
aimed a poisoned look at First Mandarin.

"Disasters," the old man murmured and waited until everyone had a chance to shiver. "But history is full of disasters. The
careful scholar always questions his sources, and the one fact that
seems quite indisputable is that the records become unreliable
for a time after the Portal opens. There are huge gaps. We believe
that it has opened five or six times since the count of years began,
but not on any regular schedule. We suspect that the breaks in
the record are caused by widespread panic, but we are not certain
even of that. There are tales of great slaughter, all unexplained.
We know that the Third Dynasty fell, but we do not know the
true name of the Emperor who founded the Fourth, or when he
claimed the throne."

"It is unfortunate, then," the astrologer said with a smirk,
"that my advice about the Firstborn was ignored. You may recall,
Your Majesty, that back in the Year of the Osprey I ventured to
remind your council that the Urfather, as the vulgar call him,
perished in the 246th cycle."

He hesitated, as if wondering whether to remark that Emperor
Zealous Righteousness had ordered the pest put to death before

he could grow up and start causing trouble again. Discretion won; he didn't.

"Thereafter, of course, he would be reborn in the ensuing Year of the Phoenix, as always, and by Osprey would be old enough to be recognizable. I suggested that all provincial governors be directed to make inquiries. Even now may not be too late. He must be coming up to, hmm, fifteen this year? Being ageless, he should be able to tell us exactly what happens when the Portal of Worlds opens."

First Mandarin was looking to the Empress Mother for permission to respond. She gave it with a bitter nod.

"If your warning in the Year of the Osprey seemed to be ignored, Court Astrologer, it was because I had already reported to Her Majesty on the possible significance of the guest star and had made the same obvious suggestion regarding the Firstborn. He was duly located in Qiancheng during the Year of the Eagle and has been a guest of His Imperial Majesty ever since."

Court Astrologer bared a few yellow fangs in fury at being so imperially crushed. Furthermore, First Mandarin was not qualified or authorized to interpret omens. Chief Eunuch and Supreme Guardian watched with amusement.

"What progress does the warden report, First Mandarin?" the Empress Mother inquired. She knew yesterday's answer, but matters had changed since yesterday.

"Still none, Your Majesty. It is a mistake, in my opinion, to think of the Firstborn as a boy. He may look like a boy at times, but he should never be treated as one. The warden has applied all the pressure Your Majesty permitted, but the prisoner still refuses to cooperate."

If Zealous Righteousness had considered the freak revenant such a pest that he had ordered his execution out of hand, without even the chance of a hearing, why should she change imperial policy? "Unleash your warden, Eminence. Let him question without mercy or limit."

First Mandarin bowed his head with a satisfied smile. "To the death?"

"Specifically to the death. He's been there often enough before. Meanwhile, what are we going to do about the demons?"

"I presume to suggest, Majesty, that the Emperor issue a decree of fasting and penance and blame the omen on the unrest down in Dongguan, the so-called Bamboo Banner. The demons are a warning that they must be returned to obedience. His Majesty has been tolerant long enough."

She thought about it, waiting to see who else might contribute. Up until now, she had been reluctant to glorify a few rioting peasants with the status of a rebellion, despite First Mandarin's repeated pleas that Supreme Guardian be ordered to march the army south and crush what the old man persisted in calling an uprising. Something must be done about the demons, though, and it would be better to have people blame them on an insurgent rabble than on the government. On the other hand, with famine impending, she was going to be short of tax money, and the cost of moving the army anywhere was appalling. Nothing must be allowed to delay her rebuilding of the Water Palace!

They were all waiting on her decision.

"So, Supreme Guardian, it appears that you will get your chance to earn glory in the field."

The old warrior sighed and shook his head. "I fear the chance has passed, Your Majesty."

Even in the icy room, she felt a sudden chill. "Passed? What do you mean, *passed*?"

"I mean that it will be months before we can assemble the materiel to move the army. Traffic on the Grand Canal and the major rivers is already unable to carry enough food to nourish starving areas—they cannot transport the army as well. And after tonight's expenditure of powder, we should be reduced to fighting with bows and arrows, if any of His Majesty's troops knew how to use them. We spent about half of the entire army's supply shooting at demons."

"Powder? Gunpowder, you mean? Well, buy some! Where does gunpowder come from?"

Supreme Guardian ran a finger over his dangling mustaches. She had a horrible suspicion that he was trying not to smirk at her.

"Powder, Your Majesty, is made of enormous quantities of sulfur, specially prepared willow charcoal, and three times as much niter. Niter is extracted from animal droppings in a process that takes about two years. It can also be mined, but the Good Land's only niter mines are down in Dongguan, and thus under the control of the rebels. Also, I have reported several times recently, Your Majesty, on the alarming desertion rate, which will certainly continue to rise unless the troops receive their arrears of pay, which in many cases is now a year overdue. I see little prospect of being able to move against the rebellion until summer at the earliest, and even that will require a very substantial increase in funding."

How infuriating! At this rate, she might not live long enough to see the Water Palace completed.

"First Mandarin, find some adequate source of revenues. Report to me at noon. You are all dismissed."

CHAPTER 2

The Army of Admirable Cause was dying. Imperial forces led by Brass Knife had driven it back against the river and set the forest upwind of it ablaze. Now Brass Knife's archers were shooting at random into that mass of choking, blinded men, with every shaft finding a target. The Firstborn was blinded, also. Last night, he had gone on his knees to Brass Knife, begging him to give the Army a few more days to return to allegiance. Refused, he had returned to the peasants, who would have done better to have called themselves the Army of Lost Cause, or the Army of Starvation. He wept again with them. Very soon he would die with them, although that meant less to him than . . .

Someone was speaking.

"Firstborn! Urfather! Holy One!"

The prisoner pulled his mind forward a few centuries and forced open crusted eyelids. He tried to smile. "I thought I was, er . . . Sunlight now?" His voice was a croaky whisper that even he could barely hear.

The man kneeling over him gasped with what sounded like true relief. "Yes, no, not to me, Holy One. We have doctors. We have food and warm bedding. The blacksmith is coming to release you."

The Firstborn tried to lift his wrist, but pain stopped him. The flesh there had been abraded by the manacle until it was ulcerous and infested with maggots. The rest of him was little better after months of semistarvation and lying on stone, which in places had rubbed through his flesh to the bone. His body and clothes were falling apart. When winter came, they had given him a single, louse-infested blanket, thin as paper.

"Which do you need first, Holy One?"

"Warm soup? May I bless you?"

"When I have earned it, Urfather." The speaker was familiar now, one of the clerks who had read out the Emperor's questions. He was elderly, at least fifty, with a graying mustache whose droop seemed to express unhappiness and . . . guilt? . . . No, more like worry. He was going to get his precious robes dirty. There were soldiers in the background and now the workman with his tools.

"What date?" Sunlight's lips and mouth felt cracked like desert mud.

"Two nights past the full of Wolf Moon."

"Another year," the Firstborn muttered.

"The Year of the Nightingale."

The year that the Firstborn must die, if the omens spoke true. It would be soon. It was a wonder that he had survived these four months of torment.

"The warden ascended?"

The clerk twitched in alarm. "You know, Urfather?"

He didn't like them calling him that when he was young. "I knew when I first saw him that he would not tarry long in this world. How?"

"The winter sickness. Just seven days past, he began coughing and took to his bed. He has not spoken for three days. We were waiting, and just minutes ago the doctors said that he had released his spark. I came as fast as I could, Holy One."

"But much faster than you should. I am grateful." The prisoner was so incredibly weak that his eyes were watering like a child's. He was only a child, of course. That explained much.

The manacle was struck off his wrist with a clang and he cried out at the pain. Soldiers closed in to lift him and lay him on the bed, as the doctor directed. His head was gently lifted and a bowl of water held to his lips. Someone began washing his feet and legs. He gave up the effort of talking for a while.

It all came back. The people of the town had known he was being held in here. He could recall hearing musketry, but a long time ago. No one had spoken to him in an age, except to read out the Emperor's stupid questions. Renewed hope was the best of medicines. By the time he was sitting up against a pile of cushions and had sipped enough soup to warm him but not enough to make him ill, he was ready to ask questions.

The clerk was so typical that the Firstborn could have written his life story. Whatever his background—and his indeterminate accent suggested a widely traveled childhood and, therefore, a mandarin father—he had entered mandarin training and failed one of the early examinations. Barred from further progress, he had been literate enough to be employed as a clerk, and that he had remained all his life. *Here* he had remained, in Four Mountains, working in the office of the warden. Mandarins were moved to new postings every two or three years so that they could never build a local power base, while the petty bureaucrats beneath them stayed on. Theirs were the palms to grease to grease the wheels; they knew where the bones were buried, and who to see for what. Now his superior was dead, so he was nominally in charge of a great fortress, probably of the town also, and of the most valuable prisoner in the Good Land. But why was he ignoring the instructions the Golden Throne had given his predecessor? That was very much out of character.

The helpers and soldiers withdrew, so that only the clerk remained, plus an unexplained skinny youth, more boy than adolescent, who crouched low on his haunches just inside the doorway, almost as if he wanted to be invisible or should not be there at all.

"Your name?" Sunlight asked the clerk.

"I am Clerk of Records, acting as warden until the Son of the Sun can send one worthy of that position." It was typical that he thought of himself as a title and not a name.

"My mother, Eminent One?" What was her name? Ah, yes, Quail.

"She comes to the gates every morning and asks to be let in to see you. She is ignored. Someone leads her away at sunset. . . . People in the town must be feeding her and giving her shelter."

They left her outside the gate all day in the middle of winter? Why had the late warden not thought to drag her in and flog her before the prisoner's eyes?

"Will you have pity and let her in today?"

The clerk looked abashed, as if caught out in great sin. "I have already done so, Holy One. She is being fed and decently clothed and has been told that she may see you later, when you feel stronger."

"And the people of the town?"

"Bad news, Urfather." The clerk wrung his hands and the silk of his sleeves made noises like trees in the wind. "When you stopped appearing on the rampart, they tried to force the castle gate. . . . And some were shot."

"Human stupidity," the Firstborn muttered under his breath. "Nothing greater under Heaven. And then?"

"And then the scholar started sending the boy out in your stead. But it seems your mother told them that it was not you. . . . Not many come to watch now; those who do come jeer and boo."

"Forgive me!" wailed the boy at the door. He threw himself prostrate on the flagstones. "Holy One, forgive me!"

Sunlight glanced quizzically at the clerk and then said, "Come here, then. No, don't wriggle like a snake. Stand up, walk over here with your head up. . . . Now put your buttocks on the floor and cross your legs and look at me. Look at my eyes! Now, what's your name?"

The boy still couldn't meet his gaze. Trembling, he stared down at his own twiggy legs. "M-M-Mouse, Holy One!"

Sunlight suppressed a smile and again looked at the clerk, who shrugged.

"The boy did not want to, but the warden had him beaten if he refused. He is not much to blame, Urfather."

"I don't think he's to blame at all. Mouse? No, you *must* look at me. Good. You are not at fault. You did nothing wrong, and if you did, I forgive you absolutely. Can you smile? Try. Try *much* harder! That's better. Go and sit on that rug. You will stay and talk with me after. Now, Scholar, what—"

"I am not a scholar, Holy One."

"Tell me your name."

"Shard Gingko, Holy One."

"Tell me, Clerk of Records Shard Gingko, how much has the town offended the Son of the Sun? They threw stones, tried to force the gate, what else? Have they raised banners, or injured any of his guards? And how many townsfolk were hurt when the guard opened fire?"

"Injuries unknown," Shard Gingko said. Three dead townsmen had been left behind as the mob fled from the muskets. There had been no reprisals, no more insurrection than he had already reported.

The Firstborn could think questions easily enough, but it was still an effort to make sense of answers. No Emperor in all eleven dynasties had been able to tolerate loss of face, and any complaint that could not be ignored would always be stamped out with brutal repression. In this case, though, unless young Absolute Purity was feeling bloodthirsty, he could blame the town's unrest on the errors of an incompetent warden fortunately already ascended beyond imperial reach. If he did feel bloodthirsty, then there was absolutely nothing that Sunlight could do now to prevent an imperial massacre.

"How long until noon?"

"An hour or so," Shard Gingko said.

"Then I can greet my mother now. And perhaps eat a little more. But at noon, I want her to go out on the rampart, and I want Mouse to go with her. Will you do that for me, please, Mouse?"

Shocked, the boy nodded. "Anything, Urfather."

"I'm not strong enough to walk yet. But they can't see your face clearly from where they're standing, and if my mother is with you, they'll accept you as the real Firstborn. And later, she will go out to the gate and tell the people I am alive and well, and they will return to obedience."

"It shall be done, Urfather," Shard Gingko said.

"And when you write to Sublime Mountain . . . Have you written yet?"

The acting warden did not quite manage to hide a shudder. Reporting bad news could destroy a man. "I felt that determining the state of your health was more urgent, Holy One, so that I could report on it." A typical master of ambage, he was—never a straight answer. "Besides," he added, "The roads are so bad that even imperial couriers cannot get through."

"When you do write, you may tell the Lord of the High and the Low that I have answered the first question for you. You must say I did it for you personally, to reward your correct behavior." That likely would not save the clerk from the Emperor's wrath, but it was all the thanks Sunlight had to offer.

Eyes wide, Shard Gingko nodded.

"What was the first question? I forget."

"'Who made the Portal of Worlds?'"

The Firstborn sighed. "Ah, yes. It's a very childish question. The answer is, 'Whoever made the world,' of course."

CHAPTER 3

Brother Silky was meditating, his body cross-legged on the floor of his room in Jade Harmony 7's palace, his spirit far away among the stars. Even when he was a contracted aide, a Gray Brother kept up his spiritual regime. Silky's days were never empty, for he must also maintain the weapons skills needed by a sand warrior, which required several hours' practice at the House of Humble Followers of Martial Ancestors. He frequently visited the abbey to confer with the Abbot, help out with funerals, or instruct novices. He also kept an eye on his client's financial dealings, and had several times prevented him from plunging into disaster—the niter fiasco, for example. News of the Bamboo Banner rebellion having at last become generally known in Wedlock, Jade Harmony had decided to invest a fifth of his fortune in a scheme to corner the market in explosives. It had taken a ferocious lecture from his young aide to convince him that, whether the warehouse full of niter eventually went to the Bamboo Banner or the Empire, neither side was likely to pay for it. A week later, the price collapsed as this truth filtered through the financial community. Jade Harmony had yet to offer Silky either thanks or apologies.

Life, in short, was very pleasant, if somewhat lacking in excitement. The only cloud blotting Silky's sky was Verdant Harmony, Jade Harmony 7's widowed daughter. The current business plan required Silky to bed her, and his continuing lack of success was becoming embarrassing. The Abbot kept asking for progress reports, and Silky had none to offer. If today's battle with the dragon did not produce results, he would have to try something truly drastic.

The dragon! It was time to prepare for battle.

He returned to the Fourth World and opened his eyes.

Springing to his feet, Silky stretched luxuriously. Meditation was wonderful! When he began, the knowledge that he was very likely to die this afternoon had been an icy weight on his mind, but now he was relaxed and confident. If it happened, it happened. There were infinitely many other worlds after this one.

At first, Jade Harmony had been stingy in providing quarters for his sand warrior, but things had changed as soon as prize money began to appear. He had still grumbled at Silky's request for a large mirror—large mirrors were expensive and Jade Harmony was a merchant—but the third purse, the one for being the unbloodied survivor in a grand melee, had finally convinced him that sponsoring a sand warrior was a worthy investment. The mirror was impressive. The new room was sun-bright but private, with easy access to the outer wall for secret coming and going.

Silky meditated in his monk's robe, of course, which automatically put him in his Gray Helper persona. He smiled at its reflection. His scalp was as smooth as an egg, his ears stuck out, and his arms were slender—not a very convincing opponent for a dragon, even a two-clawed dragon. He dropped his robe and donned his warrior's breeches and boots, standing on one foot at a time to do so. He spread his weapons on the floor around him, within reach. Then he set his fists on his hips and ventured the magic of seeming.

He saw nothing change, any more than he could watch a flower grow, but after four or five minutes, much had happened. He had the start of a queue again, his chest and shoulders were thicker, his ears flatter. Without taking his eyes off his reflection, he squatted and began to arm. He strapped on his forearm knives, slid others into the sheath on each boot and each thigh, strapped two on his upper arms, a dagger and short sword on his belt. Each improvement made the transformation move faster. The straps began biting into his thickening forearms and had to be loosened. He gathered up his hair, tied it in the traditional top-knot with ribbons, hung his bandoliers of throwing knives over his shoulders, and rose to smile at Sand Warrior Silky.

One saw what one expected to see, in this case a very dangerous-looking young man. The "real" Silky, if there even was such a person anymore, was probably much closer now to the husky warrior than the skinny scholar of last year or the flabby, shortsighted clerk he sometimes assumed. Ironically, the inoffensive monk was the real killer, a lot more dangerous than the sand warrior with all his cutlery.

Now, all he lacked was his long sword. Most matches in the arena were fought to first blood, so the swords used were light-weight and blunt except for a few small barbs designed to rip skin and cause copious bleeding without doing serious damage. Today, he needed an authentic lethal weapon. It required his full attention and a pair of thick gloves to coat the blade with the deadliest snake venom known to the Gray Helpers—enough to kill a hundred men. Then he painted a couple of throwing knives and returned them carefully to his baldric. He wrapped a pair of similar knives in bull hide and slid them inside his boots. They made walking uncomfortable, but he would dispose of them before the fight began.

It would make more sense to carry a poisoned sword in a scabbard and not just a belt loop, but that would break with sand warrior tradition and attract attention. Even owning a poisoned weapon cost a man his head under imperial law, but Creature of Nightmare, the last man who had gone against the dragon, had been cremated in a tea caddy. The lizard hadn't overlooked much of the previous challengers, either.

But if Silky won, he would be on his way to fabulous wealth.

He gave his reflection a blessing. It grinned back at him. They headed for their respective doors. As he emerged into the corridor, someone ducked quickly out of sight around the corner—quickly, but not quickly enough to escape the eye of a sand warrior.

"Master Malachite?"

An adult-size but rather chinless face appeared, followed sheepishly by a collection of elongated limbs and bones clad in inadequate meat and excessive amounts of lustrous silk. Malachite Harmony, who would one day assume the name of Jade Harmony 8, was the elder son of the house, and a fanatical hero-worshiper of its resident sand warrior. Given the chance, Malachite would happily admire Silky's biceps from dawn to dusk.

Silky strolled closer. "May I do something for Your Grace?"

The boy shuffled his feet. "J-J-Just be sure to win!"

"I certainly intend to. Why don't you come and watch me?"

Malachite wilted. "Honorable Father says that it is not a proper act to witness bloodshed."

"Yet it is all right to make money from it?"

The boy must have tried that argument himself, because he had the answer ready. "A gentleman can own a stable without having to shovel it out."

"But if he does not watch that it is well and properly shoveled out, his livestock will not prosper."

"Oh."

The mandarinate government, steeped in the philosophy of the Courtly Teacher, deplored violence of any sort. So did merchants, because it was bad for trade. Merchants usually claimed to follow the rule of the Humble Teacher, although he had decreed poverty and abstemious living.

"I can get you in free," Silky said. "If you molt all that finery and wear only a loincloth, no one will notice you." Of course, clean fingernails and neatly dressed youth lock would be a dead giveaway, but there was no need to mention those. Heavens bless us, even the loin cloth would probably be clean. "You can ride in my rickshaw."

Malachite's eyes bulged like a dragon's. "Disobey?" The word was a breath, a shimmer of moonlight, a whisper of hope from the stars.

Silky shrugged. "Or you can go and play with your brother. He has a stuffed duck he might share." Encouraging a son to disobey his father was punishable by twenty strokes of the bamboo, whether the son was thirteen, as in this case, or seventy-three.

Malachite had turned white as sea foam. "You'll wait for me?"

"No, but if you're behind the gingko at the inner gate, I'll take you."

"The guards?"

"I can get you past the guards."

Jade Harmony 8 was gone like the morning dew.

Silky had not even reached the next corner before another figure materialized there, a much more welcome one. *Aha!* It was starting to work.

The wealthy merchant Distant Cloud had died, together with his sons, in one of those food poisoning tragedies that so often smote the dining rooms of the Good Land. His wife, Verdant Harmony, had been visiting her parents that day and had thus been saved from sharing his sad fate.

Tragically widowed, she had returned to her father's home, bringing an enormous fortune with her. She was still not seventeen and obviously frustrated close to insanity. Women in the Good Land, other than the poor, were sequestered and secluded, but a wealthy man's wife could at least escape from vapid boredom by running a household. After enjoying that authority for an entire year, Verdant Harmony was back under mother's rule and her money was under her father's. She must also miss, one hoped, the stimulation of the connubial bed. Another husband was her only possible escape, but her father was never going to part with all that wealth. She was a bird of paradise in a golden cage.

Silky had been trying for months to catch her alone. Only once had he managed to exchange private words with her, and it had been her doing. Right after his second sand warrior match, she had accosted him to ask why he engaged in such a barbaric practice.

"Because it makes me so much more of a man," he had retorted. He had gone on to explain that his sword was really quite harmless and offered to let her examine it, but she had changed color and swept away. He had registered her interest and planned accordingly. Today's dragon match was just for her.

"Sand Warrior!" she said, with a smile as thin as midwinter sunlight. "I came to wish you good fortune in your combat . . . with . . ."

Silky did not drop and touch his face to the floor as he should when a lady addressed him. He kept on coming. She retreated until she backed into the wall, and he stopped very close to her, almost touching. Verdant Harmony was large and not classically beautiful—her chin was too square, her shoulders too broad, and in a few years, she would be as fat as her father. Fortunately, Silky preferred large women. Winning friendly tussles with them gave him healthy exercise and a sense of accomplishment. Even as a booted sand warrior, he was only just eye-to-eye with Verdant; as a monk, he would be both shorter and barefoot. He was also bare-chested at the moment, and what he was doing was unthinkable familiarity. She opened her mouth to protest or scream.

"Celestial Womb," he whispered.

"What?"

Silky sighed. "You don't remember? We have met before. You *must* remember! In the third world, in one of its great ages? The Empire of Lilies, and we were young."

She shook her head dumbly. People did sometimes recognize people they had known in previous worlds, or said they did.

"You were the Emperor's daughter, Princess Celestial Womb. You were almost as beautiful then as you are now. Oh, how could you have forgotten me, after all we were to each other?"

Her face flushed under the white paint. "No! I do not remember! Now—"

"I remember you! Vividly. I was a prince, then," he said wistfully. "Noble Lance was my name." He glanced around. "I must speak with you! Tonight, when you hear a tap on your windowpane, it will be me."

"No, no! The guards will shoot you! And nobody can climb that wall!"

"I can. For you, I will. Today, I will slay the dragon. Tonight, I will speak with you through the casement. Tonight!"

He walked away without looking back.

Very satisfying! The Emperor and his mandarins would certainly have disapproved of a servant subverting his employer's son from the path of filial obedience and debauching his employer's daughter, but Gray Helpers did not think that way. A little variety would do them both a world of good.

A prince was any man descended in the male line from the Emperor of the current dynasty, no matter how many generations divided them. Being forbidden to engage in labor or trade, princes varied greatly in their state. Their smarter offspring could enter mandarin training, but this was rarely attempted, for then they must compete with sons of the gutters and paddy fields, so failure was a catastrophic loss of face. A few princes held hereditary office and even fewer had hung on to ancestral wealth. Many were paupers. The rest made precarious livings by gambling. The highest rewards were in the arena.

One anonymous noble—generally assumed to be Prince

Wondrous Fortune—had imported a two-clawed dragon at fantastic expense and offered a prize for the man who could kill it with a sword. So great was the prize that every sponsor of warriors in the city had put up his best man. Silky had drawn the eighteenth chance, and traded it for the fourth spot, originally drawn by a man with more sense than ambition. Fourth still felt about right—he had learned the lizard's style by watching how it killed its first three opponents, and could hope that the slow-witted reptile had not yet learned the sand warriors' style. He was reasonably confident of success, since he would be fighting by the Gray Helpers' rules, but there was an undeniable beat of excitement in his groin as he climbed into the rickshaw waiting for him.

The Abbot knew nothing of this madcap venture and would be furious when he heard of it, but to Silky, it had seemed like the surest way to Verdant's heart—or, at least, her bed—and their brief encounter as he was leaving had confirmed him in this belief. Faint heart never won fair lady, as one of the teachers had probably said.

Adding young Malachite Harmony to the rickshaw was literally child's play. The lanky runner was understandably unhappy at having to tow a double load, but he was Novice Mast from the abbey on discipline detail, so Silky just laughed at his woebegone expression and told him to be quick. The guards at the gate did not bother to inspect Silky's rickshaw as it left, because they were more worried about assassination than theft; besides, he was one of the household. So they did not find the boy crouched under the bench.

As soon as they were out in the streets, Malachite emerged and squeezed in beside Silky to sit with mouth and eyes stretched as wide as they would go, gaping at all the sights. He was very rarely allowed out of the grounds, and never without a parental escort and guards, so this would be an epochal adventure for him. It would also leave him vulnerable to blackmail if Silky ever needed to make use of him.

By the time they neared the Courtyard of Dancing Blades, the program was already under way, and the surging roars suggested another sellout crowd. For a long time, young Malachite had been growing more and more horrified as the crowds grew thicker, buildings higher, alleyways darker and narrower and smellier. At one point, he asked, "Why do all the streets smell like latrines?"

His education had been neglected. "Guess."

Silky was recognized as soon as the rickshaw entered the Alley of Rose-Red Lanterns, which led to the competitors' entrance. People began shouting his name and pressing forward to touch him in the hope of gaining good fortune. Novice Mast was brought to a panting halt, so Silky disembarked and grabbed Malachite's arm just before the lad was swept away by the crush.

"Stay close! Hang on to my back strap."

"How will I find my way home if you die?"

This problem was not high on Silky's agenda. "Pick out a couple of the nastiest villains you can see and tell them who you are."

"What? Why?"

"They'll ransom you back to your father."

Malachite moaned. "He probably won't pay!"

Possibly not.

The winner's share of the gate would make fat Jade Harmony drool an ocean—as long as the winner was not the dragon. On the other hand, at a rough guess, a fourth win by the dragon should pay out its cost and put Wondrous Fortune's fortunes on the right side of the abacus. Meanwhile, Silky had to get himself and his deadly sword into the arena without killing anyone, especially young Malachite.

The Court of Dancing Blades was a large, sand-floored oblong surrounded by stands. The seats at the south end were shaded by a great roof with the upturned gables typical of Good Land architecture, supported on green pillars and tiled in blue. Four drum-shaped stone booths, which were used for various purposes at various times, stood south of the center. That day, they were merely blinds, protective cover for participants in some of the contests.

Silky and Malachite entered just as the junior melee was ending. Eight youths had been bloodied and eliminated, leaving three still warily stalking one another in and out between the blinds, closely watched by the umpires. Even between roars, the arena rumbled with excitement. Having lodged his terrified but fascinated companion in the box reserved for competitors' families, Silky found a secluded corner. Confident that all eyes were watching to see which of the three exhausted boys would make a mistake first, he quickly drew his two poisoned knives and transferred them to sheaths he had sewn inside his breeches, between his legs. The result was far from comfortable, and he knew from experience that he must sit down with great care or risk dire consequences, even without the added peril of the poison. He filled the empty spaces in his baldrics with the two extra knives he had brought in his boots.

Walking carefully, he went to check in at the competitors' entrance. He laid his sword on the table and deposited all his other weapons in a basket that the officials would keep safe for him—or for his heirs if his afternoon turned out to have been inauspicious. He added his boots. These were the rules of the Court of Dancing Blades, and the prince's rules, which he just happened to be following at the moment. Having done all that, he was required to drop his breeches and raise his arms, so that the officials could see that he was not trying to smuggle in any illicit weapons. The officials, of course, were busy watching the junior melee, shouting bets at one another.

"How long do I have to stand here with my hammer hanging out?"

"That's fine. Hide the horrible thing quick. Ten more on the blue kid!"

"Done!" retorted the other official.

Silky raised his breeches carefully and tied the laces again. The senior gate officer shook out Silky's boots, threw them back at him, and stamped a record sheet, all without taking his eyes off the action. Two boys met face-to-face and engaged their swords in a duel. Boy Blue-White managed to cut Boy Orange-Brown's shoulder just as Boy Green-Pink, tracking the noise, came around behind him and ripped Blue-White's back. The crowd went mad. Sand Warrior Silky was officially checked in.

Half a dozen bouts of various types followed the junior melee but none aroused much interest. Even a grudge match fought with real blades hardly made a stir, although the winner risked becoming a murderer in the eyes of law. Everyone was waiting for the last item on the ticket: Two-Clawed Dragon versus Sand Warrior Silky. Over the winter, he had made a name for himself—mostly with his skills but partly because of the fiendishly appropriate name laid on him by his client, which was a great joy to the crowds. Other warriors invoked horror or terror in their arena names; there was only one Silky. Today he would either consolidate his growing reputation as the premier upcoming warrior in Wedlock or nourish a growing dragon.

He stood on the competitors' terrace to watch the bouts, ignoring the dwindling group of fellow competitors. They shunned him. He was doomed, ill-omened. It was very bad fortune to speak to a man on the day he died. He brought his heart back to its proper tortoise pace. It was a fine day to fight, sunny but not too bright, warm on bare skin but not too hot for the extreme demands he would soon make of his body. Imperial edicts called this Ice Moon. Here in the south, it was Budding Moon. It was even a fine day to die. What better exit could a man ask of Heaven than to die bravely before twenty thousand screaming supporters?

There were other worlds than this one, and he could see no reason why Heaven would send him to a worse one.

A straight fight on open ground between a swordsman and even a mere two-clawed would be suicide, especially when the dragon had been starved for three days. To make the odds very slightly better, the dragon was handicapped with a snack beforehand. Once it began to feed, the stupid lizard would regard a human intruder as a rival trying to steal its kill and fight defensively instead of hunting him down as prey. Even with that, the odds were heavily in favor of the dragon—fifty to one at last report. It had easily dispatched Leopard Claw, Mighty Fangs, and Creature of Nightmare. But none of them had been a Gray Brother.

None had been Silky. He was the best.

Of course, there were sure to be problems he hadn't thought of.

A wild boar lost the last-but-one bout and was towed away, the winner receiving a brief cheer. Now Silky stood alone on the north terrace and the crowd began to chant his name. They had shouted, "*Nightmare! Nightmare!*" the last time.

The western gate opened; a gazelle bounded onto the field. The stadium fell silent. The terrified beast raced around the whole arena before recognizing shelter and making a dash for the blinds. In its run, it passed directly below Silky and froze his blood.

Unforeseen problem number one: Brother Providence, seeming to be an obvious arena employee, was to have groomed the gazelle before its debut. He was also supposed to dust its coat well with opium powder, because dragons were very susceptible to opium. So was a gazelle, for that matter, and thus Providence would have muzzled it with a strap to prevent it from licking its coat and losing interest in the proceedings. The gazelle had not been muzzled. Conclusion? The bait had been spiked with opium.

Prince Wondrous Fortune had a large investment to take care of. His guards had detected and frustrated half of Silky's battle plan.

Then the east gate opened and the dragon streaked out like an opal snake, a shimmering ripple of blue and green scales. Previously, Silky had guessed its length as that of three horses end to end, but today was his turn, and now four horses seemed more likely, maybe five. Big ones. How fast did dragons grow on a diet of human meat?

There must be many newcomers in the crowd, because this first glimpse of the monster provoked just as much screaming as it had on its previous three entries.

Problem number two: In previous bouts, the dragon had writhed and snarled around the arena, terrifying the spectators, until it had caught the gazelle's scent. This time it hurtled across the sand in a straight line, right into the four blinds. The gazelle did not even break cover before it died. Icy water ran down Silky's ribs and his topknot tried to unravel. Dragons learned much faster than he had expected.

It was time to move. His feet were strangely reluctant, but he must reach the blinds before the lizard finished its appetizer and came out looking for the entrée. He hurried over to the stairwell and started down, not running in spite of his increasing sense of urgency. At the bend in the stair, for the one brief moment when no one could see him, he removed the poisoned knives from his breeches and tucked them in the sheaths in his boots. At the bottom, he drew his sword and transferred it to his left hand. An attendant opened the tiny barred door for him. He sucked in a very deep breath and walked out onto the sunlit sand of the arena. He was shivering as he had not done since fever swept through Wedlock in the Year of the Heron. For the first time in his life, the prospect of imminent death seemed real. The lizard was *clever*.

The crowd roared. "*Silky! Silky! Silky! Silky!*"

The dragon rose up on its hind legs with three-quarters of a gazelle in its mouth, rearing high to look over the blinds, straight at him. It had not done that for Leopard Claw, Mighty Fangs, or Creature of Nightmare. It had been *expecting* the main dish to appear from that inconspicuous door! It dropped down out of sight. Guessing what was about to happen, Silky began to run for the cover as fast as his boots would move sand. That was what his opponents had done, playing tag in the blinds. Leopard Claw had even managed to nick the dragon's tail. But the dragon closed off that option for Silky. It came around the blinds and the crowd screamed even louder as the two opponents streaked toward each other over the bare ground.

The lizard streaked twice as fast as he did. Obviously, it had developed a taste for man. It liked raw warrior better than gazelle, and it was certainly showing no sign of opium poisoning. Never mind a tea caddy; a tea*cup* would be enough to hold Silky's remains.

The body of a snake, the scales of a fish, the antlers of a deer, the talons of an eagle, and the eyes of a demon—never could death look more certain or more beautiful, flashing in green and blue iridescence. He must not get too close. A two-clawed was wingless and did not breathe fire, but its breath would stun. One whiff to knock you out and two to kill, it was said—worse than Brother Archives's.

The dragon had come around the blinds on his left and his instinct was to veer to his right. Seeing that he wasn't going to make it, Silky changed course and ran straight at the monster, whirling his sword over his head and yelling at the top of his voice, although there was no chance the beast would hear him over the noise of the crowd. Shouting just made him feel better.

The prince's rules said that the man was required to kill the dragon with no weapon but a sword. Silky had been prepared to argue that throwing knives might blind it but never kill it and therefore were not forbidden. If the argument failed to bring him the prize money, he would at least have won the honor. At the moment, he had no interest in honor or prize money, only bare survival. He was close enough. He stopped.

At that same moment, the reptile's tiny mind decided that all was not right. Prey should not attack! The other two-legged meats had not attacked. Puzzled, it skidded to a halt in a shower of sand and raised its great head to stare at him with huge bulging eyes. Even at ten paces, it was looking *down*.

Silky's palm was too sweaty to throw a knife. He stooped, rubbed his hand in the grit and, even as he straightened, snatched a knife from his boot and hurled. The first blade bounced harmlessly off one of the bony brow ridges. The dragon cocked its head to see what the biped was up to, and the second knife plunged into its left eye.

The lizard did not like that. It hurtled backward with a roar that echoed off the far end of the stadium. It toppled, curled, writhed, thrashed, clawed at its head, threw sand in all directions. Now what? However great its agony, there could not possibly be enough venom on that tiny blade to kill such a monster, and yet, between flying sand, thrashing tail, and poison breath, Silky could not get close enough to ram his sword into those glittering scales. Twice he ran in to try and twice had to leap back to safety.

Uttering an even more gargantuan roar, the dragon gathered itself together. With its left eye spurting blood and the right turned balefully on its tormenter, it rushed him. Silky pivoted on one boot and hurled his sword with all his might into those nightmare jaws. He threw himself flat on his face and prepared to die.

The crowd was making the loudest noise he had ever heard, but all he could hear from the dragon was a gurgling, clashing sound. He was alive? He sat up. The lizard was in its death throes,

twisting and rolling as if trying to knot itself. It was still chomp-
ing on the sword, which must have cut its tongue and palate to
shreds by now, and it was dying from the effects of snake venom,
but who could prove that? Did it matter? As Silky rose unsteadily,
his eyes caught a flash of sunlight from one of his knives. He tot-
tered over to it and idly scuffed sand over it with his foot. There
must be another one around somewhere. They might not be
found for months. Only then did he realize that the twenty thousand spectators were on their feet screaming his name.

Shoulders back, chest out!

Sorry about your dragon, Prince.

The lizard had coughed up his sword. It was bent and chipped,
but he retrieved it, went over to the heaving, writhing corpse,
and rammed the blade through its left eye, into its evil little brain.

I threw sand in its face, Prince. What did you think I threw?

When Jade Harmony heard that the afternoon's excitement had
made him twelve thousand taels richer, he was inspired to invite his sand warrior to dine with the family, an unprecedented
honor. "Family" meant the merchant, his widowed daughter, and
Morning Jewel, his lemon-sour wife, who pouted so reprovingly
at this unseemly pampering of retainers that she had to eat her
rice one grain at a time. Their underage son was excluded as
always—the guards searched incoming traffic more rigorously
than outgoing, so that socially deprived seedling had returned by
climbing over the wall. He had needed instruction from Silky on
how and where to sneak back into his own house, poor little rich
boy. The four adults sat cross-legged and paddled food from delicate porcelain bowls with ivory chopsticks, even at times talking.
Servants came and went, bringing and taking away.

Verdant Harmony just munched without mouthing a word,
causing her mother to frown thoughtfully at her, as if assessing
her for plague. Jade Harmony himself failed to notice their mood

and droned about food shortages in the north and the price of grain. He neglected to ask a single question about the dragon fight, an oversight that rankled Silky—unreasonably so, since the Gray Helpers were taught to pursue anonymity. But the Gray Helpers were also taught how to make appropriate conversation at funerals, and now was an equally good time to talk about money.

"May I venture to ask the Eminent One if he has ever heard of the Portal of Worlds?"

The merchant contemplated the question, his in-house assassin, what conceivable reason the latter should have for putting the former, and the most appropriate of several appropriate answers. "Only legends," he said at last.

"It has many of those," Silky admitted. "But there really is such a place, up in the Fortress Hills. It is the work of great ancestors, a construct unthinkable to us lesser men in these smaller days."

"What does it *do?*"

"Nothing. It's only a carving on a cliff."

"Ah."

"But there are rumors," Silky admitted, tweezing a chunk of pig liver out of the zoology-with-beans. "It is said that the gate opened at the end of the Third Dynasty and the ferocious Hauik came pouring out to conquer the Good Land."

"And eventually founded the Fourth Dynasty?" Jade Harmony displayed a hint of interest.

"Precisely as Your Eminence says. And the dreaded Karun, who founded the Eighth, claimed a similar origin. No one seems to know where else they could have come from."

The current Lord of the High and the Low was counted in the Eleventh Dynasty. Jade Harmony nodded thoughtfully as he worked it out—fourth, eighth, and then twelfth? His house assassin had made him about five times richer than he had been just a few months ago—assuming one included money that was technically his daughter's, as Jade Harmony always did. When Silky talked, it was wise to listen. What bait was the House of Joyful Departure dangling now?

"And there are omens," Silky added.

"What sort of omens?"

"Unseasonable weather, civil unrest." He did not mention the old belief that such disasters were a sign of Heaven withdrawing its mandate from the ruling dynasty. Such talk was treason. "There are tales that many sky demons have been seen in northern provinces."

"Superstitious rubbish," said the merchant, who was highly superstitious.

"Indeed, as Your Eminence says. But there is one prophecy that may bear watching. It is said that the nightingale will sing to two broom stars."

"Ah! The nightingale," Jade Harmony dogmatized to his womenfolk, "is the only eponym found in both the catalog of years and the catalog of moons. Thus Nightingale Moon in the Year of the Nightingale is especially portentous!" Everyone knew that, even housebound women. "You think that the Portal of Worlds will open then, Sand Warrior?"

"Your humble servant is ignorant of such matters, Eminence, and defers to your noble judgment. However, most sources seem to believe that it opens only in the Year of the Firebird. If, indeed, two broom stars are seen during Nightingale Moon, then many persons may speculate that the Portal must open in the *next* Year of the Firebird—this cycle!"

"And?" the merchant's piggy eyes glinted.

"There is much good grazing land near the Portal that might become more easily available to the wise investor who did not panic at foolish omens," Silky said. That was the message the Abbot had told him to deliver. The Abbot had been rooting around in Portal lore for decades.

The meal dragged to a merciful close. Verdant had not once

looked in Silky's direction. Her mother had not once stopped pouting. Jade Harmony was still blissfully contemplating his twelve thousand taels. Eventually, he moved to rise and end the gathering. At once, his sand warrior was at his back to lift him, after which he was permitted to perform the same service for each of the ladies.

And then—surprise!—Jade Harmony was suddenly seized by a pang of gratitude. "And what of our noble dragon slayer? What can I give you to reward your fine service today? What does a strong young man crave, hmm?"

That was unquestionably an offer of one of the kitchen slave girls as a concubine, which was not exactly outstanding generosity, but better than his customary stinge.

Silky bowed very low. "Your munificence is legendary, Eminence. Just to serve you is ample reward. I have everything here I could dream of." At that moment, he managed to catch Verdant's eye. The great heifer looked straight through him as if he did not exist.

No matter. . . . He enjoyed a challenge.

His nightwork costume consisted of a dark gray tunic and matching trousers, but if he tried seeming magic with those on, he would become smallish and utterly nondescript. A romantic lover should wear sumptuous courtly robes, of which he had none handy; besides not even a mythical hero could climb three stories up a sheer wall in them. He improvised by stripping down to nothing except a sword belt and sword. That worked. His reflection became tall and lean, with muscles snaking under his skin. His eyes became strangely lustrous, his queue long and thick, finely braided. And so on.

When he was satisfied, he disarmed, turned his back on the mirror, and dressed in his now ostentatiously tight burglar clothes. He slipped his lock-picking tools into one of the copious pockets, extinguished his lamp, and went to his window to watch Verdant's.

The walls of the palace were fitted with downward-facing bronze teeth to ensure that no burglar climbed very far, and flanked with spikes along the base to make certain that he would fail only once. After a very long torment of waiting—killing dragons made a man exceedingly lascivious—the lights faded, which meant that Verdant's servants had finished readying her for bed and were departing. Tonight, she kept a light on, which was not her usual practice.

In a few moments, Silky reached the terrace outside her room. By his third night in the Harmony residence, he had mastered all its locks, so it was child's play for him to creep up the servants' stair to the family quarters, exit to the roof terrace through one of the unoccupied suites, perform a death-defying walk along the narrow parapet to Verdant's quarters, and then—because he had arranged it beforehand—open one flap of the casement and peer in.

He might have lost his face to a point-blank blast from First Musket's pistols, but this was certainly his lucky day. She was alone, sitting erect in a chair and wearing a robe that buttoned to her neck and covered everything except her face and toes. It could not conceal the width of her shoulders or the wonderful depth of her breasts, nor the great cataract of gleaming black hair.

The room was hot, heated by crackling logs in the fireplace. Lit by firelight and a single lantern, it was a mist of silks, shadows, and heavy incense. The bed itself was well quilted and quite large enough for what he had in mind.

He slid a leg over the sill, smiling. "You left the window for me!"

"I did not! I thought I made sure they were all locked. You are a madman. You might have been killed climbing that wall."

He closed the flap. "I died for you once, Princess. If I must, I will do so again." He watched her scared eyes as he approached— justifiably scared, but she had known he was coming and could easily have arranged for servants or armed guards to wait here in her stead. He knelt before the delicate bare toes peeking out from under the hem of her robe. "Any more memories come back yet? The Summer Palace? That night in the Waterlily Park?"

"*Nothing* has come back, as you put it, nothing at all!" Verdant was as strong-willed as she was strong-armed.

She wanted to be wooed.

He sighed. "When I first told you, this afternoon, I thought you . . . But, no matter. You truly don't believe me?"

"No." Had there been a hint of hesitation there?

"I would never lie to you, Princess. I recognized you the instant I set eyes on you and my heart sang. I kept hoping, hoping, hoping that one day I would see that light of memory in your eyes, too."

"You never will. If I strike this gong, you are a dead man, Sand Warrior."

"Sometimes . . . Do you by any chance have a birthmark . . . about here?" He touched his chest. "Shaped like a fish?"

"*No!*" She lost color. It had cost him four taels and several sweaty nights to win that information about her birthmark. Both tattletale maids had subsequently been dismissed—for reasons that could not possibly have had anything to do with Sand Warrior Silky—so they could not now be questioned.

"Or do you recall this?" he said. He crouched down and kissed her toes.

She jerked her foot away. "What are you doing?"

"You used to enjoy having me kiss your toes, Beloved." He took her foot, raised it to his lips, and gave every toe a thorough nibbling. Somehow, he could not imagine the late Distant Cloud ever descending to such indignity.

She did not say a word, not even when he repeated the process with the other foot. He was almost tempted to tell her to stop playing virgin, as if she didn't know what he had come for or couldn't stop him easily. But his crotch was aching too much for him to risk failure now.

"Oh, that brings back memories!" He sat on his heels and used the lustrous eyes on her. "You truly cannot remember the day we met, Princess Celestial Womb? In the spring, when you were boating with your ladies and the wind caught your parasol?"

He transferred the old story of Sea Flower and the Storm Prince onshore. It was famous poetry, but the Harmony residence was no palace of learning, and Verdant showed no sign of recognizing the originals of Princess Celestial Womb and Prince Noble Lance as their romance unfolded.

"I don't believe a word of it," she said at the end. "Who are you? Really."

"Really Sand Warrior Silky, the city's best. I really, truly did slay the dragon today and made your father a lot of money."

"Why? You must love him more than life itself."

"I love you more than life itself."

"You lie like a camel trader."

At least she was talking, not ordering him out. Not that he would go if she did, not now.

"I only lie to beautiful women when I am desperate to get into their beds. Ask me about anything else and I will tell you the truth, every word, I swear. But be careful what you ask."

"Why did you fight the dragon?"

"To make money for your father, because eventually I will get a share of his wealth. That's in the contract."

"What contract?"

"That is a dangerous question."

"Answer it."

"The contract that says I am to make him very rich. I have already done so, with good advice and by other means that you definitely do not want to ask about."

She fixed him with a hard stare. Perhaps it was only the dim lighting that dilated her pupils so much. Or perhaps not. He spoke before she did.

"Now I get to ask you a question. How much longer are you going to sit here gabbling like a dowager great-grandmother when I could be making love to you in that bed? I can show you things that Distant Cloud never dreamed of. I can make you cry out in unbearable ecstasy, not once but many times."

"Words!" She stood and unfastened her robe. The birthmark was larger and nearer her nipple than he had expected. She walked across and climbed onto the bed, on top of the downy quilts. Silky put his sword down within easy reach and lay beside her, equally naked. It was only a few minutes before he got where he desperately needed to be. He thought he would have to struggle to hold himself back, but she did not want that. She pushed the pace as if she was equally eager, going quickly to climax, and if she was faking her cries of rapture, she was a very good actor. His orgasm was certainly genuine and entirely satisfactory.

She began the second round almost before he'd caught his breath from the first one. Much later, as he was climbing out the window, he said, "Tomorrow?" She did not answer, but anything not forbidden was permitted. Or rather, anything was permitted if you could get away with it.

The Abbot would be pleased to learn of his success.

CHAPTER 4

The Bamboo Banner came to Golden Aspect on a sunny afternoon in Hare Moon. As the Pearl Army had moved back inland, the countryside had risen, so Man Valor was seeing hills for the first time in his life. The town stood on a gentle rise at the edge of the plain, surrounded by paddy fields as far as the eye could see. At that time of the year, everyone was out attending to the spring weeding, so the diversion in the square attracted mainly children and old folk. The governor sent guards, but they watched from a balcony and did not interfere. There would not be much recruiting in Golden Aspect that day. Gathering nobodies, they called it.

Gathering nobodies, Man Valor had guessed, was not the main reason for this visit. He was not the only one to have noticed that the rice bowls were not being heaped as high lately. Many thousands of patriots followed the Bamboo Banner now, and they needed to eat well, for they were rarely still. They exercised ten hours every day to increase their agility, their strength, their martial skills. They ran for two hours a day, chanting battle hymns or the hypnotic, mind-wrecking doggerel of the Bamboo Song:

NOT sticks nor stones
can break my bones;
Swords and shot
can hurt me NOT . . .

Over and over and over and over and over and over . . .

That moronic jingle filled his thoughts, his dreams, his entire life. They sang it running, exercising, bathing, even sometimes wrestling. Any time they got a spare moment, they were expected to pair off and practice wrestling. They sat down exactly three times a day, to eat, but then they listened to lessons also. Even as a twenty-year-old dockworker, Man Valor had been no fitter and stronger than he was now, and he slept nine hours a night on the hard ground under the jeweled worlds of Heaven. *Swords and shot can hurt me NOT . . .*

Older than most recruits, he was doing well. In six months, he had been promoted from a nobody to a patriot of the second proving. He had learned how to endure the sort of blow he had watched Leaping Serpent take that long-ago day back in Celestial Vista Square, even strokes that should shatter bones—although that was hardly a fair comparison, because Man Valor's bones were much better padded with muscle than Leaping Serpent's would ever be. Sometimes, the strokes hurt more than he cared to admit, but no one seemed to notice his pain, and he suffered no serious hurt. The ancestors protected him.

Now Leaping Serpent had been promoted to third proving and had chosen Man Valor to be second deputy in his cadre. That meant Man Valor was running right behind Serpent as the cadre approached the town from the west. Ahead of him was Serpent's sweaty back, with a collection of fading bruises and the dangling ends of his headband with its three knots. Bamboo said, *If your men cannot count your knots, then you are not their leader.*

Twenty-eight more superbly trained and motivated young patriots ran behind them, with First Deputy Skewbald at the rear. Serpent and Skewbald had reconnoitered the town a couple of days ago and knew what part this cadre would play in the day's events. Whatever it was, the rest would do as they were told, as eagerly as any men who serve a great and holy cause—more so, because they knew they were invincible.

Every town in the Good Land was protected by a wall, but Golden Aspect's looked to be in poor repair and so low that Man Valor could have pole-vaulted over it. Three men stood guard on the western gate. They stared in alarm at this line of runners, every one of them armed with a heavy bamboo staff—all except Leaping Serpent himself, who held a thinner cane with its leafy fronds still in place. Every fifth man also carried a heavy ax.

First Musket stepped forward carrying a gun and accompanied by the elder of his two flunkies. Serpent waved his banner to signal a pause, and the cadre stopped advancing, but continued to run in place.

The junior guard bowed. "With deepest regret, we must inform the noble travelers that the laws of the Good Land and decrees of His Majesty, Lord of the High and the Low, et cetera, forbid strangers to enter cities while bearing weapons, and the most honorable governor of this ancient and peaceable town of Golden Aspect has charged First Musket to enforce this edict."

"The Emperor is dead," Serpent announced. "A woman has shamefully placed her defiling buttocks upon the Golden Throne. We come in the name of the Bamboo Banner, who will set this opprobrious affair to rights. And these staves are not weapons," he added with blatant untruth, "but badges of our allegiance to the righteous cause of Bamboo."

The guard looked to First Musket for guidance. First Musket seemed to be unnerved by the way those sixty bare feet continued their relentless rhythm. Obviously, no one had sent him orders to shut the gate and the odds were impossible.

"If the honored strangers do not now withdraw," he declared harshly, "Then I must instruct my troops to open fire."

"The learned and valiant officer must obey his conscience," Serpent said cheerfully, "but he knows that we patriots who follow the Bamboo Banner are immune to bullets. Shoot if you will. You will not harm us, but we will kill you all for trying."

First Musket chewed his lip for a moment longer, then nodded and backed away. Serpent signaled the advance and his cadre trotted into Golden Aspect.

Already drums were beating in the heart of the little town. Cadres that had entered by other gates had already begun the distraction and the clandestine looting. Serpent brought his men to a halt at a crossroads and signaled them to assemble. They swarmed in around him, eyes bright and expectant.

"Spit," he said and did so himself. Twenty-nine other wads joined the mire in the road. He unwrapped a banana-leaf package to reveal thirty precious yang leaves, then proceeded to put one in each man's mouth as they all stood around him, gaping like fledglings. He took the last for himself, dropped the wrapping. As Man Valor chewed, he felt the welcome first rush of fire in his veins. The world danced and sparkled anew. With yang in him, a man was far more than other men—fearless, untiring, invincible. Even after he had chewed the leaf to a pulp, it would not quite lose its potency, and he would hold the cud in his cheek until the evening meal. Two leaves a day was the normal ration during training, with a third issued only at the start of serious operations such as this one.

"Rice," Leaping Serpent said between chews. "We came for rice and only rice. First third will come with me this way. Skewbald will lead the rest farther along that road to fetch some mules. Go." He watched two-thirds of the cadre run off and grinned at his own little band. His eyes were brighter already.

He jabbed a thumb at the shadowed, wormhole alley behind him, where a group of naked infants watched the strangers with wide eyes. The ground was layered in filth, but the buildings were built of brick in the vain hope of keeping vermin out of stored perishables.

"Just about every door along here is a rice shop. We have ample time before the mules arrive, so we can spread the word. Nobodies stay with your buddies and watch. The rest of you take a store each, go in and tell them about the Emperor and his demon mother. Explain their duty to support the Banner. Let them hit you if they want to, but no showing off—take no more punishment than you've proven to me that you can stand. Is that clear? If they contribute a bag, put it outside the door, bless them, and leave. If they argue, take two. Skewbald's group will load it when they arrive. Use no more violence than necessary, but no less than you need. Questions?"

There were no questions. Only two of the cadre were nobodies, and the rest had all done this before. Bare feet squelched along the alley. Man Valor hung back to the end, watched men peeling off into the narrow doorways until only he and Serpent were left. They flashed smiles at each other and took the next two doorways.

As Man Valor was about to enter, the owner tried to slam the door in his face. She wasn't quite quick enough, which saved her a repair job on her door. Although large, she was elderly, and Man Valor's response catapulted her back onto the table where she usually sat to measure rice into her customers' jugs. She lay on it, legs dangling, gaping up in terror at the fearsome smile above her. The tiny space must suddenly have seemed full of half-naked man.

"The Emperor is dead," the intruder growled. He saw that the old woman was too shocked and frightened to take in very much of his lecture, but he told her anyway, and when it was finished, she nodded to agree that the Bamboo Banner was entitled to take two bags of rice—under the circumstances. Man Valor hoisted her back to the vertical, patted her head in blessing, and carried two weighty sacks from the store at the back to the doorway, one in each hand.

Outside, Leaping Serpent was keeping an amused eye on the doors that had been visited so far, making sure that no sacks vanished back inside. First Deputy Skewbald was just entering the alley with the first mule. Man Valor ran along the alley in the hope of finding a store not yet visited. He passed Carp Shining joyfully smashing a door apart with an ax. Then a man screamed.

Man Valor was closest and beat both Carp and Serpent to the noise. Still howling in agony, Mariner came staggering out with his hands over his face. Man Valor grabbed him by the shoulders. Mariner and he had been recruited in Face to the Sun on the same day, and had become friends, in as much as any of the Bamboo Banner had time in their lives for socializing or small talk. Mariner, however, was more strong than smart and had not yet risen above First Proving.

"Pepper," he sobbed. "He threw pepper in my face! I'm blind."

Man Valor shifted his grip to Mariner's wrists and pulled his hands down by brute strength. "No, you are not blind! Pepper can't hurt you. *Look at me!*"

Mariner tried. His eyes were hugely inflamed and watering, and he could barely force the lids apart to open slits. Rivers of tears had washed clean channels through the red dust on his cheeks.

"Pain is illusion," Man Valor insisted, repeating the training mantras they chanted a hundred times a day. "Hurt is lack of faith. The ancestors make us strong because our cause is just."

"I can't see. . . ."

"You don't need to see. You memorized the store when you went in, didn't you? Of course you did, good man! You're one of the best and strongest. Now go in there and bring out four bags of rice. Smash him if he gets in your way. I'll be here if you need me." He spun Mariner around and pushed him back inside.

Mariner halted. Man Valor pushed him all the way back into the dark little store. Mariner was taller than Man Valor, which was why Man Valor failed to see the blow coming. He felt the impact through his arms, and then Mariner slumped to the ground with blood and brains spilling out of a chasm in his skull. Beyond him stood an even bigger man, holding one of the Bamboo Banner's own axes.

Man Valor roared in fury and leaped over the body. The storekeeper tried to hit him with the ax, but he was too slow. Man Valor's hand closed around his throat and rammed him back against the wall of stacked rice sacks. The man gurgled, trying to batter Man Valor's ribs with the ax, but he was holding it one handed, and the best he could do was use the head as a ram. Man Valor ignored his efforts.

For a moment, he wasn't sure what to do next.

"All the way," said Leaping Serpent's voice behind him.

Man Valor crushed the storekeeper's throat until blood gushed out of his mouth, then let him slide to the tiles. Serpent had gone, satisfied that Man Valor had the situation under control. He pulled Mariner off to the side so the body couldn't be seen from the doorway, then heaved the dying shopkeeper on top of him to hide him even better. He had piled eight bags of rice in the doorway by the time Skewbald's men arrived with the mules. Man Valor passed out all the rest. The storekeeper was dead and had no need of it.

He suspected he had a couple of broken ribs, though. He whipped his hand away from them quickly when he saw Leaping Serpent coming.

"It was the pepper," Man Valor whispered. "He couldn't see." Yes, the Bamboo Banner patriots were invincible, but there were whispers. Once in a while, a man's faith might waver, or he didn't see danger coming.

Serpent smiled. "Looks like you picked up a few bruises there, Brother." He produced a rolled-up yang leaf from a pocket. "This will take the sting away. No, don't spit out the other."

Man Valor stared at the treat longingly, but also unbelievingly. He hadn't known that cadre leaders carried an emergency supply. "Two? So soon?" It would be like his first taste of the yang, the day he took the oath, flying like a bat for hours.

He tried to protest that the pain was trivial, but Leaping Serpent pushed the second leaf into his mouth anyway. "There's lots of room in there for this. Just don't try and talk for a while, right? Or you'll choke."

Mouth full, Man Valor could only nod. *Don't talk!* The Bamboo Banner might have taken other losses on this expedition, but by the time Leaping Serpent's cadre had assembled and was driving the laden mule train out of town, the double dose of yang had made him too dizzy to try counting heads.

There were no assigned beds in the Bamboo Banner and no private possessions. Blankets were handed out at random and collected again in the morning—sharing the bugs fairly, they called it. Mariner would not be missed. A failure's name was never spoken.

Before dawn, even before reveille, when Man Valor was reliving the shopkeeper's death in nightmare for the third or fifth time, he was nudged awake by an ungentle toe. He blinked up at two men standing over him, dark against first light. He threw off his blanket, snatched up his headband, and had it back on his head even before he was upright. He stood at attention, shivering as the wind stroked his bare chest and back.

One of the two was Leaping Serpent. The other he had never seen before. He looked very young, thin and short, and with a stoop that thrust his head forward, but there was no weakness in his features. His teeth stuck out like the front of a wheelbarrow, so he looked rather like a dog on a leash, straining to bite someone.

"You're going to be promoted," Leaping Serpent said. "You're reassigned to special training. If you can handle it, you'll get your third knot. Well deserved. Congratulations." He turned and walked away between the sleepers.

"You're Man Valor?"

"Yes, Leader . . ."

"My name doesn't matter," the newcomer said, scowling up at him. "I'm sometimes called Silent, because my cadre is the Silent Cadre. We work twice as hard as the others. You'll be allotted three leaves a day, otherwise you won't be able to stand it. No man could. But that's the only treat you get. Nod if you understand."

Man Valor nodded.

"And you never speak unless I order you to speak. Not to me, not to anyone. You nod for yes and shake for no and if you don't know the answer, you just stand and wait for me to speak again. Got that?"

"Yes, Leader."

Silent punched him hard enough to knock all the wind out of him and double him over. He staggered backward, clutching his belly. By the winds, the kid was faster than thunderbolts! He punched at three times his weight.

Man Valor forced himself upright, wondering whether he was supposed to take that or not. He decided he was, so he opened his fists, relaxed his shoulders, and stepped back to where he had been. It wasn't easy.

"Just this once, I'll ask you again. Do you understand?"

Man Valor nodded. He did now.

"Do you have any questions?"

Man Valor nodded again.

Silent leered his splay teeth. "Ask them in three months, when you've earned your third knot. Now follow me."

CHAPTER 5

"In the hope that Your Holiness will overlook my unforgivable presumption, understanding that it is provoked only by my extreme concern for your personal welfare," Shard Gingko said, "I do urge you to leave Four Mountains very soon. In a handful of days, no more. My letter to Sublime Mountain would have arrived before the full of Ice Moon. A new warden will be at the gate before we know it." He had been planning this speech for a week and was amazed to hear himself actually managing to say it.

The boy smiled. He was cross-legged on a cushion, wrapped in a blanket—he refused to wear anything but simple peasant clothes, although he still felt the cold very much. He was eating nuts. He ate all the time, it seemed. He joked about the Emperor owing him many meals, and costing more to keep that a battalion of guards, but clearly his maltreated body was trying to catch up. The servants brought him anything he asked for and many things he didn't, and he ate them all.

He said, "Mandarins do not travel as fast as imperial couriers, especially in winter."

"The roads are much improved. Tonight marks the start of Hare Moon."

The Firstborn nodded. "You are right, of course. A replacement is overdue. Without offense to your rank or abilities, Clerk of Records, I confess I am surprised that the provincial governor did not send a stand-in."

"And I confess that I did not send my report by way of the honored governor. The late warden's instructions were to communicate with no one except First Mandarin, and I took it upon myself to comply when reporting his ascent. But the Emperor may not send a new warden all the way from Heart of the World. He may send a directive to an official in some place near us, naming him the replacement, even if only provisionally. There are four or five towns within two days' ride for a strong man."

"You are still right," the Firstborn agreed, somber now. "I thank you for this correction, Clerk of the Tablets, and for the respite you have given me. But you know I cannot leave Four Mountains Fortress." He glanced thoughtfully across the table at the peasant woman he always addressed as "Mother." She was ignorant and stupid and rather ugly, and he treated her as if she were the legendary Jade Queen herself. He tolerated her presence day and night. He had given her his bed and slept on a mat in the corner.

The fourth person present was the boy, Mouse, who was now the Firstborn's self-appointed lap dog, never leaving his sight. The Ancient One tolerated him, refusing all offers to remove him. Servants had overheard the two of them chattering together, but Mouse almost never spoke when Shard was present. When he did, his accent betrayed his local Qiancheng origin. He had taken his bowl of rice over to a corner and ate in silence, cross-legged on the floor.

The four of them had just finished a noontime meal in the Firstborn's room. It was a good room, large and spacious, but his attachment to it was maddening. Shard had given him leave to go anywhere he wished in the castle, hinting broadly that if he wanted to go away, he would not be pursued, but he never took advantage of that liberty. As his health returned and the weather improved, he had started going out to the courtyard to exercise. At noon, rain or shine, he and the woman would appear on the parapet, where he would bless the crowd that was already gathering below. That was the limit of his wanderings. One could not argue or question anyone as holy as the Firstborn—not that there was anyone as holy as he—but Shard felt an overpowering duty to persuade him somehow.

He was a strange-looking boy, instantly recognizable to anyone who had ever seen his likeness—and who had not? His wavy hair was a curious shade of brown, his nose too big, his eyes too round. That was how the Firstborn was always pictured, not unlike some of the western Outlanders, but without their brutal look. He shaved the lower part of his face every few days because it sprouted crab hairs despite his youth. His winter ordeal showed in his extreme thinness, a bandaged wrist, and a limp that would likely stay with him throughout this life. But he would live. If he left now.

He was unfailingly gracious and even-tempered, even with the humblest. Enjoying humor, he would joke with the guards, laughing aloud in shocking disregard for his dignity. Yet he could quote the most obscure ancient texts like a high-ranking mandarin, and avoid questions he did not wish to answer so skillfully that the questioner did not even realize he had done so. Apparently, he never changed his mind on anything. Sage of sages, he knew that he was always right in all matters. But on this thing, he would have to be persuaded soon, and Shard braced himself for a supreme effort.

Before he could speak, Mouse rose to his feet and came across to the table. He stacked the used dishes on the tray, leaving only the Firstborn's bowl of nuts. Then he carried the tray over to the door, laid it there, and resumed his previous watchful posture in the corner. Either he had decided to make himself useful or the Firstborn had suggested that he do so, for any hint from his hero would be an absolute imperative for him.

He was probably very close to the same age as the Firstborn, and not unlike him in appearance, as if he had a touch of that same Outlander blood somewhere in his ancestry. Of course that was why the late governor had picked him out last fall to use as a faux Firstborn.

Shard said, "Holy One, you know that the Honored Sedge Shallows very nearly killed you. But he was not acting out of personal spite. I filed his warrants and have read them. I will show them to you if you wish. He was told to abuse you until you answered the Emperor's questions."

"I came to that conclusion quite soon in our relationship." The Firstborn popped more nuts in his mouth, his eyes twinkling. "I am surprised only that such orders were put in writing. It would seem that the Son of the Sun aims to be even more bloodthirsty than his father was."

"Oh, son!" the woman murmured, horrified at such blasphemy.

He patted her hand. "Emperor Zealous Righteousness cut off my head without a trial, Mother. Twice! The first time I had said some unkind things about him, I admit, but even the Courtly Teacher taught that Emperors may be censured when they stray from the path of righteousness."

"Twice?" If her son was the crack of a musket shot, she was the slow grind of glaciers.

"The second time I was only eight years old. I cried as they carried me out to the block, because I did not want to die again so soon."

It seemed that the Firstborn was trying to educate her to accept that he had a destiny she could not share, could barely understand. Shard had noticed him dropping many such hints lately.

"It grew worse, Holy One. Other instructions arrived. The honorable warden was ordered to torture or mutilate you in any way he wanted, to the death. Whether you were answering questions or not."

The woman looked thoroughly bewildered.

The boy's face had hardened. "And the Son of the Sun put his seal on such an edict? Truly, the poet said, *Our monuments are broken and the streams do not run.* These are small times. Why do I still live then?"

"By the grace of Heaven, I think. The honorable warden had taken to his bed when the second warrant came. I took it to him at once, but he was sleeping, so I laid it on the table by his bed. One of the doctors or servants must have knocked it off there, because I found it on the floor, unopened, after he died. He never read it."

"Dying worries me less than it does most people," the boy said with a smile that showed no humor. "But you assumed his responsibilities. Why did you not obey your Emperor's instructions?"

"I am a mere clerk, Holiness. I lack authority to administer such orders."

The boy chuckled. "Most men would not interpret your mandate so narrowly. They would see an opportunity to loose the demons that lurk within us all and use them to achieve great advancement. I am very thankful for your righteousness. Perhaps the delay in appointing a replacement for the eminent Serge Shallows is because the Golden Throne cannot find another servant willing to descend to such depths? One must hope that this is so."

The Humble Teacher had taught that one should think well of one's neighbor until he proved himself unworthy, but that maxim could be carried to suicidal lengths. Although a gentleman would not have pursued the subject further, Gingko was growing desperate.

"Serge Shallows was a man of honor. His first orders were to put you to death at once if the Bamboo Banner flew anywhere in Qiancheng."

The woman moaned, so she was understanding some of this. Even Mouse made a slight noise. His eyes were stretched wide, but then they always looked too large for his pinched face.

"*What is the Bamboo Banner?*" The Urfather did not raise his voice, but it rang with more than mortal authority and his eyes burned.

"Holy One . . . one hears tell of a rebellion, an insurrection, led by a man known only as Bamboo. It seems that he has been preaching sedition against the Golden Throne down south, in Dongguan and Kermang, for some time. The movement is spreading north. Late last year, his banner was raised in High Abode, here in Qiancheng."

The boy sighed and was suddenly just an odd-looking youth again. "And what happened next?"

"The honorable governor sent troops, Ancient One. The ringleaders were put to the death of a thousand cuts. Yet I believe that High Abode was not the main fire, only a spark carried on the wind."

"Where there is one spark, there may be more. I had hoped that, leaving here, I could travel north to Heart of the World and converse with the Emperor. I have not seriously admonished the Golden Throne since his honored grandfather reigned. The need seems even greater now, after what you just told me. But I also wish to learn what this revered Bamboo has to say. Truly, he sounds like a very upright person! If the Son of the Sun is so determined that we shall not meet, there may be good reason that we do. The problem is you, noble Clerk of the Tablets. You have already put yourself at too much risk for me, and I will not endanger you further. When the new warden arrives, he must find me here, obedient to the Son of the Sun."

"I would be greatly blessed if Your Holiness would let me accompany him on his travels," Shard said hopefully. "Such an honor would crown my existence on this tread of the staircase of worlds."

For the first time, he saw the boy hesitate.

"Would it? If you know any part of my history, you know that those who consort with me often come to very sad ends." His gaze flickered briefly to the other boy, the one in the corner.

"Holy One," Shard said. "I have nothing to keep me here. My wife went on without me many years ago. Heaven never sent me sons; my daughters are all married. My service with the Lord of the High and the Low will end as soon as the new warden arrives."

"Tell me why."

"Because the Bamboo Banner was proclaimed in Qiancheng."

Shard was arguing that he might have enough authority to cut off a man's head but not enough to torture him to death. The Urfather spotted the supposal at once and smiled. He made his familiar gesture of blessing.

"You could have held your own in wrangling with the Courtly Teacher himself, Clerk of the Tablets. It is well. You knew that you might be buying my life with your own, yet you did what was right. I am grateful and honor you for it. I cannot walk far yet, but is not High Abode on the Clay River? We could take my mother home by boat and continue on to hear about the forbidden Bamboo Banner."

It was done! Feeling as if all the air had drained out of him, Shard nodded. He had the strange sensation that the Man of a Thousand Lives had been several steps ahead of him all the way.

"I warn you again, Shard Gingko, that the paths I follow are hard and often shortcuts to the Fifth World."

"We all go there in time, Holy One."

"Except me." The boy rose. "Then let us do that. Hare Moon is auspicious for fast travel. You must call me Sunlight and I will call you Grandfather. Mother, we will take you home to Long River now. Let us accompany the honorable Clerk of the Tablets down to the river and see what boats may be heading our way."

"Today, Urfather?" Shard said. A thousand essential delays arose in his mind like midges. Farewells? Clothes? It was raining!

"The Rose Teacher did say, *Today is a gift and tomorrow an illusion.*"

The boy in the corner sprang to his feet. Last fall, Mouse had been the Firstborn's double, but he was too tall for such a pretense now; his body had not been starved and maltreated as the original's had been.

Sunlight looked up from folding his blanket and smiled at him, as if answering an unspoken question. "If you wish. Our feet will bless the road together."

CHAPTER 6

Brother Horse was shoeing a pony. The pony's name was High Stepper, and if High Stepper had been a little higher, Horse would not have had to bend over so painfully far. There were no farriers left in the ashes of Huarache, but there was one very ancient ex-farrier, Old Sturdy. He still owned many of the family tools, which his son, Young Sturdy, had been forced to leave behind as they were too heavy to carry when he went looking for work elsewhere. So Horse, wearing a ratty ancestral leather apron, was holding High Stepper's left rear hoof between his knees and scraping it with an ancient rasp. It was a splendid way to spend a hot spring afternoon.

Old Sturdy's house stood in a little paddock outside the town, and had thus escaped the fire. Beyond the strip of dry mud that served as a road, the buildings had been reduced to heaps of ash and orphaned stone chimney stacks. Old Sturdy himself was sitting on a stool in the sunshine, telling a story he had already told Horse three times in the last three months. His dog lay at his feet, happily gnawing a paring from the pony's hoof.

Ice Moon had been astonishingly mild, as if to apologize for its elder sisters' bad behavior. Hare Moon was starting off even better, so that the blossoms were out, and Horse, although wearing nothing under the wraparound apron, was sweating copiously. Tending a horse was one of his favorite occupations, and the old man's steady babble was as soothing as a trickling stream.

At sunset, he would share a convivial evening meal at the abbey and then enjoy another night with Moth. One day, all this bliss would end. Soon, his client would appear to put him to work, but Horse was certainly in no hurry for that to happen.

"And then the mandarin said . . ." Old Sturdy chortled huskily as he built to his punch line.

Out of the corner of his eye, Horse saw a youth running from the direction of the abbey.

Think not on evil or you will summon it, the Humble Teacher warned. Someone was in a hurry, and in Huarache, only one event could trigger any sense of urgency. Horse snapped at High Stepper to stand still and carried on with the hoof.

Huarache's makeshift House of Joyful Departure was woefully understaffed, with only three women and five men apart from himself, but all wonderfully friendly people. Only two were novices: Moth, whose duties were to educate Brother Horse in decorum and Palace Voice, and Simple, who was expected to do everything else, from washing discards to cooking meals. Simple was far from being simple, although he was driven to distraction by the need to satisfy six superiors. It was, of course, Novice Simple who came panting around High Stepper to accost Horse.

"Brother Butterfly . . . Sword . . . The abbess . . . is back. . . . Your client . . . wants you. . . . Now, she says. . . . At once," he gasped.

"Tell her," Horse said with deep satisfaction, "that I cannot leave a pony with one shoe off and two others loose. She will have to wait. I'll come as soon as I can."

The youth stared at him goggle-eyed.

Horse chuckled as well as he could when bent almost double. "Go on," he said quietly. "It isn't often you get to say no to a shrill like her."

"May Heaven preserve me," Simple muttered and turned tail. He had been grinning, though. Good lad.

"Now, Grandfather, finish your story."

"That was a Gray Helper!" Old Sturdy said. "Don't hold with them! Stole my mother's necklace that she was supposed to wear to her ascent."

"They're a shifty lot, yes." Horse decided he had trimmed the hoof as well as he could and released it. Straightening with a sigh of relief, he headed for the forge and the bellows.

Later, after Old Sturdy had finished story twelve and started on number eight, and when the shoe was glowing at the right heat, Horse carried it in the tongs back to High Stepper.

"If my lady would hold still for a fitting?"

He tried the fit and inspected the scorch marks on the hoof. Very good! It needed only a couple more scrapes with the rasp to make it perfect. With hammer and cutters and a mouthful of nails, he prepared to attach the shoe. And right after the first nail went in, he heard the rattle of a rickshaw. There was only one rickshaw left in Huarache, and Novice Simple was its runner. The dog jumped up and barked with excitement. Horse carried on with his work until he was addressed.

"Brother Butterfly Sword!" It was his client's agent, of course.

He glanced up at her and pointed to the nails in his mouth. Then he went back to finishing the job. This was the end of Horse, he decided. He would just have to accept that his name was Butterfly Sword from now on. What it might be in a week or two did not bear thinking about, but it couldn't be much worse than Butterfly Sword.

Then he straightened up so he could bow to her, hammer in hand. High Stepper kicked the turf a couple of times and seemed to approve of her shoe.

The anonymous abbess was still sitting in the rickshaw, which meant that Simple must stay holding up the bars to keep it level. He had been allowed to shed his robe in favor of a peasant's loin-cloth, but it was just as well that his passenger could not see the expression on his face.

"Had I known you were coming, my lady, I would not have appeared before you dressed like this," Horse remarked humbly.

"I should think not!"

She was still robed as a high abbess. She looked older than he recalled; her face was even thinner, as if she had been sick. He had hoped that he might like her better the next time they met, but he felt no sign of that yet, which was strange, because there were very few people he did not get along with. He enjoyed people, studied them, collected them. He was on friendly terms with everyone he had met in Huarache, just as he had been with almost everyone in Sheep Rocks, both priory and village, all except this woman, who had bought his absolute allegiance. She grated on him like a mouthful of grit. The first evening, they had exchanged barely a dozen sentences. The next morning, she had merely told him to study hard and wait until she returned, and that had been all. Yet, even that fleeting correspondence had convinced him that he neither liked nor trusted her. Something about her reminded him of Deputy Prior Evening Fade at Sheep Rocks, who had enjoyed reminiscing about all the scores he had made in his long, and reportedly deadly, career. But even he had some redeeming features, so perhaps the nameless abbess would show some eventually.

"We must leave this evening!" she announced. "The boat will leave before sunset."

"We should have plenty of—"

"Before that, I must have an extended talk with you. There is no privacy on those boats."

"We can talk here," Horse announced firmly. "Grandfather, how would you like a ride in a rickshaw?"

Old Sturdy had never ridden in a rickshaw in his life and was so lame now that he had not even viewed all the damage done by the fire. The offer, once it had been made clear to him, made him cackle and spray spit in excitement. Novice Simple's expression suggested that it was time to start his assassination practice and he had a good subject in mind. He was mollified when Horse told him to go very slowly so he did not rattle the old man's bones too hard, and not to be gone long.

The abbess settled on the stool with bad grace and waited until the rickshaw had left.

"Are you a fool?" she began. "I told you to study for palace life and here you are shoeing horses. I am told you also dig bone pits, chop firewood, and wash kitchen floors."

Horse was bent over High Stepper's left foreleg. "The abbey's short-staffed. It's all good exercise. I enjoy it."

"But it gives you hands like that file you are using! How do you expect to pass as nobility when you have the muscles of a stonemason and hands that will smooth planks?"

"I can easily make muscle look just like fat under courtly robes, my lady. None of that matters. I'm a Gray Helper. Ask Novice Moth if my hands feel rough on her breasts."

There was a pause. Then the woman said, "I left you five books to read."

"I'd read them all at Sheep Rocks. I can quote a lot of them from memory. Got a good memory."

"Bah! Enjoy your exercise, then, because it may be the last you will get for a long time. How much have you guessed about your future duties?"

Too much, far too much.

"Palace Voice, court protocol?" If she had wanted a mandarin, she would have chosen an older man, and it would take him years to master their way of speaking, their constant citations and literary references. "I thought, at first, that you wanted me to play a prince, although princes have families and many servants. . . . Then I saw the picture in my room. The old Emperor Zealous Righteousness, may he prosper in all higher worlds. Why a print of him and not his son, our present beloved Lord of Ten Thousand Years?"

He released the hoof and straightened up. They stared at each other.

"You tell me," she said.

"It smelled like treason, my lady. And then I discovered that Novice Moth had been given very specific instructions to discover if I am capable of fathering a child."

The abbess's gaunt face grew even grimmer. "Is that what she told you?"

He strode over to the forge, closer, so she had to look up at him. He began pumping the bellows furiously, resenting her contemptuous sneer. A brief leather apron that did not even close properly at the back was not appropriate dress for an interview with a client, especially one with the rank of high abbess, if indeed she was entitled to that.

"It was obviously what she was trying to do," he said. "And the other men's complaints confirmed it. When I guessed and refused to cooperate, then she admitted the truth and begged me to help, because she had been promised a very great reward."

"For which she is now eligible, you will be pleased to hear."

"I already knew that, and no, I am not pleased. I don't want to be a stud horse for even the Gray Order, and I fear that as soon as I leave here, Moth will receive the same reward as Prior Fraise."

That pulled the old snake up short. "Meaning what?"

"Meaning that I knew that man very well, *Your Holiness.* He never came to see me after we parted that first evening. Next morning, I was told he had left already. Quite apart from his saddle sores and his piles, which would have stopped him traveling unless his life depended on it, he should have completed the naming ceremony by explaining the leash to me. That's required so that new initiates aren't tempted to run wild, thinking they can get away with anything. Prior Fraise would have wanted to do that. He would have wanted to hear me thank him for all his instruction and so on. I know he would. He had a strange, morbid sort of interest in me. It made me uncomfortable, but he never suggested anything improper, so I never complained. Yet he just disappeared without a word? That was not in character. Wasn't like him."

Her eyes glittered. "If he didn't tell you about the leash, then who did?"

"I'm from Sheep Rocks, remember." He took a moment to enjoy her mystified frown before he explained. "It's a penal posting, didn't you know? We had some really smart initiates there and I used to ask them why they stayed. So one of them told me—she stayed because she had no choice. She'd tried to cheat her house out of some loot and her abbot sentenced her to five years in Sheep Rocks.

"Maybe," Horse added when the woman was about to speak, "Prior Fraise was there for the same reason, I don't know. If I was being posted to a new house, then he should have told you, my new superior, what my leash was. But a transfer of house is not a naming ceremony. You cannot be both my superior and my client. That was not a proper initiation, my lady."

Furious that he should be getting so close to losing his temper, Horse blatantly turned his back on her and marched over to the pony, carrying the tongs with the glowing shoe.

"I never said it was." Her voice remained calm and flat. "Have you any more spleen to vent, or are you ready to listen yet?"

He hauled the pony's leg up and gripped it with his knees. "Just that I am a loyal child of the Emperor. He is sacred and all his people owe him allegiance."

"There are higher loyalties."

"No there aren't. That's what I'm saying."

"There is one. Why don't you fill your mouth with nails again so I can speak for a change? The present Emperor is the same age as you are, and very nearly as big, but his bulk is grease, not brawn like yours. He suffered a serious illness as a child and has

never recovered. He has the mind of a two-year-old. He is incapable of feeding or cleaning himself, let alone fathering an heir.
His mother, the Empress Mother, has ruled as regent in the hope
that one day he would recover, but obviously he is not going to.
There is no clear successor."

Horse glanced briefly at her and then away. He could guess
that he had just been told a secret more dangerous than six angry
cobras.

"Have you heard of the Bamboo Banner, Brother?"

"Some bad tales."

"When the rebels claim that the Emperor is dead, they are not
far from the truth. He isn't dead, but he might as well be. Very
few people know the truth. They have kept the secret for many
years, but the time has come when we absolutely must have a
viable Emperor, a *visible* Emperor. Someone must perform the
rituals, make the sacrifices, and receive the Outlander ambassadors. And so on. He cannot hide behind childhood any longer."

Horse dropped the shoe and his tools and straightened up,
staring at her in horror.

"There is no alternative at all except revolution and civil war,"
the woman said. "I swear! I hung that picture of Zealous Righteousness in your room because I expected I would have to coach
the aide I chose to practice resembling him. But you already have
a look of him, enough that no one will question your relationship, at least not on those grounds.

"So now I ask you where your highest loyalty lies—to the
Emperor, who is an imbecile, and always will be, or to the Empire
itself? To the hundreds of millions of the Gentle People who
depend on the Empire to keep them safe from war and famine
and terror?"

After a moment he licked his lips and whispered, "My client?"

"Your client is the Empress Mother herself. She named you.
She wants to smuggle you into the imperial harem to provide

her with a grandchild who can carry on the dynasty. She will continue to run the government as she has for years with great success. In a year or two, when you have done your duty, you will be appointed abbot of a house very far away."

"But the Emperor is holy! He is the conduit through whom Heaven dispenses its blessings to the Good Land."

The woman sneered. "Heaven has accepted substitutes since you were born. You are not content just to tell the Empress Mother how to rule, but now give instructions to Heaven as well?"

"No, no!" he protested. "But how can I be pretend to be the Emperor? People will know."

"Leave that to us. You will not appear in public. You are required to perform the imperial duties in bed, not on the throne. Dozens of concubines eager to please, if that is your fancy. It is a fair offer, I think."

"Not one that appeals much to me, lady." But one that he would have to accept, because if he refused, she would speak the words of his leash and even the thought of that made him retch. "Who are you?"

"Sister Twilight. In the palace, I am known as Lady Twilight, a long-time confidant of the Empress Mother. That I am a Gray Sister is no great secret. That I have poisoned people for her on occasion is not much more of one. Will you be another of my victims, or will you accept this contract and the name she gave you, Brother Butterfly Sword?"

He bowed his head and thought about it. If the Empress Mother was still in charge and if she was ordering this in the Emperor's name, then it was his duty to obey. If he refused, then Twilight would use his leash on him and squeeze his mind through her fingers like bean curd. He had no real choice.

"Will Her Majesty give me these orders, face-to-face?"

"You think she doesn't know her own son? Of course she will."

"Well, then . . . I am true to my oath of obedience, my lady. I will obey. What happens to Novice Moth?"

"Mind your own business." Twilight stood up and beckoned impatiently, no doubt to Novice Simple returning. "Finish nailing up that pestilential horse as fast as you can and come back to the priory."

CHAPTER 7

Heaven surprises us to remind us how ignorant we are. So said the Desert Teacher. Truly, Shard Gingko had never expected to return to Long River. Only a couple of months ago, he would have dismissed the prospect of going there without the armed guards who had escorted him the first time as certain suicide. Yet, here he was, sitting on the edge of a riotous party around a bonfire in the village center, while inhabitants plied him with choice fragments of roast pork and potent rice wine. The difference this time was that he had come in the company of Sunlight, the Firstborn. He had brought their hero back, and the Firstborn vouched for him.

Six days ago, he had walked out of Four Mountains Fortress and away from his former life. He had left behind no orders or explanations. No one would take command for days. No one would send soldiers after them. But the new warden might, when he arrived, and the first place he would look would certainly be Long River, so the Firstborn must not be allowed to stay here very long. He was too recognizable to hide.

Shard was not. Not now. On their second day afloat, he had cut off his queue and his trailing mustaches. But that was not quite true. A laughing Sunlight had suggested that he ought to do this, and when Shard had reluctantly agreed that the scholarly trimmings made him conspicuous, the Firstborn had handed his own razor to Mouse and told him to do it. At first, the boy had

refused, horror-struck at the thought of demonstrating such dis-
respect, but the Firstborn had insisted. Mouse knew how shaving
was done, because he watched Sunlight all day long, never taking
his eyes off him. So he had shaved Shard's face and scalp, and by
the time he had finished, he was smiling.

Shard had never seeing him doing that before. Sunlight
caught his eye and remarked in Palace Voice, with a wink, "As all
the teachers said, *There is a first time for everything.*"

So the missing Clerk of Records had melted back into the
anonymous millions of the Good Land from which his family
had emerged three generations ago, and if the Emperor's men
came looking for him, they would look in vain. Son and grandson of mandarins, Shard had done well in child school, and
had passed the prefecture examinations, which ninety-five out
of every one hundred failed. He had then spent several years
studying for the second level and traveled to Heart of the World
for the examination. Alas, the stars had been inauspicious for
him that day, and his eight-part essay on the use of flower sym-
bolism in the work of lesser Seventh Dynasty poets had been
deemed too generalized. Unable to finance a second attempt,
and thus unable to progress to the third-level examinations,
where a pass meant a place in the mandarinate and eventually
a role in administering the Empire, he had been condemned
to the humble life of a scribe. Since then, he had lived his life
of dull mediocrity, working for various officials who paid him
a pittance, from their own private purses, that he had eked out
with no more than the usual corruption. With his daughters
gone into marriage and his family line ended, he had been
waiting until he could follow his wife to the Fifth World. And
then—wonder of Heaven!—he had somehow become a disciple
of the Ancient One, the Firstborn, who perversely insisted on
being addressed as Sunlight.

We are children of Earth, so Heaven surprises us.

Now Shard wore a peasant's conical straw hat, which kept off sun and rain and hid the gray stubble on his scalp. He ate peasants' food, wore peasants' clothes, and scratched peasants' lice in a mysterious state of bliss. He ate well, because the Firstborn shared with him and Mouse what the peasants were so eager to spare from their meager lot. He had no money, no income, no worries. How could even death be a worry around the Man of a Thousand Lives? Did not he prove that there were many more lives to come, even if he alone always remained in the same world?

The Urfather was recognized everywhere now. At times, men came close to blows arguing whose boat would have the honor of transporting him to the next village, or whose roof would shelter him overnight. He was only a weedy, stunted adolescent with bent legs and a persistent cough, but they revered him as if he outranked the Emperor, which he probably did in the eyes of Heaven. They would have kowtowed and worshipped him had he allowed it, but he did not. He responded to their excitement with unending patience and good humor, like a mother caring for her children. By nightfall, his throat was hoarse and his cough harsher, but he never complained.

He settled disputes, gave advice, and taught the wisdom of the ancients, most of whom he had met. Sometimes, he would mention them as if they had died just days ago, instead of centuries. "Yes, the Rose Teacher did say that, but he thought about it for three days before he found an answer that satisfied him!" He quoted poets long dead in their original dialects, which even Shard had trouble understanding, but which often brought back a luster their words had now lost. Then the Firstborn would smile and translate. Sometimes, when he was in the mood, he would mischievously recount local history, deeds of famous persons who had lived in that village millennia ago, or battles fought nearby.

Two days ago, they had arrived at Long River and met a tumultuous welcome. The spring planting was over, so the whole village had a few days' respite from labor, and had used it to organize a gigantic party and keep it going indefinitely. Here, Sunlight seemed content to linger, despite Shard Gingko's anxious muttering about pursuit. He insisted he had business to attend to, conceding only that if he stayed too long, too many feasts would eat up all the villagers' stores.

Now it seemed he was about to make a speech.

Since sunset, he had been sitting at the far side of the bonfire with his mother and stepbrothers beside him. They had all been laughing and celebrating, like everyone else, but now the odd-looking boy was rising to his feet. He raised a hand for silence and the whole village, from babes to bent old elders, heeded. Whispers and sniggers in the background stopped. Even the fire and the torches seemed to crackle and hiss less loudly. Moonlight decorated the scene with silver.

"Honored Mother, elders, family, neighbors, friends . . ." He spoke well. He had been practicing since before the count of years began, since long before the First Dynasty. "The great teachers all agreed on one thing, the only thing they ever did agree on, and that is that one must honor one's parents and ancestors. My true father, I cannot remember, if indeed I ever had one. I have had too many mothers to count. The latest, dear Quail, who you all know and love, sits here at my feet. None has been a better mother to me than she. Her husband, who reared me and was a father to me as much as he could be, is dead because of that, my good fortune and his misfortune. . . ."

Shard should have guessed what the "important" business was. The Firstborn was going to see the woman settled. That was what it was all about. Her brothers' wives had cared for her other children in her absence, although the youngest had died, and the rest were grown up and married now. Her husband,

Sunlight's foster father, had perished from abuse in the dungeons of Four Mountains—as Shard had admitted to the Firstborn, who had broken the news to her on the boat. The woman had wept sorely.

He would not, could not, take her with him on his travels, and the lot of a widow was ever hard, especially one too old to supply a new husband with many sons. She was hiding her face in her hands, speechless. Her other children were smiling and chuckling, even the oldest deferring to the Firstborn's authority.

"Men of Long River! Here is a strong and upright woman, and a very loving parent. She thinks she may yet produce another son or two; with some help. . . ." Sunlight waited for the laughter to end. "And she insists that she will be willing to try. I have asked her if there is any man she especially wants . . ." The entire village exploded in a cannonade of laughter at the outlandish idea of asking her opinion. He grinned, waiting for silence again. "And she is too shy to tell me his name!" More laughter. "So I must ask if there is any man here who has room at his hearth for a first wife or another wife."

The gathering rustled. To Shard's astonishment, it seemed that every male in the village was on his feet at once, from striplings to bearded antiques. No peasant could afford more than one wife, and very few even that many, if she were a prolific breeder of daughters. But to cherish the mother of the Firstborn would be a meritorious act.

Now she was on her feet also, half pushed by her other children and half pulled up by Sunlight. He led her partway around the bonfire and beckoned to a man at the rear, who was immediately shoved forward by his companions. The cheers began as he took Quail's hand in his. He was a stocky youngster, seeming little older than the Firstborn himself. There were shouts of "Grainstalk!"—apparently his name.

"A very good choice," a harsh voice commented at Shard's ear. "Strong but gentle. His wife died two months ago. Has a son already. He'll care for her."

He twisted around and recognized the speaker as Sunlight's chatty aunt Kettle, a toothless crone who might be forty and looked like a mandarin's wife would at eighty. He had met her four years ago, when he had come with the warden's men to collect the villagers' testimony for forwarding to Sublime Mountain. By that time, the Firstborn had been old enough to be discreet, but the damage of his youthful chatter had been done and rumors of his current incarnation's whereabouts had reached the authorities. The Golden Throne had sent men to confirm his identity. If Shard had dared to warn the villagers, they would have either disobeyed him or put too much trust in their Emperor's benevolence. Both, likely.

"Would you expect him to choose a bad man?" Shard remarked.

Kettle's wattled neck turned her head so she could scowl at him.

"I know you. You were the governor's spy, writing down everything we said about the Firstborn! Weren't you?"

The crowd was packed in thick around them, many eyes and ears.

"I was," Shard admitted.

"And gabby old Kettle was a big help to you, wasn't she? Took all my words and used them against Sunlight, you did. 'A fine healthy babe, he was,' I told you. 'Born in the year of the Phoenix, yes. . . . No, what the others told you was wrong, it was the Phoenix.' Played me for a fool you did. Oh yes, I go and tell you all how about the toddler who asked about people no one else had ever heard of. How, by the time he was working in the paddies, he was boasting about talking with Emperors, so we all knew that he was the Firstborn returned. I even told you how he used to tell stories about long ago, when there wasn't no Emperor and people dressed in skins and hunted in forests where our fields are now. And you wrote it all down and thanked us by taking him and his parents away in chains!"

Shard heard angry whispers at his back, but nothing that sounded like a call to violence—yet. "I did. I was obedient to the Son of the Sun, as we must all be."

Kettle snorted, but her reply was forestalled by a neighbor's comment: "Grainstalk's too young for her!"

It seemed that Grainstalk was in some way related to Kettle, so she sprang to his defense, claws out, and Shard was forgotten for the moment.

Then the argument progressed to whether it was not Quail's children's job to care for her in her old age so Sunlight should not be meddling, the holy Firstborn or not. They decided to put the question to the visiting scholar.

"Everyone in the family seems happy," Shard said tactfully. "He is very fond of her, even if she isn't really his mother."

"And why isn't she?" Kettle demanded in a gust of rice wine fumes. "You think he came out of her easy like a bee from a hive? Oh no. I was there. There was blood and tearing and screaming just as always. If you men had to bear the consequences, there'd be a lot less heaving and bouncing on the mats every night." She hiccupped. "Three Willows's got a gift for you, Scholar."

She pointed across Shard to an elderly man on his knees, who seemed to be tongue-tied, either by lack of wits or by the ordeal of addressing a stranger, for he thrust a cotton-wrapped bundle into Shard's hands, scrambled to his feet, and waddled away as fast as his wobbling legs would take him.

Puzzled, Shard, extracted his gift from the bag. It was a wooden box, the sort of box scribes used to pack their equipment, but the moonlight was not bright enough for him to see details. Then a dawn of torchlight warmed and brightened the scene. Mouse was holding the torch. The Firstborn dropped on one knee to inspect the box.

"Very nice!" he said.

It was nice enough to strike Shard dumb. It was a classic scribe's box of sandalwood, containing ancient cracked ink stones, brushes with pure camelhair bristles and ivory handles, such as were never seen nowadays, and sheets of fine paper, slightly curled and discolored by age, but well-enough preserved to be still usable. Judging by the exquisite marquetry, the box was Ninth or early Tenth Dynasty. It had probably been hidden away here in this fleck-speck village ever since.

"Belonged to an ancestor o' his," Kettle explained, chuckling. "Wants you to have it."

"Me? But this is worth . . ." Except that one could not sell an heirloom like this, and a peasant trying to do so would be accused of theft. "Why? Why me?"

"'Cause you're the Urfather's disciple. So's you can write down his words and how he was born in Long River."

"Accept it," Sunlight whispered in Palace Voice. "You must not insult them by refusing."

Shard gushed thanks to the satisfied watchers, praising the quality and venerability of the box without mentioning that it was worth more than six fine fishing boats.

"Now come," Sunlight said softly. "Excuse us, all my friends. I must be gone before the Son of the Sun's men come looking for me. If that happens, do not tell them lies. Heaven's blessing be with you all."

Go? Shard had been hoping for tomorrow, but the skies were clear and the moon was bright. Leave by night and no one would know whether they had headed upstream or down, except the men who took them, and who could remember, or be sure, who they had been? He followed as Mouse led the way and Sunlight brought up the rear. None of the villagers came after them, so this fast exit had been well planned. In a moment, he saw a boat at the jetty, and two men waiting there.

Empty-handed! The expedition's only luggage was his scribe's box.

"Mouse!" Sunlight caught the boy's shoulder just before they reached the jetty. "Are you sure you want to come? Many men in the village would adopt another mouth in return for two strong hands. You could live here in peace, buy a wife, raise children."

Mouse's recently found contentment vanished instantly. Dismay! "No, no! Do not abandon me, Holy Urfather!" He tried to kowtow, forgetting that he held a blazing torch.

Sunlight leaped back, laughing, although Shard Gingko would later see him rubbing river water on a knee as if it had been scorched. "You do not have to set me on fire, Friend Mouse! If you want to come, then come with us by all means, and we will happily share whatever we have. The provisions may be small and the privations great, but if that is your choice, then just give us your company and you will be a thousand times welcome."

CHAPTER 8

Snow Lily, as the senior, and still only, imperial concubine, out-ranked everyone in the Great Within except the Emperor and his mother. Rank had nothing to do with power, though. Hundreds or thousands of people there could overrule, forbid, or ignore her.

She did merit the attendance of thirty-two girls and twenty eunuchs. They washed, perfumed, and dressed her, held her parasol or bore her palanquin when she ventured outdoors, guarded her at all times—from what she could not imagine—and slaved over her wardrobe, although clothes of any sort would be an impediment to the exercise of her duties.

The Empress Mother had hundreds of flunkies to serve her, and the Emperor thousands. Amazingly, few of them ever saw the Son of the Sun face-to-face. Snow Lily's best count was nine-teen, including herself, Chief Eunuch, and the Empress Mother. There might be others in the mandarinate or nobility that she did not know of, but the Emperor's personal attendants num-bered only ten eunuchs and four women. On the rare occasions he appeared in public, he traveled in covered chairs, hidden from view. Emperors always did, always had.

In icy dignity, this huge river of lives flowed along the val-ley of centuries, bearing the Emperor and his palace like a great barge, but also nurturing the teeming life under its surface, the unseen dwellers in mud and weed. The main business of that great army of eunuchs was theft. Tribute and gifts and bribes flowed in the main gates and vanished unseen down a thousand private sewers.

As Hare Moon was dwindling to a dawn crescent, an unexpected ripple troubled the surface of the waters—Court Astrologer announced that the first day of Fish Moon would be extremely auspicious for the Lord of the High and the Low to move to the Summer Palace. In most years, this grand event did not take place until Nightingale Moon, so a horde of women and eunuchs were rushed there to begin preparations. Among them were four of His Majesty's personal attendants. Snow Lily had nightmares in which the four who had gone to the Summer Palace had never arrived, and worse nightmares that she might soon be dispatched to join them in whatever state of nonexistence they currently abode. It was probably a capital offense to have nightmares like that.

She had been Absolute Purity's concubine for almost half a year, and he had never touched her or let her touch him. How long before the Empress Mother gave up on her and let some other lucky girl try?

Today was the auspicious day. The journey would not be long, for the Summer Palace was just another part of the huge imperial city-within-a-city, the Great Within, but the slightest change upset him. The eunuchs were laying bets over how many days he would scream and have fits, but if the she-dragon Empress Mother said it was time to move to the Summer Palace, then what star would dare argue?

As usual, Snow Lily had withdrawn from the sacred presence at dawn and returned to her own quarters nearby. She would have a minor part to play in the day's proceedings—as a tiny part of the imperial baggage—and her maids were waiting to primp and bedeck her. Instead of dallying an hour or two over her toilet, as she usually did just to get through a little of the interminable boredom of yet another interminable day in a lonely, interminable, pointless existence, she told them to be as quick as possible.

Then she went back to the Emperor's rooms, which she very rarely had reason to visit in daylight. The guards were surprised to see her, but she had mastered the Look of Authority now, and they admitted her—without her entourage, of course. She walked quickly through deserted halls to the imperial bedroom, which the Lord of the High and the Low rarely left. There, amid grandeur of gold and jade, Precious Flower was spooning the imperial breakfast into the Son of the Sun's slobbery mouth.

Absolute Purity was a large man of nineteen winters. Although his bulk was mostly blubber, it took four eunuchs to restrain him when he was enraged. He had the mental capacity of a two-year-old, so that he could not speak in complete sentences or understand more than the simplest words and situations. Food and bed defined his world, toilet training was beyond it, and hygiene forcibly resisted, so he often reeked like a night-soil cart. He hated people touching him, and the one time Snow Lily had made a serious attempt to do so, he had given her a magnificent yellow and mauve eye. And yet—although this might be only wishful thinking—she sometimes suspected that a glimmer of thought lurked behind his moon-face. He recognized her now, and would sometimes smile or even say, "Lily!" He enjoyed music, so she spent hours every night playing and singing to him. They also played mah-jongg together, building palaces with the tiles so that he could knock them down. He greatly distrusted strangers and hated people of anywhere near his own size. His dislike of his mother was intense and mutual.

Precious Flower was His Majesty's official food taster. She fed him by hand so he didn't throw food all over the palace. She was a plain-looking servant of around twenty, taciturn to the edge of insolence, and apparently unmarried. She ranked far down the prestige ladder, yet she regarded Snow Lily with disapproval or even anger, not respect.

"You want something, Concubine?"

Snow Lily had never liked Precious Flower and had recently come to distrust her. "I just came to see how my beloved lord was doing. Carry on, or he'll start screaming." She had slipped into the others' habit of talking about him as if he were furniture.

Precious Flower spooned more soup into the gaping mouth.

"Did you taste that first?" the senior concubine demanded, and was caressed by a venomous stare.

"I always taste first. It is my duty. If you managed your duties as well as I do mine, Concubine, then your belly would be bigger than a rice sack."

"Taste it again, then! Let me see you finish the bowl."

"Go away." Another spoonful.

Snow Lily grabbed for the bowl. Precious Flower snatched it away. Half the soup splashed over the rug.

"You are poisoning the Emperor!" Snow Lily said. "You put opium in his food!"

His Majesty Absolute Purity roared for more soup. Precious Flower gave him more. "That is absurd. I will report this conversation to the Empress Mother."

"Do so. I guessed what you were up to when he went to the Cherry Blossom Viewing. Of course I knew he had been unusually well washed when I attended him that night, but he was a dead lump. And for the next three nights, he was a mad dog. You are addicting him to opium. No wonder he has no use for a woman."

"Occasional medicinal use is not pernicious," Precious Flower said, curling her lip in anger. "The first symptom of opium addiction is extreme emaciation. The emasculation comes later. His Majesty is anything but emaciated. It is true that he has to be sedated before public appearances in order to maintain the imperial dignity. He can also be rinsed off at those times. You should be grateful for that, Concubine."

"How long have you been doing this?"

Precious Flower frowned into the bowl as if assessing how much was left. "Ever since he became big enough to be dangerous."

The Emperor thumped his fists on the chair, wanting more. Snow Lily had never seen him so eager for food. So the she-rat was feeding him opium, and what other foul potions? Was this the cause of his idiocy, not some childhood disease as she had been told?

"How long have you been official food taster?"

Precious Flower sighed as if the conversation had become tedious. "Ever since I was old enough to help out my mother. My mother succeeded the taster who brought him to this sad pass." She continued to feed the Emperor. "You don't know that story? You never heard of the Scorpion Summer? Back in the Year of the Firebird, when the old Emperor died, he was followed to the Fifth World by many, many more. The imperial family suffered its own epidemic. Someone used a slow poison on the babe. His taster felt no symptoms until too late, after His Majesty had eaten enough to blight him."

"Not what I was told. Does the Empress Mother know what you are doing?"

"Of course I do," said the Empress Mother.

Snow Lily gasped, spun around, prostrated herself.

"Look at me, child." The Empress Mother stood a head taller than Snow Lily. Seen from the floor, she loomed like a pagoda. Her face had been carved from flint and her gaze was deadlier than a pit viper. Scraggy rather than lean, she held herself as erect as bamboo and was invariably a walking treasure of glorious gems and embroidery, painted like a Ninth Dynasty tea caddy. "You are too clever for your own good. As Precious Flower says, you should be bearing by now." The threat was blatant.

Trembling, Snow Lily lowered her eyes. The dowager's wrath on those who displeased her could be fearful. But that accusation was unfair. "The fault is not mine, Your Majesty."

"You presume to criticize your Emperor? Do you know what happens to unwanted concubines, you foolish girl? A new Emperor always chooses his own bed toys. He never accepts the old ones. We still have crones dating back three and four reigns, moldering away in cobwebby corners. Most of them are loopier than bluebottles."

"I have done my best," Snow Lily whispered. Then, louder, "I have tried everything I was taught, everything I could think of!" There was no reply, and eventually she looked up to meet the kohl-rimmed obsidian eyes and the smile of a demon image.

"I know you have," the harridan conceded. "And your inter-ference here today shows that you do have my son's well-being at heart. Who have you told about my son's affliction?"

"No one, Your Majesty! No one at all. I tell lies! I tell my maids he was especially demanding—"

"I know that, too. Well, since you had to be trusted with the heart of the secret and have guessed at more, I don't suppose it matters if you learn a few even messier details. Return to your quarters. I will send some dark clothes for you. Put them on. Be ready at the third gong."

Snow Lily crawled back a few paces, then rose and fled.

Why dark clothes? Snow Lily had no dark clothes, for an impe-rial possession must always wear yellow. The floor tiles in the Private Quarters were yellow, the draperies yellow, the walls pan-eled in yellow silk. But the Empress Mother was as good as her word, and a eunuch runner arrived by the second gong with a carefully wrapped bundle. When the summons came at the third gong, it was in the form of a carrying chair and a team of the Empress Mother's own lackeys. Refusing to answer questions, they bore Snow Lily away, leaving all her followers behind. The journey was a long one, into a part of the Great Within that she had never seen before, and it was followed by a suspenseful wait in an empty room until the Empress Mother herself was carried in to join her.

"This," she announced, hobbling toward a magnificently carved door that armed eunuchs were just opening for them, "is known as the Emperor's Eye. You must keep very quiet! Do not speak a word!"

The Eye was the smallest room Snow Lily had seen in Sublime Mountain, little more than a closet, barely large enough to hold two chairs side by side, facing a heavy drapery. The women sat, the door silently closed, leaving them in complete darkness, and then the curtain softly moved aside, to reveal a grille, and beyond that a vast throne room.

The Emperor himself was there, holding court in all his golden finery. His eyes were open. Once in a while, they moved, but the rest of him did not. He sat like a resplendent work of art, obviously drugged senseless. At his feet knelt a frail old man massively robed in scarlet and blue, who at a guess must be First Mandarin. Another ancient was in the process of completing his kowtow before the throne. In the back, many more waited.

"The Great Council," the Empress Mother rasped softly in Snow Lily's ear. Apparently, rules of silence applied to her no more than any other rules did. "The first time he has presided in person. Do you understand the sedation now?"

Snow Lily nodded. Without the sedation, Absolute Purity would be thrashing in a screaming panic. But what purpose did this charade serve? Even fully conscious, he would not understand one thousandth of what was being done here in his name.

"His Highness," First Mandarin intoned, "implores Your Majesty to hear of regrettable unrest in the provinces of Dongguan, Kermang, and Shiman."

"Prince Tungusic Vision," the Empress Mother explained, "senior prince of the Empire, heir presumptive. Doesn't know a glove from a shoe now."

The old man on his knees was peering around him as if lost. A mandarin of the fourth rank swept forward from the sidelines to stand alongside him and read out a report about rioting and burning towns in the south, attributed to misguided peasants calling themselves the Bamboo Banner.

"Bawolung and Jingyan will be getting infected soon," the Empress Mother remarked sourly.

Prince Tungusic Vision was thanked for his report by First Mandarin and given leave to withdraw. His purely figurative mandarin assistant helped him rise and steadied him as he backed away, bowing.

Prince Crystal Sea was proclaimed and helped forward to kowtow. He seemed even more bewildered than Tungusic Vision, and his face was a skull. Snow Lily had seen enough addicts to guess that the body hidden inside all those pleats and folds of silk was skeletal and barely functional.

The Empress Mother pulled a face. "Typical opium smoker."

Like his predecessor, Prince Crystal Sea served as a ventriloquist's dummy. A mandarin reported on famine developing in the northern provinces. He dared to compare it to the famine of the Year of the Swan, which probably meant that it would be much worse.

After him came Prince Gratify Poet to describe flood damage along several major rivers. He was a man of middle years, capable of reading out his own report, but the Empress Mother's comment on him was even more damning, possibly the most terrible accusation possible by Good Land standards. "He killed his own father." At Snow Lily's gasp of horror, she added, "Very touchy temper."

After the princes came senior mandarins, identified by office, not name. Supreme Guardian was trying to gather the widely scattered army to counter the Bamboo Banner insurrection, but spring mud, spring planting, spring floods, and a drastic shortage of funds were delaying inevitable success. Senior Gatherer of Bounty described a catastrophic collapse of tax revenue. Court Astrologer warned that a broom star was being observed in the constellation of the Fishing Net, and another in the Cart. Both were still small and hard to see, but if they grew over the next couple of moons, as some broom stars did, they would be exceedingly inauspicious and cause widespread panic. There would be an eclipse in Nightingale Moon.

That news actually provoked a reaction from First Mandarin. A warning of the eclipse would be distributed to all provincial and city governors, he said, so that ritual countermeasures could be organized in time.

The Empress Mother sent some signal then, or she had issued orders previously, because the drape silently closed, shutting off the women's view of the hall. The door behind them opened, flooding the Emperor's Eye with light. The Empress Mother rose stiffly and turned to leave.

"You will not speak a word of what you have seen."

"Oh no, Your Majesty, I won't! But I do not understand!" Snow Lily was as confused as Absolute Purity must be. Why had she been shown all this, what was the Council supposed to achieve, and was the Empire really falling apart?

The old lady stopped and looked back. "Of course you do not understand! But now you know of all the troubles the Good Land suffers, all of which may be your fault."

"Mine, Your Majesty? How could I possibly have—"

"Court Astrologer is of the opinion that Heaven is displaying its displeasure at the Emperor's failure to produce a son. I realize that he is not the most ardent of lovers, but you must redouble your efforts, for everybody's sake."

The old witch paused with a hand on her carrying chair. "But

I hope you have the wit now to see why Emperors so rarely attend meetings of the Great Council and most certainly never address it. Suppose one did and misquoted a report or decreed an impossible solution? The loss of face would be intolerable. Keep your mouth shut." She took her seat and, while her attendants were arranging her robes for her, added, "I will explain more fully when we are at the Summer Palace."

An imperial progress was a major event, with bands, horses, guards, and hordes of officials, guests, flunkies, and sweepers. The Emperor was carried in a grandiose golden palanquin on the shoulders of sixteen bearers, and his mother followed in one hardly less gaudy. His senior concubine—whom he was rumored to favor so extravagantly that he had refused to accept any others yet—came right behind, peering out through pinholes at hundreds of heads and raised bottoms, for faces were all pressed in the dirt as the Son of the Sun passed. She wondered why a procession was necessary at all when no one ever really saw it. No doubt this was a very foolish question and she was an ignorant and stupid girl even to think it.

This was the most interesting day she had experienced in half a year. She had forgotten how to handle such excitement. By the time she had been escorted to her new quarters in the Summer Palace, she felt drained and battered, haunted by troubles which she must not discuss with anyone. That her inadequacy might be the cause of so many terrible disasters! More than anything, she wished she had someone she could talk to. But her attendants certainly included spies who would report everything she said to the Empress Mother and Chief Eunuch.

And what sort of a night was she facing? If Absolute Purity was still drugged with opium, then she might be able to stretch out on the great imperial bed and sleep until dawn. At least he would not smell quite so vile, but when he woke up and found himself in an unfamiliar place, he would have hysterics. His body would crave opium and he would not know what he wanted or how to ask for it. She nibbled some food and tried to rest, but she kept thinking of the ocean of bad news she had overheard in the Great Council. The Good Land was in dire trouble and the Emperor was an overgrown baby. Could the Empress Mother continue to hold it together? And what could Snow Lily do to help?

The warning summons arrived before sunset, earlier than usual, but her usual maids followed the normal procedure of bathing and scenting her, painting her face, and pinning up her hair. The entry ritual went exactly as it had in the main Winter Palace— she stepped into an antechamber guarded by six eunuchs. But there was change, for she recognized none of them.

The one in the grandest robes bowed to her. "If it please, my lady, I have the honor to be Joyous Diligence, His Majesty's Keeper of the Hours."

She nodded. She did not like the look of him, and certainly not the unmistakable eunuch smell of him, but that was hardly a rarity. "The august Son of the Sun is alone?"

"Absolutely."

"And how is His Majesty's mood this evening, honorable Keeper of the Hours?"

The eunuch smirked unpleasantly. "Buoyant, I should say."

That sounded highly unlikely, but if it was a joke at her expense, the other five guards showed no signs of understanding it. She walked over to the other door, shed her robe, and turned around so they could see that she was carrying no weapons. She was long past being embarrassed by being observed nude, at least by eunuchs. Joyous Diligence opened the door for her, followed her along the corridor, and saw her through the second door, which he closed behind her. She heard the lock turn. He probably locked the first door, also—or perhaps the corridor was guarded all night—she did not know.

The antechamber was unfamiliar, of course, but in the fading light, it seemed no less sumptuous than the quarters she had become accustomed to. If anything, she decided, it was even grander, with lacquered furniture, silk screens, and three huge windows facing southward over the Summer Park. Yellow everywhere.

Now she must find Absolute Purity and await His Majesty's pleasure, which was usually, "Lily sing!" but tonight might be only the snores of a drug-induced coma.

There were two doors to choose from. She guessed right and stepped into the grandiose imperial bedchamber. As she closed the door, she was astonished to see Absolute Purity standing at the windows, staring out. All his absurd state vestments had been removed, and no doubt safely stored away in a vault somewhere, but he was wearing a loose robe of ornate gold silk. She had never seen him in anything like that before. The evening attendants usually left him in diapers, which he often removed before morning.

She froze as she registered the length of the queue dangling down his back. That was not the Emperor and no servant would ever be dressed like that.

With a cry close to a scream, Snow Lily spun around and fled. She raced across the antechamber and pounded her fists vainly on the surface of padded golden leather.

"You are Snow Lily, of course."

She peered around nervously. The man had followed her and was standing in the bedroom door. The *man*! He spoke with a deep voice, neither the raucous screech of a eunuch nor the childish babble of the disabled Emperor. He held a bulky golden cloth in one hand. He tossed it toward her, letting it collapse on the floor.

"Drape yourself. We have to talk." He turned away and disappeared into the other room.

Trembling, she hurried to the discarded sheet and did as he had said. A man in the imperial bedroom with the imperial concubine? The eunuchs were not going to come and rescue her before morning, obviously. Even if they did, even if the stranger never laid a finger on her, she was a corpse walking.

Talk, he had said.

He probably meant much more than talk.

But then she recalled the extraordinary events of the morning, and the Empress Mother's cryptic remarks about redoubling efforts. Was it possible that Snow Lily was about to meet the real Emperor for the first time? Had the last half year been all a terrible hoax, some sort of test?

Trembling, she went back to the bedchamber.

He again had his back to her, but he was sitting on a chair near the windows. She waited a moment. He continued to stare at the park outside and the first stars. She closed the door.

"Ready?" he turned around and smiled. "Sit there." He pointed to a divan.

Again, she obeyed, trembling. In her entire life, she had never been alone with an unaltered man. She had never even spoken with one who was not a close relative. There was some terrible conspiracy afoot, for no intruder could possibly have broken into the palace without help. A real man! She was going to be raped, ruined forevermore, put to the death of a thousand cuts as a traitor to her Emperor.

The man was close and facing her, but not *too* close and not *quite* straight on. He had a powerful, masculine face, broad, not flabby. He was a young man, but a large one—about the same size as Absolute Purity, of course, and his smile was intended to put her at ease, however insincere it might be.

"The old she-dragon didn't warn you she had changed her plans, did she?" he said. "That's typical! She is a viper. But I assure you that she smuggled me in here—the Empress Mother her-self. Nobody else could have done that, now could they? Chief Eunuch wouldn't dare. They'd melt him down for soap."

"You're pretending to be the Emperor?" New eunuchs on the doors, new servants in the Summer Palace. Only the Empress Mother could be behind such an outrage; no one else could hope to carry it off.

He shrugged. "It sounds crazy, I know, but you must have noticed that nobody ever looks straight at the Emperor, not ever? Even if they don't have their faces in the dust, kowtowing, even if they're *speaking* to him, they don't look him in the eyes. Most people see him only at a distance or behind a veil. I proved it today. She had me preside over a meeting of the Great Council. I thought I was headed for the death of a thousand cuts, but all I had to do was sit there like a temple idol and . . . What's wrong?"

"I was there! I sat beside the Empress Mother and watched you!" It had been him. She remembered watching his eyes mov-ing, and they had been this man's eyes. She had thought that poor Absolute Purity was doing very well with the opium in him. What a fool she had been!

He grinned wider than ever. "And even you didn't notice? You? His concubine!"

She felt herself blushing scarlet. "I expected . . . I assumed . . ." And the Empress Mother had been waiting to see if she would ask who that was up there, pretending. If the imposter could fool her, he could fool anyone.

He was grinning. "Most people see only what they expect to see, most of the time, and if his own mother wasn't complaining, who were you to? . . . Am I right?"

Oh! It had all been some sort of a test? A cruel test of . . . What? Loyalty? That overgrown child had been a hoax all along. How could she have ever believed? She slid off the chair to her knees and bent her face to the floor.

"Don't!" the man said sharply. "Sit where I told you. That's better. I am *not* the Emperor. You know that."

"I do? Then who are you?"

He smiled as if he approved of her progress. "That's a complicated question. Or it's a simple question with several answers. I have no family, so no family name. My friends always used to call me Horse, because I'm big and not too smart. The she-dragon called me 'Butterfly Sword.' That's a joke, too, because a butterfly sword is a large knife intended to be hidden in a sleeve or a boot. Meaning I am a concealed weapon, and no one must bring a weapon into the Great Within."

Especially his sort of weapon. "Why? I can see using you as a puppet in public. Explain to me exactly why she smuggled you in here."

He bit his lip and looked away. The mirage Emperor dissolved into a grandly robed, very large young man. An Emperor could never be embarrassed.

"Please don't make me spell it out, sweet beauty," he told the window. "When the old Emperor Zealous Righteousness died back in the Year of the Firebird, Junior Empress Jade Star contrived to get herself named co-regent, and over the next few months, she poisoned off all the other *co*s until she was the *only* regent. She also poisoned every possible rival to her infant son, all conceivable heirs. Then she settled down to enjoy running the Good Land, but her son is now of age and ought to be reigning in his own right. I gather he can't." He fell silent, leaving the story hanging.

"And he can't father an heir, either," Snow Lily said bitterly. "You can . . . er, Your Majesty?"

"Just call me Horse." He nodded. "Yes, I can give you a child. She made sure of that. That doesn't mean I have to do it tonight. And I swear I won't force you, not even to please the she-dragon. If you don't want to cooperate, then she can pull another concubine out of the closet easily enough."

"And poison me to silence me?"

"Sorry." He pulled a face. "I didn't want to frighten you, nattering about poison. I suppose it would be possible, although you are no real danger to her. Who could you tell and who would believe you if they weren't in on the plot already? The old witch obviously likes you, so maybe she'd just post you to the far end of the palace and forget about you."

Snow Lily felt as if the world was spinning, with her on it. She clutched at the one encouraging thing he had said. "Why do you say she likes me?"

"Because she let you have first chance at"—he grinned shamefacedly—"at me. She told me just today that she had decided to take that risk. You had earned it, she said. She has other girls waiting, girls who have never met the real Emperor."

"But it would be treason!" Snow Lily wailed. "You're supposed to father a child with me so the Empress Mother can pass him off as the true heir to the throne? Then what happens to me, and you, and her real son?"

The young man who insisted on being addressed as Horse turned his head slowly and fixed her with a hard stare. She felt her face flaming hot, but she endured his scrutiny because she thought that was what he must want of her. He was not hard to look at himself. An unaltered man! A young and large and strong-looking, *virile* man, and she was supposed to accept him as her husband.

"When this assignment was first explained to me," he said at last, "I was told that I would never be seen in public and all I would have to do was perform like a stud horse. I was told that when I had successfully completed my assignment, I would be given a sinecure job very far away. Then I was told that I bear so much natural resemblance to the true Emperor and his father that my role is to be expanded to include the odd public appearance. I was told that the real Absolute Purity would carry on playing with his dolls or whatever it is he does between meals and naps. I was told that the concubines I was to, er, service, would believe I was the genuine article. But finally, today, I was told that you would know otherwise. . . .

"Frankly, I believe almost nothing I have been told. The one thing we can be sure of is that the she-dragon will see that she has another twenty years or so in power. She hasn't ruled too badly in the past."

"Not badly?" Snow Lily was reminded of something beyond her own troubles. "Weren't you listening to all the reports in the Great Council? Floods, famine, eclipses, omens, riots?"

"Horrible, wasn't it?" The imposter sprang to his feet and strode back to the darkening windows. "I wanted to leap to my feet and scream at them all to *do* something to help those poor people—send food, send building materials to replace the lost homes . . . I am supposed to be Emperor and I am utterly helpless."

He sighed. "I'm sure she planned all that for a purpose. Why reveal such a catalog of disasters? Was she warning me not to try and steal the throne? Was she warning any ambitious prince that there's enough trouble already without any unrest in Sublime Mountain? Some of the mandarins in the background were horrified, so maybe she was distracting them from looking too critically at my face. Next time, of course, they'll remember me, and believing in me will be that much easier. When the Empress Mother plays chess, she moves every piece on the board, so they say." He fell silent, studying the heavenly worlds.

No matter what he said, Horse was not stupid, Snow Lily decided.

She felt stupid though. She was paralyzed. What should she do? Why didn't somebody *tell* her what to do? Never in her life had she ever had to make a decision. Her mother, her father, the eunuchs in the palace, the Empress Mother—all her life she had followed orders without question, and now she was being left to make up her own mind on a matter of high treason, life and death.

"You would be a very important person if you were the next Empress Mother," Horse told the stars. "Of course, the she-dragon would keep all the power, but stay loyal to her and you should do very well for yourself. All you need is a son."

"And then I will have done all that is required of me. And you will have done all required of you."

He spun on his heel, came striding straight to her, and—just before she panicked—dropped on his knees to stare hard at her again.

"And what happens then, do you suppose?" he growled.

"We die. Both of us. And the real Emperor . . . is . . ."

Was already dead or very soon would be. She started to cry. She buried her face in her hands. Her face paint would be all smudged and horrid. She was going to be murdered.

Suddenly, the divan rocked and a very large arm went around her. She stiffened in terror, but nothing more happened.

"I don't know what to do!" she whispered.

"I do, but I am not exactly an unbiased adviser," Horse said. "All in favor, please rise. Too late, already risen. . . ." He pulled her tighter against him. He was very strong. He smelled pleasingly musky—an intriguing scent . . . nothing like Absolute Purity or the eunuchs.

"Would you like me to help you decide?" he whispered in her ear.

"Yes."

He pulled her in even closer, using both arms, tucking her head against his shoulder. "We're both in this together, you know. And if we don't do as she wants, we're liable to die together. If we cooperate, we may have a chance. You are incredibly beautiful. I expect all the boys . . . No, I suppose not. But you are certainly beautiful enough to be an Emperor's prize jewel. Tell me about yourself, beautiful Snow Lily."

"Me? But, Your Maj— Why do you want to know about me?"

"Because I do."

She squirmed into a more comfortable position, her head against his chest. "My father is descended from a daughter of Emperor Tenacious."

"That's your father. What about you?"

"Well, so am I." She tried to collect her wits. Why did this man care about her background? "My father is a captain of a ship. I mean we were not really, truly poor, but my mother had more children than servants. And my father decided I was pretty enough to be a concubine, so when I was twelve, he took me to the School of the Sublime Arts, and they agreed. And last year . . . My parents wrote me a letter saying that Chief Eunuch had sent Father a lot of money, and if the Emperor favored me . . . Are you going to make love to me?"

She was remembering those naked people she had been shown, the frantically active young men and the girls making such extraordinary noises, sounding as if they were in pain, but not behaving as if they were.

"I hope so," Horse said, "but not until you tell me you want me to. We have the whole night ahead of us. Lots of nights. I'm in no hurry. Are you?"

"Not yet," she murmured. It was wonderfully comforting, being held like this. She had not realized that men could be gentle. "Soon, maybe. If I bear a child by you, then Chief Eunuch would pretend it was the Emperor's and First Mandarin would send my father a lot of money, wouldn't he?"

"A huge amount, I expect, especially if it's a boy. And probably give him an important job, maybe a title. Your brothers will prosper, too, if you have brothers."

Snow Lily sighed happily and cuddled closer. Everything was going to be all right. "Keep talking, Your Majesty."

"Horse."

She sniggered.

After a long moment she said, "This is nice. What happens next?"

The Marble Ship was a gazebo on a promontory in the largest of the artificial lakes in Sublime Mountain, but it was built in the shape and size of a sternwheeler riverboat, so that it seemed to float on the water. It was one of the jewels of the Summer Palace and a fine place for viewing theatrical performances or hosting large banquets, although the food would always arrive cold. It was the Empress Mother's favorite picnic place, where she could hold informal meetings without the eunuchs eavesdropping. Never before had she been able to use it so early in the year as the end of Hare Moon, but the weather continued to be remarkable. Unfortunately, while astrologers were always ready to declare bad weather a bad omen, they rarely had a good word to say about fair.

Emperor Absolute Purity, Son of Heaven, Lord of the High and the Low, and so on, must never kowtow to any mortal, only to his ancestors during certain rituals. By ancient law, no woman could rule, although, historically, several had done so as regents, most of them very well. However, the Emperor's mother was an ancestor and outranked him for ritual purposes, so she could summon him, and he came to her, not vice versa. Three days after the move to the Summer Palace, she summoned him to the Marble Ship.

As she watched him striding in at the head of his retinue, she was overcome with a nostalgia quite foreign to her normally remorseless nature. The man was an astonishingly good fit for what the public expected the true Emperor to look like. He was also a superb actor, radiating the proper imperial arrogance like a noonday sun, ignoring prostrate servants and courtiers, careful to not gawk around at the miracles of marble tracery. How big he was, how strong! This was what her son should look like now, and the knowledge that whoever had blighted him fifteen years ago had undoubtedly died for it in her mass revenge was very small comfort. His recent untimely end had been very peaceful; she had seen to that.

The imposter bowed to her with surprising grace for his size. As he took up her hands to kiss, his eyes twinkled with impertinent amusement. She met far too few real men these days, and never young ones, only ancient mandarins and decadent princes. He glowed with virility. She had been assured that he had no family of his own to comment on his unexplained disappearance, not even the girl whose unborn child had proved his fertility.

He took the chair beside hers. Ceremonial greetings were exchanged, tea and sweetmeats brought, flunkies banished out of earshot, but not out of sight, available for summons by a gesture.

"I did not even need to have the girl examined," the Empress Mother said approvingly. "Her maids report that her toes have not touched the floor since you deflowered her. Instead of dread, she rushes to her lord's embrace at sunset with eagerness and gaiety."

"I look forward to her arrival as stars await the dark," the man admitted with seemly modesty. "You chose her well, Majesty."

"There are more waiting, just as worthy. You must not neglect the others who so anxiously long to seek your imperial pleasure."

He laughed, but for the first time showed a trace of unease.

"You doubt your strength?" she inquired waspishly.

"No. And when the duties were explained to me, they seemed like a young man's dream."

"But now you feel like a neighbor's boar borrowed to improve a farmer's herd?"

He bit his lip. "It is foolish. I accepted the contract."

"It is certainly not the correct attitude for an Emperor. Most of them reveled in their prowess at your age. Even when I knew him, Zealous Righteousness summoned two, often three, women a night."

Butterfly Sword nodded. "I have warned Snow Lily that I may not be able to send for her every night in the future."

"And she wept, I suppose? Your manly heart melts for her?"

His control was too good for him to change color, but his eyes glittered. "I will do what is required of me, Your Majesty. But I cannot maintain my strength sitting around listening to music. I need exercise and variety. There is a hunting park, I understand."

He was issuing demands! Nobody had done that to her since Zealous Righteousness had died, and only he for years before that.

"My son has never been on a horse."

"But how many people know that?" He eyed her warily and then risked even worse insolence. "Since childhood, I have been trained in the arts of deception, and I presume to advise Your Majesty that the path to success does not go by dark, unseen places, avoiding witnesses, but follows the bustling sunlit highway. The more I am seen around the palace, doing things a young Emperor would do, the less likely doubts will be voiced or considered."

She knew this was exactly what Lady Twilight had been telling her, but it was a path beset with traps. "You would like to lead the army on maneuvers?" she sneered.

He took her seriously. "A wonderful suggestion, Your Majesty! No one in the army can possibly have met your noble son! I had in mind a pilgrimage to some sacred place outside Sublime Mountain, but the army would be even better."

Could he possibly be so naive? "You may risk a daily walk in the park. You may even have a favorite concubine, but you are to service others also. If you perform as required, I may allow more liberty later."

"Snow Lily!" he said. "Snow Lily is special, because she knows I am not what I pretend to be, although at times she seems able to forget that. I am safer with her than I will ever be with others, who may notice a slip and gossip. I want to name Snow Lily the Pearl Concubine, which I understand is the rank below Junior Empress. And I want her company during the day. We can go boating, sightseeing. An Emperor should enjoy himself by day. I will do my duty by the others at night."

His bizarre impudence was almost refreshing. But not quite. She had never considered the possibility that juvenile lust would lead him into something so absurd as falling in love with one of the girls. Still, that weakness made him much more vulnerable to her control. Even at his age, could he be so stupid as to make Snow Lily hostage for his own good behavior? Or was he playing a clumsy double game?

"I am unaccustomed to bargaining."

He had the gall to study her like a dealer eyeing a horse. "How long do I have?" he said brashly. "Do you have a target in mind? Three of them with child? Or four? Will you wait until my first brood hatches and you can confirm that I have sired at least one fake prince for you? Can I count on living that long?"

She threw her tea in his face. He blinked, but made no move to wipe his face or robe.

"Nobody speaks to me like that! Lady Twilight gave you absolute, ironclad assurances that you would be returned alive and unharmed when your mission was accomplished."

"She did. I did not believe that then and do not now."

Too accustomed to cringing eunuchs, she had forgotten how difficult unaltered males could be. "*Faugh!* You accepted the commission even believing you would be murdered at the end of it? You expect me to believe that?"

"I did. I do. I did not care—then. But now I think I do."

"Oh, how romantic! You have fallen in love again after only three nights' strenuous copulation?"

"One was enough," Butterfly Sword said simply. "Or maybe two," he admitted with a fleeting smile. "I will fulfill my duties better if I may have Snow Lily as my daytime companion. With respect, Your Majesty, I am not the only one at risk in this venture. If the conspiracy leaks out, the Bamboo Banner will surely overrun Heart of the World."

"Insolence! The Bamboo Banner is a peasant rabble of no account. I let you see the Great Council just so you would know the real alternatives. Which of those degenerate princes would you have as Emperor—Crystal Sea, Gratify Poet, or Tungusic Vision?"

"I would never deny that Your Majesty has ruled well, and I will do whatever I can to ensure that you rule for many more years. I hope that my reward will be to live to see them."

"Your insolence is insufferable! I made you, boy, and I can unmake you with a snap of my fingers."

"Did not the poet say, *We are promised death so that we will enjoy life?*" Without warning, he grinned at her and seemed to drop ten years and become a mere innocent boy. She was so startled that she discovered she was smiling back. She, the Empress Mother? Smiling at a common gigolo hired off the streets?

"You shall have your sweetheart," she promised, "but you must produce a boy child, whom I will serve as regent."

"I will work tirelessly to that end, Your Majesty."

That much she could believe, but it was a very long time since anyone had stood up to her like this hired stud. He would bear very careful watching. He might well have completed his assignment already. More than one Emperor had been born posthumously.

CHAPTER 9

The sun sank to rest beyond the paddy fields and a moon thinner than paper showed for a few moments in the rosy hem of the sky. Nightingale Moon! Shard Gingko turned his head and, yes, he could see a few bright stars starting to appear in the east. And a broom star, still faintly. A second would join it soon, when the sky grew darker.

He carefully cleaned his brush and placed it back in the box. He and the box were sharing a small jetty in a backwater of the Clay River—sharing it with a dozen small fishing skiffs and four million mosquitoes. It was Shard's custom to withdraw to a quiet place in the evening, some empty corner where he could record whatever wisdom he had gleaned from Sunlight's conversation during the day. The peasants were all preparing for bed, and the Firstborn himself always retired early, husbanding what little strength he had and resting up for another leg of his journey tomorrow.

Asked about the meaning of the broom stars, the Urfather said, "The Desert Teacher taught that changes in Heaven mean much to Heaven and little to us; for what good is a warning if you do not know to whom it is addressed? And again he taught, what is good for one person is often evil to another. So if a broom star presages a rich harvest, that may be good news to the fathers of many children and bad

*news to the rich merchant who has bought up much rice in
expectation of a famine. Enjoy your own world, letting the
Emperor worry about Heaven and Heaven worry about the
Emperor."*

Shard laid the paper in the box also and closed the lid. He
chuckled, remembering a fragment he had uncovered in Four
Mountains when trying to find out everything he could about
the Firstborn. It told of the great Sixth Dynasty sage, Cone
Mountain:

*Cone Mountain asked, "When so many books are filled
with folly, why is the wisdom of the Firstborn not written
for students to study?"*

*The Firstborn said, "I have no wisdom. I am not clever,
I only repeat what I have heard from persons wiser than I
and poems from fine poets."*

*Then Cone Mountain said, "But what you say is so
uplifting that this humble follower hungers to record the
words he hears."*

*The Firstborn said, "You may write if you wish, but
few will read, for many will seek to destroy what you have
written."*

Of course they would—mandarins who had spent lifetimes
studying corrupted texts when the Urfather quoted the original
versions, Emperors who did not wish to hear of their follies and
ignorance, and even rebels who thought their cause was new and
glorious. Of course, dozens or thousands of followers must have
recorded the Firstborn's sayings since the invention of writing.
And now Shard Gingko had joined their number.

He was about to rise when he sensed a shadow between him
and the western brightness. Looking up, he saw a barefoot male

peasant in a cloth and straw hat. Surprisingly, it was Mouse, apparently seeking him out, which was unprecedented.

"Friend?" he said with a smile.

The boy squatted on his heels and his somber dark eyes scanned the old man carefully, for Shard must seem very old to him.

"Master, may I ask you a question?" His adult voice had grown in, deep and tuneful.

"You may ask, by all means, but the Firstborn will give you a better answer."

Mouse shook his head. "It is his answer that troubles me. The villagers were asking him what the broom stars augur."

"And he said he didn't know, that no one knew, and maybe he told the questioners to enjoy them, because they are beautiful, like brush strokes in Heaven." That was more or less what he always said, every day, in every village.

"But later, Master, I asked him what the broom stars meant for him."

Shard said, "*Hm.*" The question had been impertinent, but he could not resist asking, "And what did he tell you?"

"He said that, for him, they were very bad news."

Shard shrugged and rose to his feet. "If the Man of a Thousand Lives wishes you to know more, lad, I expect he will tell you more. How many more days to High Abode?"

"The villagers say two days, Master."

Two more boat trips. And then what? How many more days to Sublime Mountain and the Emperor?

As he trudged back the few dozen paces to the village, Shard noticed that the smaller broom star was now brighter and closer to the larger than it had been last night. Two broom stars in Nightingale Moon in the Year of the Nightingale were a sure sign that the Portal of Worlds would open in the next Year of the Firebird. Sedge Shallows had told him that before he died, and Sedge Shallows had been a mandarin of very high rank.

❋   ❋   ❋

The mood of the villages had changed as the Firstborn's expedition neared High Abode. By then, Shard had stopped worrying about pursuit, for thousands of boats plied the great waterway, thousands of towns and villages lined its banks. Sublime Mountain would never find them now, unless some genius mandarin guessed that they were bound for the site of last year's brief rebellion, and how could anyone do that?

It was easier to guess why nobody along the river wanted to discuss the place or even admit ever hearing of the mysterious Bamboo. His Banner had certainly not been seen or heard of anywhere else in Qiancheng Province. But the governor had been forced to send troops to High Abode, which was shameful, and a dangerous association to make.

Shard could piece it together as easily as the Firstborn could. No great peasant rabble had come marching through on its way north from Dongguan to overthrow the Son of the Sun. That was how dynasties fell. This had been some local dissident picking up the rumors of southern unrest and deciding to start his own reform movement before Bamboo himself arrived. Rash youngsters had joined in and overwhelmed the elders. The nonsense might have been stopped with a few beatings or executions, but the governor of Qiancheng had chosen to defend the dynasty.

Sunlight insisted on seeing for himself, which proved difficult, for the village stood on a high bench, too far back from the river for his misshapen legs to carry him. Eventually, Mouse found a farmer with a bullock cart and an independent turn of mind who agreed to take a day away from his labors to show the Urfather the remains of High Abode. At first, the road crossed paddy fields on the river's flood plain, where every able-bodied man and woman was busily transplanting rice in the heat of early summer. Then it angled up the slope, much of which had been terraced into more fields, although the upper levels were deserted and already seemed forlorn and desolate.

Long before Shard saw the village, he smelled the stench of burned homes and the choking sweetness of decay. When the road leveled off, he saw heaped ashes of wicker and thatch, scraps of iron, broken pottery, and a few stark chimney tombstones marking houses of the wealthy. Much worse than those were human remains, scattered bones, scavenger birds too bloated to fly, waddling rats, scraps of clothing. High Abode had not just been massacred; it had been left to rot.

Mouse went chalky white with shock. Sunlight lost his temper. His outrage should have been the shrill complaint of an adolescent, but it came out as a thunderclap of celestial fury.

"Absolute *Purity*, he calls himself? Absolute *Putrefaction*, I say! Is the Son of the Sun mad? Does no one teach him history? Do they not warn him that such atrocities herald the end of a dynasty? *Go! Go now!* Go and bring honest people to give these wretches peace!"

The farmer was so overcome that he left his tortoise cart and ran off on foot, leaving Sunlight weeping in it. Shard and Mouse remained behind on the charnel ground, making vain efforts to drive away the vermin. The Firstborn continued to growl in tongues Shard did not know, although sometimes he recognized the names of infamous tyrants and celebrated battles.

Eventually, the youth's frail strength gave way and he flopped down in exhaustion and misery. Shard waited a few prudent moments, then approached the cart. He had no doubt that an army of the local peasants would come running in answer to the Firstborn's summons, eager now to give the dead proper burial as they should have done sooner.

"Master?" he whispered.

The boy looked up with eyes hollowed like caves by the cares of centuries. "I warned you that my disciples come to no good."

"Yes, Master, and I do not flinch, not yet. We'll go on to Sublime Mountain, now? So you can admonish the Golden Throne?"

The Firstborn shook his head. "We must go south. I must find Bamboo and stop him. He does not know what he is doing."

Shard remembered something he had written only yesterday.

The Master said, "No folly have I not seen before, no sorrow have I not mourned many times, no warning is ever heeded."

CHAPTER 10

"I am carrying your child," Verdant Harmony announced in a very soft voice.

She was brushing out her hair at her dressing table by the light of a single lamp. Verdant was crazy about hair brushing, always pestering Silky to do it for her. Usually, he was happy to oblige, because it made her lubricious as fast as any trick in his bag, but at the moment, he was resting, spread on the bed in much the same condition he had been when some fortunate midwife had been the first person to set eyes on him. Except that then she would have been holding his legs together, likely.

Obviously rest time was over. He summoned enthusiasm and sat up. "Oh, that's wonderful news!" Wonderful, yes, but not news. He could count. Sixty-nine nights without a single refusal? He had told the Abbot weeks ago that he had completed that stage of his mission. He held out his arms. "Come here and be smothered in kisses."

She turned on her stool to stare at him. "What are we going to do about it?" Her face, her body, would make a eunuch weep.

He rose from the bed and went to kneel at her feet. "Not *it*—*he*! He won't stop us making love for a long time yet. Come back to bed and let's celebrate!"

She slapped his face. He saw it coming and steeled himself to take it. She had muscles to stun a mule. He thought his neck was broken.

"You'd better hit the other one, or I'm going to look lopsided in the morning."

She did, even harder.

"Enough of that," he said. "Should I now put you over my knee and spank you? I don't like that sort of game. Of course you're with child! It would be unnatural if you weren't, and I'm bursting with joy. I know it's unmanly, but I love babies! Even girl babies! It had better be a quick wedding. Public or secret?"

"You'll want to get your hands on my money as soon as possible, I expect?"

"I won't touch your money. The wedding contract will leave it all in your name, every copper bit of it, to spend as you will."

She eyed him narrowly. "I didn't know that was possible!"

"That married women are allowed to own property? I simply cannot imagine why your father has never thought to mention that. I insist on it. As owner of a household, you can even obtain a permit to arm your guards. Then you can be my sponsor and I will earn my noodles in the arena. I have brought home sixteen thousand imperials for your father so far."

"*How* much?"

"Sixteen thousand, four hundred, eleven. I swear I will never touch your money. Your body, now, is another matter. I will continue to paw it relentlessly." He ran a hand along her thigh.

"But I know nothing about you," she protested.

"You know I love you and that you love me."

"Do I?"

"You certainly know that I am the world's greatest lover."

A trace of a dimple peeked out and vanished again. "Greediest if not greatest. Also the world's greatest sand fighter. And the world's slickest liar. But your family? Your parents? I know nothing about them!"

He stood up and lifted her upright to embrace. "Neither do I," he said, and smothered her protest with a very thorough kiss.

Then he said, "If I'm going to lie, I want us both lying." He lifted her, carried her over to the bed, and adjusted them into a comfortable nose-to-nose position. She did not resist.

"Now, when have I ever lied to you?"

"Telling me you climbed the wall."

"I never said I climbed the wall! You assumed it because I came in the window."

"All that nonsense about Celestial Womb, then? I heard the story of Sea Flower and the Storm Prince at my grandmother's knee."

"Don't believe everything you hear around arthritic knees. I was spinning silk to get between a pretty girl's legs. No man counts that as lying. You knew it and you consented. Noble Lance was real enough, wasn't he?"

She was starting to relax and respond to his banter. "Nobler than anything in my previous experience."

"Good." Subtly, Silky started stroking. "You should have told me sooner about your little silkworm. You have nothing to worry about, nothing at all. True, I'm an orphan and know nothing of my origin. My earliest memories are of the docks and the gutter, an orphan waif fighting dogs for the scraps, rat bites on my arms. I don't know what my real name was, even. I was adopted by a fraternity that taught me to fight. Your father is my first employer."

"My mother would rather die than see me marry a sand warrior."

"Let her make her own decisions by all means."

"My father will kill you."

He can try! "I'll bring him around," Silky said truthfully. "Just watch me! The fourth thing you must do is go to your mother and break the happy news. She has a party planned for tomorrow, doesn't she? Tell her before that and ruin it for her."

"And what are the first three things I must do first?"

"Rape me, rape me, and rape me," he said. "Break our record."

Verdant laughed and his skin chilled as it sometimes did in the arena when he sensed a miscalculation.

"Help yourself, lover," she said. "This is your last chance. Make the most of it."

"And what does that mean?" Suddenly, he knew exactly what it meant.

"Silky, dearest, I would very happily live with you forever in a permanent daze of fornication, but that isn't practical. My mother and I are of one mind."

"*She* is in on our little secret?"

They had *used* him! *How dare they?*

"It was her idea, bull. I needed a marriage to pry my wealth out of Father's talons, and only the shame of a baby would get me one. It was Mother who suggested I submit to you. She was furious that Father had polluted her house by admitting a brute warrior."

Silky sat up, too furious to think of sex now. She had let him think he was seducing her! He was the one who had won her that money by killing off her husband and brothers-in-law. Ungrateful slut! "You trapped me!"

"Of course," she said, mocking him. "You were the best stag on the hill. I'm grateful for all the hard work you put in to please me. Yes, you are a fantastic lover. If bed was everything and the rest of the world didn't matter, you'd be the only possible choice, and I'm sure you've put a fine, healthy baby in me, but this must be good-bye."

Silky knew that Jade Harmony was stupid and Morning Jewel even more so, but he had credited their daughter with some brains. "You honestly think your father will find you a husband because of this? He will never let go of your money that way. He's turned down eight offers for your hand already."

"What?" She tried to sit up. "I don't believe it!"

Silky pulled her back down and wrapped her in arms and legs. "At least eight. I go through his correspondence regularly, but I may have missed a couple. He'll pack you off to visit some mythical rural aunt for a few months and put the baby up for adoption. He may do worse than that! Your little silkworm can't win your freedom by himself. He needs his daddy's help."

She tried to move his left hand. "Stop doing that and keep talking."

He kept talking while still doing *that*. "I can offer him a son-in-law he can't refuse. Your mother will be hysterical with joy. We will head upriver and you can bear our child far away. When we return next year, I won't be a sand warrior anymore. Doesn't that sound more exciting?"

She punched him. "What sort of business? What else do you do for my father, other than slaying dragons and prowling through his accounts when he's not around?"

"Ask not what I do for your father," Silky growled, suddenly aflame with a desire to dominate, "but rather what I am about to do to you. And, if you are very good, I will then reveal the rest of your life to you."

In the middle of the morning, Sand Warrior Silky just happened to be wearing his full sand-warrior regalia when he was summoned to the master's counting room. The page muttered a warning about a bad mood.

After seven months in his service, Silky had decided that he disliked Jade Harmony very much and despised him even more. By last month, the merchant had taken to the Gray Helpers' way of doing business to the point of requesting an outing. The proposed subject had been quite young and even Archives had been unable to make out much of a case against him as a threat to the client. Silky had reluctantly made the score, cutting the man's throat in an alley and faking a robbery, but he had done it mostly so that Jade Harmony could never pretend that he didn't know what he was doing.

The fat man had a very small soul for his size, insisting on a kowtow even when the two of them were alone together. That sort of thing he would pay for, some day, but regrettably not today.

Jade Harmony left Silky on his knees. Add that insult to the list. He was depicting rage like an actor—face stark white, eyes bulging, hands shaking. "You raped my daughter!"

Temptation: She raped me. No, mustn't! "Never, Master!"

"Debauched her, then." *She seduced me first, blast her!*

"With respect, Eminence, she is a widow. When I told her I would come to her room in the middle of the night, she did not set out tea bowls and a chess set."

"You abused my trust and hospitality. I will report this to your abbot."

"I already have." *He congratulated me on a job well done.*

Probably Jade Harmony detected the threat in those three little words, because he vibrated even more in his frenzy. "You have ruined her!"

"I am planning to make her much richer. And thus you, of course."

The merchant grabbed up a bronze lion and rushed at Silky. He seemed quite surprised to find his wrist being crushed in steel fingers, his arm completely immovable, and the eyes of an assassin glaring down into his.

"May we discuss this like reasonable men?" Silky said softly. *I would so love to break some of your bones in self-defense.* He removed the lion and placed it gently back on the lacquered cabinet. "Your daughter and I love each other very much." *In bed, on the floor, and up against the wall; every one of the fifty-six positions listed in that tract you keep locked in your muniments chest—the trapeze, the plowman, the heron and turtle, the weeping birch . . .* "I will gladly marry her."

Rubbing a whitened wrist, Jade Harmony bared yellow teeth. "I daresay you would. Fortunately, imperial law forbids Gray Helpers to marry!"

"I doubt if Verdant knows that and she certainly does not know that I am a Brother unless you have told her. If she marries anyone else, you lose control of her money. Either he gets it or she keeps it. But legally, I will be a rapist, marrying her under false pretenses, so I can have no claim on it."

That caught the fat man's attention. "So?"

"The nightingale will sing to two broom stars."

"What?"

Silky sighed. "Business. Huge business. Sit down, client, and listen to the sound of gold clinking as your faithful aide weaves dreams before you."

When Jade Harmony failed to move, Silky took him by the shoulders and pushed him backward a few steps, until he toppled onto a cushioned sofa, going down like an old-growth cedar. Silky pulled up a stool for himself, putting his knees between Jade Harmony's knees. He waggled a finger.

"The prophecy, remember? The omen. There are two broom stars in the sky now and they will still be there next month for the nightingale to serenade. All the astrologers in the Good Land are gibbering already. They are all convinced now that the Portal of Worlds will open, the year after next."

Porcine eyes shrank even smaller. "What happens then?"

"Who knows? Barbarian hordes coming out? Imperial armies vanishing inside, as did Emperor Virtuous Ruler's? Legends proliferate. But the price of land in the Fortress Hills must be falling like hail."

"But what *will* happen?"

"I, for one, expect nothing to happen," Silky said cheerfully. "And do not intend to be near enough to see. Whatever the Portal does, the land will still be there afterward. Barbarians tend to be hard on herds, but you can move yours to safety in the Year of the Firebird. The Portal will close, the hills endure." He pulled the scroll from his belt and tossed it in the merchant's lap. "This is a contract of marriage between your daughter and Mandarin of the Fourth Rank Effulgent Brushwork, dated three days from now."

"Another of your impersonations?"

"No. I am not old enough to do a good mandarin. He's one of ours, Gray Brother Luminous, but his probity and erudition will leave you speechless. Having met your daughter at her late husband's house and hearing that she is now available, he has begged you for her hand in marriage. Your wife will roll on the floor, giggling. The wedding must be rushed because the Golden Throne has just posted him to a new assignment and he cannot linger."

The fish was nibbling. A merchant marrying his daughter to a top-rank mandarin would soar socially. "Assignment where?"

"Imperial secret. The seal he uses on the marriage contract will be mine, as will two of the legs in the wedding bed. Next day, Verdant and I will go up-country together to buy real estate and drop babies, respectively."

"Buy land for whom?" The conversation was now about money.

"We will buy land with *her* money in *your* name, understand? Our contract is to make you richer, not her. Next year, her official husband will suffer a tragic accident, and your twice-widowed daughter will return to the bosom of her family, bringing all that land with her. Don't tell her that bit."

"A Gray Helper cannot marry!"

Silky sighed. "Irrelevant."

"Have you told her all this?" Jade Harmony's pretense of reluctance merely made him look sly.

"I have certainly not mentioned the Gray Order. I suggest you now exhilarate your wife by explaining the solution you found, tell Verdant the happy news, and start rushing out the invitations."

"You expect me to commit perjury on a wedding contract?"

Another sigh. "Me too. I don't suppose a death of two thousand cuts is much worse than the one-thousand version."

Jade Harmony leaned back on the sofa and smirked greasily. "No! I deal in silk and spices, not real estate. I certainly will never trust you with my money or hers. You will leave this house now and never return. Tell the Abbot to assign an older, better man to my contract. My daughter does not lack for suitors, and in any case, there are much quicker ways of disposing of unwanted bastard trash."

Delighted at the opportunity thus presented, Silky flipped his right forearm dagger into his hand and poked the point into the merchant's groin. The fat man uttered a terrified squeak and shrank backward and upward until he was spread-eagled against the wall above the sofa and could go no farther. The knife went with him all the way.

"Dispose of my son, you will not," Silky said. "You are also proposing what lawyers call a *breach of contract*, Master. I will now qualify you for a job in the imperial palace. Just remember not to drink anything for three days; if you can pass water after that, all will be well. Ready?" Silky *seemed* himself a bloodthirsty monster as well as he could without a mirror.

"Mercy! Mercy!"

"You don't deserve mercy. The holy Abbot has been working on this plan for years, and we have no time to find a substitute client. I have killed nine men and worn my pizzle to a frazzle impregnating your daughter, just to get us to this point. How can I trust you now?"

Jade Harmony's teeth chattered. He could not see the dagger, because it was hidden from him by a belly that overhung like a temple eave, but he knew exactly where it was and his eyes were aimed in the right direction. "W-What do I have to do?"

Smiling, Silky repeated his instructions. "And if you do not obey my orders *exactly*, Master, you will be dead before sunset and I will marry your daughter anyway. Do you understand?"

"Y-Yes."

"You believe me?"

"Yes!"

"And you will obey every brush stroke of my instructions?"

"Yes! Yes!"

The monk sheathed his blade and stepped back. "Tomorrow I will present a list of properties she will need to liquidate in order to free up sufficient funds. It is extensive. A mandarin of the fourth rank, remember. Effulgent Brushwork. Now summon your family and tell them the wondrous news."

Pity the poor orphan not invited to his own betrothal! The Harmony household had been anything but harmonious all day, and especially so after Brother Luminous arrived in his mandarin seeming to meet his bride. The night was half gone before calm returned and the guests left. A light appeared in Verdant's window. As she was preparing for bed, Silky donned a princely robe borrowed from the House of Joyful Departure. After being exposed to the grandiose Prefect Effulgent Brushwork, she deserved to be reassured about the man she was really going to marry—Brother Luminous was a skilled philanderer and would have no compunction about cuckolding his young colleague if the opportunity presented itself.

When Silky finished seeming, his reflection in the mirror was awe-inspiring. His robe alone must be worth a couple of gold taels; his arrogance was worth thousands. That slim dark line of mustache across his lip, drooping at the ends to his jaw line— magnificent! His queue hung to his thighs and his fingernails were as long as daggers. He set off to dazzle her and celebrate their engagement.

Perversely, Verdant had locked her door. In a pitch-dark corridor, hampered by the fingernails and his cumbersome robes, Prince Noble Lance needed almost two minutes to pick the lock.

The bolt clicked, and he was free to go in. He opened the door partway to give his eyes a chance to adjust to the light, then pushed it wide and entered. Regrettably, she was fully dressed, standing by her dressing table, holding a pistol in both hands with the barrel pointed straight at him. He closed the door quietly, staying where he was. At that range, the ball could blow his entrails out into the corridor, but the chances were excellent that she would hit the ceiling instead. Those flintlocks packed a kick like a three-humped camel.

Making no hasty moves, he inclined his head respectfully. "Felicitations on your elevation, lady."

"Who are you?"

"Your future husband, Noble Lance. Have you forgotten so soon? Emperor Auspicious Grandeur begat Prince Obscene Gestures and Prince Obscene Gestures begat—"

She flicked the pistol as if trying to dislodge a fly and he jumped. "Don't *do* that!"

"I want to know who you really are, and how you control my father."

"No, you don't."

"Yes, I do."

He smiled. How could she resist him? "You'll remember me when I get my clothes off." He began to struggle with the accursed buttons, scores of them.

She pointed the gun straight up. "If you don't answer me, I will fire this and waken the house."

That was a much more credible threat. He unseemed his fingernails and continued to work on his buttons. "Silky is truly my name. I pretend to be a sand warrior to deceive your mother and a sand warrior pretending to be a clerk of accounts to deceive the servants. Now I am pretending to be a prince because I desperately need to get back into your bed. See how honest I am?"

"No. Keep talking."

"Then put the gun down."

She stared very hard at him for a moment before laying the pistol on the dressing table, probably believing it was within reach if she needed it. She had no idea how fast he was. The next few minutes were going to be interesting.

"I am a Gray Brother, employed by your father as an assassin."

She nodded, as if she had known. "And did your work on his behalf include the massacre of my husband and half his household on the one evening I happened to be absent?"

"Must you put it so crudely?"

"Yes."

"Then yes."

She did not change countenance. "Why?"

"Partly because he had arranged to have your grandfather assassinated, but mostly to make your father richer."

Now she reacted, but more with disbelief than shock. "My grandfather?"

"Jade Harmony 6, may his ancestors cherish—"

"Even if I believed that, what about my two stepsons and the rest? You killed all of them?"

"It was necessary," Silky explained patiently, untying laces now. "They would have inherited the money. An accident has to seem reasonable, my love."

"The distinguished guests and the servants who ate the leftovers?"

"Corroborative detail to add artistic verisimilitude."

"The head cook was impaled for negligence!" Verdant was attempting to look nauseated, but she was not truly surprised, clever girl.

"Certainly," Silky said, tearing off an especially stubborn button. "His kitchen wasn't any filthier or more squalid than most kitchens in town, but he should have noticed that one of the boys helping prepare the meal was a total stranger. Very careless! They should have sacrificed a few of the guards on the gate, too, for letting me in."

"All this to make my father richer?"

"And because I wanted to marry you."

"You had never met me."

"I had orders to marry you and I obey my Abbot."

That surprised her. "You were *ordered* to seduce me?"

"Yes. But I would have done so anyway, once I saw you. You're everything a man dreams of, the perfect woman."

"How many other people have you killed?"

"My tally so far is nine. Come and help me with these barbarian buttons or I'll be here all night."

"Father knows all this?"

"He knows most of it."

She laughed. She *laughed*! "This is incredible! Father employing an assassin? I never thought he had the balls."

"That was in doubt, briefly. When did you guess I was not a sand warrior?"

"The third night, when you stopped pretending to be climbing the wall to my window. I realized that nothing about you was believable. And I had missed the food poisoning disaster so conveniently."

He grinned admiringly. "Verdant, my downy chick, you knew I was a merciless hired killer and you still let me romp in your bed every night?" The woman was a tigress!

"You have mitigating qualities. So the mandarin is another imposter and Father knows that?"

"Your father made a pact with the Gray Helpers, my darling. We will make him enormously rich and take a handsome cut, but in the meantime, he does as he is told."

"Including selling his daughter?"

"He did that before he ever met us."

She shook her head in disbelief, but she was very close to smiling. "So now what really happens?"

"You win your freedom, Most Glorious One. You do not belong here in this cage! I will show you the world."

"Your tongue is smooth as bean curd, Sublime Poet. Keep talking."

"You go through the fake wedding ceremony with the fake mandarin, and then you and I will embark on the sternwheeler *River Pearl*. Luminous will accompany us, because he knows a lot about land values. We will travel up the Jade until we reach Cherish, which is in the Fortress Hills, and the last town this side of the border. There, we will take up residence. You will complete that baby-making job I assigned you. Luminous and I will start buying land for you."

"Using whose money?" Oh, she was clever!

"Yours. But the titles will all be in your name. Don't tell your father that. We anticipate that it will increase enormously in value in a few years. Aha!" He had opened the robe enough to wriggle out of it.

"And when you have made me rich," Verdant said, "you will murder me, too, and inherit it all?"

He shed lesser garments, tossing them around like confetti. "What an obscene suggestion! How can you even think that? I would never harm the mother of my child. Our marriage will be illegal, so I can't inherit, anyway." He trod down the last of his clothes, although the presence of that accursed gun was keeping him from achieving a decent erection. "And I love you madly."

"Maybe."

"Definitely. I never lie to you. You know the whole truth. You seduced me as much as I seduced you, but you kept me on after you guessed what I was. Didn't you?"

She nodded. "I found that nothing in my life seemed to matter except bedtime. Not just the sex, but the talk, the teasing, the fun . . . You saved me from going crazy."

"So you forgive me for playing rough to get you?"

"I suppose I do."

"Good. You are not just marrying beneath you, my love. You are marrying beneath anyone—marrying filth from the gutter, trained to murder and lie and cheat. But I love you and I will make you the richest woman in the Good Land. Right now, as you can see, Noble Lance urgently needs to celebrate our forthcoming union, fake or not."

He walked forward. She moved as if to take up the gun again, but he continued until he was close. "Are you going to shoot me or lay me? That's your choice."

She sighed. "Did not the Rose Teacher say, *The scum always comes out on top?*"

Howling with laughter, he grabbed her and carried her over to the bed.

Verdant's second wedding went very well, with all the aunts and cousins *writhing* in jealousy and her mother inflated like a blowfish—not just a high rank mandarin, but a *prefect*! Half the merchant elite from the city seemed to be there, including some Verdant had never even heard of. Father was grumpy, of course, but anything expensive made his belly ache. When it was all over, the bride and her official husband embarked in palanquins and were borne off in triumph to board the sternwheeler *River Pearl*. Verdant watched Brother Luminous embark in the first palanquin, she watched it precede hers all the way to the docks without stopping, and yet the man who emerged from it at the docks was Silky, almost unrecognizable in the garb of a merchant.

"How did you do that?" she demanded as he offered a hand

to lead her up the gangplank, she being cluttered with excessive finery.

"Do what, my rose?"

"Switch."

"Switch what?"

The *River Pearl* was smaller than she had expected, a smelly, smoky, and excessively noisy contraption whose cramped cabins-for-the-rich were barely large enough to hold their bedbugs, Silky said. There was scarcely room for the two of them to stretch out side-by-side on the sleeping mat, so they got even less sleep than usual.

In the morning, she discovered Mandarin Effulgent Brush-work was aboard in the guise of another merchant, Gold Luminous. He and his son—Silky, of course—were on their way to Cherish to meet an incoming caravan, traveling with their concubines, because no honorable man would take his wife on a long journey. Verdant found this new state amusing, almost laughing aloud every time she wondered what her mother would say if she heard. The other girl, Plum Blossom, was a Gray Sister incognito. She was pretty and witty but too quick to smile at any man under forty, including Silky.

The food was appalling and, on dry nights, even the cabin passengers often preferred to sleep on deck among the smelly riffraff, but none of that mattered. Silky had extraordinary ideas about a man's responsibility to organize his womenfolk's lives—as far as he was concerned, he told her, she was free to do anything she liked except bear children for other men, and at the moment, she had one of his in the pot. Verdant felt truly free for the first time in her life. She talked with complete strangers, tasted new food—mostly very strange—and discovered new scenery. She knew it could not last long. A month or less would bring them to Cherish, and by then, her condition would be starting to show and lovemaking would have to stop.

The idyll stopped sooner than that. Six days out of Wedlock, the boiler exploded, killing several sailors and leaving the ship to drift until it ran aground. Verdant and her companions found themselves stranded in a ratty little town called Humble Duty. The only room they could find would be unworthy of a traitors' prison. Plum Blossom stayed there to guard what remained of their baggage while Luminous went in search of the rest and Silky went out to hire a boat and sailors. Verdant felt unsafe without Silky, so she went with him.

The sun had almost set, but it was certainly not yet dark, thank Heaven, as they hurried along a cramped and busy alley. Two knife-bearing youths blocked their path. Everyone else in the alley turned and fled. There was a third thug behind her with a club, but she did not know that just then, and everything happened so fast that she was never quite sure what she saw. Silky threw her out of the way, so she fell; he pulled a knife of his own, parried the first man's thrust, dodged the second man's, kicked the first assailant in the crotch, and then twirled the second man around and rammed him into the third man, so he took the blow from the club. He dropped that one, got the third from behind in some sort of lock that left him helpless, and ran him face-first into a bamboo wall. The boy screamed, but he was rammed again and again, until he stopped screaming, then dropped. By that time, one of the others was trying to rise. Silky kicked him in the face, once to drop him, and several times more while he was on the ground. The third man had hobbled away, doubled over, so Silky cut the other two's throats to make sure they were dead. Then he helped Verdant up.

"You all right, love?" He wasn't even breathing fast.

She just stared at him, unable to speak. The alley had been quite busy before, but the only people in sight now were the two corpses.

"*Are you all right?*" His face was so twisted with rage that she hardly knew him. She nodded, but she was shaking too hard to stand without assistance.

"Let's go back to the room, then," he said. "Do I have to carry you?"

"No," she squeaked.

Gripping her arm, he raced her, stumbling, along the alley.

"Did you kill them?"

"Yes. They deserved it, incompetent trash. I promised I would show you the world. I didn't promise you would like it."

He had bragged of killing nine people, and she had thought she believed him, but now she realized that there were different levels of believing. Now she had seen the reality of deliberate murder and knew that the man she slept with was an animal, a monster. Would she ever sleep again without dreaming of the bloody pulps Silky had made of the youths' faces?

"Well?" he said. "Would you rather I had let us be robbed, slashed, probably murdered?"

She licked her lips. "No. Thank you. Well done."

CHAPTER 11

The so-called Lord of Ten Thousand Years was brushing his concubine's hair. Probably no Emperor in centuries would have dreamed of doing such a thing in his worst nightmare, but this one had learned his lovemaking from the Gray Sisters, who were all experts. He did not see why he should be the only one to enjoy the ridiculous performance necessary to create an imperial heir, and he knew how most women reacted to having their hair brushed by a man with no clothes on.

He was sitting on the edge of the great bed. Snow Lily sat on a stool between his knees, wearing no more than he was. She had luxurious, gleaming black hair as long as any he had ever seen, and the process was working as well as usual—on both of them. His free hand clasping her breast to steady her could detect her nipple hardening, and his own body was reacting to her reaction, signaling its readiness for another try. He wondered if she could feel that, pressed against her.

"I love you," he whispered.

She jumped. "Your Majesty!"

"How often have I threatened to have your head cut off if you call me that in private?"

She chuckled. "Horse, then. Stallion of Ten Thousand Mountings! You must not confess to human frailties, like falling in love with a mere woman!"

"Then who am I supposed to love?"

"Just yourself, I suppose. Everyone else does."

"Love me or love themselves? Silly child, I love you much more. I would do anything for you." And that was strange, because the Emperors' extravagance rewarding their favorite concubines' families was an age-old grumble among the Gentle People, and Novice Horse had always agreed with that sentiment. Now he had discovered he would do anything to win a smile from Snow Lily, even raise her family to the nobility, which is what he had recently done. "Did your father receive the rescript?" The imperial bureaucracy moved slower than a tortoise.

"I have not heard yet, Your . . . my beloved Horse. But I know he will be ecstatic, and Mother will hug the moon."

"Good. Hard on the moon, though. Now what about your brothers? How many of them are of age?"

"Three, but you don't need to—"

"No, I don't *need* to." The great imperial hand slid across to caress her other breast. "But I *want* to! Tomorrow you must make out a list of them, and include the younger ones, also. And describe what would make each of them as happy as your parents will be. Military commands, estates . . . anything in my power."

Everything was, of course, in the Empress Mother's power. Butterfly Sword would approve the list of donations, but the eunuchs would run it past her first. She would agree without a thought, because she approved of such prodigality. For one thing, her world did not include such a thing as thrift, and for another, the news would spread and help counter the Bamboo's campaign of whispers that there was no real Emperor. Next week, the Lord of the High and the Low would look after Snow Lily's sisters' dowries.

Enough! He was as hard as rock just thinking of her delight. He threw away the precious gold-and-tortoiseshell-backed hairbrush and flopped back on the bed, pulling Snow Lily on top of him with both hands. She squealed in surprise and shot her legs in the air, which let him put his feet on the stool, improving an uncomfortable position. He nuzzled her hair while his hands explored. . . .

A sudden thought of Moth made him shiver.

Snow Lily felt it, of course. "What's wrong?"

It was subtle, but there was a change in the shape of her belly. Moth had shown him when it had happened to her.

"You are with child!"

Snow Lily squirmed around, in a great tangle of limbs, so she could kiss him. "I hope so. Even the eunuchs are not sure enough to tell the she-dragon yet."

Had he completed his assignment? It would be months yet before the child's sex was known. His seed had brought death to Moth, but this time, it might bring death to him.

CHAPTER 12

Silent had been bragging when he told Man Valor that his cadre worked twice as hard as the others, for that would not have been humanly possible. But what he did make them do was not humanly possible, either. When the Pearl Army shifted camp, as it did every three or four days, the patriots ran for a couple of hours singing the Bamboo song and carrying only staves and canteens. Men of the Silent Cadre did that with sacks of rice on their shoulders, and then went back for another load. They sang on both trips.

They did everything harder, faster, and farther, and Silent's three knots were always out there ahead of them.

On any task or journey, the last man to finish was subjected to extra labor or public humiliation, usually the spitting ritual. They ate like horses, chewed three or four yang leaves a day, and could fall asleep while bathing in cold water. When they boxed, they fought until their knuckles bled. The worst torment of all was Silent himself, that weedy, juvenile, ugly, arrogant, obnoxious turd who worked as hard as any of them.

All this harshness was not to make them invincible, Silent insisted. They were invincible already. Any man who doubted that could ask to be shot at and he would arrange it; none ever did. The purpose of the Silent Cadre was to turn them into leaders, to serve Bamboo. Just do as he did, Silent said, but even the best of them rarely managed to equal him.

NOT sticks nor stones can break my bones . . .

The group's number varied from twenty to about forty. Some obviously could not keep up; they vanished without explanation. Some completed the course and were sent off to be promoted at the third proving, but the men of the Silent Cadre did not waste training time attending the ceremony, although other cadres did. Every man worked, ate, and slept in a crowd of strangers, for no one ever spoke. They chanted lessons or sang hymns to ancestors or the accursed bamboo song. That was all. They knew one another's faces, but never their names.

Man Valor missed the comfort of simple talk, of telling stories, of laughing at jokes. He even missed women, to his shame. Once or twice a month, back in Face to the Sun, he had taken a bowl of rice around the corner to a local widow, Blue Harmony, and she had let him make the blossom of eight petals with her, but spilling his seed weakened a man, and the patriots had dedicated all their strength to Bamboo. Fortunately, no women were available to tempt them.

The Pearl Army was moving steadily inland, heading westward and northward, into cooler hill country. There were several armies in the Bamboo Banner—the Pearl Army, the Jade Army, the Agate Army, and probably others, with the exact number being a secret—and they would join up or divide as tactics required. Most towns wisely left their gates open and suffered little. Those that resisted were besieged. No siege lasted longer than three days before a swarm of patriots came over the walls. Then the looting and destruction were much more serious. The governor and his helpers were beheaded or impaled. Willing young men were enlisted. Women were treated with respect and must not be touched.

The Bamboo Banner was heading to Heart of the World, of course, to dethrone the she-dragon and appease Heaven's anger, but it was going to be a very long journey.

Man Valor's torment in the Silent Cadre ended one baking hot noon in Lotus Moon. The men had eaten and were standing in line, eagerly waiting for their midday yang leaf.

"Spit!" Silent said. They all spat. But then he stopped unwrapping the packet, leaving them with their mouths open and juices flowing. He smiled. His smiles were very rare and usually meant trouble for someone. "Duteous, Man Valor, Spring Tide . . . You three have completed the course, wait here. The rest of you, fill your canteens at the spring, then run to the top of that hill and bring back a pebble. Last man in will take them all back again."

He unwrapped the yang and began feeding the salivating mouths. That trek would be grueling in the noon heat. The army was in arid country now, and the wind carried dust that stung a man's eyes, gritted in his teeth, and threatened to skin him. The cadre took their leaves and dashed away.

Poor devils! Man Valor chewed his leaf happily. He eyed the other two, wondering which was Duteous and which Spring Tide. They were eyeing him, no doubt, for similar reasons.

As Silent threw away the banana leaf, he looked up at Man Valor. "Three moons ago, you said you had questions. Do you still?"

Man Valor shook his head.

"You may speak if you have anything to say. Do you?"

"Yes, Leader."

"Say it."

"I have wanted to smash you every day for three months."

Silent showed his garden-rake teeth. "You had plenty of chances. You want to try now?"

"No, Leader. You would smash me. Thank you for showing me what a leader should be." Duteous, or possibly Spring Tide, clapped Man Valor's shoulder to show that he approved of what had been said.

For the first time since Man Valor had met him, Silent looked pleased. "You always had the brawn. I hoped I could give you some sense, and maybe I have. These two," he gestured at the others, "had too much of that. I tried to knock some brains out of them."

"They still have enough sense not to risk speaking before you give them leave, leader," Man Valor said. The other two grinned.

Silent did not. "So I see. Come and be proven." He spun on his heel and ran. His pupils followed.

There were three provings. The first came a few days after a no-body enlisted, when he had to show that he could withstand two blows from a staff, one across his chest and the other on his back, in the exact exercise that Leaping Serpent and Chestnut River had demonstrated for Man Valor in Face to the Sun. There were ways of standing the impacts, and the rest of the troop would have taught him those tricks if they approved of him. There were also ways in which his leader could strike him that seemed deadly but would not seriously hurt even a nobody, and ways that would look the same but cripple anyone except a patriot of the second proving. His leader must be able to administer the one he wanted, and Silent had taught his cadre how they would do this when they led their own cadres. Thus a promising no-body became a patriot of the first proving; all others were sent home with a couple of broken ribs. *NOT sticks nor stones . . .*

The second proving was made with a blade and was much more dangerous. Silent had given his students very careful instruction, for men who failed it died. The exact ritual was essential.

Three days after leaving Face to the Sun, Chestnut River had raised Nobody Man Valor to patriot. Leaping Serpent had promoted him to second proving. Today, he must risk all in the third proving, the grimmest of all, and he must do it for himself. *Swords and shot can hurt me NOT. . . .*

Man Valor felt that he had earned the honor and had no doubt at all that he would survive the proving. As they ran through the camp, he savored the thought of a Man Valor Cadre. It had a nice ring to it.

The Pearl Army was growing. Now it had wagons, to carry its stock of weapons and siege equipment, and also tents, although those were not needed yet. It had horses to pull the wagons and all the harness and paraphernalia that livestock required. No doubt the other armies were growing too. The she-dragon must know her days were numbered and must tremble on her stolen throne.

There were several thousand men lined up around the stony hollow, standing with arms folded. Because they were almost never still—even waiting in line to have their rice bowls filled they would run in place—they were showing that they could do so to perfection, standing like statues with only the dangling ends of their headbands fluttering.

A narrow passage had been left open, and Silent led his little troop to the open center. They took their place at the front of the crowd and bowed hastily to Bamboo himself, who sat on a throne at the far side. Man Valor had seen him twice at a distance and soon would speak to him face-to-face! He was obviously the most powerful man in the Good Land now—the she-dragon had no army to match his—but he refused any honor beyond a bow. He said there would be time enough for his men to kowtow to him after they had put him on the Golden Throne, or so the cadre leaders reported.

Second provings were already under way, with a man standing in the center, holding a sword, and Man Valor was delighted to recognize him as his old cadre leader, Leaping Serpent. That seemed like a very good omen for his own third-knot promotion. The candidate trotting out to him was Radiant Duty, one of the nothings who had served on the Golden Aspect raid.

Man Valor knew from his own proving that Leaping Serpent would perform the ritual perfectly, but he could watch it now with an eye trained by Silent. As the candidate approached, Leaping Serpent extended the long, slightly curved, sword at arm's length. Radiant Duty walked straight to it until the point was just touching the end of his nose. Leaping Serpent raised his arm and the blade vertically.

Radiant Duty took off his headband and held it straight out in front of him with both hands, as if offering it. The next move was tricky, because although the patriots were invulnerable in battle, they could suffer minor accidents just as nobodies could, and a proving sword was as sharp as a razor. If the two men misjudged, the candidate's nose would be sliced in half. Very slowly, Leaping Serpent brought the sword down. Radiant Duty did not flinch as the point went by his face and the blade passed between his outstretched hands. It went through the headband like smoke. He flickered a faint smile as a drop of blood fell from the end of his nose, nicked to perfection. That would have been his own doing, an imperceptible move of his head, and a slight scar there was much admired.

He spread his arms out to the side, a fragment of ribbon in each hand. Leaping Serpent raised the sword again, took one step forward, and *attacked*, slashing down at Radiant Duty's right arm. Had his victim not been a patriot, that brutal stroke would certainly have amputated the limb just below the shoulder, but his arm repelled the sword. It moved under the impact, of course, and he obviously felt the blow, because he winced, but he did not fall apart, nor even bleed. Instantly, Leaping Serpent swung again, another flash of steel, this time at Radiant's left forearm, and again the arm recoiled from the impact but was not severed.

Radiant Duty waved both fists overhead in triumph. The onlookers bellowed, "*Hiya!*" the salute to a new second-knot. The roar echoed back from the scabby hills. Leaping Serpent produced a fresh headband and tied it on the beaming patriot. He had one more ribbon dangling from his belt, and another man came trotting out to be proven, a man Man Valor did not know.

Then another cadre leader, with four ribbons trailing from his belt, trotted out to replace Leaping Serpent. Man Valor took a few minutes to remember his own second proving, and the two narrow bruises he had sustained. They had hurt, and his arms had turned beautiful colors all the way to his wrists afterward, but he had known from then on that he was invulnerable to mortal attack. Leaping Serpent had told his cadre that their provings were only to convince themselves. The rest of the world must learn in battle.

As the cheer went up for the fourth candidate, Man Valor could not resist a sideways glance to see how many more seconds were waiting. There were no more seconds, and two men with guns were marching in from that direction. Silent scowled at him.

"If you're so impatient, Man Valor, you can go first."

Without a word, Man Valor ordered his feet to move. His heart was beating faster than usual, the whole parade glittering for him with the glory of yang. He was to win a third knot! He was going to speak with Bamboo and see the great man up close.

He trotted across the space to the throne. Under its canopy, Bamboo was the only man shaded from the sun, but his face was as dusty as any other man's, and streaked with shiny rivulets of sweat. He wore only what his men wore—baggy unbleached trousers and a headband. His ribbon was golden instead of green; that was all. There were streaks of silver in his hair and trailing mustache, and his musculature was that of a mature man, but his thickness was not flab. He was obviously still fit and strong. Bamboo was of pure Gentle People stock, descended from Emperors of the Tenth Dynasty, before the Outlanders came. He was rumored to be more than a century old, but seemed no more than fifty.

"Bamboo, I am Man Valor of the Silent Cadre of the Pearl Army."

"You have sworn to fight for me, Patriot?"

"I have, Bamboo."

"But will you obey other orders? If I judge that some lackey of the she-dragon deserves to have his head chopped off, will you do the chopping?"

"I will obey orders, Bamboo."

"If I decree that he ought to be impaled, will you swing the hammer to drive in the spike?"

"I will obey orders, Bamboo."

"Will you die for me?"

"If I must."

"Go and prove it." The great man held out a hand. Man Valor removed his headband and gave it to him. Then he spun around and walked away. Any man who turned his back on an Emperor would die horribly, but Bamboo refused such honors from his warriors.

The two riflemen were standing at ease, guns at their side. A third man was waiting with a paint bucket, and it was to him that Man Valor went, and to him that he gave the first order: "Paint a target on my chest."

The youth smiled as he dipped his brush in the bucket. "Plenty of room for it," he whispered. He dabbed the brush over Man Valor's heart, then drew a circle around it with two quick strokes.

Man Valor did not look down at the artwork. He walked over to the sharpshooters. They were not grinning. They must know that men sometimes died in this proving; perhaps they had shot a few themselves.

"Firing squad, atten*tion*! Prepare to shoot me."

They went down on one knee apiece.

"Load."

Each produced a cartridge, inserted it in the breech, and closed the bolt.

Man Valor spun around and walked away. Not too far, but not too close, either, Silent had warned. The rifles could kill him as easily at ten paces as at five, and if he stood closer than five, the impacts might knock him flat on his back, which would be a very evil omen; men would not want to serve under him. A stagger was all right. One, two, three, four, five paces. Turn.

Sun and sweat and the wind stroking his hair. Life was very sweet. Thousands of eyes on him alone.

"Aim!"

The riflemen raised the butts to their shoulders and peered along the barrels. Man Valor was looking at two gun muzzles. They seemed enormous, like cannons, and much, much too close. He had forgotten to allow for the length of the barrels, so he was probably less than five paces away. Too late to do anything about that, though. It was permissible to wait a moment, Silent had warned, but more than a moment was exhibitionism or cowardice. Neither cowards nor exhibitionists would be trusted with a cadre.

"*Fire!*"

Man Valor had never been hit so hard in his life. He stumbled back about three paces, arms wheeling. Even through the yang glow, it *hurt*! He had not expected pain. But his heart was still beating and there was some blood on his chest, which was also good. Had the audience shouted, "*Hiya!*" already? He had missed it.

"Firing squad, at ease."

He marched back to Bamboo and bowed. The great man smiled and nodded. "Well done, Man Valor. I have never seen a third proving done better. You honor both your ancestors and your own name." He tied one more knot in Man Valor's headband and handed it back.

CHAPTER 13

"Snow in Harvest Moon again?" the Empress Mother glared out the window with her gaudily painted face pulled into a grotesquerie. "I do not know what the weather is coming to!" The few uncertain flakes drifting around had so far failed to make any difference to the golden roofs of Heart of the World. Perhaps they melted before they got down that far.

"Alas, Honored Mother, I fear this blizzard may impede Supreme Guardian's progress." Butterfly Sword kept a straight face for the benefit of the listening eunuchs. A great ceremony in the Hall of Celestial Peace had just adjourned. After two hours solemnly playing statue on the Golden Throne, he wanted to vault on a horse and go for a long gallop in the Game Park, leaving his cavalry escort frantically straggling far behind. Or perhaps swim in his personal lake with one of his concubines. The water would still be warm and the snow was nothing. That was the joke—after months of nagging and a myriad excuses, Supreme Guardian had finally been forced into action, setting off at the head of the Imperial Army to suppress the Bamboo Revolt. His commission had just been given to him in the name of, and under the eye of, the Emperor.

"It doesn't take much," the Empress Mother agreed knowingly. Emperor Absolute Purity was being seen in public more often these days, and it had become a tradition that he have tea with his mother afterward to discuss the business done. And mock the participants. Mimicry was a skill the Gray Helpers encouraged and one at which Butterfly Sword had always excelled. He delighted the old she-dragon with his imitations of her chief ministers, especially ancient First Mandarin.

The servants backed out of earshot, bowing. Butterfly Sword had questions to ask. Possibly he would provoke a temper storm, but he had resolved that today he would persist and risk her wrath.

The two coconspirators in high treason against the dynasty had come to share a strange, and very tenuous, friendship. He was a fraud, she a vicious killer. The harem was the center of all the palace gossip and Snow Lily passed it on to him, so he knew now that few Gray Sisters or Brothers could have equaled the Empress Mother's murder tally. She was a tyrant and a usurper, autocrat of the Good Land for nigh on a generation, and yet he could see for himself that the loneliness of power sat heavily on her aging shoulders. There was something almost pathetic in the way she had adopted her spurious child as a confidant, sharing secrets with him and wallowing in his flattery. He was the son she should have had, and she could not see him as a threat to her power. She took a prurient interest in his bedroom labors.

Novice Horse had always gotten along well with people just by being his own convivial, unflappable, and genuinely friendly self. Brother Butterfly Sword, recognizing that his life hung by a thread, had easily learned how to play toady and flatterer for the Empress Mother. She soaked up adulation, no matter how thickly he spread it. *Night soil makes crops grow.*

"Well, you have done your duty by Snow Lily and Devotion and, er . . ."

"Sweet Melody."

"Yes. The others don't inspire you?"

"They wear me out, they are all so desperate to please. Lack of success is not for lack of effort, Honored Mother."

"Possibly you need more variety." She displayed wrinkles in a satisfied smirk. "We will tell Chief Eunuch to round up some more virgins for you. How do you like them—plump, skinny, cultured, stupid . . . ?"

He found it hard to remember that the crone had started out as a concubine herself. He knew he was eccentric in seeing women as more than mere breeding stock, but that was because of his upbringing. Almost alone among the Gentle People, the Gray Brothers treated women as equals, because they knew that the Gray Sisters were at least as good as they were in the magic of seeming, at least as deadly with knife or potion, and could often beat them at unarmed combat, too. Novice Horse had learned that lesson from sassing Sister Lotus, his anatomy instructor, at about age fifteen. Lotus had been at least twice his age and half his size, but she had taken him to the wrestling gym and thrown him around the floor until he was so bruised he looked like a bunch of grapes. A month or so later, she had rewarded his improved attitude by ordering him into her bed and humbling him there also.

"Congenial," he said. "I don't want my seraglio to be a permanent cat fight. Let the Pearl Concubine make the final choice." Seeing the Empress Mother starting to bristle, as she did whenever he showed any trace of disagreeing with her wishes, he quickly added, "She has to live with them all day. If I don't like their looks, I can just blow out the lamp and tell them to be quiet."

She chuckled. "So you can, dear boy! So you can."

So he was her dear boy today. "Honored Mother, I am deeply troubled by so many reports of famine and floods, and yet First Mandarin never seems to take any action. Can you do nothing to ease the lot of the peasants?"

She hissed like a serpent and her eyes glittered. "You expect me to stop floods?"

"No, Your Majesty. But cannot you order food moved into the areas where people are starving?"

"From where? You think we have bloated granaries all over the Empire? Who would pay for that food, or pay to move it, and how—on men's backs? I have never known a year when people were not starving somewhere and the weather is always bad before an opening."

"An opening of what?" Surely, she did not believe the crazy myths about the Portal of Worlds? Carvings on rock faces did not *open*.

"None of your business. You work hard on all those pretty girls I give you and don't worry about history."

She hadn't started making threats yet, so he pushed on.

"I know you cannot stop floods, but I wonder about warnings. When the Golden River starts rising in Wanrong, the governor reports to the throne. But does he rush warnings downstream, to Nanling and Shashi?"

The Empress Mother slammed her bowl down, splashing tea everywhere. Her face flamed red under the face paint. "So now you think you really are the Emperor, do you? Peasant filth! I dragged you out of the gutter and I can bury you head down in a cesspit. And I will, if you start getting ideas. I'll have that Snow Lily of yours whipped before your eyes, no matter how close she is to term!"

"Mercy, Your Majesty, mercy! I was only trying to help!"

She beat on the table with both fists. "You can help with that long cock of yours, and if you meddle in anything else, I'll have it cut off and put you to work in the stables."

She had never raged at him quite like this before. Obviously, she did not know the answer to his innocently intended question about warnings. Perhaps no one had ever asked it before.

CHAPTER 14

Silky's expedition had left Humble Duty the morning after the fight in the alley, but from then on, it had traveled by traditional means. Thousands of skiffs and little junks plied the Jade River, and although they varied enormously in their smell, comfort, and resistance to rain, and although their owners might be skilled, honest, and helpful, or none of those, the journey should still have been completed in another month, or a month and a half at the most.

Alas, few of the boatmen would venture farther than three days' travel from their families at the best of times, and Nightingale Moon brought two great broom stars to blaze in the heavens, so terrifying to the river folk that only a few hours around noontime every day were judged auspicious for travel. The travelers found themselves stranded in a succession of squalid fishing villages. Not until the waning of Lotus Moon were the locals willing to believe that the world would not come to an end right away.

By then, the winds were consistently and contrarily contrary. Thunder Moon brought almost continuous rain, raising the river to dangerous rates of flow. Silky gabbled that floods were another omen foretelling an opening of the Portal, but he took small comfort from the fact. Their journey seemed to be cursed. Worse, it seemed doomed to be everlasting.

Harvest Moon's deluges ruined the crops and promised famine before next summer. Chrysanthemum Moon saw an end to the rain, but the rivers were still too high for travel. Verdant Harmony, too bloated now to find comfort in any position, swore she was going to drop triplets, and very soon.

By this time, Silky was on the verge of madness and might have stepped over it had Brother Luminous not been there, reassuring him that all journeys end and women had been giving birth to babies for a very long time. Having completed three contracts, the older man must be enormously rich in his own right, but he enjoyed the life of a Gray Helper and showed no signs of retiring or losing his deadly touch—his tally was a secret, but reputed to be more than forty. Most of the time, he seemed to be plump, fatherly, and jovial, with an armor of fat and a wispy white beard. His true appearance was another secret.

Fortunately, Plum Blossom offered Silky what help she could for stress. He denied this to Verdant, but she clearly refused to believe him.

On a bitterly cold and windy day in Falling Leaf Moon, a stinky little cargo junk finally brought them to Cherish, which was the last settlement of any size on the headwaters of the Jade and thus served as the start of the Wilderness Road. The sky had cleared at last, and the weary travelers, huddled in blankets, had a fine view of its many jetties and caravanserais, with the Fortress Hills beyond and the towering, ice-capped peaks of the Western Wall in the distance. The most distinctive feature of Cherish was an ominous stone fortress, towering above all other buildings, garrisoned by the Imperial Army, and a reminder that savage tribes lurked on the far side of Swordcut Pass. Not all the men who rode the Wilderness Road were peaceable traders.

"It is late in season to explore opportunities in real estate," Luminous proclaimed. Even he had lost his normal joviality by now; they were all so sick of travel. "But regard the fine mansions carpeting that hillside. Our first priority must be to rent a house."

"No," Verdant declared.

Suddenly, her fingers were digging into Silky's arm so hard that he realized that something must be wrong and turned to regard her in dismay.

"What's the matter?"

"Nothing yet," she replied. "But your first priority must be to find me a midwife."

— IV —
THE YEAR OF
THE RAVEN

CHAPTER 1

With a hushed rustle of silk and a faint pad of slippers on tiles, the Son of the Sun mounted three steps to the dais. Majestically, he trailed his train across to the Golden Throne and turned to set his divine buttocks on its silken cushion. He composed his features in the stoic mindlessness they would have to bear for the next hour or so; servants adjusted his draperies. The wall of golden fretwork just in front of his toes was in fact an ornate screen meant to hide these preliminary indignities. The retainers withdrew; he took a deep breath and signaled his readiness with a barely perceptible nod.

Trumpets blared, gongs sounded. The screen parted, its halves sliding wide to reveal the celestial Son of the Sun to his Universal Harmonious Beneficence, a magnified Great Council, a thousand or so Grand of the Land gathered in the Hall of Celestial Peace, all of them with their foreheads pressed to the floor and their backsides raised to Heaven like dabbling ducks. Too many people were starting to believe the Bamboo Banner's insistence that Emperor Absolute Purity was dead, so the Empress Mother was reluctantly allowing the imposter to emerge more often and to be displayed to selected worthies. Commoners never set eyes on their ruler, of course, even when he was genuine.

Out beyond the frosted windows, the park with its lakes and pagodas lay snowbound and icebound in the steely fangs of Wolf Moon. The Feast of Snowy Owls had passed without the intrusion of dancing demons that had ruined last year's celebration. This was the third day of the new year, the first sufficiently auspicious day for such a gathering. Auspicious, but cold as the Empress Mother's heart. Rows of glowing braziers did nothing to banish the chill in the hall. As the assembled worthies completed their prostrations and sat back on their heels, their breath steamed.

Snow Lily was in labor. More than anything in the world, Butterfly Sword wanted to be there with her, comforting and encouraging. Of course, no man would ever be allowed into a birthing room, even an Emperor, and he must never lose face by canceling an important ceremony after it had been announced. Why should a mere birthing interest him? He had many concubines, and although the Pearl Concubine was known to be his favorite, Devotion and Sweet Melody were also with child. He was young and fertile, so if this one was not a son to carry on the dynasty, then the next or the next . . .

Snow Lily was in labor and he kept thinking of Moth. Poor Moth! She had done her duty at Huarache, teaching him Palace Voice and proving his ability to sire children. She had known the risks. They had both guessed what was afoot when they identified the picture of Zealous Righteousness in their room, so Horse had tried to talk her out of it. She had persisted, and after three nights of abstinence, he had succumbed to her wiles. She had been small and light, flitting through life, delicate as a child, with tiny breasts and nipples like pink pearls. He had felt like such a lumbering hulk beside her! Her hands together could barely meet around his forearm. The skill in those tiny hands could make him tempered steel or a great heap of noodle paste. She had conceived, as ordered. In Hare Moon, Lady Twilight had returned to the priory to fetch Brother Butterfly Sword, and he had seen Sister Moth no more.

So why was he thinking of her now, for ancestors' sake? Guilt? Terror? The cases were quite different. Certainly, Moth would not have been allowed to come to term, even if she had survived at all. He knew enough of the Empress Mother's techniques to know that her accomplices had very short lives. *Snow Lily was in labor; he kept thinking of Moth.*

Snow Lily was bigger than Moth had been, but not by much. A big bull bred a big calf.

Today was a very auspicious day, a good day to give birth. Tomorrow would be very inauspicious. How long must Snow Lily endure the torment? Better the death of a thousand cuts than what she must be going through now, whereas Butterfly Sword, who had caused her present torment, had nothing better to do than sit there like a burl on a tree and be worshipped. The Empress Mother had learned to trust him, or else had learned to trust the stupidity of the court. The hoax had survived nine months, and no one was going to violate this sacred ritual by leaping up and shouting that the youth on the throne was an imposter. No, he was the Lord of the High and the Low. He had presided at councils, reviewed a march past of troops, performed sacrifices, gone hunting in the park, been seen boating on several of the lakes with the Pearl Concubine—he had even been observed taking the oars himself.

The Empress Mother had blazed in rage at him over that. "No Emperor ever demeaned himself so! You have shattered the precedents of five thousand years!"

"Which no imposter would ever dare to do, yes?" he had said with his best cute-boy smile, which often worked on the old terror. "And besides, what scribe would ever have dared to record such an undignified act?"

She had glared at him, then pulled a face, and finally changed the subject, which was as close as she could ever get to admitting that he might have a point. They were fellow conspirators. A very odd pair indeed—she ruled the Empire and he was garbage from the gutter, but they were cooperating to cuckold a dynasty.

And now their intrigue was literally bearing fruit. An imperial concubine was in labor with the imposter's child. How many people in this great congregation knew the terrible truth? Chief Eunuch, of course, for he knew everything. First Mandarin, probably, for the same reason. Supreme Guardian, certainly not; the Empress Mother was far too acute to trust the army to anyone with more brains than a louse. She would never let the head of the army anywhere near such a secret. The eunuch Joyous Diligence was certainly in on the plot, for he was the imposter's handler, so that all Butterfly Sword's requests or queries, and most of the Empress Mother's orders, were passed through him. He would be here somewhere, watching through a spyhole. Certainly, none of the princes suspected, nor did the ambassadors from the barbarian kingdoms who had been deliberately placed right at the back of the assembly.

Everyone who could possibly get into this celebration was there, waiting to present their New Year gifts to the Son of the Sun. Only one notable was absent, and very conspicuously so. The Empress Mother was otherwise engaged, supervising the delivery of her fraudulent grandchild. Everyone knew that Pearl Concubine was in labor.

It was ironic that the supreme ruler of the Good Land had organized the greatest of all possible treasons. If this child turned out to be a boy, the Empress Mother would have little further use for her hired stud. The unfortunate accident or sudden fever wouldn't happen right away, of course, but everyone who knew of the deception would be silenced—Snow Lily, Joyous Diligence, Chief Eunuch, and most especially Butterfly Sword.

He had known the palace was a death trap before he ever set foot in it.

The ceremony began. The princes came first, in strict order of rank, each being proclaimed, kowtowing, laying his gift before the throne—although many brought a servant along to do the heavy work. The eunuchs then removed it from the hall, and by nightfall would have removed most of the loot out of the palace altogether. Jeweled caskets, carved jade, bronze or porcelain vessels—any one piece would support a family for a lifetime, but the scale of theft in Sublime Mountain was incredible. It was a wonder the Golden Throne itself remained.

The Emperor had nothing to do but sit and look imperious. Senior princes might be awarded small nods if he was feeling benevolent, which that day he most decidedly was not. What a pathetic lot they were, too! Butterfly Sword could almost approve of the Empress Mother's deception. Yes, she was ruthless, but sometimes rue was inappropriate. Yes, she was motivated by a consuming hunger for power, but in all truth no one anywhere close to the line of descent seemed capable of replacing her idiot son. Prince Tungusic Vision had the best claim but was so senile that he had been excused from attending court now, and he was the last of his line. After him, Prince Gratify Poet was the most qualified, and he had a young grandson to succeed him. But Gratify Poet had been born under a very evil star. He alternated between periods of melancholy when he was incapable of doing anything and maniacal rages in which he had been known to kill people. Prince Crystal Sea had succumbed to his opium habit. Prince Apotheosis was reputedly a deaf mute.

Where was the real Emperor Absolute Purity now? It would be very out of character for the Empress Mother to have kept her son alive as evidence of her perfidy. Whatever crooked paths she walked, she never left witnesses behind. As soon as she had a spurious grandson to continue her regency, then the imposter would go also and the fraud would be shut down. For a year, Butterfly Sword had lived under sentence of death, and execution time was drawing near.

Another jade vase, another frightful poem . . .

He remembered the day he had been smuggled into the sacred

precincts of the Great Within in a wagonload of pillows. At daybreak, he had been dressed in finery and borne in a curtained palanquin to the Summer Palace. That evening, he had met a terrified naked child. Somehow, he had never realized that concubines began as virgins, yet she had been so desperate to please him.

And now she was in labor. His seed had killed Moth. Would it kill Snow Lily?

The New Year levee still had hours to go. They were down to mandarins of the third rank now, bringing them forward in tens to present their gifts. The latest ten were just rising, the eunuchs sweeping forward to remove the booty, and—

Boom!

The court froze. One elderly mandarin lost his balance and fell, but even he did not move after that.

Boom!

Five guns for a girl, nineteen for a boy.

Boom!

The Emperor, especially, must show no emotion.

Boom!

Nobody was breathing.

Boom!

Silence.

More silence.

The Son of the Sun released his breath very gently. He was safe for now. Snow Lily was safe—assuming she survived the birthing. Diligence and Sweet Melody would not come to term for months yet. During that reprieve, could he organize an escape from Sublime Mountain? An escape for himself and Snow Lily and their daughter? In this madhouse of corruption, whom could he possibly trust to help him?

It was late that night before the Emperor was able to view the imperial baby, named Snowbell by her grandmother. Having never seen a newborn before, he was appalled at how tiny and vulnerable she seemed. Snow Lily was asleep; they would have wakened her had he not forbidden it.

So he was a father? He spent the rest of the night staring into the darkness, spinning webs that fell apart as soon as he looked at them with any scrutiny. Concubine Dawn Clouds slept peacefully at his side, although she had been distressed earlier by His Majesty's lack of interest.

His child was safe enough, but probably doomed to a life of spinsterhood and unbroken boredom in the palace. While the throne could not descend through the female line, very few men were sufficiently noble to marry a princess. Snow Lily was as doomed as he was—more so, in fact, because he was still a Gray Brother. If he could somehow find the right clothes, he could make himself seem a eunuch or a soldier and try walking out the gate. That might work for him, but abducting an imperial concubine and an imperial princess was as unlikely as flying away on a magic carpet.

He must find help, and he decided to play by the Empress Mother's rules. She had achieved the impossible simply because it was unthinkable. Butterfly Sword's best bet was to turn her own trusties against her.

Every morning, as the imperial upper lip was being shaved— like most young males of the Gentle People, Butterfly Sword had so few chin hairs that it was easier to pluck them than shave them—Joyous Diligence appeared to receive His Imperial Majesty's orders for the day and explain which ones His Majesty's imperious mother would forbid him to accept. Large and plump, probably not much past thirty, and sumptuously dressed, of course, he had probably been altered quite recently, because he still sported a few hairs on his lip and his voice had not yet become shrill and strident. Like most eunuchs, he always reeked of perfume intended to disguise his sour urinal smell.

The barber and other servants withdrew out of earshot; the Keeper of Hours completed his kowtow and remained on his knees.

"So I am a father," Butterfly Sword said.

"The Empire rejoices at Your Majesty's good fortune. Salutes have—"

"Good fortune that it wasn't a boy."

A skilled actor stays in character at all times. Joyous Diligence pretended to misunderstand. "Of course the Good Land eagerly awaits a brother for Princess Snowbell."

"I mean, as you well know, that as soon as I have given the Empress Mother a grandson, she will have no further use for me. I will be nothing but a threat to be removed, right?"

"Your Majesty's humble servant is distraught to confess that he fails to understand what—"

"Stop that! I know who I am. You know who I am not. If either Sweet Melody or Devotion produces a boy, my days will be numbered. And so will yours be, my obsequious friend! You know too much."

Joyous Diligence remained on his knees, eyes wide, staring up at his master without a word. But he was very far from stupid.

"How many others around the palace are in on the deception?" Butterfly Sword inquired. "Chief Eunuch must be. First Mandarin? Is Absolute Purity himself still breathing regularly? How many?" He would not mention Snow Lily.

"I have no idea," Joyous Diligence said, dropping the pretense of respect. "Why ask? No one will tell you."

"Because of what I told you. As soon as she has a baby prince to play with, the tigress will pounce. I, for one, intend to make a break for it before then, and I expect you do, too, but the moment one of us disappears, the rest are compost."

This wasn't going to work, he saw. The basic requirement for bribery was something valuable to offer. He was penniless and already under sentence of death. Joyous Diligence was probably a very wealthy man, if he had managed to stash his loot in a safe place outside the palace walls.

"You would never get out of the Great Within, imposter," the eunuch said, barely hiding a sneer. "There are never less than a dozen pairs of eyes on you when you step through that door. Whenever you go riding, troops of cavalry guard every possible exit. At night, men with dogs patrol the grounds around whichever palace you are occupying."

"That's why I am suggesting we form a partnership. You could arrange a small lapse in security. And I . . ." *Um?*

"And you?"

Butterfly Sword laughed. "And I do not believe a word you say. There may be many people guarding me, but they cannot all be aware that I am not the genuine Emperor. Maybe an officer or two. The rest think they are guarding me, not restraining me. Who gets obeyed when I start shouting orders?"

"I expect the officer shoots you dead," Joyous Diligence said. "And I doubt if I am in as much danger as you think, but it is an interesting idea and I will discuss it with my father."

A shiver of alarm ran down the imperial imposter's backbone. "I am not familiar with your father."

"He has the honor of being Your Majesty's Chief Eunuch."

Oh, bollocks! The family resemblance was obvious now it was pointed out. Butterfly Sword stammered. "I . . . I find that a curious paradox."

"It is not uncommon, *Your Majesty.*" There was no respect in that title, only contempt. "My father is a eunuch, as was his father before him. Your Majesty graciously allows his servants to leave the palace as long as we return by dark. I have a house and family in town. Once I had sired the sons I needed, I underwent the operation. They may do the same in their time. When my revered father wanted someone he could trust absolutely to supervise a valuable guest, he chose me. Now, is there anything I can do for you this morning, August Son of the Sun?"

"Is there something you would particularly like to steal?"

"Your Majesty is most generous. I do have my eye on that jade horse, but it is a little too heavy to carry. I will get one of my brothers to assist me. May Heaven sustain you, lord." Joyous Diligence bowed and took his leave.

CHAPTER 2

The Firstborn was dying. His coughing in the darkness was growing weaker, and he had not eaten for two days. He did not know that they had no food to give him, because he had not asked for anything to eat. Shard Gingko lay beside him, wrapped in the same blanket, hoping thereby to keep him warm. They had long since run out of fuel, so the only thing heating the tiny cave was Splendid Steed, the donkey, and she had not eaten for two days, either. Even she was too weak to complain now. Mouse had gone away to look for help in the worst of the blizzard and must be presumed dead by now.

When the storm ended, perhaps Shard would find the strength to saddle Splendid Steed, and perhaps she would have the strength to carry him to somewhere, and perhaps that place would have some food and fuel to spare to save the First-born's life.

Back at High Abode, Shard had foreseen the journey south to Dongguan as being long but relatively easy—down the Clay River to the Grand Canal, south to the Great Fish River, and then upstream to Dongguan. Three months or perhaps four, he had guessed, but there he was thinking like a mandarin, as the Firstborn had explained.

"The Emperor will have ordered the army south by now, which means the canal will be closed to all other traffic. Rebels always stay away from the canal, because they know the army controls it and will destroy the locks rather than let insurgents use it. The Bamboo Banner will keep well inland as it heads north."

"Are you certain that it will head north, Master?"

The Firstborn had smiled his sad, heartrending smile. "Where else can it go? Rebellions almost always begin in the south, but even when one doesn't, all that rebels ever think of is marching on Heart of the World to explain to the Emperor that he must govern more wisely so their children don't starve. Sometimes, the Emperor flees and the nastiest of the rebel leaders takes the Golden Throne. More usually, the army meets the rebels halfway and routs them. When soldiers fight farmers, the farmers lose." He sighed, looking very young and frail. "Now guns have made it much worse."

All the rivers ran east. "You are planning to *walk* to Dong-guan?" Shard Gingko glanced down at the reed-thin, twisted legs.

Sometimes, the Firstborn seemed like the legendary sage of his reputation, pouring out wisdom. At others, he was only a boy, an irreverent one at that. He smirked. "You don't have to come."

"Yes, I do."

The Urfather raised a hand in blessing and his smile changed from mockery to gratitude, from boyish to ageless. "It won't be quite as far as you think. The army almost always turns off from the canal at the Golden River and heads inland. It intercepts the rebels in Jingyan, Shashi, or Wanrong. That is where we must go."

For thousands of years, that crippled boy had not met a problem he had not met before, and he had never intended to walk half the length of the Empire on his own twisted legs. He no sooner asked some elders to have a bamboo carrying chair made for him than it was done and strong young men were fighting over the honor of carrying him on to the next village. So it went—a morning's journey, an afternoon of teaching and preaching, and next day on to the next village. His bearers sang as they trotted. Mouse could keep up, but poor old Shard was usually left hobbling far behind. He worried that Sunlight was leaving an obvious trail for the Emperor's men to follow, so he always warned the village elders not to let news of the Urfather's passing spread, and evidently they never did.

Day after day, month after month.

> The disciple said, "Master, how can I tell what is good from what is evil?"
>
> The master said, "Tell me a good you know and an evil you know."
>
> The disciple said, "Giving alms is good and stealing is evil."
>
> The master said, "And which one hurts other people?"

By Fog Moon, the weather had turned, and they had been in Wanrong, in country too dry to grow rice or even barley. Rumors of famine and insurrection had been growing ever more ominous. Villages lay farther apart, too far for young men to run in a morning. Crops gave way to orchards and vines, then charcoal burning and mining. But Sunlight had said, *Miracles are only a matter of patience*, and sure enough, one village had given him a donkey. It would have cost far more than he could pay, but he had accepted the charity, named her Splendid Steed, and continued on his way with his disciples trudging alongside.

Shard Gingko had known that their luck must run out eventually. Fog Moon waned. Cold Moon waxed and then waned. Wolf Moon brought in the new year with a blizzard. Shard Gingko and Mouse would have died the first day, but the Firstborn knew the country, all the country.

"This way," he said, pointing. "There used to be a forest here.

There used to be forest everywhere. Rivers did not flood in those days. Up this valley . . ."

He led them to the cave, he riding the donkey and Mouse pulling it, although he often had to go back to help Shard also. Mouse was growing fast. Without his strength, they would have all perished. There was a spring nearby, and Mouse gathered thorns and shrubs for fuel, but the blizzard soon buried the landscape and the fuel ran out. The food ran out. The All-Wise had been running a fever and should not have been traveling at all.

A whisper in his ear: "Grandfather?"

Shard Gingko had been dozing without knowing it. He started awake to the dark and the cold. At least the cold kept down the stench of donkey dung. Water was dripping somewhere. "Master?"

"Thank you. For all you have done. It was a good try. Thank Mouse for me."

"It is not over yet," Shard said gamely. "Listen! The wind has stopped. As soon as it is light, we can be on our way. How far to the next village?" He was numb with cold and the frail youth he held was an icicle.

For a while, there was no reply. Then the Firstborn had another coughing fit, long and painful.

When he recovered, he croaked, "It was never possible. I should have told you. The Portal of Worlds is going to open."

"What has that got to do with it?"

"Know you of Humble Voice?"

"A sage of the Ninth Dynasty who wrote of the Portal. His work has been lost, but he is quoted by other writers."

The Firstborn tried to chuckle and was taken with another coughing fit. "I expect the Son of the Sun has the original and makes sure no one else sees it. Humble Voice was a big man, loud, and never humble, but he wrote an exquisite fine hand."

He paused to cough again and then continued, sounding weaker then ever. "I am wrong. It was he who said, *To claim wisdom is to reveal ignorance*. So he was humble once."

"You should save your strength, Master."

"I have none left to save," the lad whispered. "Listen, and write when you have light. Humble Voice gathered all the auguries he could find that predict an opening. The Portal opens rarely, about once in a thousand years. I know of seven openings since I first came to the Good Land. When I saw that inscription on the mountain face, the barbarians who lived near there before the coming of the Gentle People swore that it was indeed a real door, and their ancestors had witnessed it opening.

"Humble Voice listed floods, famines, and insurrection, but those can happen any time. Earthquakes the same. Most of the others are seen often in the years before the Portal opens, but not always—a fire mountain in the Year of the Firebird, an earthquake in the Year of the Raven . . . many dying stars. All of these may be seen before the opening of the gate, or in cycles when it does not open. Humble Voice knew of four portents that have never failed. *The Nightingale sings to two broom stars*. We saw this. *The dynasty falls, either just before or just after the opening*. That is why the Emperor was so anxious to have me answer his questions. His eagerness was such that I think a change of dynasty must be a good thing in this case. It usually is, for a while. Is there water?"

Shard Gingko stirred himself. "I can go and fetch some."

"Wait till I am done. My time is short." The Firstborn coughed again, but weakly, as if it hurt. "Where was I? A third sure omen is: *Demons dance at Snowy Owls*. We have heard many times that this happened last year."

"But, Master," Shard Gingko said, anxious to take over the talking for a moment and save the Firstborn's voice, "you must have seen many openings, and Humble Voice must have garnered the truth of what really did happen at those times. There are so many legends! Did Outlanders really pour out to overrun the Good Land? I wonder if it was just that the Portal stands close by the Wilderness Road to Swordcut Pass. Was that how the Outlanders came, and ignorant people assumed they had come through the Portal? Thus an opening may merely signal their coming, but does not mean that they will emerge through the Portal. And as for Emperor Virtuous Ruler—who supposedly rode into the Portal at the head of his army and never returned—is it not at least possible that he was pursuing an Outlander horde through the Swordcut Pass and was ambushed in the desert beyond?"

The Firstborn sighed. "I cannot tell you, friend, because there is an omen that Humble Voice did not know of, that only I know. And that is that the Firstborn is not there. Heaven has never let me see the Portal stand open. I very rarely come even this close. Always I die before it opens, and am not reborn until the Year of the Phoenix, two years later. Often, I am born far away. By the time I am old enough to question, men's memories are already blurred and uncertain. Whatever it is that happens, it must be dread, for I have never found a witness who stayed to watch. Men flee. Or, if they do not, they go mad, or they do not live to speak of what they saw."

Shard stared at the faint trace of the icicles that decorated the cave roof. Some were ice and some were stone, and it could not possibly be dawn already.

"Look, Master! There is light!" Splendid Steed had raised her head and Shard Gingko could make out the shape of her ears against the cave mouth.

Releasing Sunlight, he wriggled out from the blankets, painfully stiff and weak. He crawled past the donkey and rose unsteadily to his feet, leaning against one of the white stone pillars that Heaven had put there to support the cave roof. He heard voices just an instant before a man pushed aside the hurdle and flimsy old blanket that they used as a door.

"Are we in time?" the man shouted. It was Mouse, huge in thick padded clothing. "We have brought food, and oil, and charcoal. And the most virtuous Lady Cataract has sent soft bedding and warm furs. Her own physician follows with a sled and horses to pull it; they will be here within an hour."

Shard Gingko stammered, too overcome with joy to speak.

Behind him, the Firstborn whispered, "Yes. You are in time. This time, you are in time."

CHAPTER 3

Spring had come to Cherish at last. The frigid, dust-laden winds of winter had given way to warm showers. Swallows were back, hills were turning green again, cracked lips were healing.

Poor Silky had spent a very dreary morning in the gloomy fortress of Cherish, in the company of General Scarlet Meadow, the governor. Most towns and cities were run by mandarins who, while not honest, at least kept watch on one another so that any shortfall in the Emperor's taxes remained within traditional limits. Frontier stations like Cherish were run by the army, and their governors were petty monarchs.

Scarlet Meadow was a sour, wizened little man with a hideous scar across his face. He had his mandarin clerks thoroughly cowed—none of them being of higher rank than second anyway—and even the abbess of the House of Joyful Departure almost treated him as an equal, which Silky found quite shocking. Fortunately, she had bought into Silky's venture and now had brought the governor on side also, at least for the moment. He had spent the last two hours showing Silky his collection of antique swords.

Silky had enthused, of course, and had presented His Excellency with an addition for his collection, a very valuable archaic bronze blade from the Sixth Dynasty, specially made by the Gray Helpers' skilled counterfeiters in the House of Joyful Departure on the far side of the town square.

They had drunk tea.

At last, it was time to talk business.

The document that Silky had asked to borrow . . . ?

"Ah, yes." The little soldier fixed him with his remaining eye, canting his head like a chicken. "Such papers are supposed to be utterly secret, of course. Even I am not supposed to pry. . . . But I suppose that a brief look at just one, here in my study, would not endanger either of us . . . unduly."

He was trying to raise the price.

"I need to compare the details with data on several others back in my studio, Your Excellency, *as I thought our mutual friend explained.*"

Soldier and assassin regarded each other for several seconds. "You know her well?"

"Not especially, but we have many friends in common."

Scarlet Meadow sighed, and rose to fetch the scroll he had promised.

Wise of him.

Silky solemnly promised to return it within four days, five at the most. In a few more minutes, he was on his horse and riding home through the dogs, carts, camels, raucous street vendors, and chickens of Cherish, whistling happily.

His project was on the move at last.

The original plan, that complex plot that the Gray Abbot of Wedlock had worked on for so many years, had fallen like a pagoda of mahjong tiles before the fist of reality. The price of real estate in the Fortress Hills had not plummeted as the omens mounted and the Year of the Firebird drew nearer. The locals refused to heed either legends or portents. The Emperor's mandarins might have records of the Portal opening, but no folk memory could remain after almost a thousand years. The price of real estate had not risen, either. In fact it never changed, because nobody ever sold any. The Emperor relied on his holdings to supply him with the finest horses in the Good Land, while the rest of the landowners were not about to give up their petty fiefdoms. They mostly claimed to be princes, defying anyone to deny it, although all were descended from old-time brigands, smugglers, or barbarian invaders. No doubt some of them still piously followed family traditions.

Brother Silky could be just as stubborn as they. He refused to lose face by crawling back to Wedlock empty-handed. If they would not listen to reason, he would just have to show them how unreasonable he could be.

The winter had not been all gloom and frustration, though. He enjoyed being the possessor of a loud and healthy son and a very fine house, both of them provided by his wife. He owned half a dozen horses, too, and even Verdant had taken up riding, there being few other interesting things to do out there on the frontier. The house itself stood on the hillside above the town and commanded a fine view of the river. Like its neighbors, it was enclosed by a high stone wall topped with bronze spikes and hooks.

Recognized and saluted by Bold Star, the rheumatic gatekeeper, Silky rode into his domain and around to the stable yard at the back, where he dismounted. Walnut Shell came hurrying out from the stable to take his reins. The lad was young to be trusted with such an establishment, but he managed it well with the help of two boys. He was so bright and eager to please, in fact, that Silky had suspected him of spying for either the Gray Abbess or the governor. Having tailed him a couple of times, Silky had established that he was most likely reporting to the mandarins of the tax department. They would not likely be exchanging notes with the governor, and were no danger in themselves, since smuggling was about the only crime Silky *wasn't* planning to commit.

He had hired Walnut Shell at a salary about three times more than he could have expected, and then produced a couple of very sharp knives, promising to detach certain valuable portions of the lad's anatomy if he increased his income by as much as one handful of rice. So far, the arrangement seemed to be working.

"The mistress home?"

Walnut Shell's smile flashed the whitest teeth in Shashi Province. "Her Ladyship has gone riding with the Lady Plum Blossom, Master."

Good. That meant Silky could get right to work on the scroll in his satchel. Brother Luminous would still be studying ink-on-silk painting of the Tenth Dynasty down at the House of Joyful Departure.

But first, Silky went to call on Thunderbot, known to some people as Silkworm. He turned out to be awake and colicky. He was being walked by White Petal, his cretinous wet nurse. Silky took him and gave him a kiss. Thunderbot eyed him suspiciously and then smiled. As always when that happened, the heavens opened, a thousand ancestors cheered, and his father almost melted.

"Oh, that is magnificent! If you can just keep that smile, my son, the world will be yours for the taking. People will turn over all their possessions to you and die of happiness at your feet. But whatever you do, never *mean* it! That would be fatal. Lesson one, my dearest, is *never trust anyone*."

Thunderbot considered his father's advice, crumpled his face up in fury, and let rip again.

"That's my boy!" Silky said. "You didn't mean it after all. Well done." He handed the noisy bundle back to his keeper and beat a quick retreat to the workroom he shared with Brother Luminous and Plum Blossom, which the servants never entered.

There, he made himself comfortable on a cushion under the window and began to study the scroll. It was longer than he had expected, listing not only a dozen minor bequests, but also every tussock of land Sky Hammer 7 claimed to own. No doubt some of those claims lay between legend and myth, but the excessive detail was a sensible precaution against having some parcels disappear from the governor's archives; it meant more work for Silky but also a greater air of authenticity for the fake documents he would prepare. The seals were very simple and old-fashioned, which was good. New seals were harder to forge.

"You're back early."

His twitch of alarm almost lifted him off the cushion. A Gray Brother should never let himself be taken by surprise in case he wasn't who he was supposed to be. Fortunately, it was Verdant. He jumped up and went to hug her. A luscious big armful she was.

"Work to do here," he said. "By sunset, I will be exhausted and need to go to bed very early."

She evaded his embrace. "How many people did you kill this time?"

Angry, he stalked over and closed the door. "Not funny to say things like that. And that is a confidential—"

Too late. She was examining the scroll. "Who is Sky Hammer 7 and what are you doing with his will?"

She was being difficult these days. Back in Wedlock, she and her mother had played the rich lady role before their friends—although to call them that was a misuse of the word—and left the problems of the real world to their husbands and sons. Here in Cherish, she was free to act as she pleased. Silky should have kept her on a tighter rein, that was the trouble, and it was too late to start now. Gray Sisters had been treated as responsible adults all their lives, but Verdant had been brought up to be a decorative baby-making machine and servant herder. She did not know how to handle reality. He had not foreseen this difficulty.

"You're happier not knowing, darling."

Again she evaded his efforts to hug her. "Answer my question."

"Be careful! You know I never lie to you."

"I want the truth."

He shrugged. "We came here to buy land, remember? Well the landowners refuse to sell, which is very unreasonable of them. They force me to use other methods."

"Such as murder?"

"No murder. That old man owns more of the Fortress Hills than anyone except the Emperor. He is decrepit and dying, so he has no further use for them. I am going to change his will to leave everything to you. No murder needed, just a little patience."

"And what about"—Verdant paused, scanning the scroll—"Sky Rider? Won't he wonder why his father cut him out of his will?"

"Possibly. But why should he have been born into all that wealth when I was born to nothing at all? Why can he sacrifice to his ancestors back for three dynasties and I don't even know my mother's name, let alone my father's? Life is never fair and it will do him a lot of good to learn that, even at his age."

"Won't there be a copy of this will on file in the governor's palace?"

"I checked. There isn't." Not now.

Verdant threw the scroll down. "I don't want his land! Even if you don't plan to kill him, which I do not believe, you certainly intend to rob his family. I won't be party to it."

This time, he did fold his arms around her. Big as she was, he was faster and stronger. He held her despite her struggles.

"You listen to me, beloved," he said grimly. "I swore to make you rich, and rich you will be. If you don't need wealth, our son does. If I could gain it honestly, I would. If I can do it with a little forgery, I will. If you won't let me do it that way, then I really will have to go back to killing people and I truly do not want that. Which is it to be?"

"I will report you to the governor!"

"Then he will put me to the death of a thousand cuts and throw you in jail as a witness and accomplice. Is that what you want?"

She struggled more. He tightened his grip.

"You are crazy!" she said, trying to look frightened, although she knew she was in no danger from him.

"No, I am scum, remember? You should have been more careful when you put yourself out to stud." She began to cry and he waited, not relaxing his hold. "You knew what I was," he said. "I haven't changed. Now, whose name do I put in as beneficiary? Yours or your father's?"

"Your own."

"No. I don't steal from my client. The brotherhood would kill me. Your name or his?"

She was silent. He waited, although his body was starting to betray him. "Neither."

"No. Then the Order's, a pious bequest. I can do it that way and still get my cut. You won't get anything. I'll buy you a good pair of shoes and you can walk home. But you won't get Silkworm. My son stays with me."

"You swear that you are not going to murder anyone?"

"Of course I swear."

"My name, then."

"Good!" He released her. "I'll make it up to you tonight in bed, I promise. Go and see to your eyes, they're all red."

She slammed the door behind her. He probably would name the Gray Helpers as beneficiary. Nobody would dare challenge a bequest to the Order; and if anyone did, no sane judge would rule in their favor.

Plum Blossom entered. "What was all that about?"

"An attack of postpartum conscience," Silky said grumpily. He picked up the scroll of contention. "I just promised that we won't kill Sky Hammer."

"Did you mean it?"

"Of course not, but warn Brother Luminous not to mention the plan, will you?"

Murder? Grand larceny? How had she ever let herself be trapped in this madhouse? Verdant stormed off to seek comfort from her son, but for once Silkworm was sleeping like a baby. He suffered a lot from colic, and it would be folly to risk wakening him and provoke a few more hours' screaming. So Verdant just smiled and nodded approvingly to White Petal and walked out again. Even as infants, men were useless.

She had brought it on herself, she knew. As the Teacher of the Rose said, *Who can escape the wrath of ancestors betrayed?* She had resented her father's control over the money she had inherited, and had plotted against him. Even though she had been encouraged by her mother, that was not correct behavior. That the money had come to her by murder made it worse, although she had not known that. She had not deviated from her rebellion when Silky admitted the terrible crimes that had been done in her name. No, she had continued prostituting herself to a vulgar sand warrior! Small wonder her ancestors turned their faces from her now.

What was the right course? Even if her father was as guilty of Distant Cloud's murder as the assassins he had hired, she must return to her parents and beg forgiveness. But who would help her? How could she escape? And how could she leave Silkworm behind to be raised as a thief and murderer by a thief and murderer?

Half-minded to go for another ride on this fine spring day, she walked out to the stable yard. The boys were still rubbing down her horse under the watchful eye of Walnut Shell, who was sitting on a stool beside the stable door, cleaning tack with soap and water. Clad only in cotton breeches, he displayed the same dense, compact build as Silky did when he was a sand warrior, a far cry from the senile blubber of her first husband, Distant Cloud. And Walnut Shell's rippling muscle would not disappear in the darkness, under the covers, as much of Silky's did.

Sensing her regard, Walnut Shell glanced up. He flashed that incredible ivory smile of his, and in that moment, the idea was born. Why not? If she had sold her body to get herself into this pit of horror, she could sell it to get out again. The Courtly Teacher said, *A bad deed can sometimes be excused by a good motive.*

Verdant Harmony returned the smile. No lady in the Good Lands ever did that for a male servant. He noticed and smiled again, this time with meaning.

The locals all agreed that the Portal of Worlds was located about two days' ride west of Cherish, but could be seen from a lookout known as Heaven's Threshold only one day away. After a week's hard forgery, Silky had important business in that area, so he certainly intended to view the legendary Portal while he was about it.

Spring had adorned the Fortress Hills. The grass was so green it hurt the eyes, the sky was hugely blue, furnished with white cushions. This was perfect horse country—gentle, rolling hills of lush grass with long vistas to give warning of predators, whether two-legged or four. The Wilderness Road wound across it like a gray snake, an empty dirt trail rising imperceptibly on its way to the rampart peaks of the Western Wall. Lonely dust motes floating in the topless azure sky were undoubtedly vultures. And once in a while, a traveler might spot grazing herds of horses. Once in a longer while, Silky saw buildings. He would never be unobserved, though. City-boy Silky had felt safely anonymous among the teeming crowds of Wedlock, even in the cramped and smelly town of Cherish. Here he saw nobody and sensed eyes watching him all the time.

He was thumping along the trail on a homicidal chestnut known to his enemies as Red Demon and to his present rider as

Big Sponge. At his side, Novice Watersprite rode a black gelding. The wind whirled Silky's queue around and made his eyes water; he was blissfully happy to escape from Cherish after five boring months of prying information out of the locals, polishing his horsemanship, and practicing swordsmanship—and penmanship, of course. He had not, he reminded himself with a secret smile, killed anyone in ages. A man must keep his hand in.

Watersprite raised an arm to point. "Goat Haven."

Silky nodded in admiration.

The Fortress Hills were named for the exceptions. Among all the egg-smooth hills, a few stood much higher, as if they had hatched. Instead of gently rounded tops, these few sprouted crowns of gray rock—flat tables with near-vertical sides. For centuries, painters had come on pilgrimage to admire and depict these natural strongholds. Many of those great slabs supported fortified houses on their summits, for this was rustler country and border country and often brigand country. Goat Haven was the largest and most impressive stronghold Silky had seen yet, as befitted the lair of Prince Sky Hammer. Silky intended to call on His Highness before sunset, but only after he had seen the Portal.

Visible ahead now were landmarks he had been told to expect—a sprawling caravanserai close to the road, flanked by two tiny lakes. Water in the Fortress Hills moved mainly underground, rising in springs, flowing only a little way before sinking back down again. Sometimes the streamlets would end in ponds that never overflowed, sometimes they trickled away down natural drains. The directions he had been given were good; if he had come this way without Watersprite, he would have found Goat Haven without trouble.

She was good company. The House of Joyful Departure in Cherish did not compare with Wedlock's for size, but the abbess had been very helpful after being promised a generous share of the booty, if any. Novice Watersprite was dressed, like Silky, in typical rancher leathers, slung about with the usual weapons. In company, she would seem a boy, but at the moment, she was just a lean, dark-eyed, wind-flushed beauty whose flirtatious smiles kept reminding him that Verdant was back in Cherish with the baby.

They met no traffic, but caravans were starting to assemble in the town, and its big horse markets were opening already. Soon, ranchers would begin driving herds in. Swordcut Pass in the Western Wall was still barred by winter snow, but when it opened, troops would be riding back and forth between the town and the frontier fortress, taking supplies, carrying reports. The big Two Lakes Caravanserai in the Great Valley had not opened yet, either. That was part of the plan.

An hour or so later, the trail turned to the south to skirt a very long north-south-trending hill. Its rocky cap was ragged, but it was still high enough to block any glimpse of the mountains beyond. Watersprite pointed to a barely visible path that broke off from the road and led up the slope.

"To Heaven's Threshold. Let them catch their breath," she added, reining her horse back to a walk.

"You noticed the watchers?" Silky said without turning. "We're being followed."

"Of course we are. We're strangers. Horse people never trust strangers."

That was annoying but very wise of them.

The horses went slowly on that long, angled path, traveling in single file so Silky could admire Watersprite's supple back. But then they entered a narrow crevice in the rocky cap and the going became a real challenge—steep, winding, and dangerous. Some parts were almost too narrow for a horse to pass, while others skirted hideous drops. Several times, Silky called for a break to rest the horses and inspect the terrain.

Each time, Watersprite said, "Not yet. There's a better one."

Nevertheless, he memorized every scene before going on, so that when at last she stopped and said, "Here?" he could agree instantly that this one would be the place. It was Heaven's Own Perfect Ambush Site. The trail dipped into a narrow V-gorge, and crossed a knife-cut ravine on a slender plank bridge.

"Where does he wait?" Silky asked. "There?"

"No." She led him across to the far side. "There, by that rock. He'll have a clear view of them coming back, but he shoots from between those two rocks so nobody except the target will see him. They'll all be concentrating on their horses' footing anyway. They won't realize what's happened. Even a blind one-armed idiot can't miss at that range."

She was assuming that the archer would be a local man, requiring yet another kickback to the abbess, but Plum Blossom was the best crossbow archer Silky knew, and quite capable of managing such an easy shot. The best feature of the site was that the victim would fall and roll a long way, to a steep and rocky landing, certainly fatal if the shot itself had only wounded him. The bolt would be broken off, even if it hadn't gone right through him, which it likely would at that range. His companions would need hours to get down to the body. The vultures would be there first. To touch or even approach a corpse was an act of extreme ill-omen, but the Gray Helpers summoned from Cherish would not arrive for two days or so. By then, there should be no evidence of murder. Sky Hammer's death would be just another tragic accident.

At the top, they emerged onto a rocky surface of crumbling rock and well-cropped turf, across which the wind howled, blowing his queue out like bunting and dragging his hat against its tether. The terrain was too rugged to build on and too dangerous for horses or cattle that might stampede over the edge, but a dozen or so shaggy goats sprang out of the ground nearby and went bounding away. They held Silky's interest for a few moments, so that when he finally turned to see where Water-sprite was leading him, he was startled by the panorama.

He was overlooking the famous Great Valley, a huge but straight trough in the landscape, extending roughly north and south as far as his weeping eyes could see. It was wide and flat-bottomed, almost a plain between two ranges. He could see no signs of water or habitation. On the far side marched the Western Wall, a line of triangular cliffs and V-shaped ravines, as if the range had been cut off by a razor. Behind it stood higher peaks, topped in the far distance by icy pillars holding up the sky.

Below him, Silky could just make out the Wilderness Road entering the valley around the end of the Heaven's Threshold and fading away as it headed for whichever notch led through to Swordcut Pass.

"Well?" Watersprite said with a wry smile.

"Very impressive, but where is it?"

She pointed out the largest of the gable-end cliffs, almost directly across from them. "It shows up better at noon, when the sun angles across it."

"Can't see a thing."

Wearing a cryptic smirk, Watersprite handed him a small telescope. It made very little difference. After several minutes' search, he located Two Lakes Caravanserai down by the river. Then he raised the scope to look for the Portal of Worlds. Even-tually, he made out a rectangular mark on the cliff. He was still unimpressed, until he remembered that he was still a day's ride away from it. The scale of the landscape hit him like an ax. His shock scared Big Sponge, who neighed in alarm and tried to stand up straight. Silky slapped him down angrily.

"*How big is that thing?*"

She laughed, satisfied. "I've heard it said that it's almost a thousand paces high. If you laid it flat, you could build a small town on it."

"And it *opens*?"

"So the legends say."

Silky could not imagine such a thing. He could just trace out a doorway surrounded by a complex design of pillars and vines. Absurd! What ancient race could have created such a thing, even if it was just a carving? What might emerge from a door that size if it ever did open? That was an utterly terrifying thought, and now he understood why the locals so stubbornly refused to worry about it. Let it open, they said. Even if it had opened before and might very well open again, the land would stay here and so would they.

The sun was setting behind the Western Wall as two weary horses trekked up the long ascent to Goat Haven. The riders had been quiet a long time while Watersprite studied her face in a small mirror. Then she turned in the saddle and said, "How do I look?"

"Very good, but not as good as before."

She was a boy now, with his hair in a queue, weather-beaten cheeks, a shadow on his lip, and a thymus bulge in a neck as graceful as a swan's.

"Promise me you'll change back later."

She smiled provocatively. "Depends how much privacy we have."

When they reached the guard post at the base of the cliffs, Lord Silk Hand, senior secretary to His Highness Prince Luminous Aspect, showed his authority and begged leave to deliver a letter to His Highness Prince Sky Hammer 7. His Highness's rules stated clearly that the gate must be closed one hour before sunset and no visitors admitted after that, but Lord Silk Hand and his companion were such honest-seeming young men that the gate commander made an exception for them. Having surrendered all their visible weapons, they were escorted up to the summit.

The climb was narrow and steep, although it had been greatly improved by the hand of man and was easier and safer than the track to Heaven's Threshold. Not too safe, though—Silky noted gates and other barriers, and even giant stone cylinders ready to roll down the trail to turn invaders into harmless paste. Goat Haven was a fortress as well as a palace.

Most of the windswept plain at the top was divided into paddocks by dry-stone walls. There were more than a hundred horses in sight and no doubt as many again in the barns, for this was foaling time. The palace in the center was a sprawling complex of one-story masonry and timber buildings. It was obviously old, but would still be defensible against traditional weapons and perhaps even the Emperor's guns, because it stood higher than any hill within range and the attackers would have to shoot blind.

Despite the unseemly lateness of the hour, the visitors were made welcome. Their horses were led off to be cared for, and they were given a room to wash and make themselves presentable. Nor were they left to brood for long before a steward came to lead them into the prince's presence.

Complicated by centuries of alterations and additions, the palace mingled royal grandeur and working ranch house—barns beside stately pavilions, horse troughs here and ornamental pools there. The great hall, as the steward called it, was indeed great, but poorly lit and currently filled with people sitting cross-legged and eating—more men than women, almost all dressed as servants or ranch hands. None paid any attention to the newcomers being led through their midst. They were all chattering happily and gobbling what looked like generous portions of rice and vegetables, plus something that smelled like meat sauce, although scents were hard to distinguish in the thick medley of people and horses. Most couriers bearing letters from royalty would be mortally insulted at being taken to servants' quarters, but Silky's alleged royal master was a fraud, of course, and Silky knew what to expect because Watersprite had been there before, in the Year of the Vulture, when Sky Hammer's wife died. No one was going to recognize the most junior of the Gray Sisters of then in the boy warrior of now.

At the far end of the hall, the mood switched to grandeur, with a gilded throne at the back of a wide dais whose walls were draped with numerous ink-on-silk scroll paintings of fanciful landscapes. At one side, a harpist played discordant foreign music, and at the other stood two guards heavily encumbered with pistols and swords that they would obviously love to use. The floor of the platform was covered with thick rugs from distant lands, on which sat the owner of the throne, eating rice out of what looked like a Ninth Dynasty porcelain bowl.

Prince Sky Hammer had the outlander round eyes and long nose often seen around Cherish. His robes were silk, intricately embroidered with images of horses. He was elderly and sun-dried, tall and rawboned, and he watched the embassy arrive with cold suspicion, not pausing in his eating.

Silky knelt. The steward announced him. Silky touched his head to the floor, which felt gritty and had not been cleaned in a very long time.

Sky Hammer wiped his mouth on a sleeve. "Never heard of any Prince Luminous Aspect."

"His Highness's estates are mostly located in Jingyan."

His host grunted. "What're you up to, coming here after sunset?"

Silky held up the scroll. "Delivering this letter from—"

"But you didn't. You went sightseeing first."

"As my master bade me. He wanted my reassurance that the Threshold was worth a visit."

"What's he doing here, so far from home?" Suspicion came easy to people living in borderlands.

"Will His Highness graciously read my master's own words?"

Grunt again. The steward took the scroll and presented it. The prince broke the seal and unrolled about a third, but then he held it far from his eyes and scowled. He glanced around.

Another man wandered forward to step up on the dais—younger but just as sumptuously dressed. The barbarian features were less obvious in him and he was stockier, but almost certainly he was Sky Rider, who expected to become Sky Hammer 8 one day. He hung reading glasses on his nose, took the scroll from his father, and read it out, as though even his eyes had trouble in the poor light. Silky studied him carefully, because Sky Rider was a potential snag, one of the unknown factors in the plan.

Brother Luminous, in his princely guise, had written an expert harangue of pure fog. Traveling with his daughter, prior to delivering her to her future husband, he had heard that the noble Sky Hammer 7, the celebrated expert on Tenth Dynasty silk scroll paintings—which he also collected, but in a minor, humble fashion—lived in the district, and within sight, so it was said, of the legendary Portal of Worlds, which diviners and astrologers insisted was going to open in the near future . . . and so on.

The silk painting bait had come from the Gray Sisters, who took careful notes in rich houses. The caravanserais were not yet open, so how could one prince refuse hospitality to another?

The leathery old rancher showed signs of interest. "How many Tenth Dynasty scroll paintings does he have?"

"Thirty-three complete, Your Highness, and a few partial."

"Any good ones?"

"Four by Agate Shining," Silky said, "seven by Harmonious Bulrushes, twelve . . . I have the honor of being his curator . . . Twelve, as I was saying, by the Master of High Breezes . . ." If real, the fictitious prince's imaginary collection would be substantial, but well behind Sky Hammer's, of course.

"He must come and see mine."

Bait taken.

✼   ✼   ✼

Silky had expected to be assigned to a bunkhouse and intended to sneak out with Watersprite when the other occupants were asleep, but the visitors were given a room to themselves. That was annoying, because it implied that someone might be eavesdropping on them and the door would be watched. Both windows were covered by wooden lattice that looked tight enough to balk a cat. Fortunately, the wind was making enough noise that subtle whispers close to Watersprite's fine porcelain ear would not be overheard.

"Don't know about you, lad," Silky said aloud, "but my ass aches all the way up to my ears."

"As the venerable one says," she agreed, and in very few minutes they were both wrapped in their blankets and the lamp was out.

As their eyes adjusted, a faint glimmer of starlight emerged from the gloom. Throwing off their covers, they rose and tiptoed over to the nearer window, with Watersprite in the lead, testing every step for creaky boards.

"Demons! Hardest floor I ever met," she said for the benefit of listeners.

The lattice was tight as a drum skin. Whisper: "*Hopeless!*" They moved on to the next window. Here there was hope, for one of the slats was slightly loose in its the groove and they had brought a few tools, of course. They set to work, operating by sense of touch and keeping up a nonsensical muttering so that the listeners, if any, would know they were awake and not be suspicious of other noises.

"You quite sure you aren't a girl, lad?"

"You want your balls ripped off?"

"Sure a pity. Been a long time since I got my jack in the orchard. My wife dropped a babe. Hadn't got her going again yet before we left Jingyan."

"Boy or girl?"

"Boy."

"Good. What's he called?"

"Wife wanted Silkworm, but I named him Thunderbot."

"Did you say 'Thunderbolt'?"

"No."

There was a moment's pause before Watersprite remembered that she was currently male and supposed to find that funny. While Silky exerted as much bending effort as he dared on the loose slat, she managed to pull one end of it free, then work it far enough out of the weave to leave a diamond-shaped hole.

"*Big enough?*" he whispered.

She was a skinny girl, but the gap still looked impossibly narrow to Silky, who would need to remove at least one more slat, probably two, before he would have a space big enough for himself. He would have to leave all the work to her.

"*Think so.*" She crept back to the pallets to change into burglar clothes. "Those pictures you were looking at, sir—are they really so valuable?"

"You wouldn't believe." He had been genuinely impressed by some of the scrolls the prince had shown him, both in the great hall and in several other rooms. The Gray Helpers were well aware that a man's hobby was his most vulnerable spot after his groin. The mistrustful old rancher had probed hard at Silky's knowledge; fortunately, his long days of cramming had given him as much expertise as a genuine collector's curator would have. He would forget it all as soon as possible.

His accomplice was ready. He pecked her a good luck kiss and lifted her so she could put her feet into that impossibly small space. It seemed like a miracle, but somehow she made herself slim enough to squirm through, and he lowered her to arm's length, which put her toes on the ground.

✳   ✳   ✳

From then on, he was alone, dying a death of a million cuts. The day was highly auspicious for Watersprite, but for all he knew it might be pure poison for him. Life really was not fair. Since he did not know his birthday, no astrologer could cast his horoscope. He knew the good days he had experienced so far—his acceptance into the House of Joyful Departure, his first meeting with Jade Harmony, the days he had increased his tally—but there was apparently no way to work back from those to fix the day and hour of his birth.

The night was moonless, filled with sounds and movements by the wind. Sky Hammer must be assumed to have posted guards on the visitors' cell. The risks Watersprite was taking were bloodcurdling, and if she were caught, both intruders would surely endure very unpleasant interrogation before they died. Once, Silky became so jittery that he went and tried the door, confirming that he was bolted in. He felt better then, for there might not be watchers outside after all.

But the old man might even have posted guards on his bedroom, where the muniment chest stood. The Gray Sisters had made a note of that two years ago, but had not established whether there were booby traps on the chest. Nor had they been able to take a wax impression of the key, which they would have done automatically had the opportunity presented itself. Watersprite had to enter the bedchamber undetected, pick the lock, and extract one essential document. It might be the only one in there, or there might be hundreds, and she could not read in the dark. Knowing only how weighty a document she wanted and the number of seals it bore, she would have to select a few and take them to wherever she could safely make light, check each one, and then wait until her eyes had adjusted again before reentering the bedroom to replace those and repeat the process.

Only when she had found and removed the genuine will could she replace it with Silky's forgery, which was an exact copy of the version he had "returned" to the governor's archives.

Sky Hammer was old and the old sleep poorly.

But even a century does not last forever, and eventually, a small pebble tapped on the window lattice. Silky rushed over there. Her face was a faint blur below the sill.

"Done it!" she said softly.

CHAPTER 4

The winds of Wolf Moon had done with their howling and slunk away. The bitter cold of Ice Moon had glittered in the clouds, while in the palace of Lady Cataract, the Firstborn cheated death yet again. It was there that Mouse had found the help he sought during the great blizzard, and it was the lady who had sent her servants and supplies to the cave. She personally nursed the Firstborn back from the prospect of another reincarnation. She poulticed him, pampered him, fed him with her own hands, and spent an untold fortune on heating. She bullied him into living by sheer power of will.

No sooner could he stagger around on his own feet was he anxious to be off in search of the Bamboo Banner, but Death had breathed on him, and he was far from fit to travel. Shard Gingko suspected that he would never be a well man now, perhaps never live to maturity. Even if the Portal did open next year, as the Firstborn forecast, he might not be alive to see it. He was thin as a rice stalk, his hands trembled, and a feverish restlessness never left his eyes.

Lady Cataract refused to listen to his protests.

"Not in winter in these hills!" she decreed. "When you are strong again and the snow has fled, then you will make far better time. You will arrive as soon. Indeed, if you leave too soon, you will not arrive at all. A man who claims to have lived thousands of years should not be as impatient as a child. Must you relearn wisdom anew in every life?"

No one else would have dared speak to the Urfather like that, but he laughed and yielded to her bullying.

Cataract was old and at times—especially in the evenings— seemed as frail as he did, but her back was straight and her life flame still burned bright, despite many tragedies. She had borne children, all of whom had died. So the servants had told Mouse, who had told Shard, and silk portraits of three handsome young men hung on the wall of her winter parlor. There could be no greater tragedy than an ancestor burying descendants. Although the lady's husband was never mentioned by name, there were hints that he had not died a natural death and that she bore no love for the late Emperor Zealous Righteousness. Her palace, it was whispered, was all that remained of once great estates. It had been a hunting lodge of some long-dead Emperor, set high in craggy hills beset with waterfalls and forest, although the forests had mostly gone now and the game with them. She lived there year-round in decaying grandeur, kept company by ghosts and equally decayed servants. She was a daunting scholar, able to cap Shard's quotes, verse by verse, and very often even test the Firstborn, who loved her dearly.

She owned a vast collection of antique books and scrolls, which fascinated both Shard and the Firstborn. Although Shard had no difficulty reading even the oldest, only the Firstborn could read them aloud with the original pronunciation, which was almost impossible to understand, but did make the poetry sound better.

Hare Moon had come leaping and dancing, all eager springtime and impatience, yet still the Firstborn lingered. For the first time since seeing the evidence of massacre at High Abode, he had recovered his previous tranquillity of spirit, the calm courage with which he had defied Sedge Shallows's persecution. It was almost as if he had decided to wait for something. Not a sign from Heaven, of course. Shard knew the Urfather well enough now to know that he put no faith in those. Or not much. But Hare Moon departed, admitting Fish Moon, and still the Firstborn tarried under the approving eye of Lady Cataract.

One afternoon, Shard dared ease the conversation around to the subject of the Portal of Worlds, which had not been mentioned since that terrible night in the cave, months ago. The three of them were sitting in the water garden, soothed by its gentle murmurs and shaded by trees from a sun already unpleasantly hot. Cherry blossoms came late to the Wanrong Hills, but they had blazed in their brief glory and were now gone. Boisterous rhododendrons were blooming, ostentatious as ever. The hills were green, lambs and foals had been born.

Swathed in a finely embroidered silk gown, which Shard suspected might be almost as old as she was, Lady Cataract was providing tea. She approved of her celebrated guest and even of Shard Gingko. He wasn't a true scholar, of course, and he was totally eclipsed in the presence of the Firstborn, but she must be so starved for educated conversation that even a clerk of records could be tolerated.

A mere servant, which is how she saw Mouse, was expected to remain out of sight. The Firstborn permitted this discrimination for Mouse's comfort, not hers. He had told Shard—in one of the very few direct orders he had ever given him—to teach Mouse to write. He had seen what Shard Gingko had missed, that the boy had natural abilities to overcome his lack of education. He had taken to writing as a lark to singing and was learning twenty characters a day. He knew more than a thousand already, and Shard rarely had to criticize his brushwork.

Shard's clumsy change of topic provoked the glance of tolerant amusement that he now knew so well.

"I was not delirious that night, Grandfather. Wandering a bit, perhaps, but not delirious."

Lady Cataract raised her painted eyebrows but withheld comment.

"Then you do believe the omens?" Shard said.

"I believe great things happen. If they are messages from Heaven, I wonder that Heaven does not speak more clearly. It may be that our faithful Mouse, with Her Ladyship's help, balked even the will of Heaven that night. If not, and if the Portal is still due to open, there is one essential sign that has not yet been granted, as I told you. That omen was one that Humble Voice did not know. Only when that event has happened can you be confident that the Portal will open next year."

He was almost certainly teasing his hostess.

The knife-edge-thin eyebrows rose even higher. "The Portal of Worlds? You are certain, Urfather?"

"No." Sunlight explained about Humble Voice, his omens, and his own death.

"You told me that the scholar knew of four certain omens," Shard Gingko said. "I do not recall that you mentioned all four, just the broom stars, the demons, and the, um, change of dynasty." That was not a topic to discuss outside close family circles, but Lady Cataract smiled approvingly.

The Firstborn drank his tea and reached out to set the bowl on the table. His arms were still as thin as noodles. "No, I didn't. I dread it as much as I worry about the Portal of Worlds itself, or even more. But it is one I know of my own experience to be a true foreshadowing. I told you that the Portal has never opened while I have been walking the Good Land, and sometimes, when I have been reborn in an area distant from it, I have heard nary a whisper of its happening in my next lifetime, either. But," he added somberly, "every time I have been reborn just after an opening—and usually in the lifetime after that, even—people have spoken of a great earthquake."

Lady Cataract crumpled her lips together disapprovingly. "Earthquakes happen all the time, somewhere. There are little ones and big ones. Here, in Wanrong, we get a tremor or two every year."

"Most earthquakes are quite local, but I mean a Destroyer of Many Cities Earthquake. You have heard tell of the Lotus Moon Quake? Perhaps even of the Fog Moon Quake?"

She nodded uneasily.

"Those truly great earthquakes happen only once in many centuries, but always one comes just before the Portal of Worlds opens. This is the one true sending."

Shard Gingko shivered. In silence, the hostess refilled his tea bowl. A quake as great as those two might explain some of the dynasty changes that happened around the openings. People blamed the Emperor when Heaven displayed such wrath. He put it into words. "The Bamboo Banner will use a great shaking against the Son of the Sun. The rebels will say that the Golden Throne has lost the Mandate of Heaven."

"Indeed," the Firstborn said. "And it is time I continued my quest. The Bamboo Banner will bring even worse disaster. No," he cautioned, raising a hand to forestall Lady Cataract's protests, "this time, I mean it. I have enjoyed your hospitality more than any I have met in many lifetimes, my lady. It has restored me as much as I can be restored in this incarnation. Perhaps even restored my faith in humanity," he added with a smile that belied his words. If he, of all men, ever lost his faith in humanity, he must assuredly go mad. "But now I must be about my business."

"I was merely going to say that I fully intend to accompany you, Urfather. I have horses ready, and a litter for me. Your servant boy has advised my people on your needs and preferences, but if you wish to travel by litter, also, then that can be arranged. A party of a dozen or so will travel faster than you can alone."

The Firstborn smiled at her fondly. "My *disciple* has kept me advised of your nefarious plotting, my lady. Your kindness will certainly be rewarded in the Fifth World."

"And where we will go?"

"I seek the Bamboo Banner. Scholar Shard Gingko, what is the latest news of it?"

"Just what I told you two days ago, Urfather. That the governor of Kermang was preparing to meet it in battle if it entered his province."

"Other governors did not stop it, and that news must be at least a month old, so we must assume it is in Kermang and continuing north. The question is where the Imperial Army will try to—"

The tea bowls on the table rattled.

The ground quivered. The air was filled with a strange mutter of no discernible source, like some trouble very loud but far away. Birds swirled up from the trees.

Lady Cataract laughed, a little shrilly. "What did I tell you? But this little shiver is not going to shake down a dynasty."

For a few minutes, nobody spoke. The noise grew louder. The trembling continued. It came in spurts, less and then more, but Shard watched the tea in the bowls, and how the surface rippled. That never quite stopped. He looked at the pinched face of the boy across from him and saw fear there. Would this sending never end?

Eventually, it did, as it must, but by then, the servants in the house were wailing in terror and even Lady Cataract's leathery face was pale under her face paint. The birds stopped circling and returned to their perches.

"No damage," she said, "or we would have heard it."

"It was far away," Urfather said. "That is why it seemed faint to us."

"Oh, how can you, even you, possibly tell?"

"Because it went on for a very long time. Small earthquakes are brief. I have never known one to last as long as that."

Never? In seven thousand years or more—*never*?

So the Portal was going to open.

CHAPTER 5

Early in Fish Moon, the Bamboo Banner crossed the border into Kermang, where it met its first serious rebuff. Food was scarce after two poor harvests, and the provincial governor was in no mood to feed a rebellious ragtag of mystical brigands. He had spies in Dongguan reporting on the Bamboo Banner's progress, and he knew that one of its divisions was advancing up the trading road that would bring it to Spires, the largest city in the province. Spires had guarded that road for centuries; it was built for war and siege, and the governor made sure that it was manned, provisioned, and ready for battle.

The advance guard was the Jade Army, under the command of Leader of Thousands White Pine, who had professional military experience. As usual, the Bamboo Banner had sent distraction squads on ahead to persuade the inhabitants of Spires and some neighboring settlements that it was no more than a band of harmless pests: acrobats, entertainers, and preachers. In fact, these six cadres specialized in intelligence, recruitment, and subversion. The governor had prepared their reception, and not one of the two hundred or so men returned. Most were mown down by gunfire, and the rest were taken to the House of Gentle Persuasion for torture.

The Bamboo Banner had other scouts, though, many of which had been put in place long ago. When the governor set up an ambush in Wind Chime Pass, including enough artillery to shred the entire Jade Army, the deployment was quickly reported to White Pine. He sent for reinforcements, but did not wait for them to arrive. The Jade Army ambushed the ambushers by night, a thousand men streaming down from the hills on either flank. The battle was fought by starlight and the flashes of guns. It was bloody, with no quarter given. By morning, the patriots had quit the field, which would normally be a sign of defeat, but they took almost all the guns with them, and they departed in the direction of Spires, in hot pursuit of the imperial survivors.

Within days, the Pearl, Agate, and Jade armies were all encamped around Spires and the siege had begun. Bamboo himself had issued an ultimatum, promising massacre if the "rebellious" city did not surrender. The messenger was hanged from the city wall. What very few people knew was that the Bamboo Banner had only three days' rations and two days' ammunition for the captured guns. The siege must succeed quickly or not at all.

By then, Man Valor had been promoted to Leader of a Hundred, in command of Dogwood's and Chinquapin's cadres as well as his own. A hot and dusty afternoon found him directing a sapping operation at the northeast corner of the city, where a shallow gully let the attackers approach within a few hundred paces of the wall without being exposed to gunfire. Their mission was to dig three trenches up to the walls, and then mine the foundations.

It was backbreaking work, with room at the face of each trench for only two men, one with pick and another with shovel. Behind them two more would pile the spoil on the city side of the dig. All four would work in a sprint for about ten minutes and then be relieved by four more. That was the plan, and it wasn't working. The soil was mostly gravel, but it included boulders too huge to move and pockets of loose sand that caused the sides of the dig to collapse. Man Valor had no timber to brace the walls, and the three tidy, geometrical zigzags he had envisioned were developing as anything but. Near-surface bedrock was steadily forcing the Dogwood trench ever closer to the Man Valor trench. Soon, they would be close enough for a single mortar shot from the walls to collapse both together. Meanwhile, enemy sharpshooters took potshots at the men, and once in a while, an artillery piece would boom out a spray of grape.

By midafternoon, Man Valor himself had done two stints at the front of the dig and was covered with filth. To inspire his men with contempt for the defenders, he sat on a conspicuous rock, chewing his yang cud and listening to the rumble of gunfire from the south, where the Banner was trying to open a breach in the walls. He could watch the cowards on top of the walls aiming their muskets at him. If they had rifles, he would be covered in bruises by this time, but so far, they were hitting every rock in Kermang but not him. Once in a while, a bullet would pang loudly off a pebble near him, but he ignored those.

Then Chinquapin came wandering over and squatted down alongside him. He was a tall, skinny youth with a perpetually morose expression. Apart from that, Man Valor knew nothing about him, because he belonged to the Jade Army and Man Valor was in Pearl. Dogwood's cadre was in the Agate Army. The three forces had been shuffled together, and would probably all have different makeups again when they moved on.

For a while, neither man spoke, just chewed slowly and watched the dirt flying out of the far ends of the digs. Man Valor stood up on his rock and blew on his whistle to signal a change of shifts. He watched heads moving in the trenches. Then he sat down again with a despicable sense of relief.

Chinquapin said, "Feeling especially bulletproof, are you?"

"'Swords and shot can hurt me NOT,'" Man Valor quoted with all the bravado he could summon. In truth, he was feeling the strain after so many hours of this.

Chinquapin grunted. "The Pearl Army came in from the southeast?"

"Yes."

"Why, do you know?"

"Mine not to question," Man Valor said, meaning that it wasn't the other man's business, either.

"Wind Chime Pass would have been quicker."

"I don't give Bamboo advice."

"But then you'd have gone past the battlefield."

Pang! That had been a close one.

After a moment, Man Valor said, "So?"

Shrug. "Nothing. Wonder where all the birds are."

There were no birds. No doubt the gunfire had scared them all away, but without the battle, the afternoon would have been as silent as an oyster. The heat was ferocious for Fish Moon, the air completely still. Gun smoke hung over Spires like a gray cloud.

Man Valor said, "I expect they're over at Wind Chime Pass, feasting off the bitch Empress's troops. Ravens, of course, but even little birds will peck at meat if it's available."

"Me too. The congee was pretty watery this morning, I thought."

"Did you?"

"Not a breath of fish paste in it and more sawdust than rice."

Man Valor turned his full attention on the kid. "Do you talk to your cadre like this?"

Chinquapin was watching him carefully. "Of course not. But I got a lot of grumbles at breakfast. Didn't you?"

"My lads know better than to try that."

"What do you do? Hit them?"

"Sometimes. Or throw away half their yang leaf." Man Valor decided he would have to report this conversation. Young Chinquapin needed disciplining.

Then the uppity kid asked, "How long have you been a cadre leader?"

"Long enough to know that my job is to inspire my men to serve Bamboo, not to spread defeatist talk about battlefields and rations."

The youth sighed and fell silent. A bullet ricocheted off a rock between them and wailed away. They both jumped.

Neither commented. Man Valor climbed up on his boulder again and blew his whistle to signal a change of shifts. He sat down faster than he meant to.

Chinquapin noticed. "Have you ever conducted a second proving?"

"Yes . . . You?" Now what was coming?

"Two days ago. Did you take a real close look at the sword?"

Man Valor hesitated, wondering what lay behind the question. A sword was a sword, wasn't it? A sword that cut through a silk ribbon as if it wasn't there was sharp enough to cut off a man's arm, wasn't it? Or at least cut it to the bone.

"Why?"

Chinquapin made a noise that sounded close to a chuckle, although his woebegone expression did not change. "Obviously, you didn't."

"Didn't what?" Man Valor snapped.

"Didn't look. The point is sharp, right? Because some men like to nick their noses on it." He had no scar on his nose; Man Valor did. "And the part close to the hilt is sharp, because the ritual requires that part to cut the headband—it's held close to you when you lower the sword, yes? But the rest of the edge is *rounded*, not sharp. It wouldn't cut bean curd. Next time, you look. You'll see what I'm telling you."

Man Valor felt his belly chill. He recalled Leaping Serpent teaching his cadre to hit the candidate's arm with the middle of the blade. . . . Then his anger flared up white hot.

"Doubter! Defeatist! Of course the middle isn't sharp any more. Someone forgot to sharpen it again, that's all. If you chopped logs with it, or rocks, it would lose its edge after four or five strokes, right? That's what happens when it bounces off a man's arm. We're *sword-proof*, you idiot!"

"That's one explanation, I suppose."

Obviously, Chinquapin was unfit to lead a cadre. "Traitor! Coward! It's the only explanation. You've been through the second proving, haven't you, and you still have both arms? And the third? You felt the bullets bounce off your chest?"

The kid looked down at himself as if to point out scars or bruises, but he was too covered with dust for marks to show. "I felt *something* hit my chest."

"I will not listen to such chickenhearted whining. We follow Bamboo and Heaven. Heaven and the ancestors defend—"

"If they'd brought you through Wind Chime Pass after the battle, you'd have seen—"

"Silence! Heaven defends us! And Heaven will overthrow the she-dragon and set Bamboo on the throne of his ancestors. It may need a miracle or many miracles, but our cause is Heaven's cause, and Bamboo has promised. Who's your first deputy?"

Chinquapin seemed more amused than worried. "Lion Paw."

"Go and fetch him. I'm relieving you of your command."

The youth shrugged. "I wish you luck with your miracles, old man." He rose in an insolently deliberate fashion and sauntered away.

There was a great roaring sound, louder than thunder. Birds flew up from wherever they had been hiding. Chinquapin went about three steps, staggered, seemed to trip over his own feet, and toppled to the ground. Man Valor fell off the boulder. He was shaken and bounced on sharp gravel, rolling on his back, completely unable to stand. The tumult faded, then returned several times. Had Bamboo not warned the Gentle People that the Golden Throne had lost the Mandate of Heaven? Was this not proof?

At long last, the noise stopped; the land steadied again. Man Valor sat up, mouth and eyes full of dirt. In the trenches, men buried up to their waists were screaming for help. Others might have been buried too deep to scream. Man Valor scrambled up and ran to see what he could do. He helped pull out a couple, both of them with broken legs. Another was buried almost head-down under a rock and obviously dead. It looked as if about a tenth of his hundred had disappeared completely and as many had been injured.

A drum was beating. . . . Sounding the charge?

He peered through dust-inflamed eyes at Spires. The north-east corner of the city wall had collapsed. The city lay naked and open.

"*A miracle!*" he roared. "Heaven has delivered them into our hands. Patriots, get your weapons!"

His men had not yet been issued guns, but they had their staves and they had picks and shovels. Red with dust, some already streaked with blood, Man Valor's hundred began to run, with him in the lead. Thousands more swarmed over the plain toward the stricken city.

He was not the youngest or the fastest, so he was not the first of his cadre to arrive, but arrive he did. Gasping for breath, he reached the jumble of stone blocks that had been an impregnable wall only minutes before. He could hear screams and frantic trumpets from inside the city, officers shouting orders to rally the dazed and demoralized defenders. He could see smoke billowing up from fires. Men with rifles were appearing at the top of the rock pile and on all the nearest roofs. They did not scare Man Valor. He went leaping up from block to block, waving a pick, yelling defiance. Gunfire crackled.

The impact hurled Man Valor backward, down onto the jagged chaos. He did not feel pain, only the shock of the bullet and the fall, which alone might have killed him. He lay there, trying to gather his wits. He watched his men running past him, jumping over him—and being mowed down. Some were getting through, but why were the rest just lying there? Heaven had spoken through the earthquake, so why were patriots falling? His wits weren't coming back. There was a red fountain spurting out of his chest. Had his faith failed him? Or had he been gulled?

So that is why we were not led past the battlefield. Not just blunt swords, but blank cartridges, too. All that hit me at my proving was wadding. It was all a fake. I was deceived and I am dying.

CHAPTER 6

The game was the thing. Gray Brother Luminous could have bought himself a 100-ply abbey years ago, or retired as a respectable citizen of any background he cared to fake, but money didn't buy contentment. It was the chase that mattered. He had long ago lost count of his score and nowadays usually left the actual outings to the youngsters, who appreciated any opportunity to increase their own tallies. But the hunt, the being somebody else, the planning, the lying in ambush—those were the things that made life worth living. One day, Heaven would decide to move him on to the Fifth World. His departure might involve a horrible display in some city square, but even then he would have no regrets. Free public entertainment would be his final role.

Nonetheless, he was aging, and spending the best part of a day on a horse in the heat of Fish Moon was a strain. There was no shade anywhere. The rolling hills were mummified already and Luminous was close to it. Lord Silk Hand, riding beside him, looked dusty and sweaty, but quite unwearied, grinning eagerly as the play unfolded. Savoring the game. A promising lad, Silky, the best to come along in years, brilliant and deadly, if inclined to be reckless. This Goat Haven project would be an incredible score if the boy could pull it off, but the risks were enough to make a man's queue stand on end, straight up, if he had one. There would be no public entertainment at the end of this road, but the consequences might be as fatal and even more prolonged. The ranchers were as hard as their horseshoes.

Luminous glanced behind him to inspect his retinue, all supplied by the abbess of Cherish. Watersprite was there, dressed as a boy, but currently flirting with Windchime, one of the Cherish Helpers. Behind them rode another, Carp, and also the curiously named Mercy, on loan from some abbey down river, a skilled young archer anxious to add a notch to his tally stick. His crossbow was well hidden in the baggage, of course. Altogether, they were a convincing following for a minor nobleman. Private armies were strictly regulated in the Good Land.

It wasn't the deception that was the problem in this venture. Luminous was confident that his performance as Prince Luminous Aspect would be flawless, and Silky as his aide had passed the ranchers' inspection on his earlier visit. Once credibility had been established, the second presentation always went more smoothly. No, it was in the seamy underside of the cloth that the bedbugs lurked, not on the public face. Any seed of suspicion planted during Silky's earlier visit had had a week to sprout.

Watersprite had put the forged will in place on that previous call. The purpose of this one was to arrange Sky Hammer 7's death—preferably by seemingly natural causes and not during the strangers' stay. This was Silky's mission, so he must choose how to proceed. He must make the crucial decision between certainty and subtlety. The Gray Helpers always had at least two plans for an outing, and in this case, they had at least three.

The simplest and most brutal option required Sky Hammer to accompany his noble guest when he went to Heaven's Threshold to view the legendary Portal of Worlds tomorrow or the next day. The old man must have seen it thousands of times, but he might go again, just because there was so much talk of a possible opening in the near future. If he did, and did not take too many guards of his own along, then he would die with an arrow hole through either him or his horse, tumbling and rolling down the cliff that Silky had so joyfully described. A tragic mishap!

The trouble with Plan One was that it was far too obvious. As soon as that extraordinary will was discovered, screams of murder would rise to Heaven's chimneypots. Governor Scarlet Meadow, in Cherish, was party to the plot, but if the disinherited Sky Rider appealed to the provincial governor in Wedlock, or even to the Golden Throne itself, then the noodles would come unraveled.

A more insidious option was Plan Two, smallpox, which would have the advantage of not showing up until ten or twelve days after Luminous Aspect and his entourage had departed. Moreover, the resulting panic would strip the ranch of hands who might resist the governor's troops when they arrived to assess death taxes and impose the new owner. The disadvantages were that the outbreak might not catch the old tyrant himself, and Goat Haven would be unsafe to visit for some time after.

There was always wolfsbane. Having used that poison so effectively against Distant Cloud on his first score, Silky was leaning toward using it again. Luminous disliked that option for two reasons. First, it was too sudden. The subject's death while strangers were visiting, swiftly followed by the discovery of an incredible will in the chest in the same room—who would ever believe in that legend? Besides, it would require either Silky himself or another Helper to repeat Sister Watersprite's feat of entering Sky Hammer's bedroom while he slept. One toe stubbed in the dark, or one old man suddenly needing the chamber pot, and all would be lost.

Silky was bound to have other ideas he had not mentioned, and Luminous would be very interested to see which method he used. Sky Hammer's life expectancy was undoubtedly very short.

"This hill is Goat Haven," Silky said. "Those two cairns mark the turnoff."

Not a moment too soon.

✻   ✻   ✻Silky had barely left with the others that morning before Verdant strolled out to the stable to begin her morning ride. She genuinely enjoyed riding, although she had tried it, at first, mainly out of boredom and a wicked sense of daring. Back in Wedlock, her parents would have been scandalized beyond belief at the idea of any woman on horseback, let alone a respectable lady of the mercantile class. In the last week, riding had become her excuse to talk with Walnut Shell, her hope for freedom.

She was determined to escape from Silky, a thief and merciless killer. After Silkworm was born, she had refused to let him touch her. Their marriage was a sham, she had said, and her son was illegitimate. Even after three months, when the birth nurse had left, whispering that it was safe and decent for a woman to "admit her husband to her room" again, Verdant had refused. Silky had never argued, threatened, begged, or complained. He had just stood in the doorway or sat on a chair, talking of other things and looking so unbearably sexy that even watching him breathe made her want to tear his clothes off. And one night, somehow—she was never quite sure how—she had found him not just inside her room, but inside the bedcovers and her, too. As always, he had coaxed her body into betraying her with fits of the most intense passion she could imagine. Now she suspected that she might be pregnant again.

Escape would not be easy. Silky had left Plum Blossom behind, obviously to be Verdant's jailer. But Plum Blossom would find Silkworm much easier to watch than his mother, knowing that she would never run away without him. At the moment, he was still making the entire household suffer from his colic, so Verdant was free to finalize her plans with Walnut Shell.

He was waiting with the last two horses saddled, hers and the one normally ridden by Plum Blossom. Since seeing Silky off, he had donned a tunic, a garment he wore only when he escorted Verdant into town. Without a word, he offered his hands for her boot and hoisted her up to the saddle. Then he swung nimbly aboard the other mount and they trotted out of the yard together.

She half expected to see the gate keeper replaced by a platoon of Gray Helpers. There might be some in the guard house, but only the usual day man, Bold Star, was visible. Bent and toothless, he scurried out to open the gate for her, bowing low as she passed.

Verdant could now speak without fear of being overheard, but that did not mean that she could trust her uncouth accomplice, who might well turn out to be another Silky spy. He was uneducated but not stupid. She had not put her needs into words yet, but she had hinted enough, so Walnut Shell knew what she wanted of him. He had certainly indicated what he wanted of her, although his idea of wooing was to stare at her with half-closed lids and fondle his crotch. Today she would spell out her plan and, if at all possible, put it into effect.

Without preamble, she said. "I am going to leave my husband and return to my parents."

"Yes, lady." He turned on his noon-strength smile.

"Taking my baby and his nurse." White Petal had not even started weaning Silkworm.

"Yes." Walnut Shell was a man of few words.

"Will you help me?"

"How?"

"Think well," she said. "It's a crime to take a woman away from her husband. Lord Silk Hand could report you to the magistrates."

Walnut Shell snorted. "Him? He's a Gray Helper."

"How do you know . . . I mean, why do you think that?"

"He's in and out of their lair all the time."

"You're not frightened of him?"

"Not if we get away fast. How?"

"There are ships in the harbor. I will buy passage for us. I need you to come with me, because I cannot travel without a man." No captain would let an unaccompanied woman aboard his vessel unless he had a brothel license, and in that case, the girls would be his employees. "I will give you money when we reach Wedlock."

She expected him to ask how much.

He beat around no bushes. "We share a bed?"

"Of course." She returned his smile encouragingly. Why not? She had played whore to get impregnated by Silky, so she could do so again to rescue her son. Besides, the hostler was not hard to smile at. He offered nothing in the way of daytime conversation, but considered purely as future nighttime entertainment, he could hardly be bettered.

"Leave today?"

"If we can."

He nodded. "Go find a ship now?"

She felt a shudder of delicious terror. She had dreamed of this moment. "Yes, now."

Her escort nodded and let her ride on ahead, falling back to a servant's proper place in the rear. Soon they left the area of big, walled houses, passed by the gloomy fort, and entered the teeming trading dock lands along the river. She sniffed at her perfumed sleeve to deaden the stench. She would have to live with smells and fleas and bad food for at least the next two weeks.

One thing that must be said of Silky, he was never miserly. He let her have all the money she asked for to run the household and she had saved quite enough of it to pay the fare back down river. She would have to do the bargaining, because Walnut Shell would be out of his depth, but she had seen how it was done on last year's painfully prolonged trip up from Wedlock.

It turned out to be easier than she expected, because there was only one paddle wheeler in the harbor. She did not trust the small craft or their crews. Having warned her companion not to speak, she walked up the gangplank with him at her heels, hoping neither of them got soot on their clothes to arouse Plum Blossom's suspicions. Her heart sank when she saw the stokers already raising steam—she could not leave without her child.

The captain was a tall, curt man, almost as laconic as Walnut Shell. She explained that her husband's mother was very ill in Wedlock and they wished to go there as soon as possible. She needed a first-class cabin for them, a small one for their child and his nurse. The captain eyed her companion suspiciously, but did not ask if that ill-clad, black-nailed yokel was the husband in question.

He named a fare. She countered.

"No haggling, my lady. I will have to evict the passengers that have already hired those cabins."

She demanded to see them. Walnut Shell followed and inspected the accommodation, too, although she had not, and would not, ask his opinion. He came out with all his teeth showing, for there was only one pallet provided and no room for more. The second cabin was a hutch, in which even Silkworm and White Petal would be squashed, but that was to be expected. Verdant accepted the tariff, haggled over the deposit, and demanded a receipt in case the ship left a little earlier than the announced sailing time of midafternoon. The port authorities were particular about such misunderstandings, although they would be more interested in extracting a fine from the captain than recovering her money.

Trembling at what she had just done, she went back down to the horses with her accomplice close behind. Desertion, kidnapping, and soon adultery? Not that Silky would care about the last, because he was even more convinced than she that she was already pregnant again. If she asked permission to cuckold him, he would probably tell her to go right ahead and enjoy herself. He would object vehemently to the abduction of his son.

So somehow Verdant must distract Plum Blossom and return to the dock again with Silkworm and his wet nurse. And her too-eager escort, of course.

Luminous saw at once that Silky had observed and described Goat Haven well: the long grassy hillside to the guard post at the base of the cliffs; the steeper, well fortified path up to the plateau; and the maze of paddocks and buildings there. The noble Luminous Aspect's approach had been observed, so his arrival was expected, but he noticed that the escort provided easily outnumbered the one he had brought—no less than a dozen slit-eyed, stone-faced borderers armed with both rifles and pistols. Perversely, he welcomed this evidence of the locals' distrust. If they thought twelve ranch hands had a hope against six Gray Helpers, then they had no idea what they were up against.

They all wore barbarian costume of leather breeches and tunics, but Sky Rider was waiting at the top of the climb to greet the noble guest on his father's behalf, and he wore proper gentlemen's robes. He was a chubby man of medium height with a vaguely vacuous face. Not impressive at all, decided Luminous, who prided himself on judging people. Speeches were made.

The visitors were escorted to a guesthouse, comprising a fine chamber for the prince and a dormitory that would have held a dozen retainers. Silky remained impassive as they looked around, but he could not be pleased. He had hoped the fake prince's retinue would be billeted in one of the hands' bunkhouses, where they could leave smallpox-infected blankets as a farewell gift if he chose that plan. Moreover, the guesthouse had only one door, which would obviously be watched at night. Luminous soon discovered two more problems.

As soon as Prince Luminous Aspect and Lord Silk Hand—guards did not count—had washed and changed after their journey, they were led across to the main palace building and the hall that Silky had described. There was no meal in progress this time, the floor looked as if it had been freshly swept in the guests' honor, and their host was standing on his dais to greet them. Low bows and flowery greetings were exchanged, and then the two princes sat down on cushions to drink tea and discuss the mess the world was in. Luminous noted that Sky Hammer leaned on his son's arm to do so, but the implication of that escaped him at the time. Attendants withdrew to a respectable distance.

Despite his fine silken draperies, all adorned with fat artistic horses, Sky Hammer was far too sun-dried to be mistaken for the sort of noble who would be welcome in Sublime Mountain. His grating speech bore more resemblance to the sound of paddle-boats than to the Palace Voice spoken there. He was tall, lean, and aging, yet he still looked capable of holding his own in a fight. He would be far harder to deceive than his son.

How official his title might be was immaterial. The governor's clerks in Cherish classed him as a rancher and landowner, but in practice, he was a clan chief or minor warlord, a semidomesticated brigand. Yet his pleasure at meeting his visitor seemed genuine enough. Real princes coming to call must be as rare as whales in these hills, although many of his neighbors likely claimed the same pseudo-royal honors he did. That Luminous Aspect was a self-promoted corpse washer must not become a topic of conversation, or the mountebank and his companions would descend from the plateau much faster than they had come up.

It was easy enough to steer the talk around to Tenth Dynasty scroll paintings. Many were hung around the three walls enclosing the dais, but Luminous had memorized the inventory taken by the Gray Sisters two years ago and knew that this was only a small part of the Goat Haven collection. He let his eyes wander.

"You are a collector yourself, Noblest?" the rancher inquired.

"In a very humble way. Indeed, what you have on display here quite overawes my few trifles, and I cannot believe your magnificence would expose his greatest treasures to the vagaries and odors of a dining hall."

"But I like to keep some of my favorites by me. The one by Smoke Hand is not without merit, I believe." *Serve. . . .*

Without hesitation, Brother Luminous glanced up at the scroll his host referred to. "His treatment of wind in long grass is quite unmistakable." *Return. . . .* "The waterfall behind me cannot be a genuine Agate Shining though?"

Even the dour Sky Hammer seemed as impressed as he should be, for the fraudulent Luminous Aspect could have had only a few seconds on his way in to observe the waterfall, let alone study it. "A clumsy imitation by one of his pupils. The original hangs in my chamber. If Your Excellency would care to see?"

That was when Luminous discovered a major snarl in the web that Silky had been hoping to weave. The moment Sky Hammer began to rise from his cushion, it was obvious that the effort cost the old man considerable pain. Sky Rider strode forward from the shadows to help. Of course one could not ask why and must pretend to be so engrossed in the paintings that he had not noticed. But if the rancher had sprained his back, come off a horse, or was even suffering a worse-than-usual attack of hemorrhoids, then he would certainly not want to go sightseeing at Heaven's Threshold tomorrow. Abandon Plan One.

The prince's bedroom was in a separate building, connected by a tiled and roofed breezeway. Sky Hammer walked slowly, but no slower than was seemly, and his only sign of discomfort was a clenched jaw. When they reached his bedroom, though, he sank into a padded chair with a long sigh of relief. The chamber was spacious and bright, as the Gray Sisters had described it. Twenty-three paintings hung on the walls, their subtle tints emphasized by the brilliant colors of the soft quilts on the brick sleeping platform and the floor's wool carpets. Luminous stopped and drew a deep breath, as if inhaling the essence of beauty.

"Magnificent! Oh that my revered father could have glimpsed such a miracle, just once in his life!" He did not look anywhere near the muniment chest under the center window, oak and iron, black with age. In there lurked the fake will that was the essence of this entire scam. Nor did he look at the bed, because if Silky decided on wolfsbane as the agent of choice, it was there that the deadly dust would have to be sprinkled.

"It was my own grandfather who began the collection," Sky Hammer said. "But take your time, Highness. Wallow! Drink deep. Sometimes I feel like a miser, hoarding such beauty all to myself."

"Who could bear to do otherwise? This is the true Agate Shining waterfall you mentioned. Yes, the brush of the master is unmistakable." Just for now, Luminous Aspect was a true expert. In a few months, Luminous would have forgotten it all, but he was confident that Sky Hammer would not unmask him.

The old man seemed to have lost any desire to test him. He clearly adored his scroll paintings. This hobby must be most of his life now, and the chance to share it with another enthusiast was a treat. He watched eagerly as his guest worked his way along the wall, scroll by scroll, judging and admiring. The two old men chattered like children. But then . . .

"Observe up there," Sky Hammer said, pointing a gnarled finger at a painting, "how the curl of the cloud matches the bend of the tree branch?" A true gentleman should have smooth fingers with long, dagger-like nails. His were chewed and none too clean, the skin ingrained with dirt.

Luminous did not observe the curl of the cloud. He was staring in horror at Sky Hammer 7's wrist, paler skin exposed where his silk sleeve had fallen away. In this brighter chamber, he could see the distinctive pits of smallpox scars on the old man's wattled neck also. They might be half a century old, but if Sky Hammer

had once survived a bout with smallpox, then he would not suc-
cumb again, and Silky's best plan lay in ruins.

When the visitor came to the ugly muniment chest, he ignored
it, but paused to admire the view. He was surprised to see that the
building was perched almost on the edge of the cliff, with only
a narrow paved terrace and a low wall separating them. Beyond
those lay more long vistas of the Fortress Hills—the rounded
green *females* and the larger, taller *male* ones, with their flat hats
of white limestone. Then—in the far, far distance—the great icy
peaks of the Western Wall.

"The great masters would appreciate this monumental view,
Your Highness. The world does homage at your window. Can
you see the Portal of Worlds from here?"

"Regrettably, no. That hill is in the way. I keep meaning to
have it moved." Clearly a standard joke. "But Sky Rider will be
happy to conduct you to Heaven's Threshold tomorrow. The
lighting is best in the late morning."

"Incredible!" There was no point in killing Sky Rider yet.

The roof creaked. The sky roared.

Luminous turned to the door as his host leaped from the chair
with surprisingly agility. Before they had moved three steps, the
windows shattered behind them, and the floor began heaving
under their feet so they could no longer stay upright. Luminous
grabbed his host and they went down together, twisting so he
ended up underneath the old man. Although the impact was
heavy enough to knock all the breath out of him, he had his host's
body to shield him from falling debris, as the roof writhed and
began to fail. Both men were screaming in terror.

Brother Luminous had experienced earthquakes before, but
nothing to compare with this. The building was flapping like a
rug shaken by a housemaid. The noise alone was stunning. He
fully expected to die, or be beaten to a pulp by repeated bouncing
on the floor. Daylight showed above him as the roof collapsed,

massive beams dropping in a hail of tiles. He burrowed in under Sky Hammer as well as he could.

His head bounced up and down on the tiles hard enough to daze him. He may even have been unconscious, briefly, for he had distinct feeling that some time had passed, yet the earth's rampage still continued. He was buried in darkness, and dust made his eyes water so hard he could not have seen anything anyway. The pressure on his chest was such that he could hardly breathe. The entire roof seemed to be lying on him.

Suddenly, there was light. He was looking at hazy blue sky. He was falling.

When Silky went with Brother Luminous to wait upon Sky Hammer, he had ordered his band to explore the ranch. If challenged, they were to say they had been told to check on their mounts, and thereafter they should try to make friendly and get shown around. Shortly after, when Luminous and Sky Hammer went to the prince's quarters to study the stupid paintings, Silky followed. The door was shut in his face.

The air was still, hot, and heavy as lead. Pretending to admire the scenery, he sat on the low wall flanking the shady side of the connecting breezeway and leaned against one of the posts supporting the roof. Another hill blocked his view of the Portal of Worlds, which he no longer expected to see on this trip— certainly old Sky Hammer hadn't been moving like a man willing to spend half a day on a horse for esthetic reasons. Smallpox was drastic and unreliable, strictly a last resort. Fortunately, Silky had brought along a selection of useful toxins. While he was mentally reviewing them, he realized that the vapid Sky Rider was standing just outside the hall, watching him. Likely every member of the team was being similarly shadowed.

"What's it like here in the winter?" Silky intended to stay at Goat Haven until at least then, once he had taken possession.

For a while, the heir stood and scowled at him resentfully, but eventually he succumbed to Silky's winning smile and came to join him. He sat on the wall opposite, looking offensively suspicious and untrusting.

"Cold. Windy."

"How many head do you keep up here in summer?"

Long pause, then a shrug. "Just working stock."

No surprise. The breeding herds would be out in the hills, growing fat on lush spring grass, while the limited grazing on the plateau would be saved for winter.

"You have much trouble with rustlers?"

"Not after we shoot 'em."

Conversation was a struggle, answers always shorter than questions. Silky very soon concluded that Sky Rider wouldn't know which end of a noodle should be eaten first. He did admit that he had buried two wives and had several sons around. The exact number had perhaps escaped him. Silky made a note to identify them, because they might have to be outed also.

About then, the boring conversation was enlivened by an ear-splitting thunder, almost immediately joined by a major earthquake. Silky found himself on the ground, which kept tossing him like a salad, so that he was unable to stand or even sit up. The breezeway collapsed. Somewhere, people were screaming. It all seemed to last a lifetime, and he wondered what would be left of Goat Haven.

When the ground stopped leaping and the incredible noise ceased, he heard himself coughing in the dust, and assumed that he was still alive. He had far too many bruises to count, but probably no broken bones. Although the breezeway had gone, spilling him out on the grass, the worst of the debris had missed him. Sky Rider had not been so lucky, for the roof had toppled in his direction as it fell. He was lying on the shattered tiles, moaning, buried from the chest down under beams and tiles. The air was thick with dust and a hundred horses were screaming in terror.

Sky Hammer 7's personal quarters, where the two self-appointed princes had been inspecting paintings, had vanished altogether. The quake had taken a great bite out of the plateau, and only the front doorstep remained on the cliff's new edge. The next step would be one's last. . . . Luminous Aspect and Sky Hammer 7 and the muniment chest must be far below, buried under thousands of tons of rock. So the princely domain of Goat Haven was to be the personal property of the ninny lying at Silky's feet, who had now recovered enough to start bleating for help. He would assume the name of Sky Hammer 8 and rule all he surveyed. Or would he? Where was Brother Silky's great inheritance? Why was Silky not equally worthy? Had not Heaven just sent a sign?

"How badly are you hurt?"

"Help me! I'm in pain. Help me! Help me!"

"I can cure the pain." When a Gray Brother surrendered his weapons, only visible weapons were involved. In an instant, Silky could whip out a thin cord and scrag the new prince, but a ruptured trachea and cyanosed face would not be consistent with death by earthquake. He found the largest balk of wood he could lift and flattened Sky Hammer 8's skull.

Now to restore some order to this chaos. The dust had gone. At least three buildings were on fire, but they must be left to burn out. Horses were still tearing around the meadows in panic, on ground strewn with rubble from fallen walls and buildings. Probably much of the stock here at the ranch had already suffered fatal injuries, and the rest soon would. Fortunately, the greater part of the stud was out on open grassland. Those might have stampeded, but they should have escaped serious harm.

Men were arriving, looking for orders, and the only man around wearing a gentleman's robes was Lord Silk Hand. He called on all his seeming magic to portray authority. Soon he was facing a crowd of about a score of men and almost as many women, plus sobbing children of all ages. His own four helpers were all there, and had come to the front. He raised his arms. Three Gray Brothers and one Gray Sister sank to their knees, and of course the shattered and bereaved inhabitants of Goat Haven did the same.

"The noble prince, Sky Hammer 7, and his noble son, Sky Rider, have both mounted to the Fifth World. May Heaven speed their passage! We must do all we can to salvage what is left of the stud they held so dear, as they would have wished. Who is senior here?"

Who indeed? After some glances and muttering, one man sank to touch his face to the grass. "Assistant Stablemaster Granite, my lord."

"Up, up! I appoint you Chief Foreman Granite, or whatever the top title is, until we see who has lived and who died. For today, at least, you are in charge. You must detail men to collect and calm the horses as well as you can. They will not settle properly until all the injured ones have been silenced, and you must see to that also. Assign about half your people to locating and rescuing the injured. Women can help with that. Set up a place for the wounded. As for the departed . . ."

He paused to watch the horror spread, the dread of contact with the ill-omened dead.

"Where is the nearest House of Joyful Departure?"

"In Cherish, my lord," said Granite.

Cherish? What had happened in Cherish? So large an earthquake must have done some damage there. The full horror of the disaster struck Silky as he realized that his beloved Thunderbot might be among the slain. And his second child, as yet unborn? Realizing he could do nothing about them now, he struggled to put them out of his mind, which was not as easy as he expected. Verdant, too, kept coming back to haunt him and muddle his planning.

"The town will be in ruins. There will be hundreds or thousands of dead there needing care. The road is probably impassable." Even the trail down the cliff would be. "My men will gather the departed. Prepare a great pyre—"

Quick-witted Carp shouted out, "No, no, my lord!"

Windchime joined in with even louder protests.

"Yes!" Silky thundered. "The bane is greatest for family and household. We, being strangers, may even acquire some merit for a charitable act. So prepare a worthy pyre, Chief Foreman, and my men will lay out the departed for their ascension. I have attended enough funerals in my life to recall most of the blessing, I believe. I will chant a simple farewell for them."

He saw the relief in their eyes and knew that he had won their respect. They would accept him, for the present. In a few days, it would become a habit. They were humble people who had lost loved ones and security, whose world had shattered under their feet. They needed a leader. If Brother Silky played this right, he would soon be Prince Silk Hand of Goat Haven by the decree of Heaven. Mayhap Heaven was starting to right the many wrongs it had done him.

CHAPTER 7

Verdant had still not worked out how she would smuggle her son out of the house without her jailer noticing. She had ordered Walnut Shell to bring the horses around to the front door after the midday meal. After that, she would have to improvise.

Plum Blossom had welcomed her back from her ride without the slightest sign of suspicion, which meant nothing. While Verdant was certain that Plum Blossom was spying on her, she found it much more difficult to spy on Plum Blossom. She disappeared for the rest of the morning and none of the servants seemed to know whether she had gone out or if she was still around somewhere. At worst, she knew exactly what Verdant was planning and enjoyed playing cat to her mouse.

Just before noon, though, she appeared in street clothes to say she would not be present for lunch, was there anything Verdant needed from the town?

"Nothing, thank you. You going anywhere special?"

"Down to the nunnery to wash a few corpses. I always find it uplifting."

"Or plan a few murders?"

"That, too." She smiled sweetly and departed. She left in a rickshaw, pulled by Mountain Mist, the senior porter, whom Silky called Dense Fog. So both horses were still in the paddock behind the house.

Hoping that she might manage to be gone before her jailer returned, Verdant hurried to her room to start packing. She would not take much, just a few clothes for the journey, all the gold she had collected, and the pistol that had belonged to her first husband, Distant Cloud. Silkworm would need much more baggage than she would. He was half a year old now, still ferociously self-centered—just like his father, his father said proudly.

She had barely laid out a couple of dresses before the door swung open.

"By the way," Plum Blossom said, leaning against the jamb and folding her arms, "I forgot to pass on a message Silky left for you." She was rangy, almost scraggy, and had no dress sense. Now she seemed about forty, but when men were around, she looked plumper, sleeker, and ten years younger.

Caught red-handed, Verdant turned at bay. "Why did he not give it to me himself?"

"Because he did not want you to think he does not trust you."

Worse yet! "And the message is?"

"Just that Thunderbot is his property and stays here. He also hopes you will wait for a better ship than the *Jade Swan*. That's a very inauspicious name."

"I have no idea what you're talking about."

"Jade doesn't float, it sinks. Don't pretend to be any stupider than you really are." Plum Blossom was very good at contempt. "As far as Silky's concerned, you're free to leave anytime. He admits you're a good bounce, but he can ride any mare he fancies. He doesn't love you. Silky can't love anyone except himself. He's possessive about his son, though."

Verdant flopped down on the edge of the bed. What had she expected?

Plum Blossom waited for comment, then shrugged. "You're a fool. Silky lets you live like a princess. You really want to go back to that small-minded, money-grubbing father of yours? He's a murderer, too, with a lot less excuse."

"That's not true!"

"Yes it is. Why did he not warn your husband after Silky told him what was going to happen? Jade Harmony 7? Tell me about Jade Harmony 1."

"A trader, I believe."

"No, a pirate, sentenced to impalement for murder. He died with a cangue around his neck, sitting on a spike in the public square."

"I don't believe you!" But Distant Cloud had made that same sneer about her family's origins.

"Silky told me, and his research is always flawless."

"Pillow talk, I assume?"

"We were in bed, yes, but the pillow was under my ass at the time. I believe him. All the great fortunes start with theft and murder. *All* of them! Emperors win thrones with wars that kill thousands. When they come to power, they make laws to stop other people doing what they did. That is how all the great families begin, girl—with robbers, pirates, and killers. They end with stupid, pampered, spoiled trash like you."

There was no way to answer such filth. Verdant stood up and went back to selecting clothes.

"Have a nice voyage," Plum Blossom said. "There are more guards on the gate now, and they have orders to let you out, but no babies. Have a nice trip. Walnut is hopeless on technique, but great on stamina." She went away, closing the door softly.

Verdant nibbled her midday meal alone, torn between rage and despair. If it weren't for Silkworm, she would be gone in a flash, but she could not desert him, leave him to be brought up by his monster father. Where he went, White Petal must go, too, although the girl was so stupid she didn't care who she worked for, or where. Given two bowls of rice a day, she would do whatever she was told quite happily. Especially for men. She would be pregnant again an hour after she weaned Silkworm.

Eventually, Verdant pushed away her bowl and went to the nursery in search of comfort. White Petal was walking Silkworm, who was having trouble staying awake so he could keep up his yelling. She looked even wearier than he did.

"I'll take him for a while." Verdant laid him on her shoulder—despite his continual colic, he was growing like a mushroom and weighed as much as a full sack of rice. He fell silent, knowing that this was not the one who fed him. Patting him and crooning softly, Verdant wandered out the back, meaning to tell Walnut Shell to abandon his hopes of a romantic voyage, but Walnut Shell wasn't there. Nor were the horses, so Plum Blossom was taking no chances, and now there was no question that Verdant was a prisoner.

She decided to go around to the front and sum up the new guards Plum Blossom had mentioned. Turning the corner of the house, she caught sight of a pillar of black smoke behind the gates. It looked close, but it meant that the *Jade Swan* had steam up and would be leaving soon. There were two men on the gate, both new to her, both armed with swords, and they stared at her as if daring her to try to run past them. Fools! Did they imagine she would try to run away in a house robe? She wanted to howl with frustration.

As if it agreed, the world roared. The gates swung open of their own accord and then fell down. Verdant fell, too, twisting to avoid crushing her child, then rolling on top of him to shield him from the hail of roof tiles shattering as they hit the paving. He screamed right in her ear but she could barely hear him over the almighty din. The ground roiled like a soup pot. The guardhouse collapsed as if built of bean curd. One gatepost broke in half; the other sank into the ground; trees were thrashing; the wall collapsing in a stately dance. She could not think for the excruciating noise or breathe for the dust.

The racket ended so suddenly she would have thought she had gone deaf had Silkworm not been providing ample evidence to the contrary. She sat up, feeling bruises but nothing worse, no broken bones. She hugged him and made comforting noises, but her head was spinning. She couldn't think.

The fog of dust was thinning. The once-smooth yard looked like paintings of the sea. The house had gone, fallen into an amazingly flat heap of rubbish. The forbidding boundary wall had gone, as had the guards, the other walls, and the other houses, but although she should have had a clear view down to the town, the town had vanished. There were no buildings in sight anywhere, only mounds of rubble and trees, some leaning at strange angles. As the rest of the dust settled, smoke trails began to coil upward.

No one was emerging from the ruins of the guardhouse beside the gate. But beyond the bamboo garden—where minutes ago there had been a wall, a street, and more houses, now was only wreckage. She could see Walnut Shell, manfully wrestling with two terrified horses, clinging to their cheek straps, and spending more time in the air than he did with his feet on the ground. He had been bringing them around to meet her, as instructed.

Verdant struggled to her feet, hearing faint screams coming from the rubble of stone, mud, and timber that had been the house. Plum Blossom appeared, limping badly and holding one arm as if it were broken. A few weeping servants trailed behind her.

"Nice to be alive, isn't it?" Plum Blossom said. She waited, then said, "Isn't it?"

"You're hurt."

"I noticed. Broke my collarbone. Can you tie a sling?"

"No."

"It's not hard. But don't worry about me. Get out of here while you have the chance."

"What?"

Plum Blossom came close and peered into Verdant's eyes. Her own face was painted with dust, streaked with blood. "Pull yourself together! You're gaping like a fish."

No one spoke to Verdant like that. She opened her mouth and then closed it again. Maybe there was truth in it. Silkworm needed her.

"I'm all right."

"Good. Then take those horses before somebody else does. And ride! Follow the Wilderness Road. Silky's at a hilltop fort called Goat Haven, about a half a day's ride west. Got that—*Goat Haven*? You can't stay here."

"His nurse! I need—"

"She's dead. A roof beam flattened her. I saw. Lord Silk Hand, remember? And Prince Luminous Aspect. Repeat what I just told you."

"Goat Haven, Lord Silk Hand, Prince Luminous Aspect."

"Well done. Now go!"

Verdant spared a glance for Walnut Shell, who was now managing to keep all ten feet on the ground most of the time, although the horses were still rolling their eyes and shivering like leaves in a hailstorm.

"Go!" Plum Blossom insisted again. "Even if the ship is still afloat, it'll soon be swamped by all the people trying to get on it. You can't even get to it if all the roads are blocked. Refugees will come here soon and take the horses. Go! Oh, I wish I had a free hand to slap you."

"Yes," Verdant said, abandoning efforts to comfort Silkworm. "Come, darling, we'll go and find Daddy."

Her clothes, the gold, the pistol, all the rags for Silkworm— all were buried under the house. She hurried along the bizarrely lumpy driveway and clambered over the rubble of the wall. She knew enough to approach the spooked horses gently. Painted with sweat and dust, Walnut Shell flashed his toothy smile at her. He had certainly proved that his muscles were genuine.

"Go to the ship now, lady?"

"Help me up!" But he daren't let go of the horses.

She looked around desperately for a safe place to lay the sobbing Silkworm and found one. Then she went back to Walnut Shell, took the knife from his belt, and slit the back hem of her robe. She replaced the knife, ripped the silk as high as she could, then went to retrieve her child.

"I'm really looking forward to getting those legs wrapped around me," Walnut Shell said.

She should have stuck the knife in his chest, not his belt. She fashioned a sling from Silkworm's blanket and somehow she managed to mount a terrified horse while cradling a terrified baby. Now what? Walls everywhere had collapsed, so the road was littered with rubble. The smoke rising from the town did not include the *Jade Swan's* black plume, so it had either sunk or been swamped, and in any case, it was out of reach as an escape. People were wandering blankly, some heading down to the town, others in the opposite direction, and one or two already carrying loot. Plum Blossom had been right. Desperate people were dangerous.

"Out of town," she commanded. Escape the looters first. But not in search of Silky. Oh no! She knew what he had intended to do to gain possession of Goat Haven, and she would have no part of it. If she couldn't take a boat down the river, she could still ride that way. It would take longer, but she must head home to Wedlock.

The gently rolling hills above Cherish were too stony for cultivation, but good ranch country. In a few places, the ground had cracked or slid, but the going was fairly easy. Houses had collapsed, herds had scattered, and the surly mounted guards who normally harassed strangers were far too busy to bother Verdant and her escort. Silkworm went to sleep within minutes, which made her wonder why she had never thought of trying to carry him on horseback before.

Her own shock had begun to wear off. As her mind cleared, she felt the stirring of hope that she had escaped from her monstrous captor. Behind her, the remains of the town still burned. The distant river was muddy brown and littered with debris. Walnut Shell refused to push the horses any faster than a walk, but even that slow pace was carrying her ever closer to home and safety. Let her father have the money, whatever was left of it! All that mattered was safety for her son and herself. And soon, maybe another child.

Her rosy daydream crumbled when Walnut Shell, who mostly rode in silence, suddenly pointed and said, "Look, lady!" He was pointing straight ahead. "Little River."

She saw a wide valley and a tributary joining the Jade. Although much narrower, it was a frothy brown torrent, and even from there she could see that it was laden with debris. "It doesn't look very little to me."

"That's its name, Little River. But it isn't, not today."

"How do we cross?"

He shrugged his big shoulders. "Bridge is down, see?"

"You mean we'll have to ford it?" That would be dangerous, especially so soon after the earthquake, when the water would be full of debris, either floating or unseen on the bed.

"Can't, not here. Have to go upstream, long way upstream."

Idiot! She should have realized that traveling along a riverbank was not as easy as sailing on the river itself. She wondered about the Wilderness Road, whether it was equally impassable. Even life with Silky would be better than being trapped in the ruins of Cherish. No, it was too early to give up.

"Then we go upstream," she said. At that moment, Silkworm wakened and began to cry. This time, he had reason, for he needed to be changed and fed.

Later, there was a brief aftershock. The horses panicked, but somehow Verdant managed to stay on and keep hold of Silkworm. Walnut Shell rode alongside and caught hold of her mount's bridle, bringing it under control again.

He had been staying well clear of any sign of living people. Two horses were too valuable to risk, he said. But suddenly she realized that he was heading to the remains of what might have been a family home, not far from the river. Now it was a heap of mud, timber, and roof tiles; the barn was badly canted, but still a recognizable building, and the paddock rails had survived.

"Horses need to rest and eat," he said. "There's water here."

There was no goat, though, and Silkworm desperately needed milk from somewhere. While Walnut Shell tended to the horses—removing their tack, loosing them in the paddock, and fetching hay—Verdant cleaned her child as best she could, and wet a corner of his blanket at the pump, so he could at least have something to suck. He wanted a nipple, but he was either too tired or already too weak to do more than whimper. She laid him on the softest-looking patch of grass she could see, and sank down beside him. She was bone weary and worried that Walnut Shell would no longer accept her orders if he didn't like them. Why should he? She didn't even have money to offer him now.

Walnut Shell came over to join her, sitting on the far side from Silkworm. He inspected the piteous morsel.

"It'll die in a day or two."

"No!"

"Yes. Might be kinder to settle it now." The stableman leaned over her and closed his great hand around the baby's tiny throat. Verdant screamed and tried to hit him. He laughed, and pushed her down so he could lie on top of her.

"I am with child!" she protested.

"Then I'll make it twins. I don't like that husband of yours, lady—that snooty Gray Helper prancing around, putting on airs, pretending to be a great lord."

She didn't like his breath, nor his face so close to her. He was heavier than Silky.

"I don't suppose he would like you if he saw you like this."

"But he's not here, is he? That's why I'm going to fuck his wife for him now. I'm going to fuck her long and hard. And if you don't cooperate, that'll be just fine, too. Now take your clothes off." He moved off her.

She did as she was told. Distant Cloud had been clumsy; Silky had been greedy. Walnut Shell liked to be rough, and he laughed every time she cried out or protested. Plum Blossom had not been lying when she said he was long on stamina. His hands were rough as rasps.

When she reached for her clothes, he roused himself to block her and said he was going to go for triplets.

It was almost dark before he was satisfied. Sore, battered, and utterly humiliated, she just lay there as he dressed and walked away. But when she heard him calming the horses, she realized that he was quite capable of riding off into the night, taking them both, and leaving her there to die. She scrambled into her clothes, snatched up Silkworm, and hobbled over to the paddock.

To her relief, he let her mount up, and they rode off together.

"Small way upstream from here's a village called Tutu," he said. "I was born there, but telling them so won't make them any friendlier."

"We're going to stay there tonight?"

"You are, and your stinky brat, too."

Tutu was in ruins. Some of the debris was still burning and people were wandering like sleepwalkers through the mess, perhaps looking for anything worth saving.

Walnut Shell reined in a short walk away. "Desperate people," he growled. "Dangerous."

"My baby needs milk."

He laughed. "You can ask. You may have to pay the same sort of fee you paid me. Now get down." He had caught hold of her reins.

"You're not going to leave me!"

"Oh yes I am. Do it!"

He rode away into the dusk. Having no choice, she began to plod in the direction of the village. This morning she had been rich, and now she was literally a beggar. Who was going to worry about some anonymous murdered stranger on a day like this? She owned nothing but a tattered robe, shoes, one blanket, and a doomed baby. But even the odious Walnut Shell had praised her body while abusing it, so perhaps some man would take pity on her. Food was never overly plentiful in the spring, and famine must be very likely now, with all the warehouses in ruins.

She was seen before she reached the ruins. Half a dozen men and a few women lined up to scowl at her approach, but then one couple came forward to meet her. The woman was short and plump, and she had already opened her robe to display milk-swollen breasts. Oh yes! Eagerly, Verdant moved toward her, but the man stepped between them.

Older than the woman, short but wiry, hardened by toil, he regarded the offered baby sourly. "Boy or girl?" he growled.

"Boy."

His nod of satisfaction implied that he would have plucked a girl away from his wife's nipple and discarded her. Heaven had taken his child and now offered him another, which would be acceptable only if Heaven had replaced a daughter with a more valuable son.

"I am very hungry," Verdant said, despising the beggar's whine in her voice.

"And we have very little. You work for me?"

"Feed me and my child and I'll do anything you want," she said.

CHAPTER 8

The fraudulent Son of the Sun was dining with Snow Lily, the Pearl Concubine, supping delicacies out of exquisite Fourth Dynasty porcelain bowls. Outside in the twilight, Nightingale Moon hung above the skyline like a silver smile, promising that spring was here, even in Heart of the World. With a small orchestra warbling discreetly at the far end of the hall, Butterfly Sword savored the romantic moment, although it added to his torment. He was desperate to welcome Snow Lily back to the imperial bed, but Court Astrologer had not yet determined an auspicious evening for their reunion. No doubt the Empress Mother was masterminding this so that Butterfly Sword would impregnate a few of his other concubines first.

He was certain that Snow Lily was as eager as he was, but this evening she seemed upset about something else. He would not pry; she would tell him when she was ready.

"How can it be," he asked, "that I rule all of the world that counts and yet my food is always cold? It makes no difference where in the palace I eat."

Her dimples flickered into view for an instant. "I expect they only have one kitchen worthy of your service. And after it arrives, it must be sampled by the tasters."

"At least we do have food." Had not the Humble Teacher said, *Count your blessings to be happy and your troubles to be sad*? "Two years of bad weather have punished crops everywhere. And now the earthquake!"

Being privy to many, if not all, state secrets, he knew that millions of his supposed subjects were growing hungrier by the day—homeless and starving. He was supposed to be their father, and yet he could do *nothing*!

It was easy enough to blame misfortune on last year's broom stars, but knowing the cause of last month's earthquake did not find a cure. Day by day, news came dribbling in: news of entire cities so flattened that it was impossible to tell that there had ever been cities there, news of floods and landslides, of bridges fallen and canal locks shattered, fires, rivers half-choked with bodies. The worst destruction seemed to have been in Shashi, but some had extended well to the north, into Nanling and Wanrong. The lack of real news yet from south of the Jade River was itself very bad news.

One thing was certain: The Bamboo Banner would be drawing strength from this disaster, preaching that the Eleventh Dynasty had lost the mandate of Heaven. The Empress Mother herself seemed almost convinced of that now, half-terrified of what her own actions might have provoked. When Butterfly Sword had pointed out that the Banner would have to cross all that devastated country to meet the army, she had allowed herself to be relieved by this comfort, even though it came from her puppet, whom she preferred to regard as an ignorant lummox.

Snow Lily dropped her gaze. "Your Majesty flatters me by sharing confidences." She gave him titles in private only when she was unhappy.

"You are the only one I can share them with." He wrapped one of her hands in one of his much greater ones. "You already know the greatest secret of all. I trust your discretion, and if the she-dragon did not, we should never have met."

"It is so hard! We have nothing to do in the concubine quarters except laze around all day and gossip. I am always frightened that I will let slip something I am not supposed to know."

"Then I will not burden you with any more state business," he promised. She had given him a child, he had given her a title; the other women probably picked on her mercilessly.

She pouted. "Sweet Melody is in labor."

So that was the problem! "I wish her well."

"I don't. I hate her. I wouldn't mind Devotion. She's nice. But if Melody gives you a first son, you will appoint her Empress."

"Not I. Not even the most Junior-Junior-Junior of Empresses." Sweet Melody was a total bore whose only interest was her own advancement. She was as ambitious as the Empress Mother, but nowhere near as clever. "And just because her son would be older than any of the dozen sons you are going to give me doesn't mean that he would inherit the throne. You know that an Emperor chooses which son will succeed him."

"The she-dragon will make her an Empress whether you like it or not," Snow Lily said sulkily.

Butterfly Sword sighed. "She may. Listen, my love. I am in danger. If Sweet Melody does produce a son, I won't be needed anymore."

"Oh. No!" Snow Lily's eyes widened in horror. "She wouldn't . . . Not right away, surely? That would be too obvious."

"Obvious to whom? Her deception is so enormous that no one can imagine it. As the Desert Teacher said, *A man atop a mountain can see all the world except the mountain.* I could jump up in the Great Council and shout out that I am a fraud, but no one would believe me. Nevertheless, the she-dragon knows the truth, so my future here is not auspicious. I must make my escape while I can."

"How?"

"I don't know," he admitted. "It seems to be much easier to become an Emperor than it is to unbecome one. She has me watched night and day." He was fairly sure that Joyous Diligence had lied to him about patrol dogs, but the human surveillance was certainly very tight.

"I'll come with you."

He shook his head. "Even if I get away, I'll be a penniless, friendless fugitive. You must stay on in the palace and look after Snowbell."

"Bah! You're being stupid." How many concubines in the history of the Good Land had ever said that to an Emperor? "They don't let me near Snowbell without other people watching me. I wasn't allowed to nurse her. You told me you loved me."

"I did. I mean I did tell you and I do still love you."

"No," she said suddenly, her rose-petal mouth suddenly determined. "You are right. We concubines are guarded more closely than rubies. Even you could never smuggle me out of the Great Within. I am safe here because I am Snowbell's mother. You must leave us and escape by yourself." Her eyes glistened. "But I will miss you, miss you, miss you!"

He sighed. "I cannot bear to leave you." The problem had no solution.

"You must! You are not safe here and I am."

She was not safe, that was the trouble. She knew that her daughter was a fraud and the baby prince, also, whenever one chose to appear. Sooner or later, the Empress Mother would decide to clean house of all potential troublemakers, and she held all the—

Drums? Gongs! Bells! The orchestra froze into icicles as the doors flew open and guards rushed in. Close behind them trotted a dozen bearers, carrying the palanquin of the Empress Mother. Now what? The tigress rarely announced her approach and had never come calling on her fake son before. But unpredictability was one of her strengths, one that Butterfly Sword admired. He admired many things about the woman who ruled an empire that was supposed to be ruled by men. Even the Gray Helpers could not match her for ruthlessness.

The chair advanced to that end of the hall and was set down. The drape flew open. There sat the Empress Mother in all her splendor, looking furious at the entire world. Snow Lily slid to the floor and kowtowed.

"I stopped by," the newcomer proclaimed, "to let you know that you need not waste sleep tonight waiting for news of Sweet Melody. She is attempting a breech birth, stupid girl, so nothing will happen until tomorrow at the earliest. And tomorrow is a highly inauspicious day."

"You are kind, August Mother," Butterfly Sword said.

The old harridan scowled even harder. "You were clumsy, putting it in the wrong way up. I assume you were indulging in perverted acrobatics. You still lack an heir, *Your Majesty*!" And with that, she slammed the silken drape shut. A guard called an order, the bearers lifted the palanquin, and the Empress Mother departed as swiftly as she had arrived.

Butterfly Sword gestured permission for Snow Lily to resume her seat. Such imperial graces were second nature to him now. "Um . . . what is a breech birth?"

Snow Lily was ashen pale. "The baby is the wrong way up. Poor, poor Melody! She'll struggle for days and when she is exhausted they will cut her open to get it out."

He put down his chopsticks. He had never known that childbirth could be so horrible. His seed had killed Moth. Now Sweet Melody?

A trill of harp music soared through the hall, and a voice began to sing.

"Blossoms come with the moon
And die before it.
If I mourn their passing
What of the bud that never bloomed?"

It was almost finished before the words registered as familiar—an old poem by a minor poet, nothing special. If the singer had overheard the Empress Mother's news, the song was so glaringly inappropriate that it might merit the death penalty for sedition, but the hall was very big, so the boy had probably just made an unlucky choice. Now Butterfly Sword remembered where he had heard it, and who had sung it. He turned to study the orchestra. Judging by the hand waving and other body language, the soloist had performed without permission and the orchestra leader was furiously warning that he would suffer for it later.

The Emperor clapped his hands. The Emperor beckoned! The orchestra leader rushed over and kowtowed, practically sliding to a halt on his forehead in his haste.

"That was well done. The singer's name?"

"Eunuch Arpeggio, Your Majesty."

"We will hear more of Eunuch Arpeggio's magic."

As the music director scampered back to his ensemble, Butterfly Sword carefully avoided meeting Snow Lily's surprised expression. He was having great difficulty keeping a straight face, because the last time he had seen or heard Eunuch Arpeggio, he had been Sister Lark in the House of Joyful Departure in Sheep Rocks. How had she arrived here in Sublime Mountain, and why was she deliberately attracting the attention of the man she had known as Novice Horse?

That the contact was intentional seemed even more likely when "Eunuch" Arpeggio plucked a few strings and then sent her superb alto voice soaring to the rafters in a famous celebration of a herd of horses galloping over the hills, another work she had sung back in those days that now seemed so long ago. Did that choice imply that she had come to rescue Novice Horse? Could he race away from his captivity in Sublime Mountain?

Sister Lark was at least ten years his senior and a confessed would-be murderer, serving a life sentence in Sheep Rocks. She had given the leggy young initiate some of his first lessons in sex and they had remained casual lovers, like every other heterosexual combination in the Sheep Rocks priory. They had never been friends. So how and why was she now in the imperial palace?

The Emperor applauded Eunuch Arpeggio's recital and sent over exquisite porcelain rice bowls as rewards for him and the music director, a standard gratuity that cost the throne nothing, because such items would normally be stolen on their way back to the kitchen.

The Emperor—and there were times now when Butterfly Sword could almost watch himself performing—then dismissed the Pearl Concubine. He had promised not to burden her with more secrets, and Sister Lark's presence in the palace was a hair-raising one. He told her to give Sweet Melody his best wishes and prayers, and to send him word of her progress. He then retired to the imperial sleeping quarters, where his valets stripped him of his dress robes and clad him in a loose silk gown embroidered with five-clawed dragons. Eunuch Joyous Diligence bowed and snidely inquired which lady or ladies His Majesty required as company that night.

If Lark had come to help him escape, she might have organized his departure for this very evening, although more likely she would need him to help by issuing specific orders to somebody. Either way, she would almost certainly call on him tonight.

"None of them. Tonight we are oppressed by the thought of Sweet Melody's travails."

The Keeper of Hours sighed. "Yes, indeed. A breech birth killed my sister. A long and terrible death!"

Butterfly Sword clenched a fist. "Go away and stay away."

Which was what he intended to do if he got the chance, but what would happen to Snow Lily? The thought of leaving without her was agony, and yet he had nothing to offer her in the world outside Sublime Mountain except danger. Earthquakes, revolution, and many lesser disasters were spreading death over the Good Land like sauce over rice. He could do nothing about those. If he was certain to die soon, he had nothing to offer her inside the palace, either.

So began the agony of waiting. By the light of a single lamp, he paced around his great bedchamber. Had he misunderstood the hint about horses? Armed eunuchs stood guard outside his door all night. More guards patrolled the grounds—he had watched them often enough and knew that they kept to no regular schedule, although he had never seen dogs with them. He trusted Lark to know where he was sleeping, but every now and again, he would go to a window and stare out, so she would see him if she were in doubt. The moon had set and the park was a pattern of shadow upon shadow in the starlight.

How had she escaped from the penal house of Sheep Rocks? She had been tethered there by her leash, commanded to stay and obey the prior. It was she who had warned Novice Horse about leashes, thereby breaking one of the strictest of rules. Lark had never been much for obeying rules. In her previous posting, she had tried to poison her abbess, or so she claimed. She cynically maintained that her real crime had been failure; had she succeeded, she would have been promoted.

Whatever her mission here in Sublime Mountain, it had to be illegal and almost certainly treasonous. So why had she been chosen for it? Because the fake Emperor knew her and would recognize her, obviously. But after that, Butterfly Sword's thinking ran into a wall. Who was planning to do what? To, and for, whom?

Her presence in the Great Within strongly suggested the supple, subtle hand of Lady Twilight, who was the only link between the Order and the court and probably the only person in the entire Empire who knew all the details of the conspiracy. It was impossible to imagine the Empress Mother making a quick trip to Sheep Rocks in person.

If Lark had been sent to kill him, she would never have shown herself to him beforehand. The Empress Mother had many ways of causing people to die without having to recruit Lark, and that reasoning also eliminated Lady Twilight. An outsider, then? A new player in the game? Some minor prince seeing himself as a contender for the throne had offered a fortune to some House of Joyful Departure to dispose of His Imperial Majesty Emperor Absolute Purity?

That was the only theory that came close to explaining why Lark had revealed herself during dinner. He was both an impregnably guarded Emperor and a trained Gray Brother. Had she approached him without warning, he could have yelled for his guards or just snapped her neck himself.

He had expected to have to wait for half the night, but the stars had hardly moved in their courses before something creaked in the darkest corner of the room. A vertical strip of light appeared low down—light so faint he might not have noticed it at all had his eyes not been completely dark-adjusted, but light where there should be none. It widened to a rectangle and was obscured as a black-garbed figure entered on hands and knees. She straightened up and advanced into the lamplight, blinking at its brightness.

Palace servants were excused the excessive formalities required of princes and other high ranks. So were assassins. Lark did not kowtow.

He bowed to her instead. There could be no legal explanation for their meeting like this in this place, so the Order's normal insistence on staying in character at all times did not apply. He did not embrace her, for they had never been friends and he certainly did not trust her. He admired her as hard-bitten, meticulous, and an excellent operator. Tonight, she even smelled like a eunuch.

"You are a sight for sore eyes, Sister. Your arrival here is a miracle, and I congratulate you on it. But don't come any closer until you have explained why I should trust you."

She acknowledged the tribute with a nod. "You have done wonderfully well, Brother. I was amazed when I was told what you were up to."

"It is the she-dragon's doing. Her audacity is amazing. No one else could have pulled it off. They call her the tigress. She is quite a character."

"She must be." Lark was implying that she had not met the Empress Mother, but that meant nothing in such a fog of intrigue.

"I see you have resources I do not," he said. "How ever did you learn about that sneaky backdoor?" An assassin's door into the Emperor's bedroom was unthinkable, which strongly suggested that the Empress Mother must be behind this. Had she sent Lark to kill him? That was possible if the tale of the breech birth was a lie and Sweet Melody had in truth been delivered of a healthy son, but the timing seemed unlikely. He ought to be able to count on a few more months so that his death would not seem such a suspicious coincidence. And why alert him beforehand?

Was this a rescue attempt? Surely, that was too much to hope for.

"I had a helper," Lark said. "She's fetching some dark clothes for you, be along shortly."

Lady Twilight, any odds.

"Tell me why I need dark clothes! Are you going to smuggle me out tonight? Is there any chance of taking my lover along with us?"

Lark's eyes shone silver in the lamplight. "Is Moth so soon forgotten?"

Ow! How did she know about Moth? "Never forgotten, but my orders take no account of my feelings. It was almost two years ago, Sister."

"It is now. Well, the answers to your questions are all no. You know Twilight, the so-called Lady Twilight?"

"Yes!"

"She's been the Empress Mother's closest confidante for more than twenty years—confidant and chief poisoner. Her tally in the imperial family alone is about a dozen. Listen . . . *Clusters of vermillion blossoms . . .*

Moonlight leaves the eastern window . . ."

He recoiled and thought he would lose his dinner. A stallion kicking him between the legs would feel no worse, for every heartbeat became a surge of agony. His skin puckered into goose bumps and his muscles trembled violently. So that was his leash?

"Sorry," Lark said offhandedly.

He was drowning in a world of pain. All he could see was her face in the darkness. "Quick, quick! Tell me what you want. And then stop it, please. Oh, please stop it!"

"Just do as I say and speak quietly. Don't give us away."

He nodded miserably. *Hurry! Please hurry!* He wanted to scream and his throat was so tight he could hardly breathe. Sweat coursed down his face and body.

Suddenly, it was over. He straightened up, his breathing steady, not a trace of discomfort. He stared suspiciously at his new mistress, wishing he could wring her neck for inflicting such pain on him. "Why can't I remember?"

She laughed. "You always manage to appear stupid, but I knew you back at Sheep Rocks before you got so good at it. Why do you think?"

"Because you don't trust Twilight. She must know my leash, so you just used it to cancel it and substitute another."

Lark chuckled agreement and wandered over to the great bed to inspect the sweetmeats laid out there for the Emperor's refreshment when his evening exertions had made him hungry. "Of course. Do you remember the words I spoke to bind you?"

·"*Clusters of vermillion blossoms . . . Moonlight leaves the eastern window.*"

Lark popped a sugary treat in her mouth and chewed with obvious pleasure. "Correct. She may try to double-cross me by changing your leash, but she won't do it until the two of you are alone together, so my first command to you was to kill her the moment she speaks those words."

Butterfly Sword felt as if he were sinking in mud and it was up to his shoulders already. Palace games were played for top stakes. "I hope you will warn her."

"Certainly not."

"Can a brother or sister have more than one leash?"

"Certainly. But usually only one is in effect, and any others are booby traps, as your old one now is." She wandered closer to the window.

He went and sat on the edge of a chair where he would have his back to a wall. "How did you escape from Sheep Rocks?"

She laughed without turning. "Sheep Rocks is an ocean of talent, Brother. After you and Prior Fraise disappeared, a new prior arrived. Pretty soon, the others began disappearing, one by one. No farewells, no explanations. New novices and brothers turned up to replace them and by the time I was relieved, it was obvious that anyone who had been there in your day was being separated and possibly silenced. I was pleasantly surprised when I discovered that I was being given a new life. Or any life at all, I mean. Have you spoken with Twilight in the last month?"

"No." Not that he remembered, but memories could be removed.

"Good. I came an hour earlier than we agreed, so I could get to you first. . . . And here she comes, only forty-five minutes early."

A faint scuffling from the corner announced the arrival of the helper. The moment she rose and stepped into light, Butterfly Sword recognized the fake abbess who had enlisted him in Huarache, who had later conveyed him to Heart of the World and smuggled him into Sublime Mountain. But he also recognized Mulberry, one of his food tasters; for months, he had looked at her every day without making the connection. Now she was just a plain, aging, and weary-looking woman clutching a bundle of cloth. Death had always been much nearer than he had realized.

"You had me completely fooled, Sister."

Twilight shrugged. Her expression was unreadable in the dim light. "Of course. But you have fooled everybody, Brother. You have done better than we ever dreamed possible."

"It's all the Empress Mother's doing. I'm just her puppet."

Two Gray Sisters, but which one was in charge? If the Empress Mother was involved, almost certainly Twilight, although she might be cutting her own hay here.

"She was desperate. She is delighted by your skill. She likes you a lot and—"

Lark said, "Stop!" She spoke very softly, but Twilight's grimace suggested strongly that she had been leashed also and Lark was running two slaves. He had guessed wrong. Who could possibly be behind this conspiracy? Lark had known both his leash and Twilight's. He had been told that no one except a helper's abbot knew his leash. . . . But common sense would dictate that there would have to be written copies, kept in a safe place. Someone had found his leash at Sheep Rocks and Twilight's at . . . at wherever she had come from, umpteen years ago. That suggested that this coup had been organized by someone very high up in the Brotherhood.

Lark said, "Take the clothes and get dressed, Horse."

He took the bundle and unrolled a set of Gray Helpers' all-enveloping nightwork garb of dark gray silk. They brought back memories of old times, when he was Horse, practicing burglary in ranch houses around Sheep Rocks. Feeling absurdly shy, he went to the far side of the room and unlaced his robe. "Where did you find these?"

"Made them," Lark said. "It's easy to smuggle things out, but anything coming in is searched for weapons. Hurry."

He obeyed as he must. The hood he could understand, but why gloves? The women were not wearing those. By the time he was done, nothing of him would be visible except his eyes.

"Time to go," Lark said.

The secret passage was totally dark, and the conspirators proceeded by touch. Twilight led the way, Lark brought up the rear, and even they found it a tight squeeze in places. Twice, Butterfly Sword almost became jammed and never did he have enough headroom. He began collecting bruises and scrapes, trying always not to tear his black garments. After several twists and turns, they descended a long staircase, emerging into the open through a hatch behind some shrubbery. Twilight closed it behind them.

The Great Within comprised hundreds of buildings, separated by open courtyards or parkland. Gray Helpers' training still helped, but even seeming magic would not let a person look like nothing at all. Had there been a moon, they would certainly have been seen, but they were black on black, and in more danger of losing one another than being observed by a guard. Butterfly Sword had never worked out the complete geography of even the Great Within, let alone all of Sublime Mountain, but the stars told him that he was being led inward, not out to the perimeter. He was not heading to freedom.

Eventually, Twilight knelt alongside a wide flight of stairs, leading up to an imposing entrance. The sides were made of latticework. She opened a panel in this and the other two followed her in; Lark closed the door. Lying in the evil-smelling dead space under the staircase, Butterfly Sword wondered what else inhabited it. Rats? Snakes? Scorpions? He must be lying on the detritus of years, blown in through the sides, and probably the excrement of small vermin. He could see nothing.

"You know where we are?" Twilight asked.

"No."

"Practically underneath the Empress Mother's bedroom."

Then he knew what was to be required of him. "Does she know it has an assassins' door?"

"It is an emergency exit," Twilight said. "Normally, it cannot be opened from this side. I explored it while she was attending the girl's lying-in this evening, and removed the safety catch on the inner door. This one I left ajar. You crawl about twenty paces straight ahead, then turn left and go up very steep stairs. They stop right at the secret panel, dead ahead. Don't break your neck or bloody your nose."

He nodded. He was about to make his first score, and his subject was the most closely guarded person in the Good Land, probably in the entire Fourth World. The void in his belly would hold an ox.

"Which way does it open?"

"Away from you."

He shivered. "No lacquered table standing against it, laden with porcelain figures and vases?"

"No," Twilight said. "There should be, of course, but it opens into the privy. That is bad design."

He did not want to do this. He had been too long away from the House of Joyful Departure, where the youngsters talked hopefully of murder every day and the girls favored boys who had scored. He was an Emperor now, not an apprentice assassin. He was out of training. Why him, not one of the women?

"She is my client," he whispered, appalled.

Lark said, "That is why we leashed you. Twilight has served the subject for forty years, so a death order would probably drive her insane. Besides, it may need more physical strength than we have. I will give you the command in a moment."

"Thank you." He was sorry, because he had become fond of the old she-demon, but she had ruled by knife and poison for years, so a violent death was fitting. This was what he had trained for since he was a child, and he did have more to gain than either of the women, more than anyone in fact. It would save him from an early death. It would be an epochal score, even for the Gray Order.

"Guards?"

"None in the chamber," Twilight said. "In summer, she has servants to fan her all night, but not now, just a maid sleeping behind a screen. The privy is in the northwest corner, facing east. A chair against the wall, main door center west, handle on your left. Guards outside that door. A freestanding screen, and then a mat in the southwest corner, where a maid sleeps . . ."

She detailed the Empress Mother's bedchamber, which was a large room containing many items of furniture, but he had not lost his training. When Twilight finished her description, he repeated the list back to her twice.

Then: "Why? Who is the client?"

"You are," Lark said. "As soon as you have produced a son, you will die, and the Order does not want to lose you. We will wait here for you." Then she gave him the direct order: "Butterfly Sword, go and out the Empress Mother!"

He was grateful for it, because he could not refuse.

Twilight opened the panel for him and he crawled into a pitch-dark passage.

She had been right about the steepness of the staircase; it was almost a ladder. He could see a faint line of light at the edge of the panel at the top, and when he pushed it ajar, he found that the privy was illuminated by a candle burning brighter than the sun. Now came the tricky part, the reason for the shoes, gloves, and hood. Although he was covered in dust and cobwebs, he must leave no footprints or fingermarks to show that there had been an intruder. Balancing at the top of that steep staircase, he stripped to the skin and went through the hatch stark naked, having a waking nightmare of the Empress Mother throwing open the door and finding him there. Then he would have to use violence and marks on her neck would shout murder to all the world. She did not appear, but when he started to open the door, an angry roar shattered the silence beyond and he stubbed his toe hard enough to bring tears to his eyes. More silence. . . . Then another leonine roar ripped the darkness.

The snores were encouraging, for he had often heard the subject complain of insomnia. The maid remained a serious complication, and he stood and listened a long time, until he had analyzed her breathing and was quite certain that she, too, was asleep. A clock ticked. The air was heavy with the scents of flowers and spices, overlying the body smell of a bedroom and long-used clothes too ornate ever to be washed. The only light was the single candle behind him, and he left the privy door ajar, as he had found it. Silent on bare feet, he passed the high display cabinet loaded with treasures, the dressing table, a stool that was not where Twilight had predicted . . . and came to where the subject slept.

He arrived at the left side, farthest from the snores. The bed was huge, built of brick, with space underneath for braziers to warm it, but winter was past and they were not lit. He parted the muslin draperies and climbed onto the slab, then crawled closer to where the subject lay, on her back, about two thirds of the way across. He selected a spare pillow, stuffed with sweet-smelling rose petals. Although the subject lay on additional padding, she would certainly struggle and that was where his strength would be needed. An old woman dying in the night without a mark on her would raise no questions, but one with bruised heels and hands would.

He recited the mantra to steady his heartbeat until he felt calm and filled with purpose. Swiftly, he pushed the pillow down on her face and threw his far greater weight on top of her, restraining her arms and legs as much as he could. No more snores—would the abrupt silence alarm the guards outside? Her initial struggles were stronger than he expected, but they did not last long. Very likely, she died more of terror than suffocation, but he held the pose until he knew she must be dead.

Reaction hit him. *Oh, Ancestors, what happens now?*

In a way, this murder was her own fault. The Empress Mother had used the Gray Helpers to subvert the Empire for her selfish purposes, as only she could have done, but now someone had stolen the plot away from her.

The client would be pleased. What client? Probably no one would benefit more than the former Novice Horse would. If he could keep up the deception for even a few days, he would be Emperor in fact as well as in name. He would be the richest man in the Fourth World. But whoever was behind this conspiracy must also expect to benefit enormously.

Sister Lark held his leash.

He would rule the Good Land, but the Gray Order ruled him.

He closed the panel and descended the stairs carefully, collecting everything he had brought, counting until he had seven garments. Then he paused briefly to dress before retracing his steps. He peered out of the hatch under the stairs.

"All well?" Lark's voice whispered.

"All . . . What's happened here?" There was just enough light for him to recognize the pale blur beside her as a naked body.

"She had outlived her usefulness. In fact, she was a danger to both of us."

He shivered. People were no more than tools to Gray Helpers like Lark, and yet he could not deny her inhuman logic. Twilight had known far too much ever to be trusted.

"Stars preserve us! What are we going to do with her? Two bodies in one night will—"

"*You*," Lark said grimly, "are going to drag her into the secret passage and leave her there. I've stripped off everything that can serve to identify her. You will turn her over and pound her face against the tiles until it is unrecognizable. She may not be found for centuries."

What of the smell? His gut writhed. Of course a bad stench might be attributed to evil demons. "I must obey if you insist, of course. But I will get blood on me, and I have no way of washing it off before my servants come to tend me in the morning. You'd better do that yourself, Sister."

She muttered angrily then said, "Very well. Take her inside and just leave her there. Her real face may not be recognized, but make it look as if she were leaving, just in case."

He obeyed, turning the body around and dragging it in feet first. The worst part was climbing back over the corpse to get out, for the passage was very narrow.

Lark said, "I'll stay around as Musician Arpeggio—I was promoted two grades because you praised me last night. The night I sing 'Four Cranes Crying,' that means I need to speak with you, understand? You arrange it. Develop insomnia and summon musicians to play to you. I may change roles later and have you appoint me as one of your concubines. Don't count on too much joy from that, though. You know I don't do voluptuous."

"I hear and obey, Jewel of the Lotus," the Emperor said. With all the luscious young girls he could ever want eager to serve him, why should he lust after her bony body now? Then he remembered that his official mother had just died. The court would go into mourning for two years, during which no sex would be allowed. Other men might manage to cheat, but the Emperor's love life was a state function. He might be very glad to entertain Eunuch Arpeggio.

Except that music would be forbidden, too. Obviously, Lark had not thought of that, so he did not mention it. He could order all the musicians sent away. She might not have thought of that, either.

They crept out from the hiding place and began their perilous journey back, shadow to shadow to shadow. Lark carried Twilight's clothes. The eastern sky was starting to shed its night attire.

As they crouched under cover, waiting for a cloud shadow, Butterfly Sword said, "Is the real Emperor still alive?"

"Of course not."

So the old dragon had murdered her own son. Knowing that, he did not feel so bad about killing her. Lark's orders had left him no choice. He had never had any choice. His decision had been made for him when he was a child, when his mother had died and the Gray Sisters who came for her corpse found him hiding in a closet. No one had ever asked his opinion of murder as a way of life; it was just a given, like eating. And it certainly paid well, or would do so if he could keep his skin whole for the next couple of months. By then he would either be agonizingly dead or the unquestioned ruler of the Good Land.

Except that Lark would be holding his leash. Who held hers? Possibly no one at all! Some houses held hundreds of Gray Helpers, so no abbot could possibly remember all his subordinates' leashes; every abbot or abbess must keep a written record somewhere. Lark was an expert, and Prior Fraise had been a donkey—she could have found that list in Sheep Rocks. Then she could act entirely on her own. No, that didn't work, for how could she have known that the former Novice Horse was now the Lord of Ten Thousand Years? How could she have known Twilight's leash? Someone much higher in the Gray Order must have masterminded the Empress Mother's death.

"I have more orders for you," Lark whispered. "You will behave like a genuine Emperor. You will hold on to the throne at all costs, as the real Absolute Purity would, had he grown up in his right mind. You will never leave the palace."

"You are contradicting yourself, my lady. The rituals for the

Empress Mother's funeral will require me to leave the palace."

"Then I amend your instructions to say that you may leave the palace only to perform the Emperor's recognized duties."

"State processions, obviously. No hunting trips?"

"We'll see, in a year or two. Your immediate problem is to keep yourself in one piece and not a thousand and one pieces."

Never a truer word spoken! First Mandarin and Chief Eunuch would be inclined to support the imposter, for they could not denounce him without dooming themselves to the thousand cuts as well. There was no obvious legitimate successor to the—

Boom!

"Flay me!" Lark said. "She did it! Already?"

Boom!

"Or they cut it out of her," Butterfly Sword said unhappily. Poor Sweet Melody! Then the clammy touch of danger registered. "Oh, Heaven bless us! If it's a boy they'll try to waken the Empress Mother!"

Boom!

"And then you!" Twilight cried. "Quickly!"

Boom!

Throwing caution to the winds of Heaven, they began to run. People running would be much less suspicious now, with the glad news of another royal baby echoing through the night. The palace staff would be thrown into turmoil. Sacrifices and celebrations must be organized at once. But would the confusion be enough to justify ignoring people dressed completely in black?

Boom!

"How many is that?" Butterfly Sword said. "Was that *six?*" He tore off his hood, the better to see where he was going.

Boom!

That was certainly more than five, so Sweet Melody had given the Emperor a son. If she still lived, she would have to be promoted to third-rank concubine or even Junior Empress, but that would be his decision now. He plunged into the shrubbery and stripped to the skin while Twilight struggled with the panel. Then he went wriggling and squirming along the passage to his chamber, gasping in his haste.

After that it was all an anticlimax. No one burst in to tell him the awful news of his mother's death. The guns had told him the other news, and if the Emperor chose to ignore it, then who would dare disturb him? He composed himself, calmed his racing heart, and pondered his next move. Finally, he decided to face the day and thumped the gong by his bed.

He was not surprised that Joyous Diligence chose to answer the summons in person. They both knew that the birth of a prince changed the imposter's status considerably. For once, he kowtowed. He was left on his knees.

"A large, healthy son, Your Majesty."

"And the woman?" Butterfly Sword inquired with a shiver.

"Well, I believe."

"Send to find out. I will rise now. Have my tea and congee brought."

Eunuchs washed him, shaved his lip, plucked a few chin hairs, and dressed him. Still no word came. Surely the servant girl would have been awakened by the guns? The guards had perhaps panicked. Or they had reported to Chief Eunuch and he had panicked. Or—most likely—the eunuchs were busy stripping the bedroom of everything in it but the corpse, robbing the dead. Only when there was nothing left worth stealing would they tell the world that the tigress had gone.

Butterfly Sword found himself nervously reviewing his memories, convincing himself that, yes, she had been really dead.

Suddenly, Joyous Diligence reappeared, his face paler than ivory. He even forgot to kneel, which was a serious error when the valets were still present.

"Something wrong?" Butterfly Sword inquired.

"Your Majesty, the Empress Moth— Your august mother has ridden the golden chariot to a higher world."

"No! When? How?"

This game must be played out at several levels. Butterfly Sword knew everything, or hoped he did. Joyous Diligence knew the Emperor was a fraud but could do no more than guess that his supposed mother had been murdered—and unless he knew that Butterfly Sword had once been Novice Horse, he could not suspect him of doing the job personally. The servants listening with horror knew neither secret.

"I will go and see her," Butterfly Sword said. "At once. . . . But I cannot, can I?" The Emperor must not be tainted by the presence of death. The rules of mourning were incredibly restrictive and complicated at the imperial level. "Have the Gray Sisters been summoned?"

"I do not know, er, Your Majesty." The eunuch's eyes burned with rage, or possibly fear, and very likely both. If the imposter could win acceptance, then he would truly be Emperor, and he would remove all witnesses to the truth.

"Send for Chief Eunuch at once. Summon my chair and inform First Mandarin that I will receive him in the Abode of Wisdom." Who else would a bereaved and now liberated Emperor consult? He mentioned a few others, and hastily added Court Astrologer to the top of the list. Joyous Diligence departed, no doubt relieved that he had an excuse to rush to his father for instructions.

Three, Butterfly Sword decided: Chief Eunuch, First Mandarin, and Supreme Guardian—if those three supported him, then the rest of the world would have to. Supreme Guardian was leading the army south to meet the Bamboo Banner. His representative in Sublime Mountain was a nonentity.

Almost before the Lord of the High and the Low was ready to receive Chief Eunuch, the gross old pudding had come waddling in, arriving so quickly that he must have been on his way already. Butterfly Sword dismissed everyone else, and Chief Eunuch watched them go with a meaningless smile and without moving from his place by the door. Only when it closed did he begin to move, waddling forward.

Was he going to stop and make obeisance?

Butterfly Sword did not wait to find out. He beckoned and pointed to cushions nearby. "Come and sit down." It was an admission of equality or even subservience, and the old man's eyes glittered slyly as he spread himself on and over the seat.

"May I offer my deepest condolences on—"

"Crap. The old cat is dead and none of us expected that. Let's talk about this. Just this once, we'll speak openly. I'm a fraud and you know it. But if you denounce me, you're likely to be torn to globules before you've started your second paragraph. Correct?"

The eunuch nodded, moving his smile up and down on the mountain of butter that was his face. He was so vast he was scenery.

"And even if you survive that, who's going to believe you? The harridan accepted me, fawned over me in public, claimed me as her son. Didn't she know her own son? That's what they'll ask."

"Oh, dear me. I could probably find a number of witnesses."

"I daresay. And I don't know who most of them are, so I can't silence them first, correct?"

Another smile, even more blubbery. "As Your Majesty says."

"But they will only be eunuchs, and who will take their words against the Emperor's? Oh, you may pull me down, but you'll go to the chopping post, too, my fine accomplice, and all your witnesses with you. A man your size will need twenty thousand cuts. You've made fools of the court, the country, and the aristocracy. You'll do better staying aboard than swimming among the sharks. What do you want out of it?"

What could a eunuch want? Not women, not estates to leave to nonexistent children. Power? Retirement would be too dangerous for him, because he must keep an eye on the fake Emperor to ensure his own survival. Revenge on old enemies? But of course, this eunuch did have children.

"I have seven grandsons. I do not wish to see them forced to follow the family tradition."

"A palace apiece?"

"Two palaces," the fat man said automatically.

"One."

"With a hundred rooms apiece. And the title of prince."

"One medium-size palace apiece. I thought princes had to have imperial blood in their veins."

"Today the Empire gained another who does not."

That was a low blow. Butterfly Sword had a son he had not set eyes on yet. "What I meant was, how do you propose to fake their ancestry?"

Lard Face sneered. "Two-thirds of the princes in the Good Land are descended from overactive imaginations."

"Then it's agreed. You make the arrangements and the imperial clerks will press the imperial seal to the imperial paper in the imperial presence."

There was something about Chief Eunuch's smile that suggested he had expected more of a battle. Or wished he had asked for more. Or was going to ask for more tomorrow and tomorrow and tomorrow. "Also, those other witnesses will not come cheap."

They would undoubtedly come cheaper than the ultimate cost to the treasury. "I rely on you to deal with them in the most appropriate fashion."

The fat man detected the threat, of course, and his smile narrowed slightly. "Your Majesty is most generous."

"I can afford to be," said Absolute Purity. "One other thing. . . ." He paused a moment, thinking it through. Yes! *Where*

there is no honor, there is no dishonor, as the Humble Teacher had
taught. If the Good Land must be ruled by an imposter, that was
still better than having it ruled by a puppet of the Gray Order.
Now that the Empress Mother was gone, Butterfly Sword could
hurl the full power of the Empire at Sister Lark. Any mention of
Eunuch Arpeggio would make Chief Butterball writhe in fury,
for he would certainly have heard of the fake Emperor's curious
interest in the singer, and to suspect a plot in the Great Within
that he did not understand must be agony for him.

How could Butterfly Sword explain his sudden interest in a
third-rate vocalist? Easy: *I thought he sounded more like a woman
than a castrato; his voice was not strong enough to come from male
lungs. So I demanded another song, and after that, I was sure of
it, but of course I could not denounce her as an imposter in case
I might be wrong. It seemed no more than a harmless prank then,
but since my dear mother . . .*

No, no, no! Hint at assassination to anyone in the Good Land
and they would immediately think of the Gray Helpers. Imposture likewise, and Chief Eunuch knew what Absolute Purity was.
To go down that road would be suicidal.

"No matter," the Emperor said. "It is unimportant at a time
like this. By the way, I understand that Joyous Diligence is your
son?"

"That is correct."

"I hereby promote him to my chief food taster, and he will
perform his services in my presence."

Chief Eunuch displayed bad teeth in a quite horrible snarl.
"As Your Majesty commands, so will it be." He turned his back—
which would normally be a capital offense—and waddled away.

In any case, Lark would slip out the gates without question.
Gray Sisters would be called in to remove the ill-omened imperial carcass from Sublime Mountain as fast as possible, and she
would blend right in with them. The toughest guards Chief

Eunuch commanded would never interfere with the death-tainted pariahs.

Butterfly Sword must remain bound by the compulsions she had laid upon him. She need not return to the palace as Eunuch Arpeggio; she could find a hundred ways to sneak up on him. Even were she to be caught and put to death now, it was a safe bet that she had acted under compulsion herself, so her superiors must know the words to control the Emperor.

Unless she had managed to double-cross them, which was more likely.

He called for a carrying chair, one of the informal small ones used only inside the Great Within. He dismissed the trumpeters, bell ringers, and gong beaters who came with it. Accompanied only by a dozen eunuch guards and carried by a mere eight bearers, he was borne swiftly and silently to the Robing Room, which led to the Abode of Wisdom. More flunkies waited there, ready to dress him in his formal robes, but he waved them away. No amount of silk brocade and jewelry was going to impress First Mandarin. A fully draped Emperor could barely move.

He beckoned Sandalwood, who was chancellor for the Abode. He was an elderly eunuch, scraggy and croaky as most of his kind became when they aged, but sharp-witted and seemingly efficient. Butterfly Sword had noticed the Empress Mother playing him off against some of Chief Eunuch's faction, and suspected he might be a future ally. His was an important office, for the Abode of Wisdom was a meeting place between the inner and outer palace complexes, and was therefore well guarded.

"Has First Mandarin arrived yet?"

Sandalwood bit his wrinkled lip, hesitant before an unfamiliar new ruler. Young, newly empowered Emperors were dangerous. "Not when I looked a moment ago, Majesty. I will check again. . . ."

"The matter is urgent, Chancellor. Will you please make sure he is not unduly delayed in answering our summons?" Butterfly Sword had no intention of cooling his heels while First Mandarin played dominance tricks.

The retainer blinked in amazement and then smiled. "With Your Majesty's permission, I will send men to fetch him at once." Any chance for the eunuchs to score off the mandarinate was too good to miss. Palace politics was a cesspool as deep as the ocean.

"You have our permission to be quite insistent. But admit no others until I have conferred with First Mandarin."

Butterfly Sword went out to the alcove where the throne stood. The lamps there were lit, but he could see through the fretwork screens that boys were still lighting lamps in the main hall. They spun around in alarm as he pushed the sliding doors apart. "That will do. Go!" boomed the giant, yellow-robed autocrat in a very unaltered-male voice. They fled in terror out the side doors, trailing sparks from their tapers.

He stepped down from the dais and headed over to a window. Dawn was fast approaching and he had not slept. Would he ever dare sleep again?

Could he hope to escape alive from this epochal hoax? Would he try to disappear even if he could, knowing that the alternative to the Adopted Son of the Sun must be civil war? At worst, the Empire would collapse into warring states that might contest with one another for a century before order could be restored. At best, the Eleventh Dynasty would simply be replaced by the wild-eyed fanatics of the Bamboo Banner, but all reports indicated that the provinces they had overrun just fell into chaos. And the earthquake would have turned rats into tigers, as some poet put it. Peasant revolts had rarely led to a stable government in the past, so far as he recalled. First Mandarin would know. New dynasties usually sprang from Outlander invasions led by military geniuses; internal uprisings produced only decades of chaos. So the ethical course was to press on.

A man pleads his own case best, the Courtly Teacher said.

And pleads the case of a son he had not seen yet. If he could pull this off, he would found his own dynasty.

Could he reasonably hope to? Chief Eunuch had been easy game, for he was motivated by greed and a lust for power; his wits were dulled by over-indulgence. First Mandarin, though, was distilled essence of fox. His mind was sharper than assassins' daggers and his training had cast him in the bronze of tradition and duty. His principles would not exclude theft to enhance his salary but they would stop far short of treason, and although the late Empress Mother had bent them enough to encompass her own usurpation, she had probably stayed narrowly within the bounds of legality.

Or had she? The realization that Butterfly Sword was not certain of the rules came like a deluge of ice water. He had assumed that the old man was in on the hoax, but maybe he was not. In fact, on second thought, that was a far more likely guess. And how to find out? Probing for hints would never work. First Mandarin was as inscrutable as the moon to a blind man. The imposter would have to gamble, rolling dice blindfolded, with his life on the table.

After gratifyingly few minutes, one flap of the great door at the far end of the hall swung open. First Mandarin stumbled in as if shoved. The door slammed shut.

And Butterfly Sword could relax again, knowing the answer to his question. Obviously Sandalwood's men had been assiduous, perhaps even to the point of manhandling the head of the imperial government. The old man was so furious that he had forgotten about inscrutability. For what might well be the first time in half a century, he had lost his temper, standing at the door glaring flames at the usurper. He would never look at a real

Emperor like that. To be dragged before a real Emperor in that way was a recipe for sheer, bone-melting terror.

Butterfly Sword waved for him to come close, and he shuffled over. The Emperor went back to studying the dawn. He decided a poetic mood might be appropriate. "*Night's fears wither as the east blossoms.*"

No mandarin could let a quotation go by without topping it. "*The greatest sorrows come guised in hope.*" He did not kneel, just scowled up at the imposter, seeming much smaller than Butterfly Sword had expected. It was the first time they had ever been close, the first time they had spoken together.

"Can we be overheard here?" Butterfly Sword whispered.

"What does it matter?"

"It matters for my life, your life, and the lives of millions of the Gentle People. Nobody expected this to happen, Excellency. The hand of Heaven did this." Actually, the powerful hands of Brother Horse. "Let us decide what we can do to solve the Good Land's problem."

"I say that *you* are the Empire's problem!"

"I don't want to be. I did not choose this. Give me my favorite concubine and our daughter, then show me the door, and we will willingly be gone." Oh, if only! By himself, Butterfly Sword might have a good chance of vanishing in the mass confusion of the Empress Mother's death, but Snow Lily and Snowbell were hostages in the Great Within, hostages of both Chief Eunuch and the mandarinate that ruled the Great Without. "But what happens then, Excellency? Who holds the Golden Throne if not I? And what happens to the Empire?"

The mandarin twisted his papery lips as if about to spit. "You think you can rule the Good Land, boy?"

"I think you can. And despite what the late Empress Mother believed, I think you have been doing so since Zealous Righteousness died." Flattery was the only arrow Butterfly Sword held in his quiver. "She told me many times that she knew of no one who could do it better and I certainly do not. You cannot expose me as an imposter without laying yourself open to charges of high treason. The Empire needs you and you must tolerate me."

With a visible effort, First Mandarin had recovered his composure, returning his face to its normal rice-flour color and texture. His straggling mustache and wispy beard were snow white, his queue an iron gray. Even his eyes wore a film like thin ice, and maggots would find more meat on an icicle.

"Oh, must I? You are too sure of yourself."

Which was certainly what Butterfly Sword himself suspected, faced with that ancient confidence. This discussion ought to be held in secret, of course, but there was no secrecy around Emperors. Their talk might not be overheard, but they were certainly being watched, and probably by spies from every faction in the palace, however many there were.

"Who succeeds me if my supposed mother's death proves infectious?"

"Prince Boundless Shore. A fourth cousin or so. A youth still, but he is said to have promise."

The Empress Mother had insisted that there was nobody, but she had been pleading her own indispensability. No doubt First Mandarin was currently doing the same, and he could be extraordinarily convincing.

"Will his claim be uncontested? Will he leave you in charge, as I would? Can he unite the Empire against the rebels? Open one tiny crack in the imperial facade and it will crumble before the onslaught of the Bamboo Banner."

"You try to bargain when you should be on your knees begging for mercy."

Maybe. But the old man was making no attempt to leave, which was as good as bargaining under the circumstances. The longer he stayed, the more he must seem like a fellow conspirator. The issue might balance on a knife blade, but it had not tipped yet.

"Venerable One, I just bought Chief Eunuch with pretty trinkets. I will not insult you with bribes. All I can offer you is my cooperation to save the Empire from chaos and interregnum. Tell me what you need that the Empress Mother refused you."

The milky eyes studied him for a moment. "You could start with Supreme Guardian's head in a bucket."

Saved again! Now they were haggling, and all that need be settled was the price. Butterfly Sword realized that he had watched First Mandarin in action often enough in the last year, but the old man had never seen him do or say anything, just sit. The man had no way of judging him. The imposter had been a stuffed dummy on a throne, no more. Now he must show that he was clever—but not too clever.

"Supreme Guardian is a loon," he agreed. "Who will you put in his place?" *Will,* not *would.*

"Iron Spur. A brilliant general. He crushed the barbarian uprising in Siping five years ago, driving them back into their desert with great slaughter. The army worships him."

"Can you trust him? A relative, perhaps?"

"A grandson," the old man admitted shamelessly.

"I must meet this hero. Where is he now?"

"Moldering on the Siping frontier, where he has been stationed ever since."

Where he posed the least threat to his grandfather's rival, Commander-in-Chief Supreme Guardian. With his grandfather's help, the doughty Iron Spur might tip the scales in the coming struggle to control the palace.

Butterfly Sword produced his best cute little boy smile. "Can I summon the noble Iron Spur without alerting Supreme Guardian's allies here at court?"

This time, the appraisal was a little longer. "No. But I could."

"Do so without a moment's delay. And tell him to bring as many men with him as the frontier can spare without leaving the door wide open to barbarian raids."

That was a surprise. "What do you plan to do with troops, imposter?"

"Rat catching. I want you to use them to drive the vermin out of the palace. I have seen how they behave, how the Empress Mother favored them, how they manipulated her, how they have appropriated the government. They are roaches."

"Dreams, dreams!" But First Mandarin was starting to listen. "What else are you dreaming?"

Better and better. They were closing in on a deal.

"And summon this Boundless Shore lad to court. Is that not what the real Absolute Purity would do—to keep an eye on him?"

"Or to kill him."

"Not my intention, I swear by all the worlds. Give him any guarantee you can think of. I am much more likely to give him the Empire and run, but don't tell him that. Tell him I am anxious to meet my relatives. When will the army meet the Bamboo Banner? Can Iron Spur come here to receive his commission and still catch up with the army before the battle?"

"The army is probably marching in the wrong direction entirely."

"Or in circles. What else, First Mandarin? I am gravely concerned about famine and the devastation in Jingyan and neighboring provinces. I got the impression, from what I was allowed to overhear, that the Golden Throne is not doing as much as it could to move food to the areas that need it the most."

The old man scowled. "I have no money. Famine and insurrection cut off a third of the imperial revenue. Mobilization of the army took another third. Now the earthquake must have swallowed the rest."

The numbers quoted at the last Small Council meeting had

sounded like fanciful gibberish, but no one had dared question them. Oddly enough, Novice Horse must know far more about commerce and accounting than First Mandarin ever dreamed of, because mandarins were trained in history, philosophy, and classical poetry—trade and business were far beneath their notice. A graduate of the House of Joyful Departure in Sheep Rocks was no stranger to the principle or practice of economy, a word unknown on Sublime Mountain. But for Butterfly Sword to start meddling in fiscal details might alienate the old man faster than anything. He could only ask, not suggest.

"Where can we find money?"

"You could shut down the obscene expenditure on the Water Palace."

"Done! Arrange it. Of course we cannot leave all those workmen unemployed, but I imagine you could put many of them to work repairing the Grand Canal. The little I saw of it last year was a disgrace. In many places, it is so silted up that the barges have to be dragged over the shallows by teams of men or oxen. The lock gates leak like sieves. What other economies can you suggest?"

First Mandarin's ancient eyes widened a fraction. He glanced around and lowered his voice even more. "Disposing of six or seven thousand, um, roaches would help. Shut down ten or twelve palaces."

Whispering was contagious. "We are in agreement. We must plan well, though. If one word gets out ahead of time, the roaches will strip Sublime Mountain bare at best and poison both of us at worst. "

The old man shook his ancient head in amazement. "You are crazy, boy! A crazy child!"

"I have experience no Emperor ever has. I have known hunger, Excellency."

For a long moment, First Mandarin stared blankly at the pink downy sky as if trying to see what lay behind it. At last, he said softly, "So did I, long ago."

"Then we will make a good team. You will have my complete support but I need yours. Do it. Let us clean the stable! The eunuchs are termites. The scale of their larceny astounds me. You could denounce me, Excellency, but only at great risk to your own venerable skin. I cannot possibly survive without your backing. Do I have it or not? Are we partners or enemies? The decision is yours, but I think you have to make it now." Sandalwood and his eunuch guardsmen were outside; which way would their loyalty jump if they had to choose between these two? Or between a horrified Emperor and an elderly mandarin suddenly dead of grief? That was another option.

The silence continued.

Emperor Absolute Purity turned and dragged his silken train across to the throne. He sat and made an effort to convey splendor. "Excellency, we require that you speedily call a meeting of our Great Council to consider the matter, manner, and consequences of our dear mother's tragic demise. You have our leave to withdraw."

First Mandarin followed him and knelt to kiss his slipper. "All things will be done as the Son of the Sun commands."

Today, yes. Tomorrow, maybe.

So far, so good. Butterfly Sword leaned back on his throne in a very unritual posture to plan his next move. The imposter had crossed two very rickety bridges.

What happened after this? Chief Eunuch might try to have him poisoned in the hope of ruling through the infant Emperor. First Mandarin might send in his grandson at the head of his troops to take over the palace and start a new dynasty. Butterfly Sword was utterly alone. The only person he could trust was Snow Lily, and she was powerless. Anyone else he tried to enlist to his cause would sell him out to one of the main players. And if an enemy could gain possession of Snowbell, even her mother could be turned.

The safest course would be to summon Prince Boundless Shore and offer to abdicate in his favor in return for a fast horse. Regrettably, Lark had ordered him to hang on to the throne, so that might not be an option—Butterfly Sword's vocal chords might not obey him. The first time he tried to disobey her commands, he might freeze, or be convulsed with agony. He must devise some test to establish the strength of her control over him. Until he knew that, he could make no plans.

He realized that a group of people in the white of mourning were waiting at the far end of the hall. Waiting for what? He sat up in proper form and tried to look wooden, the Emperor recovered from his sudden grief and ready to press on with his duties.

Chief of Protocol came scurrying to kowtow and—eventually—announce that the most senior courtier in attendance at the moment was Court Astrologer.

"Send the noble sage to us."

The white-queued ancient arrived, crumpled to the ground, touched his forehead to the floor three times, crawled forward, and repeated twice.

"Court Astrologer, you have news for us?"

The old man lifted his eyes to study the Emperor's shoes. "News from Your Majesty's augurs and diviners: We, in our ignorance, have consulted the stars and oracles, and Chief Calligrapher also, and we most humbly offer a choice of auspicious names in the hope that Your Majesty in his ultimate wisdom will see fit—"

Huh? Oh . . . "To name our son? What of our dear mother's funeral rites?"

Court Astrologer was so shattered that he actually looked the Emperor straight in the eye, while his toothless jaw dropped.

Had Butterfly Sword made a major gaffe, putting a woman's death ahead of a son's birth?

The old man hastily averted his eyes. "But . . . It is traditional . . . May it please Your Exalted Majesty . . . Your esteemed and eternally mourned father, Emperor Zealous Righteousness, did not require the funeral auguries for his departed mother to be presented until nine days after her departure." Grovel, mumble about failure, humiliation, and so on. . . .

"Your dedication and devotion are unquestioned, Court Astrologer. I see that I let my grief drive me into making unreasonable demands. We all miss my dear mother's guiding hand. . . . Take all the time you need to make your divination. As for the child's naming, let Concubine Sweet Melody choose from your auspicious list."

That was another mind-wrenching shock. "*The mother?*"

"She did all the work," the Emperor said cheerfully. Omnipotence did have its little pleasures. "Almost all of it." Besides, the poor little tyke had been born on an inauspicious day, a day so inauspicious that his supposed grandmother had died on it. With that sort of start, he would never be allowed to ascend the Golden Throne.

Absolute Purity dismissed his Court Astrologer. While he waited for Chief of Protocol to come and announce the next suppliant, he wondered if any man had ever been quite so alone as he was, trying to steal an entire world singlehandedly.

CHAPTER 9

Silky had not needed long to decide that he enjoyed the princely life. He had restored order, overseen the funeral rites, and been accepted by the three hundred or so surviving residents of Goat Haven as their lord, at least until someone else might come and tell them otherwise. The other Gray Helpers who had come with him—Carp, Watersprite, Windchime, and Mercy—had all survived the disaster and had worked to bolster his support among his subjects. He was confident that he would soon learn of any unrest. A hasty survey of the storerooms showed him that Goat Haven could survive for the next year or so.

About fifty ranch hands had been absent when the earthquake struck. Probably most of them still lived, somewhere out there in the open, but they had no way to return to their homes and families because the trail up from the road had been destroyed, much of it either completely buried or torn away by landslides. Silky was in no hurry to open the path again, for thousands of homeless refugees had come wailing to his doorstep—a very high doorstep—and he was content to wait until hunger drove them away or killed them. He had far more dead horses than the remaining inhabitants of Goat Haven could eat before the flesh putrefied, and he had already ordered it dropped over the edge. The refugees found it and ate it raw.

He worried about Thunderbot, for the sheer number of refugees proved that Cherish must have suffered severely. Sometimes he stood on the edge of the cliff and stared down at the wretched throng, wondering if any of his colleagues among the local Gray Helpers were in there, or even Verdant and his son, but there was no way he could rescue any of them. If there were, he would be overwhelmed by the starving mob.

Not his fault. Heaven sent earthquakes to reprimand the Emperor. It was not concerned with Prince Silk Hand.

The only opposition to raise its ugly head had appeared on the third evening while Silky was enjoying a bowl of horse with heavenly noodles while seated on his throne in the newly refurbished hall, overseeing the first seating of his subjects, a hundred cross-legged ranch hands. Women and children would eat later. Suddenly, a boy of around ten stepped up on his dais uninvited and scowled at him, hands on hips. He was nut brown and wore only the skimpy loincloth of youth. His behavior would have been an absurd insolence if the hall had not suddenly gone silent.

"Who're you?" Silky demanded very coldly. The kid was too young to have thought this up by himself, or at least without receiving encouragement from adults.

"I'm Sky Musket, Sky Rider's oldest son, and that's my chair you're sitting in!"

Silky threw the contents of his bowl in the kid's face, then backhanded him so hard that he fell off the dais, flat on his back.

"Get up!" Silky roared, on his feet now, staring down at the kid, who was pale with shock. Probably no man had ever so much as raised his voice to him before. "From now on, you address me as Your Highness! Is that clear?"

Sky Musket obeyed, holding one eye and streaked with meat sauce.

"Right up where you were before, in case I need to hit you again."

Even when he stepped up on the dais, the brat was forced to bend his head back to look up at the monster. His chin was quivering.

"What's my name?"

"Your Highness."

"Right. What you said was wrong. Your father had no right to inherit Goat Haven and I have proof of it. Can you read?"

Sky Musket shook his head and then, seeing Silky drawing back a hand, hastily said, "Just twelve characters, Your Highness."

"Then you're a stupid, ignorant brat! Aren't you?"

A whisper. "Yes, Your Highness."

"From now on, any more evil talk like that and I will have your back flogged raw, understand?"

"Yes, Your Highness."

Silky handed him the bowl. "Fetch me more meat and noodles. Run!"

Everyone else went back to eating.

Goat Haven was disgustingly lacking in the tools and materials required for forging documents—old silk, sepia ink to look faded, true camel hair brushes, and so on. Silky collected what he could, retired to the room he had commandeered as his personal office, and set to work. It wasn't much of a room, a former bedroom too far from the hall to be convenient; its tiled floor had cracked in the quake and the window shutters rattled all the time. He must put up with it while he was making his plans to rebuild Goat Haven.

He spent the rest of the evening and half the night producing a brief affidavit, sealed by Sky Sword—which, as Silky knew from his painstaking research, had been the name used by the late lamented Sky Hammer 7 before he inherited the throne—granting his senior wife permission to pay a visit to her parents' palace with her infant son. That she had never returned could be explained verbally. It was expected in the Good Land that rich men would have concubines or multiple wives.

It was a neat solution to the inheritance problem that Silky had rejected earlier because the Gray Helpers would have seen it as his attempt to cut them out of the deal. Now, with Cherish, and possibly Wedlock, in ruins, both the law and the Brotherhood would need years to start functioning normally again.

Soon after breakfast the next morning, he sent for Sky Musket. The boy appeared quickly, looking gratifyingly terrified and sporting a satisfactory black eye. At his age, Silky had been washing corpses. Who said life had to be fair?

The prince leaned back in his chair—the most imposing one he had been able to find—and did not tell his visitor to sit. He did not tell him to kneel, either. That might be pushing his luck, and these frontier hillbillies did not go in much for courtly manners.

"Good morning."

"Good morning," Sky Musket said, and hastily added, "Your Highness."

"You told me you can't read. Is there anyone here who can?"

A nod, quickly followed by speech. "Yes, Your Highness—Weaverbird, Grandsire's clerk."

"Fetch him."

Weaverbird, when he arrived, proved to be a gangling youngster with a clubfoot and his right arm in a sling.

"*You* were Sky Hammer's clerk?" Silky asked disbelievingly.

"I was the most junior secretary, um, Your Highness. The roof came down and—"

"Spare me the sanguinary details. Read this to the boy." The affidavit would not stand inspection by a lawyer, but it ought to suffice here and now. Silky could prepare a better one at leisure, in case it would ever be needed when the access road was fit for lawyers.

Weaverbird tried, very hesitantly, but had to keep stopping to ask Silky to explain the many legal characters he had used.

"Oh, just tell him what it means. The woman mentioned was

my mother, and I was the baby referred to as Sky Silk. You will note that it is dated two months before Sky Rider's birth."

White as newfallen snow, Weaverbird said, "Then it means that you are Prince Sky Hammer 7's true heir, Your Highness."

"Correct. You may go. Boy, you wait." When the door closed, Silky said, "Tell your brothers about this. Sky Musket is a stupid name. You are not to call yourself that anymore. From now on you are just Musket, understand? If you behave yourself, in a year or so, I may permit you to address me as uncle. Now go away and make yourself useful in the kitchen. Tell chief cook she's to whip you if you don't work hard."

It was true that Silky did not presently look older than Sky Rider had, but he could if he was ever required to.

A few days after that, Silky returned to the cliff edge to inspect the refugee crowds below. They had pretty much all gone, probably in search of water to die beside, and vultures were tidying up the few who remained. Aftershocks had become rarer, and the restoration work was sure to take several days anyway. It was safe to begin work on the access road.

The first problem was deciding where to put the new path. The landslide screes did not look stable enough to build on, and the scars left behind were all very steep, sure to require a lot of digging. Most of the gates and barriers had been swept away; the booby-trap stone cylinders had all been loosed from their nests, so anyone who had been going up or down when the quake hit must have been smeared to paste, one way or another. Silky needed a whole day's mountaineering on the end of a rope just to scout out the best route. To start at the top and work down, with only two or three men able to work at the face, would take months. He would have to use three or four crews, and all but the uppermost would have to be lowered on ropes when they went to work every morning. On second thought, he decided they could probably be fed from above, so they could stay on their work site until the open trail reached them.

Organizing a major project like this was not as inspiring as murder or impersonation, but it made an interesting challenge.

The hands labored hard, but they still needed two weeks to open a usable path. Even then, it was mostly too narrow for horses to pass one another, with a few wider places on the gentler slopes. Bringing the approach back to its former standards would take years.

A couple of days before the last gaps were closed, Silky called a meeting of his four Gray Helpers. They crowded his office and he did not sit, or invite them to do so.

"We will need checkpoints at both the top and bottom of the trail," he said. "I expect to see refugees returning when word gets around that we are accessible again. They will all be turned away, of course, because we are going to be hard-pressed just to feed ourselves this winter. But I will see that at least one of you is posted at the bottom gate to identify and admit any Gray Helpers who turn up. The only other people we will let in are the missing Goat Haven hands. Having horses, they have probably survived better than the city homeless, and some may have been granted shelter in neighboring ranches."

He looked around at the nods, then continued. "What we must avoid is forty or fifty men riding in here in a block and deciding they do not approve of the change of dynasty. Somehow we must only let them up the hill in small bunches. Any suggestions on how we can do that?"

Glad to be consulted, they tossed the problem around, and decided that only men with families still surviving should be allowed in, with shortage of food given as the reason. Bureaucratic delay in processing the applicants ought to thin out the rush, if there was one.

"When do I get to go home?" demanded Mercy, the archer who had been borrowed from a house somewhere downriver from Cherish. "I'm about due to become a father."

"I suggest you don't go into labor until we get some news," Silky said. "Have you noticed the lack of caravans? We're almost into Lotus Moon and there hasn't been a sign of them on the Wilderness Road. The earthquake must have closed passes in the mountains—that I can understand. But why have we seen none heading west? No horses in Cherish, or no docks, or is the Jade River no longer navigable?"

They wouldn't know the answer until they completed the trail down the hill.

Fair Visions had joined the Bamboo Banner after the Heaven-sent triumph at Spires and had regretted that decision almost immediately. Now, a couple of months later, he cursed the day.

Fair Visions had not been so named by his late father, who had been a hardworking carpenter. Fair Visions had nothing against carpentry as such; it was the hardworking part he disliked. He would have preferred to be an artist, but a profession so respected was not available to sons of an artisans. As a compromise, he had taught himself to sketch imaginary buildings faithful to all the essential precepts of ancestral and astrological design. Under his new and more auspicious name, he had taken up the career of itinerant house builder—itinerant because after contracting to build magnificent dream homes, he would itinerate with the down payments. Of necessity, he had become a skilled horseman, too.

His father had never mentioned that his younger brother had been born some seventy years before him, which was one of the strange beliefs held by Bamboo's followers. Nor had he ever mentioned that the family had imperial blood in its veins, which seemed odd now, when his younger brother was claiming descent from Emperors of the tenth dynasty. Fair Visions did not argue such points with Uncle Bamboo.

He did not argue anything with Bamboo, and that explained why he was currently out on patrol. The company of an armed escort would be flattering if it meant that he was valued, but it might indicate that he wasn't trusted. Although, in the beginning, the Bamboo Banner had traveled only on human feet and been armed with staves, it had collected some horses and real weapons as it prospered. Fair Visions had expected to find a troop of cavalry waiting outside his billet that morning. Instead, he faced a cadre of a dozen boys led by a juvenile monster named Silent. They carried staves and wore only cotton trousers and headbands—not even sunhats or shoes. They stood in lines without speaking, chewing their yang cud.

Of course, Fair Visions did not realize right away that Silent was a monster. He looked like a fat-free adolescent tangle of hemp cords painted the color of badly weathered skin. His head stuck out forward over a hollow chest, as if to emphasize the worst case of overbite in the Good Land.

Fair Visions was not impressed. "I will be riding a horse."

Spittle splashed insolently close to his feet. "We can outrun a horse."

"I will be taking a spare with me."

"We can outrun two horses." His cadre all grinned agreement.

Fair Visions could do nothing then except stroll over to the army's stables to collect the mounts he had picked out yesterday. So began the nightmare.

His mission had sounded simple. The closer the Bamboo Banner came to Jingyan Province, the worse the earthquake damage it saw. At Spires, part of the city wall had fallen to give the Banner its greatest triumph so far, but much of the city itself had survived. Here, whole villages had collapsed. Bridges were down, roads often impassable, and food had become desperately hard to find. Had Heaven sent a miracle victory, or an impossible roadblock?

In the baking heat of Lotus Moon, even water was a problem, with most streams fouled by corpses or animal carcasses. Bamboo needed to know what lay ahead. Should the revolution continue northward on a direct line to Heart of the World, or should it detour to east or west? And if so, which?

Fair Visions rode out at a trot, planning to convince Silent that he must acquire horses, either by going back for them, or otherwise. But Silent convinced Fair Visions. His men did do better than the horses; the horses needed to rest first. Fair Visions called for a break in the early-morning shadows of a ruined toll house, and proceeded to inspect his mounts for foot or saddle troubles. Silent kept his men running on the spot.

Fair Visions grinned at one of the toughest-looking. "He works you this hard all the time?"

The man did not answer, just stared at him and kept moving.

Fair Visions addressed another, with the same result.

"I beat any man who speaks in my cadre," Silent explained smugly. "Only women chatter all the time."

After that, things just got worse. When Fair Visions pointed out, some hours later, that Silent had set out leading a dozen men and now only had ten, he was told that this was defeatist talk and Silent would kill him if he spoke that way.

"My blue headband means that I am a member of the Supreme Leader's Council."

"I know, but I will still kill you."

By then, Fair Visions almost believed him. The lout's treatment of his own men was brutal. At the end of a solid day's running, the cadre came to an inhabited village. Silent promptly had them put on a gymnastic display for the inhabitants. When a crowd gathered, he harangued them about the need to overthrow the she-dragon who had purloined the Golden Throne and brought the wrath of Heaven down on the Good Land. They, of course, could now help by providing food for the visitors. Two men tried to argue and were promptly clubbed down.

Silent was a sadistic maniac and was doing everything he could to make his men as crazy as himself. They laughed as they competed in brutality to prove to their friends that they were not weak. Any peasant who talked back or failed to show respect was savagely beaten. Recruiting had been suspended because the revolution could barely feed the men it already had, so the villagers who wanted to join were told to organize on their own and await Bamboo's summons.

Because he had not undergone the murderous training that other patriots endured and had not been forcibly addicted to yang, Fair Visions might be the only completely sane man in the entire revolutionary horde his uncle had created. During the next few days, he often considered making a break for freedom, and was always deterred by a conviction that Silent would run him down and kill him. Whether or not Silent had been sent along as his jailer, not his guardian, that was certainly how he saw himself.

After a week, Fair Visions led Silent and his surviving followers back to headquarters to report. Even finding Bamboo was tricky. He had been forced to split the Banner into a dozen armies so it could spread out widely enough to gather sufficient food. Eventually, Fair Visions 3's men encountered foraging parties and followed their directions back to the source. Now he could see a band of patriots walking along the skyline. He was getting close.

His way led up a valley of nightmare. The hills themselves had never been fertile enough for farming, but small villages had sprung up along the river itself, and their people had grown rice on the flats and in carefully terraced paddies on the lower slopes. The violence of the earthquake had shattered most of those, destroying the work of centuries, burying houses under mud slides or drowning them in temporary lakes. The road was close to impassable, requiring innumerable detours. Here and there, Fair Visions saw signs that people had begun to rebuild their homes only to be driven away—by hunger, disease, or perhaps just fear of the Bamboo Banner, which was preying on the corpse of the Good Land like some gigantic vulture.

Bamboo would not be pleased to hear that comparison. Bamboo was a very strange man to be a revolutionary. A mystic and dreamer, yes. Not a soldier, not a scholar. He was fifty-two years old and had been a potter until three or four years ago. He had no children living, so his plans to found a dynasty would require much hard work in the imperial harem when he had won and staffed it. One asset he did not appreciate fully was a nephew willing to help with the dynastic part of the job.

As was his custom, Bamboo had appropriated the best accommodation for his own use. In this case, it was a sprawling ranch complex that had incurred little damage, probably because it was built on rock under the thin upland soil—almost every building sited on a river flat had collapsed. He was holding court in a gazebo whose massive tiled roof was supported at the corners by wooden columns. The columns had shifted on their bases, but they and the roof had moved as a unit and were still intact. Low stone walls between the posts had suffered more, but enough remained to give an impression of privacy. The view was memorable and the cool shade a joy. There were insects. As some teacher must have said, *You can have flies without horses, but not horses without flies.*

Seven men sat there. Six were on cushions and Bamboo had a chair, no doubt the grandest that could be found. He was a heavy man, little of him being muscle, with dense eyebrows and a receding hairline. He had massive hands and wrists, but his eyes were what you noticed—the eyes of a man who sees visions and believes them ahead of other people's reality. How an aging widowed potter could have dreamed up such a madhouse as the Bamboo Banner defied explanation. He was no scholar, yet he could spout astrologers' jargon when he chose and always seemed to believe what he was saying, no matter how like a singing fish it might sound.

When not prophesying or commanding, he came across as rather stupid. Only in the last few weeks had he accepted that a would-be Emperor needed advisers, and so he had begun assembling a council. It spent a lot more time listening than advising, and its membership was in constant flux. Disagreeing with the chairman was a life-threatening act.

Fair Visions stopped at the entrance and waited to be recognized. Of those present, all intent on their leader's words, he knew White Pine, long past whatever his best had been, but having genuine military experience; Alabaster, who had not revealed his history but was probably a defrocked mandarin on the run from imperial justice; and Bright Shadow, the Bamboo Banner's quartermaster, a former tea merchant. He and Fair Visions had summed each other up at first glance, and neither would ever trust the other to guard an empty piss pot. The other three were strangers.

". . . the Red Eye enters the House of the Scroll," Bamboo said. "And the Slow One will yet loiter in the House of the Sea Dragon. That means death, of course. Then will be the time to strike! Then Heaven will deliver our foes bound at our feet."

Six heads nodded eagerly.

"Early in the Year of the Firebird, you think, Majesty?" asked White Pine.

"*I know!*"

"Know, of course. Know! We will have to think about warm clothing as we move north." The old man looked meaningfully at fat, greasy Bright Shadow, who rubbed his fat, greasy hands.

"Just give them more yang," Bamboo said. "Patriots do not feel the cold."

Fair Visions suppressed a shiver. He had no idea where and how his uncle had acquired the enormous quantities of yang he had used to habituate so many thousand men. Heaven alone knew what would happen when the supply ran out and they all went berserk. The patriots believed they were invincible, but Fair Visions had seen far too many dead ones to believe that. He had no faith that a change of backside on the golden throne would improve anything for anyone except the owner of that anatomy. Any day now, the Imperial Army would appear in their path and slice the Bamboo Banner off the face of the earth like an ugly wart.

So why was he here? Because even a remote chance of being nephew and heir presumptive to the Son of the Sun was worth a throw, even a gamble as insane as this one.

He realized that the council was being dismissed and he was being beckoned. He walked forward and bowed low—Bamboo was not demanding the kowtow yet. That would come.

"You are welcome back, nephew."

"It is a joy to be back, thank you, Bamboo."

Bamboo gestured for him to sit. Of the others, only old White Pine had remained. Fair Visions was perhaps being encouraged to believe that he was part of an innermost council, but any such assumption would be dangerous until it had been spoken before witnesses. Their leader had not started handing out political titles yet.

"So what can you tell us, nephew?"

"You would weep, Bamboo. Disaster everywhere we went. We headed north at first, trying to follow the road to Wedlock, which stands at the junction of the Jade and Golden Rivers. I should say 'stood' not 'stands.' We did not reach it, but all accounts agree that it received more damage than anywhere. Wedlock itself was swallowed up by the earth. The Golden River flowed backward and by nightfall there was no trace of the old city above water. We were told that the lake continues to grow, but mandarins are warning that it will soon cut through the barrier and return to its lower course with great fury."

Fair Visions waited for comment, but Bamboo just sat very still, obsidian eyes never leaving his informer's face. That was a trick of his, flattering to the speaker and hinting at great wisdom, but there might be nothing at all happening inside that big head.

"We turned west and everywhere saw disaster, hunger, and, yes, sorrow. There is great anger against the usurping sow in Heart of the World, she who has brought this trouble upon the Good Land. Had we been permitted to recruit, we could have brought you a thousand eager young warriors, all breathing fire. If the weather continues to favor the farmers, some may yet harvest a good crop and fend off starvation, but not all, not everywhere."

Still no response.

"If you do me the honor of wanting my humble opinion, the way northeastward seems closed, for this year and perhaps next year also. To go near Wedlock would be . . . would seem to my ignorant self to be folly. To pass it on the east means crossing the Golden River. If the predicted flood occurs, it will leave no bridges or boats or shelter, only a desert of mud. Um . . ." The deluge would be as disastrous as the quake itself. Again Fair Visions wondered if these might be a sign from Heaven that Bamboo Banner should not proceed at all, for had not the Desert Teacher taught that omens, like coins, always had two sides? But even to hint at that might result in Fair Visions being assigned to weapons training, as the target. So the least unfavorable option must be the best. "Bamboo, if you ask me, I would say that you should veer westward, across Jingyan and Shashi. The army may grumble if you give it more horse or sheep flesh than rice, but the hills seem to have suffered less than the plains. This concludes my report."

Bamboo nodded and glanced to White Pine.

The old man smiled, showing a few lonely teeth protruding from shrunken gums. "History tells us of many complaints that have arisen in the south and headed north. The Emperors have always sent their armies south along the Grand Canal, for it is by far the fastest way to come. Then they move inland up the Golden River, to cross the rebels' path and cut them off. Will Heaven so bless your cause, Noble Bamboo, as to destroy the army with this flood your nephew foresees?"

"No," Bamboo said. "I just told you, old man. For your benefit, nephew, since you arrived late, I repeat that I have consulted the stars and I have cast the bones, and they agree in every respect. I have already decreed that we will proceed into Shashi Province. There we will meet the army of the she-dragon and destroy it utterly. There the Portal of Worlds will open to acclaim a new dynasty. So it is written."

Crazier than a five-legged camel.

CHAPTER 11

The Firstborn had planned to travel southeastward across Wanrong, roughly paralleling the course of the Golden River, but not going close to it until he reached Wedlock. For several weeks after leaving Lady Cataract's palace, this is what he did.

Despite the lady's grand plans, her expedition did not travel as fast as the Firstborn had done when he rode a donkey and his two disciples walked. Her retinue had swelled from an estimated dozen people to twenty-two, because she needed two teams of bearers for her litter and had forgotten to count in a cook, hostlers, and wagon drivers. Unless horses were given many hours a day to graze, they needed huge amounts of grain and hay, which meant more wagons, and wagons needed guards.

Shard Gingko expected the Firstborn to grow impatient at their lack of progress, but he did not seem to mind. The old man was reluctant to complain to the Firstborn, but one evening, as he was watching the servants pitching camp, he grumbled to Mouse that they had achieved nothing since morning except cross a single wide valley. Mouse looked down at him with a gentle smile obviously modeled on the Firstborn's. Even when Shard stood as straight as he could, Mouse was the taller now.

"There is plenty of time, Master."

"There is? Time for what?"

"Time for him to reach the Portal of Worlds before it opens."

Shard felt a jolt of what he ashamedly decided might be nothing more than jealousy. "The Urfather has told you this is what he plans?"

Mouse shook his head and looked puzzled. "No. No, he hasn't. But somehow I feel sure that this is what he plans. He expects to meet the Bamboo Banner at the Portal of Worlds."

"The Desert Teacher said, *Knowledge not based on learning is built upon quicksand.*"

"I thank you for this wisdom, Master."

"Can you write it?"

"All except *quicksand*, Master."

"The character for quicksand is water followed by sand. Write out that maxim in your fairest hand and show me."

The following day, as the cavalcade approached a village, four men came out to meet them, three carrying clubs and one an ancient musket. They lined up across the road, obviously hostile. The Firstborn slid off his horse, handed the reins up to Mouse on his, and hobbled forward to speak with them. They recognized him. One knelt, but the others stood their ground, looking uneasy. By then, Shard had also dismounted and caught up.

"We come in peace," the Firstborn said.

"But you bring many hungry mouths," replied the eldest.

"And our own food. Are you so short that you grudge hospitality to strangers?"

The old man shifted his feet uneasily in the mud. "We still eat, but starving hordes are pouring out of Shashi. They are walking dead, with pebble eyes, but they are also locusts. Must our children starve to feed strangers?"

Sunlight shook his head. "But eat as little as you can and share what you save. In some other life, on some other world, they will return the favor. Tell us what other news you have."

"News from the north is that the Empress Mother has mounted the golden chariot."

"Has she indeed?" The Firstborn glanced thoughtfully at Shard. "And what difference will that make? What do you think?"

"You are the Bearer of Wisdom, Ancient One, not I." Shard discovered that he was smiling, and hastily rearranged his face into proper scholarly impassivity. Normally, one would look to history for answers, but here, history gave far too many answers. Released from ancestral control, some Lords of the High and the Low had been freed to follow their own course at last. Sometimes, the immortal army of palace eunuchs had been raised to power instead, able to rule an inexperienced stripling more easily than his sly old harridan mother. And this case might not follow any precedent, for the Portal was due to open, signaling a change of dynasty.

"We will have to wait and see," Sunlight said thoughtfully. "Heaven will reveal its will soon enough."

By then, the villagers were reassured—and of course charmed—enough to invite the Urfather into their homes. He, Shard, and Lady Cataract drank tea with the elders, refusing solid food. Mouse sat cross-legged in a corner, silent and attentive as always.

Whether the report of the Empress Mother's death was true or not, the elders told many tales of death and devastation, of shattered homes and flooded lands. Warehouses that had survived the trembling had been destroyed by fire or water, creating famine that could only grow worse, for the spring planting had been washed away by landslides or inundation. The great city of Wedlock had been totally destroyed. Heaven's rage had been aroused against it by the devilish boats they used, breathing fire and moving without oars or current.

The Firstborn's eyes filled with tears. "If such trouble is a sign from Heaven, then only someone much wiser than I can tell you what it means. The great teachers gave many answers. The Courtly Teacher said, when asked to explain a famine, *It is an examination, such as the candidates for the mandarinate take, and our promotion will be based on our response."*

Then he quoted other precepts, none of which, in Shard's opinion, offered any more comfort. *Light will always cast shadows*, the Desert Teacher said, but the Urfather knew better than to mention that one.

Later that day, when the expedition moved off along the trail, four stalwart villagers begged to go with them a way, carrying Sunlight's chair. Shard Gingko was able to walk alongside and hold a private conversation with the Firstborn when no one else could overhear. It was an opportunity that arose rarely now. They spoke, of course, in Palace Voice, which would be close to gibberish to the locals.

"You spoke originally of heading for Felicitous Wedlock of Waters, Master. Now that it is reported destroyed, will you change your plans?"

The Firstborn chuckled. "We had to head for somewhere. The problem is never where we were going yesterday, only where we should be going today."

Shard Gingko wondered if that was a memorable quotation, but decided not to ask. At times, the Firstborn could be maddeningly hard to pin down. The twinkle in his eyes suggested that this might be one of those times. He was being Sunlight, not the All-Wise.

"Where I want to go depends on where I think the Bamboo Banner is going. Where would you go, if you were Bamboo, my learned friend?"

"Home, Master."

That won a boyish laugh. "A mandarin of the fourth rank could speak no greater wisdom! But he must cross the Golden River somewhere if he wishes to reach Heart of the World eventually. I think he will veer west, planning to ford it, for he cannot hope to capture enough ferries to transport a host across downstream from Wedlock. He will, I believe, go westward, into Shashi, not north to Nanling."

"Toward the Portal of Worlds, Master?"

"Heaven does seem intent on bringing Bamboo and the opening of the Portal into conjunction, and perhaps the Emperor's army also. I will be very disappointed with it if it does not succeed." He fell silent for a few moments. "And, just maybe, this time I will be invited to the party also. Whenever I am near the Portal, I always try to visit a fort known as Goat Haven. It is a stronghold to dream of, and it has been held by a varied succession of brigands. The last one I met was Sky Hammer 3, a lovable scoundrel. I am interested to see if his descendants still rule there."

CHAPTER 12

"I was wondering," butterball Chief Eunuch intoned in a voice that would have lit a thousand lamps and greased the stairways of the Empire, "whether Your Majesty has made a decision regarding a state contribution to that worthy cause I had the honor to bring to Your Majesty's attention a few days ago?"

His attempts at blackmail were becoming blatant. Butterfly Sword was tempted to step down from the stool on which he was presently standing, grab the obese obscenity by the throat, and twirl his head around until it came off. Would anyone dare intervene? At the moment, the Emperor was being dressed in the state robes by a team of six valets. A dozen others were wandering about, pretending to be busy. It was a highly inappropriate moment to importune him for money, carefully chosen to maximize the threat. He made an effort to restrain his temper.

"To which cause are you referring? You have mentioned so many."

"The fund for funeral rites for former palace servants, lord. Eunuchs lack sons to smooth their ascent to the Fifth World, and many are so impoverished after a lifetime in imperial service that they are practically indigent. Your honored mother and equally honored father both gave generously in their time." He sighed and mopped his streaming forehead with a richly embroidered sleeve; the Robing Room was hotter than an iron foundry.

He was lying like wet snow, of course. He had claimed seven grandsons and the average palace eunuch was richer than a wholesale opium dealer. Theft and bribery were their daily fare.

Butterfly Sword had no time for this nonsense just then. In a few moments, he would hold court. Prince Boundless Shore had arrived at Sublime Mountain three days ago, with an entourage of guards and concubines, of course, and must be officially received. General Iron Spur was to have been smuggled in last night. Butterfly Sword had been anxiously awaiting both of those men, because they were part of a plan he had devised. No one else knew it yet, but today he would make his bid for freedom.

"The Gray Helpers charge such extortionate fees," Chief Eunuch murmured, dragging the threat of exposure out in the open while there were many witnesses present.

"The Gray Helpers are thieves and extortionists," the Emperor said sincerely. "I am thinking of launching a campaign to expose their larceny and bring them to justice. Just at present, though, the so-called Bamboo rebels are posing a threat to our throne, and we intend to crush them without mercy." How was that for a counterthreat? "Besides, our treasury is sorely strained by the millions of our beloved subjects suffering from famine and homelessness. They regard me as their loving father and expect me to help. Mention your cause to me again next week."

"Your Majesty is most gracious."

But next week, His Majesty would have escaped from prison and Chief Eunuch would be in one. If all went well, that was.

Absolute Purity was the Son of the Sun, Lord of the High and the Low, Emperor of the Good Land, Father of the Gentle People, Lord of Ten Thousand Years, and so on, and he was a prisoner. In the two months since he murdered the Empress Mother, Butterfly Sword had learned just how close his confinement was. Not just he, but all preceding Emperors had become captives of the palace eunuchs. The whole palace system was designed to imprison its most important resident.

Everything came to him by the hands of the eunuchs—his food, his clothes, his entertainment, even his concubines. Although he was out of practice at playing roles other than Emperor, he was still a Gray Helper. He could don a eunuch's costume and walk out the gate as a eunuch, unnoticed and unchallenged. Alas, to obtain a eunuch's costume, he would have to ask the eunuchs. Anyone who came at him with a blade would learn his mistake very rapidly, but a Gray Helper was as vulnerable to poison as the next man. Assassination was not an impossible move in the current palace game, especially with Boundless Shore at hand.

Likely, Butterfly Sword was more conscious of this imprisonment than most of his predecessors had been, because he had not been raised in the system. Unless he did something to smash it, his children would be raised in the same traditional way. All their lives they would be nurtured, surrounded, and educated by eunuchs, so they could never relate to ordinary people. The Empress Mother had not been palace born, but she had been tended and pampered by eunuchs since she was twelve. They were as universal as fleas in a bazaar.

Long ago, the Eleventh Dynasty had fallen into the same trap as its predecessors. Because palace intrigue raised the mortality rate among imperial heirs to atrociously high levels, Emperors tried to ensure their lines' survival by fathering many sons. To do so, they needed, or thought they needed, hundreds of concubines. Therefore, they needed thousands of eunuchs to guard them. Every concubine sought to promote her own sons by conspiring with eunuchs in murderous palace intrigue, continuing the vicious spiral.

Mandarins and eunuchs were historical foes, but Butterfly Sword had few means of reaching the mandarinate except through the eunuchs. Ever since that first climactic huddle with First Mandarin, their meetings had been public and formal. Had they tried to exchange notes, the eunuchs would have opened them, read them, and expertly resealed them before delivering them. If they ever did deliver them.

Still, his hasty agreement with First Mandarin on the day of the Empress Mother's death seemed to have escaped his jailers' ken. The speed with which the two men had moved to establish a common front, combined with the mass confusion in the palace that morning, had let their plot pass undetected. Now everything depended on the safe arrival of General Iron Spur, the old man's grandson.

Today, the Emperor intended to speak in open court. That had not happened in three reigns, but it *had* happened, and a little experimentation had shown him that the compulsions Lark had laid on him allowed him to do anything that any of his predecessors had done. That gave him all the scope he would ever need.

In the past few weeks, he had read all the government reports he could get into his hands and a lot of history from the imperial library. The day after the death of the Empress Mother, he had inspected her quarters, finding them looted to bare planks as he had expected. But in the ruins, he had discovered a secret cupboard whose door had been ripped off by the pillagers. Finding it full of papers and nothing of market value, they had lost interest. The Emperor had recognized the late unlamented's confidential records, and ordered them collected and delivered to his own quarters. Those had been the most interesting reading of all.

There had been very little else to do during official mourning—no sex, no music, no masques. But he had built his kite and now the time had come to fly it.

The eunuch on the stool finished adjusting His Majesty's absurdly tall headdress, stepped down, and bowed. Butterfly

Sword examined his reflection in the enormous mirror. Swathed in yellow brocade, towering over all his attendants, he was impressive to the point of absurdity. Did majesty really require such trappings? Strong as he was, he found the robes' weight oppressive in the baking, airless heat of early summer.

"Well done," he said. "Are we ready to proceed?"

Of course they were. Everyone else would have been ready for hours.

With two youths holding his train, he rustled forward, marched through the hidden back door into the vast Hall of Celestial Peace, and took his seat on the Golden Throne. Eunuchs adjusted his robes and withdrew, except for two who swung giant fans to waft air at His Imperial Majesty and keep the flies off him.

Out in the main hall, beyond a fretted screen, lesser officials were already present. As the doorkeeper proclaimed each name and title, the owner would scurry in, approach the invisible throne, and perform the three genuflections and nine head knockings. Then he would sidle away to kneel on the sidelines. Many of the ancients had trouble kowtowing. Respect for age was all very well, but the Empress Mother had left far too many old familiar faces in place long after they passed their usefulness. An imperial court should also include a dozen or so royal princes. She had disposed of those long ago.

The Hall of Celestial Peace was a magnificent place, every surface decorated with bright-colored tiles. The balconies were already crowded with spectators, although the Emperor had not expected to see people up there and no idea who they were. Certainly, Chief Eunuch would be watching from somewhere.

Minister of This . . . Prefect of That . . . Slowly, they progressed to more senior titles, officers of the second rank, then the first. Gatherer of Imperial Bounty . . . Court Astrologer, old fool . . . Last came First Mandarin, so honored because he normally represented the Emperor. He took his place at a corner of the dais.

Butterfly Sword nodded. Trumpets blared and the screens slid back to reveal him, although not the boys with the fans.

First Mandarin signaled. The herald at the door proclaimed His Highness Prince Boundless Shore, followed by a list of estates and titles. In trotted a double line of flunkies bearing the prince's gifts to the Emperor, which they laid before the throne. Butterfly Sword noted porcelain and jade and silk carpets and mysterious carved chests and wondered how much of it would be swallowed by the eunuchs' bottomless greed before even being listed by the imperial household.

Then came Absolute Purity's fourth cousin, His Highness Prince Boundless Shore, the boy who had the best real claim to the throne. He was about fifteen, tall but still youthfully slender, and he moved a great deal more nimbly and gracefully than anyone else had done. As a prince, he was required to knock his head on the floor only three times, not nine.

"Rise, cousin," the Emperor boomed. "You are welcome in court, a jewel to brighten our house."

The court gasped. No one living had ever heard the Lord of the High and the Low speak in such an assembly.

The boy rose to his knees. He was not supposed to look at the Emperor, but he could not resist a hasty upward glance, which Butterfly Sword pretended not to notice. The kid must be terrified at being summoned to court for the first time, knowing the bloody ways Emperors had for dealing with possible rivals, but he was hiding it very well. Butterfly Sword had no such vicious intentions, for he was in firm possession now, despite Chief Eunuch's smarmy threats. No one questioned his identity, and he had not one but two infant sons to succeed him if necessary. He had summoned the young prince for quite different reasons.

"That my insignificant existence," the prince began, reciting a speech he had probably found in some ancient record, "should thus so unexpectedly, by the honor of imperial regard . . ." And so on. He did not stumble once, which was more than could be said for most courtiers haranguing the throne. ". . . can have no greater honor than to kneel here and solemnly dedicate my life to your honor and service, My Lord."

"We intend to take you up on that offer, noble cousin. You are most welcome to our court and will be treated with sublime royal honors during your stay. You will drink tea with us in the Garden of Arboreal Splendor as soon as this meeting has adjourned. Meanwhile, sit there, opposite His Excellency, while we deal with another matter."

Butterfly Sword gestured to a fat cushion in the place of second honor. To be told to sit, rather than kneel, was a stupendous honor, of course, the sort of wonder to be passed on to future generations.

First Mandarin signaled again. The herald proclaimed General Peach Harvest, Deputy Supreme Guardian. The ever-cautious Empress Mother had always kept an incompetent in charge of the army, and an incompetent would always choose incompetents as his subordinates. The old man who came tottering in from the side of the hall had probably been worth little forty years ago and now his prose was tortuous, his logic nonsensical, his brushwork almost illegible. Butterfly Sword had ripped the last report apart in fury.

Having already kowtowed, Peach Harvest merely knelt and humbly begged the Lord of All Under Heaven to receive General Iron Spur, His Majesty's military prefect on the Siping frontier. He stumbled over even that little speech, having learned of it only that morning.

The trumpets announced the general. Butterfly Sword watched with interest as the alleged hero approached. Even unarmed, barefoot, and performing the undignified shuffle required to approach the throne, First Mandarin's grandson revealed traces of a soldier's bearing. He was younger than Butterfly Sword had expected, although that might be just because he had grown too accustomed to the company of eunuchs and geriatrics.

After the newcomer had kowtowed, the agenda called for Peach Harvest to beseech His Majesty to approve a long over-due commendation to Iron Spur for his victory over the barbarians five years ago. Before he could gather his wits, the Emperor spoke, in tones that echoed from the walls.

"Honorable Peach Harvest, your reports are rubbish. Where is our army?"

Jaws dropped. The court cowered back. Peach Harvest himself just gaped in horror.

"*We ask you again, where is our army?*"

The old man made strangled noises, then addressed the floor tiles. "Your Majesty, I believe it is still in Gongshan Province. Its progress to the south is being delayed because the Grand Canal is almost dry. The level of the Golden River has fallen so low that—"

"You believe? You don't know? And why is it going south? Where is the Bamboo Banner?"

After several *um*s and *er*s . . . "Jingyan Province, Your Majesty?"

"You are asking me? You don't know? You are dismissed from office. Go away."

In a murderous silence, the crushed old soldier crept backward, out of the imperial presence. Previous Emperors might have now sent him "permission" to commit suicide, and he might not wait for it, but Butterfly Sword had better targets for his wrath. Meanwhile, nothing would happen until he told it to. He noticed that First Mandarin had so far forgotten his practiced inscrutability as to lower his snowy eyebrows in disapproval of the upstart imposter who was departing from the agenda.

"First Mandarin, can anyone in this hall tell me where the Bamboo Banner is?"

The old man almost smiled as he caught up with the unwritten script. He had sent Butterfly Sword the answer to that question only yesterday and would certainly have discussed it with his grandson already.

"Your Majesty, if anyone can advise you on the military situation, it will be General Iron Spur."

"Do so, if you can, General."

Still kneeling, the soldier took it in stride. Having been granted the floor, he now addressed it, being unworthy to look directly at the Emperor. "My understanding, Your Majesty, is that the Bamboo Banner is presently in southern Jingyan Province, and there is some recent evidence to suggest that it is veering more to the northwest, away from its previous northeasterly path. The army, as of the time of the earthquake, was in Gongshan Province, and Supreme Guardian was concerned by reports that the Golden River had ceased to flow. In other words, Lord of All Under Heaven, the two forces are still on opposite sides of the Good Land."

"So if the army does cross the river without being washed away, it may even miss the Bamboo Banner entirely and have to chase it north?" Butterfly Sword did not wait for an answer, in case he had been wrong. "If I now appoint you Supreme Guardian, can you find our army, assume command, and deal with the rebels before they do any more damage?"

The audience gasped again, but there was only one possible answer to that question. Iron Spur gave it without a twitch, although he might be putting his neck on the block.

"My life and sword are Your Majesty's to command."

"I so command. It is time to stamp out this upstart rabble. You will meet with us in the Garden of Arboreal Splendor shortly. You also, First Mandarin, and of course our worthy cousin, Prince Boundless Shore."

He raised a hand very slightly, and instantly the screens closed.

There! He had begun. And eunuchs were the first target on his list.

The Garden of Arboreal Splendor, in the Great Without, comprised several acres of artfully sited groves, lawns, flowerbeds, and lotus ponds. Butterfly Sword was carried to where his three guests sat in a small gazebo he had not seen before. It would be ideal for private dalliance with Snow Lily, except that she must never leave the Great Within. It was not overlooked by any windows, and there was no undergrowth close enough to conceal listeners. He ignored the throne provided and joined the others in sitting on the mats. All three of them must be wondering why Boundless Shore had been included in a council of war.

"I waive palace formality for this meeting," Butterfly Sword said. "Our business is too important to be complicated by ceremony or undue politeness. Disagree with me if you think I am in error. Flat-out contradict me if necessary. I am as human as you are. I spit and shit and fart. The only difference is that when I fart everyone has to look pleased."

First Mandarin stiffened in horror. Iron Spur studied his knees. The young prince choked back a grin. Butterfly Sword was relying on his Gray Helper training, as he had when he went rowing with Snow Lily. An Emperor who deliberately did the unthinkable must be genuine because an imposter would not dare. Then conversation had to wait while the tea arrived. It was cold, of course.

As soon as the servants had left, Butterfly Sword said, "General, give us your reading of the military situation."

Iron Spur must have foreseen the question. "Based on the information I have been given, Lord"—he glanced briefly at his grandfather—"the earthquake devastated large parts of three provinces: Nanling, Shashi, and Jingyan. With bridges and cities in ruins, with food and shelter critically short, the Bamboo

Banner must either return to the south or detour from its previous track. The Golden River is temporarily dammed just east of Wedlock, bringing a real risk of catastrophic flooding downstream from there. For that reason, I believe the army's present course southward may be impeded. I would humbly advise Your Majesty that your forces should head west to cut off the rebels in Wanrong or even Shashi."

"The army will have farther to go than the rebels do."

"But it will be moving over the plains. The rabble will be cutting across the ridges, up and down hills. We have an organized commissariat. They will be foraging for food in a not very fertile land. I believe Your Majesty's forces can cut them off in Wanrong."

"There is reason to expect that the interception will occur in Shashi."

After a moment's hesitation, Iron Spur said, "I am inexpressibly grateful to Your Majesty for this guidance."

"There is no military reason for my conclusion, but the Portal of Worlds is expected to open shortly, probably next year, but even that date is uncertain."

No one was going to say that a change of dynasty might follow. Very few knew that one had already happened—long may it last!

"Does Your Majesty order me to proceed on that assumption?"

"No. Do what you are paid to do as you think fit. I like your plan, though. When can you leave?"

"Tonight, Your Majesty, if my commission can be ready by then."

The difference between this young firebrand and the Supreme Guardian was noon over midnight.

"You are a man after my own heart, General, but there are a few details I must take care of first. How many men did you bring with you?"

"Ten thousand, sire. They can be here within hours."

"How trustworthy are its officers?"

"My second-in-command is my brother, Iron Fist, Majesty."

"He and the troops will stay here. You will lead our army against the Bamboo Banner. Its followers have claimed for years that I am dead. To prove them wrong, I will come with you."

First Mandarin's tea bowl shattered on the paving.

"Like Emperors of old, I will march against the rebels," Butterfly Sword continued calmly. "If a battle can be avoided, or after it is won, I will decide what terms to offer this Bamboo and his gang. But I will not presume to tell you how to lead an army or fight a battle, Supreme Guardian. First Mandarin, prepare documents to raise the Pearl Concubine to the rank of Empress and to appoint a regency council of yourself and Prince Boundless Shore to rule the Good Land in my absence. If the two of you disagree on a matter, you will consult the Empress to break the deadlock."

He waited then to let them unravel it all. First Mandarin was very pale, but he was being offered more power than he had ever had, and a chance to put Boundless Shore on the throne if the usurper failed to destroy the Banner. Boundless Shore had turned bright pink. Instead of some token job on the fringe of government, he was starting at the top, for regent was as high as he could ever honorably hope to rise in the Empire. Iron Spur just looked thoughtful.

Butterfly Sword asked him first. "Questions, Supreme Commander?"

"How will Your Majesty travel?"

"On horseback, and I will set a pace that makes you scream for mercy."

The soldier must have doubted that, but he said, "I am overwhelmed by the honor and trust you bestow on me, sire."

"And his men?" First Mandarin dared to ask.

"The Empress and the mothers of my sons will move to the

Turquoise Palace. The rest of my concubines or prospective concubines will be returned to their families with appropriate gifts. The Empress will provide a list of up to one hundred eunuchs she wishes to retain in my service. I command the regency council to impose martial law on Heart of the World and evict all other eunuchs from the palace. Start tonight. I want Chief Eunuch arrested and his house searched for evidence of stolen property."

The old man beamed blissfully. "Your Majesty, he owns two palaces packed to the rafters with treasure. It will take weeks to move it all to the imperial vaults."

"If that is confirmed, cut off his head and mount it on the Gate of Memory."

"The thousand cuts? Impalement?"

"No, it must be quick." Butterfly Sword was not going to have the fat man taking days to die, screaming allegations of treason against the Emperor. "And then move against the next layer: his sons, his accomplices. Seize their property, but go slowly, so that any who choose to flee the city may do so, but allow them to take only what they can carry. None of them should starve."

Butterfly Sword glanced around his three accomplices and resisted a desire to laugh aloud. Power certainly had its enjoyable moments. He would be wagering his life by leaving the capital, but his life was barely worth a sneeze at the moment. If he failed, Snow Lily and all his children would die. If he could overcome the Bamboo Banner, he would rule unchallenged.

"Do you have any questions? Cousin?" He went around the circle, and none of them had questions. They were all stunned.

"In that case, First Mandarin, Supreme Guardian, you have our leave to go and be about our business. No formality—and *don't* walk backward! You'll break your necks on that paving."

As the two were leaving, First Mandarin glanced back and nodded very slightly. Only Butterfly Sword saw, and he took it as a welcome sign of commitment, the old man indicating he approved of the imposter's performance so far and would support him.

In Heart of the World, anyone who trusted anyone else had a very short life expectancy.

"Well, cousin . . . ?"

"Your Majesty?"

"Family can look me in the eye in private conversations."

Startled, the boy looked up and flushed. "Sire!"

Butterfly Sword smiled. "Were you worried that I would cut off your head?"

"Oh no, sire! But . . . Of course not, sire."

"Poison or a silken cord? You were right to worry. I hope I have reassured you somewhat in this little chat?"

"I am overwhelmed, sire."

"So you should be! I just dropped the entire Good Land on your shoulders. First Mandarin is efficient, and I believe honest, but he is also set firmly in the ruts of a long life. Don't be afraid to push a younger point of view if necessary. When you were a child, did your family have a pet name for you?"

Bewilderment. "My sisters called me Sandfly, sire."

"That's too obvious by itself, but we can stretch it to insects in general. When you write to me, always mention insects of one kind or another, and that way I will know it is really from you, and you are not writing under compulsion. Any mention of spiders or webs will mean that you are not writing freely. In my youth, I was known as Horse, so I will always mention horses or cavalry somewhere. The warning will be 'mule.' Is that clear? Good. Now, is there anything you need from me?"

"Um . . ." An even deeper blush. The boy looked down at his perfectly groomed nails, and then forced his eyes up again as he remembered his orders. "Money, sire. My grandmother once had a thousand servants and now we have less than a dozen. Your esteemed and well-loved mother . . . I mean I had to sell art and jewels to pay for my journey here, the hired retainers, the gifts . . . We have only one house left."

Butterfly Sword sighed. How many houses did one boy and one old woman really need? Millions of the Gentle People were dying of starvation already. But unless he rewarded his vice Emperor lavishly, his would be one of the shortest reigns in the history of the Good Land.

"Why don't I begin by just giving you one of Chief Eunuch's palaces and all its contents? That will probably make you the richest man in the Empire after me. Once I have quashed the Bamboo Banner and can start to reign in earnest, I will honor you properly. No, you do not have to kiss my shoes."

CHAPTER 13

Lady Cataract advanced on the staircase of worlds at the full of Harvest Moon. Shard Gingko was not surprised. She had asked for the caravan to stop earlier than usual, pleading weariness, but after that, the Firstborn had sat for many hours, cross-legged beside her litter, chatting softly with her. Shard Gingko recalled how a brutally chained youth in Four Mountains Fortress two years ago had foreseen the death of Mandarin Serge Shallows, and suspected that he was seeing that same skill here. In the last two weeks, the lady had seldom emerged from that litter. At night, her attendants wrapped it up to make it into a tent for her. With a soft mattress raised off the ground, it made a better nest than anyone else in the group enjoyed.

She had not chosen a scenic place to die. Once these hills had been tightly terraced with rice paddies, but the earthquake had broken all the dikes, sending huge floods of mud and seedlings hurtling down into the valley. Whoever had lived there must lie there still, deeply buried—may their sparks find their way onward! Now the land was a desert, a maze through which the travelers were struggling to find a way along the slopes, high enough to be out of the mud slides and fairly even underfoot.

Soon after daybreak, Shard was wakened by a great lament and keening from the lady's body servants and knew his guess had been right. The Firstborn rose from his blanket and calmed everyone. No, they did not need to find Gray Helpers to conduct her rites, he said—just build a pyre and he would take care of the rest. Unlike them, he did not fear corpses. As he had told Shard more than once, the dead were much less dangerous than the living.

There being no wood in sight, the litter itself and her carrying chair were chopped up and piled together with anything else that seemed likely to burn. At sunset, Sunlight laid the corpse on the pyre. Shard noted the Firstborn's new strength with approval, although Lady Cataract had weighed very little by the end. Everyone gathered around.

"The farewell I will sing for her," the Urfather said, "is a very old one that she found in the most ancient of all the manuscripts in her collection. I will chant it as it would have been sung back in the Sixth Dynasty, and you will not understand a word of it. But she would recognize it and her spark will obey my instructions and rise to find happiness in the Fifth World."

The Sixth Dynasty had seen a great flowering of the arts. Shard did understand a little of the old tongue, and he agreed that Lady Cataract would have enjoyed the tribute. The well-seasoned wood blazed well, and sparks soared up to mingle with the stars.

The next morning, after the pyre had collapsed into ashes, Sunlight himself gathered the charred bones and wrapped them for Cataract's servants to take home.

"Her Ladyship told me," he said, "that she knew of no family to inherit her estate, and she did not want the Emperor to have anything more than he must. She hoped that her servants would divide her goods equitably and burn the house when they leave. I charge you all not to be greedy and see that even the lowliest garden boy receives a fitting tribute."

For himself and his companions, he took three horses and their tack, plus what he decreed to be a fair share of the remaining rations, although it would have made little more than a single meal in better times. He had stopped insulting his two disciples by asking if they wanted to stay with him. As so often happened, he surprised them. Instead of continuing to try and find a passable way along the slopes, he led them straight up the hill.

Mostly, they went in single file, but once Shard found himself riding alongside Mouse, who was no longer the downcast child of Four Mountains. He was now a strapping young man who smiled a lot.

"Master? Do you think you and I will be remembered in history for accompanying the Firstborn to see the Portal open?"

Shard needed time to think about that. "You mean are our ancestors watching us?"

"Assuredly, our ancestors are, but I mean other people's descendants."

"I think you should ask the Ancient One that."

The grin widened. "I already did."

"And what did he say?"

"He asked why that should make any difference to the way we behaved."

"Quite," Shard Gingko said testily. "Do you remember the Humble Teacher's warning on the dangers of pride?"

"Yes, Master."

"Write it out for me at the first chance you get."

The smile wavered. "All of it?"

"All of it, and in the decorated style."

"Yes, Master." Glumly.

At the top, when they stopped to rest their horses on the bare and windy summit, the Firstborn pointed to the southwest, where far-off icy peaks glinted in the morning sun, like many rows of teeth.

"The Western Wall, my friends! We will follow the ridges to reach the Great Valley that flanks them on this side. This is not a route I would try to bring a litter, and will at times be hard on our mounts, but we have plenty of time."

"Then we are close to the Portal?" Shard asked.

"It is still a ways south of us, but journeying along the Great Valley should be much easier than what we have been doing lately." Sunlight smiled. His happiness was Lady Cataract's legacy. He had hope now. He did not expect to die this year.

CHAPTER 14

The day after Verdant found shelter at Tutu, she learned that Silk-worm's new wet nurse was named Monkey Flower. This did not bother him, though. He took to her like a leech. Seeming much happier with her milk than he had with White Petal's, he gave up colic and smiled blissfully at people on the rare occasions when he wasn't either sucking or sleeping.

Monkey Flower had lost a girl child in the earthquake, so her husband, Thornbush, was well satisfied with the exchange. Verdant understood that she had just given away her son, but the alternative had been to watch him die, so she would have to accept the situation and love him from afar. She was less pleased by the prospect of becoming Thornbush's junior wife, for he was a nasty, foul-mouthed little man with bow legs and a fixed sneer, clearly well past his best, if he had ever had a best. Several more attractive options were walking around, if she were truly doomed to spend the rest of her life in Tutu, but Thornbush, despite his lack of stature, seemed to be the local headman, so there were going to be no other options. Then a prospect worse than marriage presented itself.

The villagers had slept on grass well back from the huts on that first night, for the aftershocks continued, and sometimes more mud-brick walls collapsed. Wounded children wailed in the night, but the weather remained fine and there were no more deaths or injuries. Monkey Flower produced very meager bowls of congee for breakfast, but her own helping was no larger than Verdant's, so Verdant made no complaint. The entire Good Land was going to be on short commons this year.

"I must find some better clothes," she said after wolfing down her snack. The tattered remains of her gown made her feel like a beggar, which was horribly close to being true.

"Come!" Thornbush commanded. He led her around to what had once been the main, and only, street. He gestured at the ruins of the village. Half the houses, including his, had survived, but the rest were heaps of rubble and mud. "You can have anything you want off the corpses. You see there?" He pointed to where a gang of men was stacking timbers. "We're building a pyre. You bring the bodies there. That's your job now."

Verdant was at a loss for words. Yet now she understood: She had offended her ancestors by marrying a Gray Helper, and their punishment was that she must become one. The nasty glint in the headman's eye confirmed it. Silkworm was welcome; she was not. She had expected that she would have to earn her keep, but she had not anticipated being assigned the worst job in the Good Land. What choice did she have? She nodded, and headed for the nearest ruin in the hope of finding something to wear.

There was a brief digression then, when a group of strangers was seen approaching. The villagers rushed out with bamboo spears and a few swords. They blew trumpets and banged drums, and the refugees turned away. It was a scene that would be repeated several times in the next few weeks.

Verdant labored for days to collect all the corpses. Whenever the men dismantling the ruins uncovered another body, they would shout for her. She would dig the corpse free, lay it on a blanket, and drag it to the makeshift mortuary beside the rising pyre. The moment she had touched the first body, she had become ill-omened and unclean, of course. After that, she had to sleep and eat apart from everyone else, and people fled from her.

Children shouted insults at her. On the bright side, she was not required to serve as anybody's concubine.

She had plenty of time to muse on her own incredible folly. Why, oh why, had she not taken Plum Blossom's advice after the earthquake and headed west to find Silky instead of east? Silky was no ideal husband, but he had provided generously for her. Fool, fool, fool!

She was not dead yet. She must fulfill the penance the ancestors had prescribed for her and hope for their forgiveness. And then she must do whatever it took to improve the situation. Silkworm would stay there, in Tutu. She would go in search of Silky and return with him to reclaim their son. And if she couldn't find Silky, she would go back to Wedlock and seek help from her father. Such plans must wait a week or two, until the Emperor came to the aid of his people, as he surely would.

The weather broke, bringing spring showers, but at least they made the world feel cleaner. Verdant found lodging in a ruin at the downstream edge of the town, a nook that was at least dry, if not warm, and her repugnant status ensured that even the raunchiest youths in the village would not dare molest her. There she could store anything she found near the corpses that might be useful to her later. She even retrieved pots of dried fruit, salted fish, and unspoiled bags of rice.

By the fourth day, the corpses were swelling and their stench was making the whole village unbearable. Thornbush declared the pyre big enough, but then came the problem of lifting the bodies to lay them on top. Verdant was not strong enough, so the men rigged a derrick, and it became her job to tie the rope around a body's ankles, so it could be dragged up a ramp. Then she had to climb up there, see that it was correctly positioned, untie the rope, go back down for the next one. The worst ones were the small children, because she had to carry those up by herself.

The bale fire burned for a day and a night. The smell before had been bad enough, but the reek of burning flesh was infinitely worse.

Even then, her work was not finished. She still had to gather the bones, dig the graves, and bury them. If she complained or balked, Thornbush threatened to cut off her food and drive her away altogether. The children alone could do that just by throwing stones at her. A few more bodies were found, so the whole process had to be repeated on a smaller scale.

At last came the day when the dead had gone, damaged huts had been more or less repaired, and the men felt free to start replacing those that had been totally destroyed. Verdant was ordered to help the women gathering the straw that would stiffen the mud bricks. It was backbreaking work, and she had to work far apart from anyone else, for she was still unclean and always would be.

The Little River no longer carried so much floating debris. Yet still she lingered, waiting until the dribble of refugees tapered away and the villagers stopped posting night guards. After that, she could begin planning her escape, and it was amazingly easy. She had found many useful things in the ruins while collecting corpses and had hidden them in her den. Tired as she was, she stayed awake until the village had fallen silent and a last-quarter moon had risen. Then she heaved her first bundle onto her back and headed for the little jetty where the boats were kept.

Voices ahead stopped her—the sound of adolescents enjoying themselves, and no doubt enjoying one another. Somewhere, a baby cried, quite possibly Silkworm, whom she had not held in her arms for so long. She crept back to her lair to wait. The temptation to fall asleep was torment, but she knew she must try again in an hour or two. Soon, the old folk would be stirring their cramped old bones to face another day.

This time, she reached the jetty unchallenged. The village owned three boats, and she chose the smallest, dumped her bundle in it, then hurried back to fetch her second bundle, the one with the food.

The Little River would carry her down to the Jade. From there, she could row upstream to Cherish and appeal for help from the Gray Helpers, who would certainly have benefitted greatly from the earthquake toll. They would guide her to Silky. If she couldn't row against the current, she could let the Jade carry her down to Wedlock, where it joined the Golden. And there she would find her parents.

The little dory was leaky, so her feet were in water, but it was outfitted with oars and a pole. She had never tried rowing, but she had watched it being done on her long trip upriver with Silky in the Year of the Nightingale. She cut the painter with a very sharp knife she had found on a dead man's belt. The current caught the boat, swinging it around so suddenly that she lost her balance, almost fell overboard, toppled over her bundles, and sprawled headlong, banging her head on a thwart.

After that, she knelt in the bow and tried to steer with the pole, for the water was mostly shallow. She could not always stay clear of obstacles—mostly stranded debris brought down by the earthquake—so the boat took several hard knocks. After an hour or so, more by accident than design, it ran aground on a sandbank. She had come a long way from Tutu. She was trembling with weariness. She made herself as comfortable as possible in the bow—the bilge had all collected in the stern—and fell into a dreamless sleep.

She was awakened by a blaze of sunlight and her own cry of alarm as her robe was ripped open. A man was kneeling over her, leering down at her. He was young, he was large, and he was naked. He grabbed both of her breasts and laughed.

"Good morning to you, woman! I've got a real treat for you to start your day with. See the lovely present I'm going to give you?"

"No! Go away, stop that . . ."

"Struggle all you want," he said. "I like that."

She tried to heave him off her, which was hopeless. But her hand found the knife she had dropped. Her right hand. Thinking of the child she carried, she thrust the blade into the man's ribs.

His eyes and mouth went very wide. He made a few whimpering sounds, and then vomited blood all over her. His death throes shook the boat loose, and in a few moments she found herself floating downstream again, soaked in blood and pinned under a corpse.

She had married a Gray Helper who was also a murderer. If she ever did meet Silky again, he would laugh himself silly.

Her ancestors had helped her escape from Tutu, but now she had proved unworthy of them. She had killed a man. Would they ever forgive her?

She struggled free of the corpse, but she could not throw it overboard, and would tip the boat over if she tried. The extra weight was making it ride lower in the water and leak faster. It was sinking. Her store of food, which she had counted on to feed her until she found sanctuary somewhere, was already ruined. Everything she tried went wrong.

She saw obstacles ahead and could not even free the pole, which was trapped under the body. She watched in frozen horror as she headed to disaster and the remains of the ruined bridge that she and Walnut Shell had seen on the day of the earthquake, which now seemed so very long ago. The boat struck the debris and the impact hurled her bodily into the river. She floundered, hampered by her clothes and the current, and then by a violent collision with a vertical post. She grabbed it, hung on, and got her head above water.

It took her several minutes and many bruises to fight her way ashore and climb onto dry land. The boat was gone. Her precious stack of food, clothes, and useful things had all disappeared. She was stranded on the bank of the Little River with nothing but the soaking wet clothes on her back, and for a few minutes, she could do nothing but sit there and fight back tears.

Her face was bleeding, her eye swollen. She had other bruises. She was barefoot.

She had even climbed out on the wrong bank, and her only hope now was to walk back to Cherish and appeal to the Gray Helpers. She didn't think she could ford the river on foot. Horses obviously did, for she could see where trails had formed on both banks, opposite each other. What had she done to offend Heaven so grossly? Why couldn't she have just died in the earthquake with so many thousands of people?

Then she heard the sound of hooves and saw a band of four people riding in her direction on her side of the river. One of them was certainly a woman, who might just possibly take pity on her. That was extremely unlikely, of course, but possible. Verdant rose and hobbled over to the trail to approach them.

They reined in and stared at her in astonishment.

Then her ancestors smiled at last!

Did not the Rose Teacher say, *However dark the night, the sun will rise*?

Verdant knew the old man on the front horse—pudgy, with his face all scarred by smallpox, and the foulest breath she had ever encountered.

"Honorable Pearl White 11! You came to my wedding."

He beamed at her. "Indeed, I do remember. You are Verdant Harmony. You married Mandarin Effulgent Brushwork! How fares your noble husband?"

He meant, of course, Gray Brother Luminous. "I have had no news of him since the earthquake struck, but I can lead you to where he is."

CHAPTER 15

"We are presently camped one day's march east of the city of Prosperity . . ." the Emperor said. He was dictating to his secretary, Mandarin of the First Rank Ash Staff. "The capital of Jiading Province," he added to save Boundless Shore from having to ask someone. First Mandarin would know, of course. "So far we have seen no sign of earthquake damage, although we are told that the Golden River is higher than normal for Harvest Moon."

He waited for Ash Staff to wipe his brush and take more ink. First Mandarin had been appalled at the idea that the Emperor would inscribe his own correspondence. Emperors wrote poetry, and some had been known to dabble in landscapes, but nothing more. Butterfly Sword knew that his own calligraphy was suffering from disuse, and would be regarded by his regents with silent contempt. Besides, writing with a water cask as a table and a saddlebag as a chair did not lend itself to creating the best art, although Ash Staff produced excellent script under those conditions.

Ash Staff had been recommended to His Imperial Majesty by First Mandarin, and might well be a grandson or great-grandson of the old rascal. He would certainly be writing his own reports back to Sublime Mountain, tattling on what the Emperor was up to but hadn't thought to mention.

"Our progress has been slower than we had hoped since we left the Grand Canal."

In fact, it had been appalling. The canal's advantage had been that the Emperor's small flotilla of two boats had been able to transit the problem locks and shallows much faster than the army's huge fleet had done. But since leaving the canal where it met the Golden River, Iron Spur had proceeded upriver by land, on horseback along the towpath. As a result, he was closing the gap only very slowly. He was still a month behind the Imperial Army.

Back on Sublime Mountain, Butterfly Sword had fantasized about outracing the wind across the Good Land, but that had not happened. Emperors could not speed along like imperial couriers. Of course he had not expected to travel in his formal robes, acres of golden silk embroidered with pearls and precious stones, but there might be occasions when he would want to dress up. That meant bundles and more bundles, and valets to look after them, and the only trained valets were eunuchs, of course, and few eunuchs knew how to ride. Even his traveling clothes must make a statement: Did he outrank General Iron Spur or didn't he? If he concealed his rank too well, some uppity officer might set him on latrine duty. Not that Butterfly Sword would mind that very much—he had attended to such matters for years back in Sheep Rocks, and it was not a skill that required constant practice—but the officer would necessarily have to be beheaded. Also, Butterfly Sword needed privacy, which meant a large tent all to himself. And so, despite his bragging to Iron Spur, his presence slowed the general's progress, which was galling. The worst of it was that everyone in the company soon knew who the big "Captain Dragon Claw" was. Notwithstanding all his protests, guards were posted around his tent at night.

So his dream of a small, fast-moving group had bloated into a nightmare of about two hundred people, crawling along at the pace of the slowest horse. Butterfly Sword was now convinced that Iron Spur was being overprotective of his Emperor's safety. Without him to guard, he would take to the river. Of course, he could be overruled, but that must be done tactfully, for Butterfly Sword had promised not to interfere in the way the army was run.

The lantern flickered; wind flapped the tent. The air was permanently full of bugs and a dust that worked its way into everything. Why should Butterfly Sword complain? Even here, bivouacking in a swamp on the banks of the mighty Golden River, he was better off than nine-tenths of the people he had seen on his journey so far. *His* people, but he would not sleep tonight if he thought much about that.

"We have received your report inscribed on the First Day of Harvest Moon. We approve of your actions regarding the unruly eunuchs, for truly they are vermin."

But they weren't, not really. They were thousands of wretched, mutilated men he had thrust out into a contemptuous and unforgiving world with no means of earning a living, but if he wrote that, First Mandarin and Boundless Shore would think he was insane.

"Try to find useful employment for the dutiful."

Now what?

"The Grand Canal," he said, "is in a much worse state than we expected."

Years of neglect had left the banks and locks in dismal condition, and vast stretches of the channel in need of dredging. Butterfly Sword had long since stopped feeling sorry for what he had done to the Empress Mother. For years, that murderous old crone had wasted the revenue of the Empire on megalomaniacal plans for a totally unnecessary Water Palace. Even if the Bamboo Banner could be stopped in its tracks and Heaven granted the phony Emperor Absolute Purity a long reign and the wisdom of all the teachers, he would be hard put to restore the Good Land to the happy prosperity it had known in the days of Zealous Righteousness.

Ash Staff was waiting again. . . .

"On land, we are held back by the slowest horse." He had to mention horses somewhere, so that Boundless Shore would know that his letter was genuine.

"We have therefore decided to continue from here by water."

Ash Staff looked up in alarm, then remembered his manners and wrote what the Lord of the High and Low had spoken. The local peasants were still terrified that the Golden River would break through the upstream obstruction caused by the earthquake and come roaring down upon them in gigantic waves. But the river here was so wide that its far bank was out of sight. Butterfly Sword could not believe that such an enormous expanse of water could behave like a mountain stream. He could even see traces of debris left on the shore above the current waterline. That was why he had sent Iron Spur ahead to talk to the local governor.

"Who goes there?" demanded a voice outside.

Iron Spur's voice gave the password.

"We will continue in the morning," the Emperor told his secretary. "Enter!"

Ash Staff obediently corked his ink bottle and put his tools away in his scribe's box.

The general entered and bowed. It had taken two weeks to train him not to kowtow out here in the field. He was very effective as a leader, Iron Spur. His men adored him, and he organized their fodder and comfort meticulously so he could drive them hard. Quite likely, he was a very able tactician, but a strategist, probably not. Butterfly Sword tended to think of him as "Young" Iron Spur, although he must have at least five years on Butterfly Sword himself.

"Greetings, Supreme Guardian. I haven't seen you smile like that in a month. You have good news."

"Indeed, yes, Your Majesty! The learned governor completely confirms what your imperial wisdom had already discerned.

The great Fish Moon Earthquake did dam the Golden River just downstream from Wedlock, and when the river did escape from its chains, it indeed displayed its anger with a great flood, but its fury abated downstream. Many vessels are now riding its vast waters again untroubled."

So now it was safe to bathe? Mustn't say so, mustn't make jokes. At times, Butterfly Sword had to restrain himself from sharing confidences with Iron Spur, for he was not in on the great conspiracy. His grandfather First Mandarin would not have told him that he was to serve a phony Emperor, because if the deception were ever revealed, all those in the know would face the death of a thousand cuts, or worse. Only Butterfly Sword, First Mandarin, and "Empress" Snow Lily knew the truth—plus Gray Sister Lark and unknown members of the Gray Order, of course.

"Let us drink together to celebrate your news."

Of course, the general had to unwrap the flask from its cooling wet wrappings and fill the goblets. He even had to drink first, to show that it was not poisoned—or if it were, that he was not party to the fact.

It didn't seem to be. Butterfly Sword took a swig.

"And has the noble governor any vessel he might put at our disposal?"

"Indeed he had, sire! The *Starlight Dream*, a recently commissioned but well-tested paddleboat scheduled to leave tomorrow laden with rice for the stricken lands. He promised to continue coal loading through the night and have accommodation arranged for us on board."

Had Iron Spur hinted that his party included a very important person he must not name? Had he threatened force? Or was the governor just a loyal servant of the throne? Stranger things could happen, but not often.

"Is he dispatching the food for charity or to make a profit on the famine prices upstream, do you know?"

Iron Spur smiled respectfully. "He implied the first, sire, and the truth should be available when we arrive near the disaster."

"Wherever the truth lies, we will hold him up as an example to others. And once we are safely afloat and on our way, I think the noble *Starlight Dream* should fly our imperial flag, so that the people may know we are attending to our duties."

And if the Emperor ever did manage to catch up with his lost army, he could appropriate more ships, load his troops on board, and sail them up the Golden and Jade Rivers to Cherish, which he hoped to reach in time to intercept the Bamboo Banner. But that would depend on events.

"What did the governor say about the passage of our army through Jiading?"

"He was reticent, sire, but I believe your orders against looting and uncompensated expropriation were not fully carried out. Evidence for a court-martial could be readily obtained hereabouts."

"I will have Ash Staff collect some statements before we sail. You have other news?" Butterfly Sword could read Iron Spur quite easily now. He was fairly sure that the warrior's loyalty had ripened from duty to sincere respect. Yet how many Emperors had died believing such improbabilities?

"His Excellency reported some news of the Bamboo Banner, reports he had received from Jingyan Province. The governor there is convinced that the rebel rank and file have all been addicted to yang leaf, sire. That might explain some of their alleged miracles."

"Inform us about yang."

"A narcotic, sire, grown in tropical lands. It dulls pain, makes the user both gullible and submissive. Apparently, Bamboo has been doping all his followers with it. The governor personally questioned some prisoners—three of them, all skinny as ferrets and raving imbeciles from yang withdrawal. They begged him to put them to death, Your Majesty. He refused to oblige traitors, and just chained them up in public to starve. Which did not take them long, regrettably."

"And where is Bamboo getting this invidious yang?"

"That we do not know, but he cannot have an unlimited supply."

"You mean that his army may explode into thousands of raving lunatics swarming in all directions?"

"As Your Majesty says." Even yet, Iron Spur had not quite adjusted to the idea that Emperors sometimes had brains.

"Would that be an improvement?"

"It would be a shame, if Your Celestial Majesty will forgive my saying so, to come all this way and not find anyone to fight."

"Spoken like a true warrior. You may pour more wine."

The collapse of the Bamboo Banner into a crazy rabble would not be the worst of events for the Son of the Sun himself, but it might be harder on the Gentle People than a straightforward military massacre. The Empress Mother had never said that running an empire was easy.

CHAPTER 16

When the new road up to Goat Haven became passable, Silky gave strict orders that all visitors must be carefully vetted at the lower checkpoint. Strangers would be turned away. He set the guard roster, making sure that at least one longtime resident and one Gray Helper were always present to vouch for those he would allow in. Moreover, the upper-level guards were to notify him as soon as anyone was seen coming up the hill.

For the first few days, only strangers appealed for admittance and the lower guards allowed none of them through. About noon on the third day, he was told that two horsemen were on their way up, and replied he would be there to meet them when they arrived. He had been working on a better version of the affidavit that made him rightful owner of Goat Haven, but he hid that away and wandered outside to enjoy the fine summer sunshine.

He was delighted to see that the report had been in error, and that the leading rider was Plum Blossom, his accomplice from Wedlock. She was thinner and showed signs of prolonged stress, which she was making no effort to dissemble. Behind her came a youngster from the Cherish abbey, whom Silky remembered as Noodles, as he had once been Tug. Silky stood at the upper gate to welcome them, backed by half a dozen guards, all of them Goat Haven men.

"Your Highness!" Plum Blossom slid from her saddle and dropped to her knees. "We were so worried that you might have perished in the earthquake."

Noodles joined her. One of the lower guards at the moment was Watersprite, who would have dropped enough hints to bring the newcomers up-to-date on the situation.

Silky laughed and urged them to rise. "And I rejoice that two such worthy retainers have been spared. Are there any more of our company alive?"

"Another five, Your Highness. We found shelter about two hours' ride away. We have been anxiously waiting to see whether you and Prince Luminous Aspect were safe!"

"Alas, he ascended the ladder of worlds in the disaster, as did my esteemed father, Sky Hammer. Can you"—he turned to Noodles— "I confess I have forgotten your name, warrior."

"North Star, Your Highness."

"Can you ride back and bring the others?" An extra seven supporters in Goat Haven would practically guarantee that Silky could survive any effort to evict him.

Making a good show of deference, North Star asked if he might eat first.

"Of course. How thoughtless of me! And do the others have horses?" Silky quickly ordered that North Star be conducted to the kitchens, be well fed, and then be provided with three horses and a sack of rice to take with him. He also ordered a meal for Plum Blossom to be brought to his study and led her there.

The moment the door closed behind them, he kissed her with intimations of serious intent. They had been sex partners since they were children copying the big folk. She would be a welcome change from Watersprite, but her response was less fervent than he had hoped for.

When they broke apart, he said, "How are you?"

"Very weary." Plum Blossom sank gratefully onto a divan. "Weeks and weeks of just me and six Brothers?"

"Still, nice work if you can get it."

"Nice work if you don't have a broken collarbone."

"Cherish must have been hit very hard?"

"You haven't heard? Totally flattened: the House of Joyful Departure, your house, everything. The abbess died of her injuries. General Scarlet Meadow . . . The docks and all the shipping, too. Hasn't Verdant arrived?"

No, nor Thunderbot. Demons take the abbess—who cared about her? Silky shook his head and sat down to hear the worst.

"Last I saw of her, she was riding away with Silkworm and Walnut Shell. It was a miracle all three of them were outdoors and escaped the calamity. With my broken collarbone, I couldn't go with her, but I told her where you were."

Silky was surprised at how dismayed he felt at the prospect of never seeing Verdant again. He had won power and fortune beyond his dreams, and yet it felt strangely empty without her to share it. Even if she had come in search of him—and he knew that it was far more likely that she had headed off back to Wedlock—then she must have starved to death on his doorstep with all the thousands of others. To have lost her to the earthquake—well, that was the will of Heaven. For some reason, it hurt much more to know that she had survived the cataclysm and then perished in the chaos.

"Any news of Wedlock?"

Plum Blossom shrugged. "Wedlock has gone completely, so they say, at least all the old town. The Golden River backed up and made a lake of it. Now the water level has started to drop, so the flood is moving downstream to claim more victims." She smirked. "So we're free! Nobody knows our leashes anymore."

"That's right," he said, although he knew her leash. The Abbot had told Brother Luminous before they left Wedlock, and Luminous had later told Silky.

Only a couple of ranch hands were admitted during the next few days—no one of any importance, older men greeted with hysterical joy by their wives. Then came news that a party of five was on the way up, and that moved Silky to reinforce the guard at the upper gate. By the time he arrived there, the five had reached the steep slope at the top, so he couldn't see their faces until they were right at the gate.

He recognized the first one instantly as the former Happy, one of his childhood friends in the Wedlock House, one of the two who had taught him to wash corpses on his very first day. When he had been assigned, his client had named him Chariot Driver. They both stayed in character, of course, Chariot Driver dismounting and bowing to Prince Silk Hand.

Right behind him came Tooth, that other teacher of corpse washing, later renamed Specter. His eyes lit up on seeing Silky, but he copied Chariot Driver's lead.

So Silky had gained two good men who would support him in his control over Goat Haven. And right behind them was Niello, another contemporary, and in her case, a very early sex partner. The fact that all three had made their way here suggested that their clients had all died in the disaster.

The third rider was another woman: *Verdant*! She had survived after all—weather-beaten and thinner, certainly, but smiling and apparently uninjured! But, alas, no Thunderbot? Small wonder. All babies were vulnerable, and the poor little tyke could have had little chance in the sort of catastrophe Plum Blossom had described. Verdant could give him more children. No pretense of royalty with her: It was with great delight that he held out his arms to catch her as she slid down from the saddle.

"Darling!" He kissed her passionately. She responded with an enthusiasm she had not displayed since very early in their marriage. When they broke free, it was to mouth all the predictable platitudes about missing you, it being wonderful to see . . . and so on. Then another long kiss.

"Silkworm?" he asked eventually.

"He's safe."

"No! Really?"

"Yes, really. I left him with a woman who lost a child in the earthquake. I can lead you right to him."

"And you will! I'll take a troop along and we'll reunite him by force if we have to. Where—" Silky suddenly became aware of a vaguely familiar, but peculiarly revolting miasma. Looking past Verdant, he met the unwelcome smile of the Brother Archives from Wedlock.

"Oh, darling," Verdant said, "this is the Honorable Pearl White 11, from Wedlock. He rescued me from— Is something wrong?"

"Of course not! This is indeed an honor and a pleasure, Your Excellency."

But plenty was wrong. Brother Archives had trained Silky and would expect to continue outranking him even if he was claiming to be the Emperor himself, let alone a mountain warlord. He had always been renowned for his memory, able to quote anything recorded in the house's annals without having to look it up. He would not have forgotten Silky's leash, so Silky must be very careful never to be alone with him. A tragic fall over the cliff edge might be justified.

"The pleasure is entirely mine, my lord," Brother Archives said with a toxic laugh. The glint in his eye indicated that he was speaking the truth, for once.

At the back of the gathering crowd, Plum Blossom must have seen the danger, because she looked aghast.

But that problem could wait. The importance of the moment was that Verdant was back. Silky barked orders that the phony Pearl White 11 had to be assigned a room and made welcome as an honored guest. Likewise, his retainers were to be fed and housed. Then Silky wrapped an arm around Verdant and led her to his bedroom, where they could cuddle and kiss in private. It had been Sky Rider's, so it was large and commanded a fine view of the hills and the icy mountains beyond. Something would have to be done about the furniture, but that could wait for another day.

"I was such a fool. I should have ridden right here—"

"But you would have died! There was no way up the hill then. Your ancestors guided you. You were very fortunate that you were even allowed in today." Silky had just realized that the Gray Helper currently in charge of the lower guard post had been Mercy, who could not have recognized Verdant had she arrived alone. Nor would he have recognized any of the Wedlock crowd with her, but the Gray Helpers had signals to identify one another.

Silky brought out wine and settled beside her on his couch. They drank together while they exchanged stories. He told of how Luminous and Sky Rider had fallen to their deaths.

"So Heaven gave you Goat Haven?"

"It felt like that."

"You always claimed you didn't have any ancestors to worship. I think that you do and they are looking after you very well!"

"Indeed they are."

"You didn't have to kill anyone to get it all?" Verdant had a very steely eye at times, but there must be no lies between them now.

"He was dying anyway. I put him out of his pain, is all. And everyone else just wanted a leader. I saved them from chaos."

"Good for you, my lord. That is what aristocrats are for."

"And your ancestors protected you from harm?" He topped up her goblet.

Verdant admitted that Walnut Shell had raped her before abandoning her. Silky had already guessed that, for she was a very desirable woman and even Plum Blossom had grumbled that Walnut Shell was a greedy lover. But at least the man had helped Verdant escape from the shattered city, and had left her at a village, not alone in the empty hills.

"And they gave you shelter in return for Silkworm?"

"I had to work for my keep." She hesitated, then smiled. "I was worthy of you, darling. I collected corpses."

Yes, that was funny in retrospect, but he would not have expected her to see the humor in such a grisly situation. He laughed and hugged her again. Their reunion ought to be moving rapidly toward coition, but her pregnancy was probably too far advanced for that.

But then Verdant narrated her escape by boat and the assault by a total stranger while she slept. Silky's amorous mood changed, he felt his dander rising. That was cause for retribution, but how to find the brute?

"Again I was worthy, dear."

"What do you mean?"

"I stuck a knife in him and killed him. Can you forgive me?"

"Forgive you? I worship you! I adore you!"

Ever since the night when he had pretended to climb up to her window to seduce her, he had known she was a determined woman, but this was stupendous. She was warrior, tigress, vengeance of Heaven! They embraced again. The wine was taking effect. Unable to wait longer, Silky scooped her up in his arms and carried her to the bed. She did not protest; she made approving sounds.

He had barely begun to undress her when the door flew open, and Specter burst in.

"Scat!" Silky said. "I'm busy."

But Specter came running with Chariot Driver right behind him. Too late Silky saw the danger. He leaped off the bed, dagger flashing into his hand. A Gray Brother could trounce two laymen anytime, never two Gray Brothers. Friends, yes, but they had been enslaved by Brother Archives. Specter threw a mugful of tea in Silky's face, and Chariot struck his hand to make it drop the knife. Then they grabbed his arms.

Brother Archives strode into the room. *Ugly the rock, but beautiful the ripples spread. . . . Jade and garnet, summer dawn.*

Silky screamed. His captors released him, and he toppled to the ground, writhing in agony.

CHAPTER 17

The Firstborn laughed. "You don't believe it, do you?"

"No, Master," Shard Gingko admitted. "My eyes are no longer what they were, and after seeing this, I don't believe I can trust them at all."

"My eyes are as perfect as the stars," Mouse said, "and they will never again see anything so wonderful."

For four days, they had been traveling south along the Great Valley, easing westward, closer to the Western Wall, a giant's saw of rocky triangles divided by green canyons. The highest peaks were permanently ice-capped, and soon the snow line would start creeping down the slopes, for last night at sunset, Shard had glimpsed the slender crescent of Chrysanthemum Moon.

The great march of mountains would have been impressive enough by itself, but they had arrived practically underneath the Portal of a Thousand Worlds. It had been visible for some time, but now they had just emerged from a sizable patch of forest, and it was noon, with sun striking diagonally along the front of the range. *Legendary* could never do it justice. It dominated the world. Shard Gingko's whole experience rejected the thought that such a mass of rock could actually move, and even the carvings on it made him want to look away, for they were unlike any inscription or illustration he had ever seen.

"Master?" he whispered. "What does the writing on it say?"

For a long time, he received no reply. The Firstborn was staring up at the mountain with a worried frown. Eventually, he said, "I don't know. I did once, I think, but I must have forgotten."

His companions looked at each other in astonishment. He had never used that word before.

"Why don't we rest the horses here, Master?" Mouse said.

The Urfather dismounted without a word, barely taking his eyes off the Portal. He walked over to a fallen tree, and sat down without even inspecting it for ants. Shard was happy to do the same. More and more he was coming to realize that he had become a burden on the two youngsters. Thanks to Lady Cataract's ministrations, the Firstborn was now as healthy as he could ever expect to be, and at sixteen was probably close to his adult stature. Mouse was a staunch young man, with squared shoulders and chin held high. It was old Shard who wearied first. He was showing his age, holding the others back.

Fortunately, the Urfather was in no hurry, or so he claimed. He never said why he was so certain that the Bamboo Banner and the Imperial Army would meet somewhere close to the Portal of Worlds, but who would doubt his word on anything? He believed that it was his duty to make peace between the two sides, which seemed like a totally impossible job to Shard. The Firstborn said that he had done this before, although he admitted that he had failed much more often. If it came to battle, he would die in the ensuing massacre. Thousands of sparks might rise to the Fifth World, but his would remain here, in the Fourth. And once again he would be absent when the Portal opened next year.

The Portal—clearly a doorway, with carvings all over its surface and the frame around it, but so gigantic that the inscriptions at the top glistened with frost, while those below did not. The base of the door was hidden in forest, so how could it open? The base of the Great Valley was not perfectly flat, and a ridge trended out from one side of the Portal. Shard wondered if it could have been created by previous openings, pushing trees and detritus aside. If that slab of mountain could move, he decided, then anything was possible.

Having settled the horses, Mouse came to stand beside him. "We're going to have company, Masters." He was staring south. "Trader caravan, I think." His earlier boast about his eyes had been quite justified. He could see a lark blink.

Shard hoped they would have some food to offer. Pickings had been slim lately. Undoubtedly, Mouse would be thinking the same, for he ate more than the other two together. He squatted down.

"This valley seems fertile. Why don't more people live here, Master?"

He had put the question to Shard, but it was really intended for the Firstborn, and he answered it.

"Because it's a no-man's-land. The Emperors claim it, but they keep their army posts well back from it, behind the Fortress Hills, at places like Cherish. The mountain folk regard it as their winter grazing. Traders use it in summer, going north and south, east and west."

Mouse frowned and looked to the east, at the hills. Most were round and grassy, but the taller ones had flat tops. "Those are part of the Good Land, though?"

"They belong to the strongest. Officially, their owners are of the Gentle people, but most of them are anything but gentle. We might go and call on some of them if there's time. Let's wait and hear what our visitors are going to tell us."

They did not have to wait long. They were sighted by a couple of horsemen, scouts for the caravan, who spotted them and came cantering up, armed with lances and swords. They reined in uncomfortably close, both large men, richly dressed in leathers and furs, and their faces disfigured by barbarian mustaches.

"Declare yourselves!" demanded the elder, his lance aimed at them.

The Firstborn rose. "My name is Sunlight—in this generation."

Enlightenment struck. Eyes widened. Both men slid off saddles and knelt.

"Ancient One, forgive us!"

"Nothing to forgive." The Firstborn made a sign of blessing. "Who are you?"

The spokesman gave his name in a strange tongue, and then translated it as meaning "Grassfire."

"You are obviously heading north," the Firstborn said, adopting the same grating accent. "What news can you give us of the Bamboo Banner?"

Grassfire spat. "Scum! Madmen! They claim to be immortal. They look very surprised on the end of a spear."

"Understandable! I know the feeling."

The warriors hesitated and then laughed.

"Where is the Banner now, and which way is it going?"

"It is in the Great Valley, following us, but we travel faster than they do. And eat better." Grassfire smirked, showing heavily stained teeth.

"The pickings are slim in the Valley," the Firstborn said.

Right on cue, Mouse's stomach rumbled.

Grassfire heard and raised his heavy eyebrows. "They are indeed, Ancient One. We tell everyone to leave until the locusts have passed."

"And when will the swarm arrive here, do you think?"

"In a month, unless they turn off to loot elsewhere. They travel very slowly. The Bearer of Wisdom and his servants are most welcome to break bread with us today."

"We will gladly accept your hospitality, fierce Grassfire."

"It will be arranged!" The two barbarians sprang into their saddles, wheeled their horses, and took off at a showy gallop.

"Your intervention was well timed, Mouse," the Firstborn said.

Mouse turned pink, but grinned anyway.

"A month?" Shard said. "We still have time to starve if we wait here."

"Of course. But we also have time to make some new friends." The Firstborn turned to regard the Fortress Hills. "And perhaps learn when the Imperial Army is due."

CHAPTER 18

Emperor Absolute Purity needed only a couple of weeks aboard the *Starlight Dream* to find his lost army. It was strung out for several days' march along the north bank of the river, plodding along like an endless herd of oxen, although the locals probably thought of it more as a plague of gigantic locusts. Iron Spur was almost speechless with contempt, swearing that the troops would all die of old age before they caught a glimpse of the enemy. Eventually, he spotted the banner of Supreme Guardian, safely located in the center of the host.

The replacement Supreme Guardian went ashore at the nearest jetty, armed with the imperial rescript that appointed him. He also asked for—practically demanded—imperial permission for his predecessor to commit suicide. Butterfly Sword was reluctant to provide this because the old man had dragged his feet for months before setting out to find and engage the Bamboo Banner; his reluctance had been close as he could dare go to asking to be relieved—which the Empress Mother would have regarded as treason. He had probably never wanted the title in the first place, but competent generals were dangerous and she had been an excellent judge of incompetence. In the end, Butterfly Sword agreed to seal the death warrant. If Iron Spur wanted to make failure in his new office a capital offense, then he should be encouraged.

Once his appointment took effect, he proved to be a dragon of efficiency. Junks and more paddle boats were lined up, and the army hustled aboard, horses, cannons, ammunition, commissariat, and all. When the wind was unfavorable—and the junks could sail very close to the wind—then the paddleboats could tow them.

Thereafter, the Imperial Army leaped ahead, traveling night and day. Stokers and sailors worked until they dropped, eager to serve their beloved Emperor. Even more impressive was the reaction of the locals, who flocked in their thousands to line the banks and cheer as the Emperor's personal dragon banner journeyed past. They brought their children, even babes in arms, so they could tell their grandchildren what they had seen. That flag had not been flown outside Heart of the World in four or five reigns.

The sight of all those people made Butterfly Sword feel very small and humble. He wondered if his ancestors—his personal herdsmen ancestors—were proud of him or ashamed. He could guess what the true Absolute Purity's ancestors must think, but they no longer had a direct descendant to honor them, so perhaps they had lost interest in the Good Land on the Fourth World.

Just before reaching Wedlock, the expedition sighted the huge upheaval of landscape that had dammed the river. Mighty dragons of the underworld must have raised it, but the river had stubbornly chewed through at the south end, refusing to be confined. The current was still so strong there that few junks could make it through unaided, but the paddle boats could, and great loads of coal were expended moving the fleet.

Where that great city, Felicitous Wedlock of Waters, had so recently stood, there was now only a desolation of landslides and mud-buried ruins. Even the urgency of war could not allow the Emperor to ignore such misery, and Butterfly Sword spent a couple of days there, sacrificing to Heaven and his imperial ancestors, but also doing what little he could to speed relief.

He had sent most of the army on ahead, up the Jade River, but he soon caught up with it. Iron Spur now assured him that they would reach the Great Valley in time to confront the Bamboo Banner and stop it in its tracks.

CHAPTER 19

A man can know true contentment only by complete submission to the will of his ancestors. So said the Courtly Teacher, more or less. And if it wasn't him, it was another of the old bores.

And Silky would gladly submit if he only knew what his ancestors wanted, or who they were. They were undoubtedly very mad at him because he did not sacrifice to them, and now they were punishing him most subtly. First they had bequeathed him everything he could ever dream of: his private kingdom at Goat Haven with more than two hundred subjects eager to do his bidding, a wife as scalding as a smelter and tough as steel, who had already given him one and eight-ninths children. Secondly, they had arranged—as Brother Archives had assured him—that both Jade Harmony and the Wedlock House of Joyful Departure itself had perished in the Fish Moon Earthquake, so Silky had been released from any obligation to share his hard-earned gains.

But right after that, his nameless ancestors had snatched it all away again, by sending the former Brother Archives, now calling himself Pearl White 11, who had used Silky's leash to enslave him. To have loved and lost was much more bitter than never to have loved at all, and the same went for wealth and power. How those ancestors must be cackling up there in the higher worlds!

Oh, he was still Prince Silk Hand, and in the eyes of the inhabitants, he still ruled Goat Haven. But for the last month,

Pearl White 11 had posed as an honored guest, one who showed no signs of ever wanting to continue his travels. He would wait and see the Portal open, he said, without any hint that he would then move on elsewhere. In fact, he ruled Goat Haven through Silky like a tyrannical Emperor. He had chosen a pretty girl and ordered Silky to order her into his, Pearl White 11's, bed. Her parents had been very unhappy about that, and no doubt there would be more pretty girls in future.

Thus Prince Silk Hand moped, standing on the edge of certain death. The small terrace outside the bedroom he shared with Verdant was a private and enchanting place to sit on an autumn evening, watching the sun set behind the Western Wall. The earthquake had not damaged the cliff at this point, but it had taken out the low stone wall that once had topped it. Having no fear of heights, Silky did not care, although Verdant stayed well back from the edge, especially lately as she neared term and her balance became uncertain.

Silkworm must be almost ready to walk now, so one day soon he must be rescued and brought home. Before that, Silky would have the wall replaced, but Goat Haven needed many other repairs. Most urgent were the fortifications on the entrance trail. The Bamboo Banner was coming.

The door from his bedroom opened to excrete the odious Brother Archives as Pearl White 11. One of the monster's most infuriating habits was to violate Silky's privacy by treating that room as a public thoroughfare and the private terrace as common property. He did it as a deliberate demonstration of his dominance. Silky would have loved to grab the old brute and throw him off, but his orders forbade it.

"Silky, dear boy! Come and sit down. We must talk."

Silky obeyed without a word.

Brother Archives settled himself on the second chair, the one that should be Verdant's. "There is wine on the way."

And Silky knew who would have been told to bring it. In the last stages of her pregnancy, Verdant was so swollen that she had trouble being comfortable anywhere, but she had been resting on the bed when Silky left her a few minutes ago. It amused Brother Archives to use her as a lackey. He could not bind her as he had bound Silky, because it took years of "Outlandish poetry lessons" to break a person's mind to the leash, but she had been present when Silky was enslaved, so she knew what was involved.

The old man read Silky's fury, and his eyes glinted with malicious amusement. "Repeat your orders."

Silky swallowed hard. "I will obey all your commands and serve you in every way. I will never seek to harm you or counter your wishes. If I ever learn that my wife has told anyone about this arrangement, I will kill her at once. And I will repeat these orders to her every night when we go to bed."

"Very good."

The door opened again, and Verdant emerged, moving with awkward care and carrying a tray bearing two golden beakers and a flask of rice wine. She set these down on the table between the two chairs, then filled the beakers.

"Forgive me if I do not kowtow to you, *Lord* Pearl White 11. I am terrified of not being able to get up again after I get down."

Silky gave her an approving smile. She walked away, but her tiny show of insolence had amused the tyrant. He raised his beaker and waited for Silky to drink before tasting the wine. The sky beyond the mountains was turning red as blood.

"We must discuss the Bamboo Banner, dear lad. And also the Imperial Army. You heard what we were told today by the carter from Cherish?"

"That the Emperor himself is coming?"

"Quite. Not just him, but his entire army, coming to deal with Bamboo."

"Is that good or bad?"

"Hard to say." Archives frowned, as he did when he had to dig deep in his cavernous memory. "Emperors rarely lead armies unless they are certain of victory, but several have miscalculated when facing rebellions coming from the south—which is where such nonsense usually begins. Three Emperors have perished in or near the Portal of a Thousand Worlds."

"We can withstand the Banner, we decided, because they will starve if they do not keep moving on. Can we refuse the Emperor?"

"That is what we must discuss. An autocrat who has been pampered all his life must soon tire of campaign conditions. He will impose himself and his train on some wealthy local, and to refuse His Majesty hospitality would be treason. The legitimate inhabitants will be ejected to fend for themselves during his stay. . . . We could bury all our valuables and excess food supplies, except that the soil here on Goat Haven is extremely thin. He may take all our horses. He will certainly leave here before the Year of the Firebird in case the Portal opens and swallows him up, as it has been reported to do in the past. An opening is always a sign of a change of dynasty, remember."

"But like the Banner, his army cannot stay in one place for long."

"Especially in a year when harvests have been poor. Nevertheless, the Banner is the more urgent danger, which is why I have a small job for you."

Physically, Silky could choke him with one hand. Or pick him up and throw him over the cliff. But his hand would not obey him if he tried.

Archives could see his slave's anger, and took a long drink to enjoy it while watching him over the lip of the beaker. "If Bamboo dies, his rebellion must fall apart. That is why I am going to send you to advance him."

"*What?!*"

To penetrate a mob of thousands of yang-crazy rebels and slaughter their chief? That was totally impossible. And certain suicide. Oh, how malicious could ancestors be? How they must be laughing now! "Why me? Why not Chariot Driver or Specter? Or both of them?"

"Because you are the best, dear boy. I have reviewed the archives, and the Wedlock House has not seen one like you in three centuries. You will do it easily. And after that I will require you to dispose of the Emperor, also. Then Goat Haven will be left in peace."

Leave Verdant, about to bear his second child, one that he would never see? Leave Silkworm languishing in some peasant hovel, unaware of the glory that should be his as rightful heir to Goat Haven? Silky could feel the sweat breaking out on his forehead as homicidal hatred battled with irresistible imposed loyalty.

Archives frowned at his wine goblet.

No! No! No! Silky leaped to his feet and fled.

One word would do it: "Wait!" or "Stop!" But no such word came before he hauled the door open, entered, and slammed it behind him. There was no sign of Verdant as he tore across the room and out into the courtyard beyond. She and Watersprite were sitting on a bench there, and they looked up in terror at his urgent arrival. They both tried to rise, but Verdant was hampered by her condition. Watersprite sprang in front of her to defend her.

"I didn't tell her!" Verdant shouted. "She guessed and gave me instructions."

Silky relaxed, and laughed with relief. "Then I am not obliged to kill you!" He nudged Watersprite aside and sat down to hug his wife gently and kiss her fiercely.

"It worked?" Watersprite asked.

"It's working," he said. "What did you use?"

"Midnight Blue."

A few drops in the bottom of a metal beaker would not be noticed, and Midnight Blue was very fast-acting.

"I daren't do it sooner," Watersprite said. "I had to wait until he let his guard down, or he might have switched drinks on you."

"He did do that, several times, but not tonight, thank Heaven. He was about to order me to—" But Archives hadn't issued those orders, just said he was going to.

"I'll check on how he's doing," Watersprite said, and sauntered off.

Silky stole another kiss and murmured in joy. He had misjudged his ancestors. They played jokes, but they weren't cruel in the end.

Verdant said, "Oops!"

He looked at her, eye very close to eye. "Something starting?"

"Maybe. Nothing may come of it. The sooner the better. Get the little nuisance out of there."

Watersprite opened the door and looked out. "Hey, boss—Give me a hand putting out the garbage?"

"I am forbidden to harm him," Silky said, but he followed her out to the balcony.

Brother Archives wasn't dead yet and was still writhing in agony. Watersprite had gagged him so he was he unable to utter orders.

"He is in terrible pain," she said. "I don't think putting him out of his misery would count as harming, would it?" She caught hold of the victim's ankles.

"Let me ask." Silky bent over the dying man. "Would you like us to end the pain, *My Lord*? Mm? I'll take that spasm as a nod."

Silky gripped his wrists. One . . . two . . . three . . . and the former Master of Archives was on his way to the Fifth World. Or would be when he landed.

Silky kissed Watersprite. "Thanks. Celebrate tonight?" Verdant was currently not available for what he had in mind.

"It's traditional after an outing, isn't it? What do we say when we're asked where Pearl White 11 is?"

"Who?"

"My Lord?" said a male voice. It was Chariot Driver's turn to peer out. "Three horsemen are coming up the hill."

It was almost dark; no one should have been allowed past the check point after sunset. More trouble!

"I'll be right there," Silky said.

By the time he reached the upper gate, the night guard was in place. The day guard from the lower gate had been relieved and was on its way up, following the three unknowns. Torches had been lit.

The visitors were already so close to the top that all he could see of them were their hats. Their horses were weary, and their saddlebags slim. Why had they been allowed in? They might be Gray Brothers who had given the recognition signal. Not likely three Goat Haven herders trapped outside when the earthquake closed the path—that had been six months ago, and none of the three was riding like a professional horseman.

Silky watched as they dismounted and his waiting stable hands took charge of the mounts, but he was still puzzled. One man was elderly and should therefore be the leader, yet he stood back in the shadows. His companions were both young enough to be his grandsons—one tall, one short.

"I am Prince Silk Hand. Identify yourselves."

It was the short one who limped forward into the torchlight. "My name is Sunlight," he said.

"So?"

The boy smiled. "This time around."

Recognition struck like a thunderclap.

"*Urfather?*" Silky sank to his knees, and all the guards and hands hurriedly did the same.

* * *

Was this yet more ancestors' trickery? Was Goat Haven once again going to be snatched out of Silky's hands? One thing was certain: The entire workforce would obey a mere hint from the Firstborn before any orders Silky uttered. If that puny, fragile youth denounced him as a fraud—not a lord, just a Gray Helper helping himself—then he would be following Brother Archives to the Fifth World before you could say "bounce."

And the Firstborn had a curious twinkle in his eye whenever he glanced at his host, as if he could read him like a scroll. Perhaps he looked at everyone that way.

The visitors had been provided with the best available guest quarters, with wash water, towels, clean clothes. And then food, the best available, which was rice, squash, and fresh carp from the fishpond. They ate in Silky's office, hastily refurnished as a private dining room. The youngster called Mouse ate as a man of his age should—with zest and speed, as if he were close to starvation. The Firstborn and the scholar Shard Gingko just nibbled by comparison.

Verdant dropped in briefly to make her excuses for not being a better hostess. The men all rose in respect, which was a surprise in the Fortress Hills.

"You are certainly pardoned, my lady," the Firstborn said. "My blessings on you and your daughter." He glanced momentarily at Silky, eyes twinkling again.

Silky was not to be baited. "I will forgive her for a daughter this time, Ancient One. We already have a boy child, who is temporarily absent."

Shard Gingko congratulated Silky on the wine. But a meal could not last forever. Even the boy called Mouse had to be filled eventually. Then to business?

"May I assume that you are come to these parts to witness the opening of the Portal, Urfather?" The Year of the Firebird would not even begin for three full months and would last twelve, or even thirteen, if Court Astrologer in Sublime Mountain decreed a Cuckoo Moon for the year.

"That is my hope. I have never seen it do so."

Never? This from a man who could remember lives all the way back to the invention of people? Who had met everybody's ancestors, spoken with half the Emperors, and all the great teachers?

"But," the boy added, "we will not impose on your hospitality that long. We have just come from a very pleasant stay with your neighbor, Knifeblade 5, the Lord of High Vista."

Mouse glanced at old Shard Gingko and smothered a grin.

Silky said, "I have not yet had the pleasure of meeting the noble lord."

The Firstborn nodded slightly, as if confirming something. "Do not pine for the experience. The last time I came by here, Goat Haven was ruled by Sky Hammer 3."

That statement was a question, and Silky's intestines had all knotted into a tiny brick inside him. "A long time ago, then."

"Certainly."

"Sky Hammer 7 and his son, Sky Rider, both perished in the recent earthquake. I belong to a, um, cadet branch of the family."

The Firstborn laughed, and poured himself more wine. "Shard, dear friend, you are out on your feet, or would be if you stood up. Mouse, you can't possibly stay awake much longer after that banquet you just downed. Why don't you both take your leave of our host? He and I have some matters to discuss."

Silky excused them, of course. Shard looked relieved and Mouse piqued, but they both rose obediently and departed.

As the door closed, Silky sat back to hear his fate.

"Your accent tells me you are originally from Wedlock."

"Yes, Ancient One."

"The Sky Hammer 1 was a barbarian raider, you know that?

He took this place by treachery, then threw every man and boy over the cliff edge. He kept the women."

Silky said, "Oh?" and suddenly relaxed.

The Firstborn was leaning back, wearing a very boyish grin. "So whatever you did to steal this place, Gray Brother, you weren't that bad. Tell me about it."

How did he know Silky was a Helper? "The whole gory mess?"

"Every scarlet drop."

The story took a long time and sounded even worse than Silky had expected it to, but he held back nothing, even that Sky Rider just might have survived if the earthquake had not been given some help. His audience of one said not a word until he came to the end.

"Gruesome! But that's one of the best stories I've heard in centuries. So who holds your leash?"

Startled, Silky said, "You know a lot about us, Ancient One."

"The Gray Brothers are not as old as I am, but we have tangled often enough over the centuries. Who holds your leash?"

"The Abbot of Wedlock died in the earthquake. His second . . ." Silky told of that day's execution of the former Brother Archives. And still the Firstborn did not denounce him as a monster.

"The lion defending his kill?"

"Um . . . I suppose so, Ancient One."

"Is there anyone left who has a better claim to Goat Haven than you?"

Silky had admitted so much that a little more matter could not matter much. "Sky Rider had three sons. The oldest's about ten or so."

"And what did you do to them?"

"The eldest, Musket, tried to challenge me. I scared him silly and threatened to flog him if he ever said anything like that again. He's still around. He'll be asleep right now, of course, but tomorrow you can—"

"Good for you," the Firstborn said. "Not prudent, but pleasing to the ear."

"So what are you going to do about it?" Silky could break this kid's neck in an instant and tell him to come back in a thousand years and try the Portal again. Regrettably, the Urfather's disappearance would lead to a lot more questions than Brother Archives's had.

"Nothing," the Firstborn said simply. "This is how it works, here in the Fortress Hills. The Emperor claims to rule, but he keeps his army posted well back from the Great Valley, you notice—at Cherish. The Fortress Hills are well named, not just because of their shape. Many of them, like Goat Haven or High Vista, are giant castles, and pay only lip service to the Golden Throne. Their rulers do not tolerate Outlander raiders, either."

Silky said, "Oh." Not being a soldier, he hadn't seen that.

"In the Fortress Hills, the strongest always rule, so you have every right to keep what you've won." The Firstborn smiled. "I won't betray your confidence, but I may ask a small favor of you in a few days. Now, if you'll excuse me, I'm going to bed, and you had better go and comfort your wife, because she's just begun labor."

CHAPTER 20

Back in the spring, when Fair Visions had joined up with his uncle Bamboo's army, it had been an awesome force, a tide of angry warriors marching north, dedicated to overthrowing the obscene rule of a woman and putting its leader on the Golden Throne.

That had been then. Now was the start of Falling Leaf Moon, and not only trees were shedding. The Bamboo Banner had shrunk and also scattered. Small groups spread out to scour the countryside in search of food. The yang ration had been cut to almost nothing, and men fought over every scrap, murdered their cadre leaders for it, and sometimes stole it out of the mouths of the corpses. Men went suddenly mad, wandering around in homicidal stupors, screaming their rage at the skies. Hungry men catch fevers easily. The army left a trail of unburied bodies behind it, and not only its own dead, for now it was more dangerous than it had been in the days when it was disciplined. Back then, it had always demanded food, but any place or person that gave generously to the cause had been left in peace. Now every hovel and larder was looted bare. Not a chicken or dog was spared.

Now it was heading roughly north again, along the awesome and aptly named Great Valley, channeled between the peaks of the Western Wall on one hand and the lesser Fortress Hills on the other. A turgid, swampy river flowed southward along the Great

Valley, and contained some evil-tasting fish. There was little else to eat anywhere, and winter crept closer every night.

Fair Visions stayed very close to his uncle, because he felt less endangered there, although by no means safe. Bamboo traveled on a litter within a personal bodyguard of about a hundred top warriors, now led by Silent, that egregious maniac. These elite received a pittance of yang, and so were hated by all the rest. Not safe, no, because one day the outsiders would fall upon the insiders, and the revolution would implode in blood.

Bamboo himself was even crazier than he had been, but at least he rarely spoke now, so his madness was less obvious. He lay in his litter like a ball of warm lard, staring at the invisible, pondering the meaningless. He was unwashed and repulsive. At night, he slept in the curtained litter, still within his protective bubble of guards and a pentagram of bonfires, so that no one could sneak up on him. Fair Visions stayed close to the leader's snores, warmed by one of the bonfires. All around him lay the army, its galaxy of tiny fires gradually winking out as the fuel was consumed.

He longed to escape, and dared not even think about it. Everyone knew who he was. He was so resented as Bamboo's nephew and toady that he would not even make it out of the encampment before being stabbed or clubbed so that his corpse could be searched for yang.

But then, as daylight gave way to another long moonlit night, a distant sound of hooves on hard ground roused the guards around Bamboo. The dying fires to the north brightened as their embers were stirred. Torches were approaching. Shivering, Fair Visions sat up, pulling his blanket around him—by day it was his cloak, and much envied. He had foreseen the change of season before most others did, and had thought to pillage some warmer wear from a wrecked village.

Silent shouted orders, and the guards came alert, ready to withstand attack. Now it was not just a few horses coming; they were being followed by an angry growling like the noise of surf on a stony beach. It could be only the sound of hunger, for horses were edible. The newcomers might soon find themselves forcibly dismounted and their mounts slaughtered by the starving horde that was closing in around them.

Six horses, six riders.

As they reined in, Fair Visions scrambled to his feet and backed up against Bamboo's litter, while the guards closed in to form a wall of muscle around it. He recognized the leader of the newcomers as Ominous Scroll, a youthful ex-scholar who had been a member of Bamboo's short-lived advisory council.

"We bring news!" Ominous bellowed. "The Empress Mother is dead!"

For a moment, there was no reaction. For months, they had fought and endured for the sole purpose of dethroning the unnatural she-dog who had usurped the Golden Throne. Then a long roar that slowly died into its own echo, coming back from the mountains.

"And the Emperor himself is leading his army against us!"

This announcement was greeted by a rumble as it was spread out through the army.

"*He lies!*" That was the voice of Bamboo himself. He had hauled the draperies open, and was sitting up, his eyes wide and crazy in the firelight.

"I do not lie!" Ominous Scroll bellowed. "We heard the news from everybody. The she-dragon is dead and her son the Emperor leads his army even now into the Great Valley."

Tumult.

Fair Visions thought of guns. The army would certainly have guns, probably cavalry. The Bamboo Banner was mostly armed with clubs. The men were starving, maddened by the yang craving. This, surely, was the end.

Silent had a war horn and blew a long blast to call for silence.

"This cannot be!" Bamboo declaimed. "Absolute Purity died years ago. I am the rightful heir. Whoever leads that army is an imposter."

Fair Visions saw a tiny chink of hope and went for it.

"Then send me to denounce him, Bamboo! Send me and others you can trust to go and investigate this army and bring back the truth. We will proclaim the rightful heir."

It was insane. Why should Bamboo ever trust him to return? Or anyone? And yet Ominous Scroll and his companions had returned. Whoever was leading that army, Emperor or imposter, would surely move to block the few passes leading out of this gigantic ditch—and very probably had already done so. The revolution was trapped.

"Go then!" Bamboo yelled. "You and Ominous Scroll, go and find this fake Emperor. Silent, go with them and keep them honest."

He fell back on his cushions, exhausted. Silent closed the drapes on him and turned to leer his ill-fitting teeth at Fair Visions 3.

"Ready?" he said.

CHAPTER 21

Shard Gingko wiped his brush and paused in his writing so that he could admire the scenery again. He had found a sheltered nook just outside the main hall, a paved path that ended at a ramshackle, obviously temporary, wall on the very brink of the cliff. It must have originally led to some building that the earth-quake had removed. A servant had brought a chair out for him, and he had been trying to describe the view of the Western Wall. It was breathtaking, quite beyond his literary powers. He wondered what artist, even, could ever have done it justice? Agate Shining, perhaps?

A shadow moved into the edge of his view, and Mouse squat-ted down by his side. The private part of Shard's mind briefly sighed for the days when his joints had moved so easily.

"Heaven bless," he said quietly, although he regretted having his meditation interrupted.

"And you likewise, Master. You prefer Goat Haven to High Vista?" Mouse had developed a quietly mocking smile exactly like the Firstborn's.

"I certainly prefer the inhabitants. Knifeblade 5 is barbarous even by Outlandish standards." And his minions were worse. Shard had enjoyed the last couple of weeks in Goat Haven more than any days since those months in Lady Cataract's palace.

Mouse chuckled softly. "You know how long Prince Silk Hand has been ruling here?"

"You've been gossiping."

"Um, yes Master. I humbly beg pardon for earning this justified rebuke."

"How long?"

The subtle smile became a grin. "Since the day of the earthquake. The previous ruler was Sky Hammer 7. He and his son both perished. By the will of Heaven, Prince Silk Hand, who was actually the rightful owner anyway, happened to be visiting that day and—"

"I suspected something like that when the Firstborn excluded us from their meeting on the evening we arrived. It is apparently not our business."

"No, Master. I humbly beg—"

"Mouse?"

"Master?"

"You must stop calling me that. I have taught you much. You have been an apt and dutiful pupil. I hope you will continue to study and learn for all of a long lifetime. I strongly advise you to continue to serve the Firstborn, but I cannot continue as your teacher. I am too frail to keep up with you and the Urfather. At present, Prince Silk Hand has no private secretary, and he has graciously accepted my offer of service."

Shard Gingko could remain at Goat Haven and record the opening of the Portal next year. His account would be the only eyewitness report in history, and would bring great honor to his name. So would his report of two years on the road with the Firstborn. *The pupil asked, "Which teacher was the greatest?" The Urfather replied, "The Humble Teacher, for he was the first. The others passed on much of his wisdom as their own."* The imperial schools would argue ferociously over that for centuries! Shard Gingko had disgraced his ancestors by failing the imperial examinations, but this would please them, and perhaps lead them to help him do better when he reached the Fifth World.

After a long pause, Mouse said, "It would please me greatly if you would allow me to continue addressing you as my master, honorable one, for as long as our lives may run together."

"As you wish. But the Firstborn has warned me that he will be leaving soon."

"That is why I am here, Master. He sent me to tell you that he will be riding out today. Lord Silk Hand has agreed to accompany him and provide an armed escort."

"Armed? The Firstborn wants an *armed* escort?" That was surprising, even astonishing.

"Yes, Master. In this case, he does. He says that it is almost the only way to get attention. He is on his way to meet the Emperor, and if he goes alone, he will probably be put to work digging ditches around the camp, or worse. Armed escorts are noticed. He sent me to ask if you would like to come with us."

For a moment, Shard Gingko was at a loss for words. The Urfather had surprised him many times, but this surpassed everything. This was suicide!

"You are certain? He was not joking? Does he not remember Four Mountains? There the Emperor chained him, and when that failed, ordered torture and death. He cannot be serious!"

"He seems so, Master. Prince Silk Hand tried to discourage him, but he would not listen."

Shard Gingko wanted to weep. Every instinct told him to stay where he was, at Goat Haven, and try to be useful for the few years or moons left to him. But he knew he wouldn't; he had to see the end of the story.

When he had been Postulant Tug in the House of Joyful Departure, Silky had several times experimented with some of the powerful drugs stored in the pharmacy. Inevitably, the results had been disastrous, and he had eventually realized that the labels were deliberately falsified. But even in the wild hallucinogenic nightmares that had racked him then, he had never imagined himself going to call on the Lord of Ten Thousand Years.

For that matter, he had never imagined himself playing host to the Urfather. At times, it was still hard to believe that the puny, weather-beaten youth with the wistful smile and an Outlandish cast to his features was anything more than a farm boy wandered in from the paddy fields. But when he glimpsed the wisdom of untold centuries blazing out of those eyes, his soul believed and his knees turned to jelly.

The Firstborn's mere presence had transformed Goat Haven. It revolved around him. Everyone there was his lifelong slave. He knew them all by name, which was more than Silky did, and he would listen to all their troubles. Silky himself had been a distrusted newcomer until the Urfather came, but he had become a revered ruler as soon as the Firstborn had accepted him. Verdant had promptly discarded all the foolish names she had previously been suggesting for their daughter, who became Sunlight from the moment of her birth. Her father had been happy to agree.

And so Prince Silk Hand, King of Goat Haven, rode out with the Urfather at his side, followed by the boy's two companions and ten armed men. Going to call on His Imperial Majesty, Lord of the High and the Low.

The Fortress Hills had changed from green to brown since Silky had ridden in, back in the spring, which now seemed a lifetime ago. Many white bones lay in the brown fall grass along the Wilderness Road, and sometimes pans, pots, and other discarded household items. Heaven had laid harsh judgment on the people of Cherish.

He entered country new to him when he rode past the turn-off to Heaven's Threshold. Soon, the road dipped into a winding gorge, which seemed like good ambush country, but still they saw no living creatures. He did not doubt that he was observed, though. Knifeblade 5 or some other local lord would be keeping watch on travelers going by, just as Prince Silk Hand now did.

The Imperial Army, for reasons unknown, had not come from Cherish by the Wilderness Road, but by some other trail to the north. About halfway down the long descent into that valley, the Firstborn's expedition came to a viewpoint and paused to gaze at the overwhelming scenery. The Portal was in shadow. The boggy river glinted here and there in the low light. Silky looked in vain for the Two Lakes Caravanserai that had once been part of the devious web he had spun to destroy Sky Hammer 7. From what he had heard, no caravans had come over Swordcut Pass this year.

"According to the very best rumors," Firstborn said, "were we to wait here until after sunset, we might see the lights of the Bamboo Banner to the south of us, and the Imperial Army's to the north."

Plus mountains to the west and hills to the east. They were riding into a killing ground.

"We can camp by the river," Silky said.

"A wise man does not drink downstream from armies." The Urfather spoke the words like a quotation.

"Which teacher said that, Master?" Shard Gingko asked automatically.

"No teacher. I was so advised by a bloody-handed warlord of the Second Dynasty." The Firstborn looked around at their faces and laughed.

They found Two Lakes Caravanserai where the road forded the river, half a dozen fenced paddocks, each capable of holding thirty or so horses or camels, and each having its own watering trough and well. For humans, there were as many shelters, each comprising a raised deck with a roof but no walls. A single sturdy stone building clearly belonged to the owners, but there was nobody home there, and the neglected grass had grown long this year. A couple of Silky's guards produced nets and went fishing.

Everyone else except Shard Gingko went for a dip in the nearer of two horseshoe-shaped lakes. The Portal was in the mountain face just to the south of them, but invisible against the sunset. The Firstborn did not refuse fish caught downstream from an army, but they were pathetic eating.

Shard Gingko wanted to write, but the light was too poor. Fourteen men sitting on logs around an open-air fire pit with sparks swirling up to the skies—the scene made him think of funerals, which should be inspiration for a poem, because he knew that his journey with the Firstborn, the greatest experience of his life, was about to end. The Emperor might have them all put to death. Even if he did not, there would be a battle, which was no place for bystanders. And the very best solution for Shard Gingko would be to creep back to Goat Haven and try to put his final days to good use.

"I will help with the guard duty tonight, my lord," the Firstborn said.

"No need, lad."

Lad? Shard Gingko looked across at them in astonishment. How dare a jumped-up horse rancher address the Firstborn like that? Then he realized that the youth Prince Silk Hand was addressing was not the Firstborn but Mouse. He not only looked like the Urfather now, he even spoke like him.

"Then I respectfully suggest that you do something now, my lord, because I can hear horses."

Two of the Goat Haven men threw themselves down to put ears to the ground. They jumped up very smartly. "He is right, my lord," said one. "Three or four horses coming. They will have seen the light of our fire." He began barking orders to the other guards. Prince Silk Hand sat in silence, letting him do so. In a few moments, there were only seven around the fire, and the rest had vanished into the darkness.

Then came voices. . . . Challenge. . . . Response. . . .

Three figures appeared out of the darkness, men leading horses.

The one in the center was wrapped in a cloak; the other two wore rags.

"They admit, my lord, that they are from the Bamboo Banner, but they come in peace."

Prince Silk Hand rose. "But do we receive traitors in peace? Master?"

He seemed unusually unsure of himself, looking to the Firstborn for instructions.

"Why not? They seem underfed to me. Offer them a good meal and see what information they offer in exchange."

One of the ragged rebels said, "We are loyal followers of Bamboo, the true Emperor, and we will not be bribed by—"

"Be quiet, Silent," said the one in the cloak. "My name is Fair Visions 3. I am Bamboo's nephew, and I was sent to establish whether the rumors of the Empress Mother's death are true."

"Everyone says they are," the Firstborn said.

"And who leads the army that lies to the north?"

"It marches under the banner of the Golden Dragon, so its leader is Absolute Purity himself. And if it isn't, he is still claiming imperial honors and has ten thousand rifles at his back. Me, I wouldn't argue with him."

Which was amusing, because the Urfather was supposedly the only man who always did argue with Emperors.

"He does not know!" shouted the one called Silent. "More lies! More rumors!"

Fair Visions looked around the circle. Unlike Silent, he was a thinker, and he had sensed the hint of humor. "And who are you?"

The Firstborn rose and stepped forward to the fire, so the light was full on him. "I have had many names. In this life, I answer to Sunlight. You must have seen my likeness?"

Fair Visions sank to his knees, and his unnamed companion followed, but the one called Silent did not.

＊　　＊　　＊

The three visitors were fed—and ate more than their horses, the Firstborn said. And when they were satisfied, it was he, the All-Wise, who spelled out the problem for them—and offered a solution.

"I have stood between rebels and Emperors many times. I always try to negotiate peace, although I rarely succeed. When I fail, and there are battles, the Emperors almost always win. Nowadays, he has guns, more guns than rebels can hope to have, so the odds are enormously in his favor.

"Tomorrow, I go to entreat this Emperor, whoever he is, to beg him to be merciful and forgiving. Whether he is Absolute Purity or a usurper, he may wish to begin his reign with a great victory. Or he may choose to show that he rules with the mandate of Heaven, his enemies melting away before his majesty. In your place, I would fear to approach him, but since I am who I am, I must and I will."

Madness, Shard thought. *Utter madness!*

"If you will trust me," Sunlight continued, "I will plead for all your lives. If I am able, I swear that I will return to this camp and tell you what he said. If I fail to arrive, you may assume that I am dead. Can you trust me?"

"Of course, Ancient One," Fair Visions said. "We will wait here and pray to Heaven that you will be allowed to return in safety."

One of his companions agreed; the one called Silent remained so.

The next morning, they emerged to see the Portal a little to the south of them, lit by the rising sun. It seemed to be almost overlooking them, although it must be many miles away. *The closer one got to it,* Shard Gingko thought, *the more impossible it seemed.* But that was a problem for next year, the Year of the Firebird.

The Firstborn's party ate congee, saddled up, and rode north, leaving the three Bamboo warriors to wait on their return.

CHAPTER 22

Dawn came to Butterfly Sword in a glorious golden blaze, sunlight shining through the silk of his tent. He had not known about this imperial pavilion until he disembarked near the ruins of Cherish. Had he known, he would have forbidden Iron Spur to bring such a useless luxury, but the general assured him that it would save many lives, because every one of his troops would fight like a hundred if he knew he was doing so under the eye of his Emperor. Thus, every night now, the imperial banner flew over the camp and the great golden pavilion was erected so the fake Emperor could lie on a very comfortable cot and reflect on what a despicable fraudulent turd he was.

Today? Today he was in the Great Valley, and great it was, as depicted on many landscape scrolls. Today, the army was to rest, because the horses needed a break, and the oxen that pulled the guns were slow and needed a day or so catch up. Today, perhaps, Butterfly Sword would ride ahead and take a closer look at the celebrated Portal of a Thousand Worlds. No, Iron Spur wouldn't allow that. He couldn't forbid it, of course, but he would send an escort of several thousands along, and those men needed a day off just as much as the horses did. So the Emperor must behave himself and try to stay out of sight.

Butterfly Sword leaned over and rapped a knuckle against the bedside gong to inform his valets he was ready for his breakfast.

Food was usually served much faster and hotter than it was in the palace. Campaigning was tough.

The pavilion was not the imperial palace, of course, but it would have slept fifty men easily. It was entered through an open patio, fenced around by yellow silk curtains for privacy, so the Emperor could sit in the sunshine and study his correspondence. If there was trouble back in Heart of the World, First Mandarin wasn't telling him. Nor had he declared the throne vacant and promoted Prince Boundless Shore, which he undoubtedly would if the Bamboo Banner won the battle that now seemed inevitable, three or four days from now.

Iron Spur was supremely confident that no such disaster was remotely possible. Refugees confirmed what army scouts sent to study the enemy through spyglasses reported: a disorganized, starving rabble with no guns and few swords. Canister shot would blow them to fragments; any survivors could be mopped up by the cavalry. This Emperor did not want to start his reign with a massacre.

It was about midmorning when something happened to break the monotony—shatter it, in fact. The Emperor was standing precariously on a stool so he could see over the fence and study the Portal with a telescope when the sounds of the camp seemed to change. Then he heard a command very close to his castle: "Squad halt!"

He jumped down, put the stool to its proper use, and took up a scroll to look busy. He was absolute autocrat of the Good Land, and yet, in some ways, he was a prisoner of his own imperial resplendency.

Three discreet taps on the signal rod outside meant that Iron Spur himself wished audience. Bade approach, the general entered through the curtain and bowed, kowtowing having been strictly forbidden in the field. His normally impassive face looked eager, almost excited.

"Your Majesty . . . There is a youth out here who was apprehended riding in this direction with an escort of about a dozen, most of them armed. He claims to be the Firstborn."

Butterfly Sword's world skipped a beat. Stories of the Urfather were legion. Many previous Emperors had granted him audience—possibly even taken his counsel, although, of course, that could never be admitted. He was credited with superhuman powers, and that he should turn up virtually on a battlefield, offering to mediate, was certainly in keeping with the legends. But the present situation was not normal.

In snooping through the late Empress Mother's private papers, Butterfly Sword had discovered "his own" orders to the warden of a certain castle to torture a certain prisoner to death. The questions the warden had been required to ask proved that the unnamed prisoner could only have been the Firstborn. The said warden had died before he could obey, and the prisoner had escaped. If the newcomer was genuine, he might not be very well disposed to his supreme ruler.

Furthermore, if the supernatural stories were correct and the revered Ancient One exposed the present Emperor as a fraud, the army would tear one or other of them to pieces. Or both.

Noticing the imperial hesitation, Iron Spur drew a finger across his throat and raised his eyebrows. Butterfly Sword shook his head angrily. "Ask the youth where he last enjoyed our hospitality."

Iron Spur bowed, backed out, and returned in a few seconds. "He says Four Mountains, Your Majesty, and the warden was Mandarin of the Third Rank Sedge Shallows."

"Then we must meet this, um, youth." It was hard to reconcile that word with a reputation for immortality. "Have the guards moved back from the tent so that our talk will not be overheard. I will receive the Ancient One alone." Seeing the soldier's jaw stiffen, Butterfly Sword added, "As long he is unarmed, I am confident I can handle any man long enough to yell for help."

He rose and went into the pavilion, where he moved a stool close to his chair of state, upon which he proceeded to sit. It wasn't the Golden Throne, and he was not wearing his imperial robes, but he doubted that either would impress the Urfather much.

The Emperor was not much impressed by the youth who was marched in by Iron Spur himself. He looked to be about seventeen. Having been stripped down to a loincloth, he was obviously both skinny and thoroughly chilled already by the fall temperature. He bowed, and kept his eyes lowered when he straightened up, as was expected in court—no one ever looked directly at the Emperor. His hair had a brownish, Outlandish tinge.

"Untie his hands!" Butterfly Sword snapped, more angrily than he intended. "And bring his clothes!" As the general ran to obey, he added, "Welcome, Bearer of Wisdom."

"Your Majesty is gracious."

"I am sorry for the bonds and the clothes. You deserve better."

For an instant, the Firstborn glanced up in astonishment, revealing the oversize eyes always shown in the drawings. He was unimpressive, not what one would expect of a man who had lived thousands of lives. Dress him in the Emperor's state robes and he would still not overawe anyone. Butterfly Sword was not much older, but he had the advantage of size.

"And I assure you that the treatment you received in Four Mountains was not by my order. My late mother grew somewhat cranky in her old age." Butterfly Sword considered what he had just said and laughed. "Vicious, even bloodthirsty. Ah."

Iron Spur brought in the missing clothes and cut the rope binding the Firstborn's hands. Then he gave the Emperor a furious and highly illegal glare, and stalked out. The visitor dressed himself hastily.

"You may sit there," Butterfly Sword said. "Now, what brings you?"

"Two concerns, Your Majesty. The Bamboo Banner, for one."

"What of them?"

"They are a rabble of starving peasants, deluded by a maniac, who tells them that Your Imperial Majesty has risen to the Fifth World and he is your rightful successor. I have not visited them yet, but three of them came to my camp last night. They were on their way here to learn whether there is any truth in the lies they have been told. I offered to investigate and go back and tell them—subject to your imperial will, of course."

"And?"

"As I will report that the rumor is obviously untrue, I most humbly beg Your Sublime Majesty to forgive them and send them home."

"Granted. I will be much happier to see them departing in peace than being cut to pieces. Will they go?"

Another quick glance of surprise. "I hope so, sire. If the rest are like the three I met last night, they are all desperately hungry."

"I'll see if we can spare some of our rations. And what is the second thing?"

This time, the Firstborn looked up and stared the Emperor straight in the eye. "The second thing is that you do look very like Emperor Zealous Righteousness, but your behavior could hardly be more different. He cut off my head—twice! I have met more than a hundred Emperors, and only four of them waived the kowtow, even when I was laden with chains and standing in muddy cow pasture. Maybe a dozen allowed me to try to mediate with rebels. And not a single one ever offered me a seat or an apology."

Butterfly Sword felt a cold trickle run down his back. Had the sun not continued to shine, he might have looked up to see if the roof were leaking. "I can have you loaded up with chains if that will improve your manners."

"You speak Palace Voice with a slight accent, probably from rural Chixi Province. And it is well known that the Portal of a Thousand Worlds is due to open very soon. This always indicates a change of dynasty."

"You are insanely impudent. I believe I will be guided by my father's precedent and have you decapitated. Once should be sufficient."

Without any change of expression at this threat, the Firstborn quietly rubbed his right eyebrow with the tips of two fingers held together.

For the second time that morning, Butterfly Sword felt an earthquake. "*You too?*"

But of course it was not only possible but extremely likely. Pick a boy with roughly the right sort of looks to start with, then teach him seeming magic until he was good enough to fit the sketches, plus enough history and philosophy to get by . . . When one dies, launch another. Or even run several Firstborns at the same time—who would ever know in a nation as huge as the Good Land? The hallowed Firstborn was only a long-running Gray Order fraud?

The boy smiled, but there was more scorn than mirth there. "No, I'm genuine. I do not go around robbing the dead. Not that the Gray Helpers have not tried to impersonate me in the past."

"You are saying that I am an imposter. So the question is, which one of us will the commander believe when we denounce each other?"

The Urfather shrugged. "Death doesn't scare me, even the death of a thousand cuts. It is only a nuisance. I judge by results. Your reaction to my appeal on behalf of the Bamboo Banner was totally out of character, but I found it very welcome. Convince me that you will be a worthy ruler and I will gladly accept a secret change of dynasty. I have known it to happen before now. There is nothing I have not seen at least once."

So now His Imperial Highness, Son of the Sun, Lord of the High and the Low, Father of the Gentle People, et cetera, was about to be judged by this barefoot waif, was he?

Yes.

"Back in the Year of the Firebird, when Zealous Righteousness died . . ."

Butterfly Sword talked, the Firstborn listened, watching the Emperor's lips as if he could mark every word as true or false. He did not comment once, but soon he began to nod slightly, and then he started to smile. He pursed his lips at the death of the Empress Mother, yet still did not speak. When the story reached the expulsion of the eunuchs, he actually grinned.

And when Butterfly Sword had finished, the Firstborn slid off his stool to his knees, and knocked his forehead three times on the rug. The tent was too small for the required two repetitions. The Emperor stood, took him by the arm, and raised him. Then he went to his refreshment bar and poured his guest a goblet of wine. "Ancient One?"

"Thanks. My name is Sunlight in this life."

"You can call me Horse when we're alone."

Thus did two young men seal a pact. There being no other goblet handy, Butterfly Sword drank straight from the flask.

"So who holds the Emperor's leash?" the Firstborn asked, sitting down again without waiting for permission.

Butterfly Sword bypassed the throne and pulled up another stool. "That I do not know. Sister Lark, I suppose. She's too smart to tell anyone else the secret, but someone else must hold hers. I can't see how I can rule with that hanging over me."

"I can," the boy said with a smile. "Just forget them. Yes, the Gray Order is the second biggest gang of thieves in the world, right after the palace eunuchs. But the Humble Teacher said, *Fret not over them that loot the rich, for the rich gained their wealth by looting the poor.*"

"He *did*? I have never heard that before."

"He did say it," Sunlight said. "Often. But it is among his many aphorisms that have been suppressed."

"Well the Gray Order does rob the rich, but they also murder the rich, and I am richer than anyone. Do I start with the impossible task of finding Sister Lark?"

The Urfather sighed. "Lark is undoubtedly dead. She knew too much. Look at the situation from the Gray Order's point of view. The Empress Mother was old, and when she died, you would become the first Emperor in history who knew all their secrets. They were afraid of you and what you might do. Lady Twilight was also old, and likely to follow the Empress Mother to the Fifth World very rapidly—if not by your hand, then by one of her uncountable enemies'. Only she knew your leash! So the Gray Order disposed of them both and secured you with a new leash to control you directly. Undoubtedly, someone gave Sister Lark very definite orders, most likely the primate of the House of Joyful Departure in Meritorious Aspect, who must have been Twilight's accomplice when she found you. But the Order has survived for centuries and no Emperor has dared tackle it since Celestial Mercy, who promptly died a sudden and very painful death. My advice to you, Horse, is to forget about them. After all, someone has to dispose of the corpses! The Gray Helpers serve a useful purpose and they cannot legally marry, so they leave no legitimate heirs. I'm sure they won't trouble you if you don't trouble them, and you have more pressing problems to worry about."

Butterfly Sword emptied the wine flask while he thought about this outrageous suggestion. He decided that it did make sense. "Thank you. I see why you are called the All-Wise. You have lifted a great weight off my mind."

"Even the Emperor cannot solve all the problems of the world, sire. Remember that, or you will go crazy."

"I need such advice! Will you return to Sublime Mountain with me and accept a post as imperial advisor?"

The Firstborn laughed. "I have believed for several centuries that nothing in the world could ever surprise me, but that does! Most Puissant Father—that's a Third Dynasty honorific—on what could I advise you were I shut up in the palace as you are? The right of access, now . . . that would work! Then, when I find something that needs the imperial frown, I could bring it to your attention. That would be wonderful. It isn't seeing what needs to be done that is the problem, it is getting it done."

"Which teacher said that?"

The Urfather scratched his untidy mop of hair. "I think it was Half-Dead Tiger. Then he cut off the man's head himself."

Butterfly Sword roared with laughter. Suddenly, he felt young again, drinking with a friend. It was illusion, of course, and he must remember so.

Sunlight was smiling, too. "I'll proffer Your Celestial Majesty one piece of advice as a free sample. If the Portal of Worlds does open next year, as predicted, and you survive, as I hope, then I think you should proclaim yourself first Emperor of the Twelfth Dynasty."

"Can I do that?"

"You can do anything, but that would make it easier for you to change all the customs and throw off the shackles of tradition. Like eunuchs, for example."

Brilliant! Simple but devastating. The Emperor rose and returned to his throne. "If you would be good enough to strike that gong, friend Sunlight, I will order lunch for us. And later, you can take an hour or two to describe to me the best of all the Emperors you have ever known, and to instruct me in all the things that a truly benevolent ruler must do to serve his people well."

CHAPTER 23

Shard Gingko spent a long day sitting on the ground with the rest of his companions just outside the army camp, watched over by a score or so of armed, distrustful soldiers. The antagonism waned soon after the Firstborn was led away, which indicated that he had been made welcome by the Emperor. The weather was pleasant, neither hot nor cold, windy nor dead calm, and the scenery was memorable. But the prisoners were not allowed to talk, and he dared not open his scribe's box to write anything lest he be suspected of making notes about the army. The soldiers were having a day off, squad after squad running over to the river to splash and laugh and horse around. Even the horses were horsing around.

Bowls of rice were handed out at noon, but after that, the monotony returned. And then, without warning, the Firstborn returned, accompanied by the senior officer who had taken him away. Everyone jumped up—other than Shard, who scrambled upright with the help of Mouse's strong arm. Their horses were being led back, already saddled and bridled, with a packhorse they had not seen before.

The Firstborn came straight to Shard Gingko and Mouse. He was smiling.

"All is well, Master?" Mouse said.

"All is well so far. His Imperial Majesty has agreed that he will not pursue if Bamboo's followers disband and head for home.

He will send some food wagons tomorrow to give them a good meal before they start. I have to witness that Bamboo himself has repented and recanted, but everyone else is pardoned already."

Shard's instant reaction was to wonder whether the Emperor could be trusted, or whether he was just hoping to catch the rebels off guard as they scattered. But if anyone could detect a lie, it must be the Firstborn.

The sun was setting as they came in sight of the caravanserai, where the three rebels already had a fire burning. They stood in a row, regarding the Firstborn's party with dark suspicion while they dismounted. As Sunlight walked over to them, three of the Goat Haven men moved in around him as a bodyguard, hands on swords.

"I have spoken with the Emperor," he said. "He pardons you all, provided you now turn around and go home. He will send wagons of food in the morning. The only exception is Bamboo himself. He has to recant his claims, and I must witness his oath of loyalty. After that, he too is free to go."

Fair Visions and Ominous Scroll smiled broadly.

The one called Silent scowled. "How do you know he is the true Absolute Purity and not an imposter?"

The Firstborn did not lose his good cheer. "I know he looks quite like Zealous Righteousness, his father, and even more like his grandfather, both of whom I met. He has given us a load of dainties to brighten our diet, so that we may feast tonight, and bless his name."

"A cheap bribe!" Silent shouted.

The Firstborn sighed. "Any man who has the Imperial Army at his back and flies the Golden Dragon banner is good enough for me. Don't argue with him!"

"He is right, Silent," Fair Visions said. "Let sleeping tigers lie. This is incredible generosity."

"I don't trust him!"

"Will you fight him alone?"

The Firstborn walked away, and his escort went with him, leaving the three rebels to argue it out among themselves. Shard had met fanatics like Silent before, men who could not allow any evidence to change their minds.

Everyone else was content. Only the Firstborn had seen the Emperor, but that was to be expected. Even to be close to him was the highlight of a lifetime.

Moonless darkness closed in. Stars glittered overhead like a river of diamonds, and seventeen men sat around a fading campfire, feasting on the treats the Emperor had sent from his own supplies—and drinking the best wine Shard had ever tasted.

Conversations were quiet and local. Shard felt again that sense of completion. His great adventure was over: He would retire to Goat Haven to complete his memoirs; the Firstborn and Mouse, his ever-faithful disciple, would go with the food train to Bamboo's camp, and the world would roll along as before.

At last, the Firstborn rose, stretched his ropy arms, and yawned luxuriously. "I foresee a long day ahead tomorrow, so I bid you all good night and safe sleep. Don't worry about noise. I can sleep through thunderstorms."

Almost everyone else had risen out of respect, cutting off the firelight, so that no one foresaw the tragedy. Silent leaped forward and twisted a long dagger into the Firstborn's belly. He cried out and fell. One of the Goat Haven men whipped out a sword, but Silent slashed his throat, incredibly fast. Other swords flashed, but it was Prince Silk Hand himself who dealt with the killer. Moving almost too fast to see, he grabbed Silent from behind and broke his neck with one quick wrench. *How did he do that?* Shard was appalled—snap a man's spine with bare hands? But then he awakened to the real disaster, the wounded Urfather. Prince

Silk Hand knelt at his right, Mouse at his left, and everyone else cleared out of the way to let the firelight reveal the awful scene. He was writhing in agony, struggling to suppress screams, and pouring blood.

"Master! Oh, Master!" Mouse cried. "Somebody help!"

"There is no help," Prince Silk Hand said. "The demon knew how to strike."

"You are right," the Firstborn muttered through clenched teeth. "The wound is fatal. But this has never been my favorite way to die."

"No!" Mouse roared. He leaped to his feet, turned to the mountains, and bellowed, incredibly loud. "Open! Open now! He is here this time, but you must be quick. Hurry!" Not even an echo replied.

"It isn't the Year of the Firebird yet!" Shard protested. No one answered.

Mouse screamed the message again, louder then ever.

The ground shivered.

Mouse fell silent. Someone said, "Another earthquake?"

If it were another quake, Shard thought, they were in a very safe place, where nothing could fall on them.

Whatever it was, it was not stopping. Shard sensed a strange low rumble, somewhere between a noise and a shaking, something both heard by his ears and felt in his bones. He wondered if he was detecting landslides in the mountains. Then a knife cut of light exploded into the darkness, painfully bright. Men cried out in terror.

Lord Silk Hand said. "It can't be! Not this year."

Shard Gingko thought, *Will you teach Heaven to eat rice?* a saying of the Humble Teacher.

"No it isn't, but he is here!" Mouse shouted joyfully. He stooped and scooped the Firstborn up in his arms as if he weighed no more than a rolled blanket.

The light was certainly coming from the Western Wall, a vertical slash on the cliff, the southern edge of the Portal. Across the valley, the Fortress Hills were bright as day.

The Portal was opening, pivoting on its north edge, swinging forward. The sepulchral rumble grew stronger, the light unbearable. Surely, the sun itself must be right behind that vast door. Now came waves of sound as trees and hillside were forced apart. Even to look across the campfire hurt now, so bright were the Fortress Hills.

"Oh, listen!" Fair Visions said.

Yes, there was music, very strange, very distant, growing louder. To Shard, it seemed to combine the essence of every timbre he had ever heard: gongs and bells, but also reeds, strings, silk, and brass. There were voices in it, and birdsong, and he thought that his ears could not detect all of its range, yet no other music would ever sound worthy again. It plucked at his heart.

The horses were shrilling in fear, racing around their paddock. Men whimpered in terror—and nothing had come out of that door yet.

"Do not be afraid!" Mouse cried. He alone was on his feet, holding the dying man, dribbling blood, yet balanced against the trembling of the ground. "They do not come for you."

Who didn't? What did he know about it?

Shard slid off the log he was sitting on and sat on the trampled grass instead. He couldn't fall any further, although he could foresee himself being bounced if the earthquake grew any stronger. The Portal was wider now, and the valley southward was an unbearable blaze of reflected light.

Somebody—probably Ominous Scroll—was muttering "Bamboo!" over and over. The rebels must be more exposed to the intolerable glare than the Imperial Army to the north, but no one in the Great Valley could be unaware now that the Portal of a Thousand Worlds was opening. The glow must be visible as far away as Cherish.

The ground shuddered when the great door stopped moving, standing at right angles to the mountainside. The ground stilled, but the music grew louder, closer, denser. Shard had never been so frightened in his life. He was infinitely glad that he wasn't just a mile or so farther south, where he would be able to see inside that gigantic opening.

Something had emerged. It was hidden for a moment by the door, but the light had grown even brighter. Then the new source of that light moved forward and was visible—except that human eyes could not bear to look at it.

It . . . He . . . She . . . The figure was as bright as the sun and stood as high as a mountain, impossible to comprehend. And yet, squinting through a slit in his eyelids and a narrow gap between his fingers, Shard had a sense of shining feathers, or iridescent tiles, or butterfly wings, all the colors he knew and more beside, but not clothes. Nothing so gorgeous would hide its beauty under garments. It was bipedal but not human. Every step it took made the world move slightly, giving under its weight like a cheap wooden floor, and the forest crunched below its feet like grass. It seemed to peer around, as if looking for something, and it uttered great choirs of sound, not a voice or music or birdsong and yet somehow all of these and sweeter yet. But even at that distance, Shard had to clap his hands over his ears or be deafened. Echoes roared back as the mountains sang in chorus.

"Come!" Mouse shouted. "He is here at last."

The Firstborn was trying to speak, apparently protesting what Mouse was doing, but clearly in terrible pain.

"Peace, Master," he said. "The time has come. You are forgiven!" Mouse alone was upright, and only he seemed able to stare right at the vast apparition towering over the valley. He began to run, carrying his burden as if it were weightless.

He grew larger, shouldering his way through the trees.

The gigantic visitor's music became unbearably sad and began to fade as she, or he, turned away, back toward the Portal, as if giving up. Tears ran down Shard's old cheeks and he wanted to shout to the vision not to leave.

But now both Mouse and the Firstborn were changing, their clothes flying away in shreds, their skin shining like opals or pearl. Mouse ran toward the Portal, growing visibly, shining brighter, towering over the treetops until he trod the forest like turf, and the world shook with his every step. The rhythm changed; there were two of him, the Urfather running at his side. They called out in the same gigantic song-voice-music as the visitor had used.

It heard, and turned, and the three of them flowed together in an unifying embrace. Their glorious chorus soared to the stars. Still singing, they went in through the Portal clasped together, all three of them. Then they were gone.

The light began to fade.

The world trembled again as the Portal swung and reverberated as it shut. A moment's pause, then the whole side of the mountain collapsed in a gigantic rock fall, like a curtain falling. Boulders rolled and bounced through the forest, almost as far as the caravanserai. A brief gale swirled dust through the camp.

At last, the night was still again, but darker than a cavern. Yet Shard's vision was full of shapes and colors. His eyes hurt. It might take days for them to recover, he thought. But his writing could wait until they did—he would never forget what had happened.

Mouse? He thought how Mandarin Sedge Shallows had so conveniently found a boy who could pass as the Urfather, even if only at a distance. He remembered the death warrant that disappeared so that Sedge Shallows never got to read it. He thought of the cave, where the Firstborn almost died before Mouse brought help, and how Mouse's strength had brought them here.

Everyone was still blind, of course. No one was talking. Eventually, Fair Visions began muttering about Bamboo again. The rebels would have seen more of what lay behind the Portal. It would be astonishing if they had not fled in a terrified mob from that intolerable brightness. Perhaps the Imperial Army had done the same. The inexplicable absence of historical witnesses was explicable now.

And then two powerful hands grabbed Shard Gingko's shoulders and hauled him upright. He was helpless in the grip of Prince Silk Hand.

"What happened?" Prince Silk Hand bellowed, right in his face. "What did I just see?"

"I don't know, my lord! I saw it, too, but . . ."

Prince Silk Hand shook Shard Gingko like a rug. "You're the scholar, you must know. Tell me what I just saw."

"I saw it also . . . It's just . . . Just that . . . *Some questions have no answers in this world.*"

"Ah." The viselike hands released him. "Who said that?"

No one had. Well, Shard Gingko himself had, but he was nobody. . . . "The Humble Teacher, my lord."

"Then I suppose it must be so." His Lordship turned away.

But Shard Gingko would write it all down and his name would be remembered for it.

— V —
THE YEAR OF
THE FIREBIRD

In Hare Moon, His Imperial Majesty Absolute Purity returned to his capital after a progress through more than half the provinces of the Good Land, an imperial inspection not matched since the previous dynasty. He was hailed everywhere as a warrior Emperor, conqueror of the Bamboo Banner, and the people rejoiced when he promised that he would be making similar tours in future.

Half his army had fled when the Portal opened. These men were rounded up, sentenced to death under military law, pardoned by imperial clemency, and marched off to work on repairs to the Grand Canal.

The Bamboo Banner dissolved in the light of the Portal, and few survivors returned to their homes. Bamboo himself was found about five *li* from his final camp with his throat cut.

In Fish Moon, a year after the great earthquake, Prince Silk Hand and his wife, with an armed escort of twenty men, rode into the village of Tutu to reclaim their son, Prince Silkworm. The young prince was not happy with the transition at first, but soon became reconciled to his new mother, father, and baby sister, and also his new home in Goat Haven. Many years later, he was to take the name of Prince Silk Hand 2.

In Harvest Moon, Clerk of Records Shard Gingko ascended on the ladder of worlds. His passing was peaceful, and Prince

Silk Hand himself sang the farewell at his pyre. The scholar's final request, made to Lady Verdant as he lay on his deathbed, was that his account of his travels with the Firstborn and of the opening of the Portal should be sent directly to the Emperor.

Few mortals could have honored that plea, but Prince Silk Hand had many influential friends, and the scroll was indeed laid before the imperial eyes undamaged. None of the multitudinous mandarins circling the throne had a chance to eviscerate the text to match traditional beliefs, for the Emperor read it in the original and ordered it printed that way by the new steam presses. The light it shed on much traditional scholarship caused a literary revolution, but its description of the opening of the Portal was dismissed as a poetic conceit.

Silkworm-Thunderbot lived to inherit Goat Haven from his father and his descendants ruled there for over a century, until Prince Silk Hand 5 lost it in a poker game.

Millennia will roll on, but the Urfather will never be reborn. The Portal cannot open again, for obviously it could never have existed, except in folktales. Mouse will be forgotten, the Firstborn will become a legend, and Shard Gingko remembered as a poet who collected the stories and created the epic.

Only Emperor Absolute Purity, founder of the Twelfth Dynasty, will be accepted as genuine.

ABOUT THE AUTHOR

Dave Duncan was born in Scotland. After graduating from the University of Saint Andrews, he moved to Canada, where he worked as a petroleum geologist for thirty years. He is the author of many science fiction and fantasy novels, among them *A Rose-Red City*, *Magic Casement*, and *The Reaver Road*, as well as the historical novel *Daughter of Troy*, which he published under the pseudonym Sarah B. Franklin. Under the name Ken Hood, he wrote the Longdirk series, which includes *Demon Sword*, *Demon Knight*, and *Demon Rider*. *Children of Chaos* (2006) was nominated for both the Prix Aurora Award and the Endeavour Award. Duncan is a founding and honorary life member of SF Canada. He continues to live in Canada with his wife, children, and grandchildren. Visit the author at daveduncan.com and openroadmedia.com/dave-duncan.

DAVE DUNCAN

FROM OPEN ROAD MEDIA

OPEN ROAD

INTEGRATED MEDIA

Find a full list of our authors and titles at www.openroadmedia.com

FOLLOW US
@OpenRoadMedia

CPSIA information can be obtained
at www.ICGtesting.com
Printed in the USA
BVOW08s2354060117
472888BV00001B/1/P